the

Dead Kid

DETECTIVE AGENCY

Loyalist to a Fault

EVAN MUNDAY

ECW

Published by ECW Press
665 Gerrard Street East, Toronto, Ontario M4M 1Y2
416-694-3348 / info@ecwpress.com

LIBRARY AND ARCHIVES CANADA CATALOGUING IN PUBLICATION

Munday, Evan, author
Loyalist to a Fault / Evan Munday.
(Dead Kid Detective Agency series; 3)

ISBN 978-1-77041-074-9 (pbk)
Also issued as: 978-1-77090-743-0 (epub); 978-1-77090-742-3 (PDF)

I. Title. II. Series: Munday, Evan. Dead Kid Detective Agency ; 3.

PS8626.U54L69 2015   jC813'.6   C2015-902782-9   C2015-902783-7

Editor: Erin Creasey
Cover and interior illustrations: Evan Munday
Cover and text design: David Gee
Typesetting and production: Lynn Gammie
Printed and bound in Canada by Marquis
5   4   3   2   1

The publication of Loyalist to a Fault has been generously supported by the Canada
Council for the Arts, which last year invested $20.1 million in writing and publishing
throughout Canada. We also acknowledge the support of the Ontario Arts Council
(OAC), an agency of the Government of Ontario, which last year funded 1,681
individual artists and 1,125 organizations in 216 communities across Ontario for a
total of $52.8 million, the Government of Ontario through Ontario Book Publishing
Tax Credit, the OMDC Book Fund, an initiative of the Ontario Media Development
Corporation, and the Government of Canada through the Canada Book Fund.

I'm on a boat!

– The Lonely Island

Broke Into the Old Apartment

Many mysteries open with a heinous crime in progress. Yet so few begin with the hero — in this case, the plucky and darkness-loving thirteen-year-old October Schwartz — committing said crime. How heinous this crime actually may be is up for debate.

It was a cold morning in early January, when October Schwartz found herself about to steal a telephone from an abandoned building — which more closely resembled a pile of wood randomly nailed together — strangely named the Crooked Arms. You are probably asking yourself, *Why?* Has October developed some sort of crippling gambling addiction to competitive curling (faithful followers of the Dead Kid Detective Agency's exploits may remember October's short stint on her school's team) for which she now must thieve and pawn antique telephones to cover her debts?

The truth is, perhaps, even more sinister. As established in our previous pulse-pounding installment, the Crooked Arms was the childhood home of October's dead Scottish friend Morna MacIsaac, and the old telephone on the lobby's front desk may be, bafflingly, the one connection October has to her long-absent mother, aside from a snazzy ankh necklace she often wears. During the Dead Kid Detective Agency's investigation of Morna's century-old death, a voice on that telephone provided clues and advice at pivotal moments, and it was only once the case was closed that October suspected the voice might belong to her mother.

That was why she had to steal the phone.

Under other circumstances, October would have simply continued to visit the Crooked Arms to speak with the faintly rasping voice she thought might belong to her missing mom, but there were two key issues: 1) since October had asked the voice if it was her mother, the voice had stopped talking entirely; and 2) the Crooked Arms was scheduled for demolition the following day.

In under twelve hours some construction company — more like a *de*struction company (am I right?) — was going to go Godzilla and make the Crooked Arms its own personal Tokyo, and October was certain there wouldn't be any phone left by nightfall. She couldn't let that happen, so larceny it was. She'd broken into places before while on a case, and she had technically assaulted someone with a broom, so she wasn't *that* concerned about adding petty theft to her rap sheet. She was collecting crimes the way an eager Boy Scout accumulates merit badges.

October trudged through the mid-January foam mattress of snow. Snow hadn't fallen in over a week, but given that the Crooked Arms was condemned, nobody seemed too concerned about shoveling its walk. And October was alone, as she wouldn't be able to revive her dead friends until the end of the month, what with the lunar cycle and the weird mystical undead rules governing the dead kids and all that. October had her dead friends' ghostly guidelines mostly sorted out:

1. The dead kids arise from their graves only during the full moon and return upon the appearance of the next full moon. (They stick around for about a month. This rule is clearly the most important in the current situation.)
2. The dead kids can become tangible and intangible at will, passing through the world of the living or interacting physically with it as they so choose.
3. The dead kids are invisible to nearly all living people, but certain people — those who have experienced untimely, mysterious deaths in their close family or friends circle — are sometimes able to see them.
4. The dead kids can harm each other and themselves with no pain or lasting consequences. Severed arms will grow back.

5. While they can physically interact with living people, they cannot knowingly harm them. Punches don't land.
6. The dead kids are to remain ghostly corpses until their unfinished business — namely, finding justice for their terrible childhood deaths — is complete. (This was the theory, at least. October had solved Morna's case in December and she still seemed to be kicking around, so this rule might be a little hand-wavy.)

October tucked her mittened hands into the armpits of her black peacoat, carefully sidestepped the plastic orange construction netting, and plunged her boots where she assumed a staircase must be under all that snow. When she reached the building's battered front door, she was astonished to find it locked. The burnished brass doorknob just wouldn't give, though it had been unlocked throughout December whenever she and the dead kids had been here to investigate Morna's death.

Instead of trying to kick in the door, October found a loose two-by-four on the front porch, glanced around in a totally *not* suspicious way, then smashed one of the ground floor windows, which was already partially broken. October made sure the frame was clear of all those jagged little glass teeth before she hoisted herself up and tumbled into the lobby. She'd had about her lifetime's fill of broken glass when she and her friends Yumi and Stacey were in a telephone booth when it was tipped over, thank you very much.

Seeing nothing in the darkness but some glittering shards of glass and her own breath, October produced a flashlight from her coat pocket and flipped it on. This process was not as easy as it sounds, as October was sure if she took off either of her mittens, she'd lose both her hands to frostbite. Either that, or she'd have a flashlight forever fused to her hand, which actually wasn't that bad an idea, as far as detective work goes. Still, the light went on, illuminating the words "Asphodel Meadows" graffitied in red on the wall. Almost instantly after turning on the flashlight, October could have sworn she heard footfalls from upstairs. October figured they were probably squirrels or (less adorable) rats nesting in the abandoned house, but given her track record, you'd think she'd have been more suspicious.

As quietly as she possibly could, October crept over to the black telephone resting on the desk under the "Asphodel Meadows" tag. In her huge boots, October's "creeping" fell somewhere within the "Metallica ballad" volume range. And given that she'd just smashed her way into the room like a confused seagull, sneakiness was not really the order of the moment. She picked up the receiver of the phone and tried one last time to communicate with the scratchy voice at the other end.

More shuffling came from the floor above.

"Am I alone here?" October whispered into the receiver. More than her mom's voice, she would have given her collection of black eyeliner for any voice — Mr. Santuzzi's, that lady from *The Nanny* — to say "yes."

The shuffling sounds moved to the far corner of the lobby. October tried to angle her neck so she could see into the room above via one of the holes in the ceiling. October had been attacked by three men armed with baseball bats while searching the Crooked Arms, and the ensuing fracas had added a few new skylights in the first floor of the tenement building. Still, all she could see through the holes were shadows.

"Is there someone upstairs?" October asked, feeling more paranoid by the second. "If this is Kirby or one of you kids, I'm going to be *so* mad."

But the phone remained silent and uncaring. It wasn't out of character for the dead kids to prank her, but she had no idea how they would have raised themselves to orchestrate such an elaborate escapade.

"Okay," she relented. "Bye, Mom . . . if it even *is* you . . ."

With a final click of the receiver, October crouched down to find the cord and yank it out of the wall. Almost on cue, a riotous crash rang out from the floor above, like someone had knocked over a wardrobe filled with mirrored clothing. (Which is something I think we can all assume *wasn't* included among the furnishings at the Crooked Arms.) October's stomach dropped and she felt her underarms begin to dampen. That was no squirrel. Or it was a *man-sized* squirrel, which would bring its own set of massive problems.

She glanced at the end of the phone cord, seriously doubting she'd be able to plug it in at home, but there was no time to think about that now. No time to stare at the wall and wonder again what "Asphodel Meadows" meant. Something big and angry (or possibly just clumsy) was just beyond the darkened stairs before her.

She wound the phone cord around her left hand, hopped over the window ledge, and took leaping strides through the snow until she was several massive-squirrel-lengths away from the Crooked Arms.

☠   ☠   ☠

Dear readers, if October had any tiny remaining doubts that something in Sticksville was more rotten than a month-old banana, her mind was forever made up that evening. Historians of the supernatural — if such a profession does or ever will exist (fingers crossed) — may find it difficult to pinpoint when, exactly, grade nine student and founder of the Dead Kid Detective Agency, October Schwartz, realized her town had something very, very wrong with it. That night she stole a telephone from the decrepit old boarding house might be a good guess, but given that that moment was preceded by months of paranormal misadventures, it's tough to be sure.

After all, it was only four months earlier that October had accidentally raised five kids — each about her own age — from the dead one night in the Sticksville Cemetery. Despite some initial trepidation about interacting with the ghostly youngsters, October soon formed a friendship with them, and since then, she and her dead pals had found no shortage of bizarre mysteries, crime, and skullduggery just steps from her front door. As you may remember from October's last two escapades, she and her five dead friends are fairly good at solving mysteries, even if they often expose October to life-threatening dangers in the process. As part of a friendly arrangement, October and her dead pals were hoping to solve the mysteries of each of the kids' own mysterious deaths. In turn, the dead kids were going to help October Schwartz find her missing mother (the one who may or may not have been using the telephone October swiped).

If you don't remember October's last two adventures, I highly recommend you hightail it to a bookstore or library or one of those ebook sites that are so popular with the shut-ins these days. Unless you have some sort of medical problem that prevents you from remembering things, like that guy in *Memento*. Then you're on your own. Reading this book and not the previous two in the series — while totally fine — is a bit like starting the Little House on the Prairie series with *On the Banks of Plum Creek*. (Ludicrous, right?) Now let's return to our regularly scheduled morbid mystery.

☠ ☠ ☠

The following afternoon, October Schwartz took the overly long way home to walk by Turnbull Lane, the now-former home of the Crooked Arms, where bulldozers were already dozing and backhoes were busy hoeing. The site of the Crooked Arms looked like an explosion at an olde-time lumberyard, if that lumberyard dealt exclusively in, like, rotting and termite-infested wood.

Looking past the orange construction fencing to the razed building, it was almost difficult for October to believe that this was the very spot where, in 1914, German saboteur Udo Schlangegriff lived and tried (pretty successfully) to ruin the life of Sam Cheng, another resident of the building, seemingly so he could take over his business, a laundry. The Crooked Arms is also the very same building where that aforementioned Udo Schlangegriff killed October's ghost pal Morna when Morna fatefully discovered his confusing schemes. So, in that sense, it wasn't so bad to see the

Crooked Arms go. It was kind of like throwing out the sweater you were wearing when you got dumped.

Taking a final look at where the Crooked Arms used to stand (or lean precariously), October buttoned her coat to the very top and shoved her tingling hands into her pockets. While October had solved the mystery of Morna MacIsaac's death, she still had four more friends with unsolved cases. On January 29th, she would be able to raise her friends from the dead again . . . or so she hoped.

☠ ☠ ☠

Are you ready, readers? October and her dead friends are about to embark on their third adventure and — trust me, I've read ahead — it's a doozy. Not only are the shenanigans to which they get up to more elaborate than ever, but they will also be rooting around the underwear drawer of Sticksville — figuratively, of course — to find all the skeletons (maybe not-so-figuratively) hidden in the town's overstuffed closet. (Yes, they'll be looking through the drawers to find things in the closet. It's a full bedroom search.)

If you *aren't* ready, please take this time to enjoy an herbal tea or have a short nap. Whatever works best for you. But those of you that *are*, in fact, ready, then imagine a passage-of-time film montage, as if Rocky Balboa were training for the big fight or the dancers of *Step Up: Revolution* were rehearsing for their next public dance intervention. In this case, our montage features our intrepid October Schwartz going to school, writing in her *Two Knives, One Thousand Demons* composition book, and watching episodes of *Dark Shadows* with her living friends Yumi and Stacey. Basically, killing time until she can reunite with her dead gang of crime-solvers.

☠ ☠ ☠

Even though Stacey MacIsaac was still, for the time being, the drummer in the moderately popular high school pop-punk quartet Phantom Moustache, he and his two best (maybe only) friends sat alone at the far end of a table in the far corner of Sticksville Central

High School's cafeteria. On January 29th, he was observing a heated debate between Yumi Takeshi and October Schwartz regarding the relative merits of weirdo '80s band Oingo Boingo.

"The lead singer is weird," Yumi declared. "Why is he always wearing a white tank top and tan chinos? He looks like a banker on day five of a hostage crisis."

"That weird lead singer is Danny Elfman!" October spat incredulously, jabbing an accusatory spork toward her friend. "Like, composer of all the best Tim Burton soundtracks."

"*Beetlejuice*," Stacey grunted with a mouthful of tuna melt.

"Right," October folded her arms across her chest and narrowed her heavily lined eyes. "*Beetlejuice*."

"Don't say it again," Yumi waved her hands in warning, her spiked bracelets and chains sounding like a hansom cab passing by. "I admit, he makes good musical scores. I just don't like his band. They're too goofy. I need my musicians to be more serious. I mean, music is *serious* business."

The three friends nodded in agreement. Aside from the recent bullying Yumi had faced, nothing was more serious than music.

"Shame about the radio," October sighed, sporking some macaroni salad.

"Even if we *did* have a show, we wouldn't play any Oingo Boingo, October." Yumi was steadfast in her opinion.

"Still," October said. "Stupid Santuzzi."

Stupid Santuzzi, called "Mr." Santuzzi to his face, was October's math teacher, an imposing man over six feet tall with a chest span that was nearly as broad. Because he was not particularly forgiving or easy an instructor, and because he dressed like an airport lounge singer and (allegedly) wore an unconvincing jet-black toupée to match his impressive handlebar moustache, he was often the object of much student scorn. Yet because of that aforementioned broad chest and rumours of his past military service, very little of that scorn was ever demonstrated in full view of the man himself, except the day that Yumi and Stacey devoted one full hour of their radio show to making fun of him. Though it was popular with the student audience, it put an end to the school's radio program.

An hour before lunch, Mr. Santuzzi, just like a military man, had dropped a bombshell on October. "You know he expects me to tutor Ashlie Salmons?" October complained.

"What?!" Yumi was outraged on her behalf.

The Magneto to October Schwartz's Professor X, Ashlie Salmons sat with her sisterhood of evil maidens two rows of cafeteria tables over. Salmons was holding court with the people October knew only as Goose Neck, the little girl with a big laugh, and the ever-fashionable Novelty T-Shirt. Today, the shirt read, "Keep Calm and Carrie Bradshaw," which didn't even really make sense. October realized she had been looking in their direction too long.

"Stare much, Zombie Tramp?" Ashlie shouted across the tables. Little Girl, Big Laugh became a Vesuvius of laughter. (It didn't take much.)

Ashlie Salmons was the first to dub October "Zombie Tramp," a label that — hot tip — is hard to shake. Now nearly everyone, save her friends and a few teachers, used it to identify her. October felt she was definitely more of a *vampire* tramp — zombies don't typically wear black — but you can't choose your nickname. If you could, everyone would be a "Maverick" and no one would be a "Goose."

"Are you even good in math?" Stacey asked.

October had to think about that one. French was easily her strongest subject, but she did little else — when there wasn't a mystery to be solved — than study and write her burgeoning literary epic, *Two Knives, One Thousand Demons*.

"I'm okay. Not amazing, but I guess better than Ashlie is," October decided. "It's more like it's some weird kind of punishment.

We're not even in the same math class." In truth, October wasn't so sure it was a punishment. Santuzzi had basically saved her from a painful death by baseball bat that night at the McGriffs' house, and he probably felt she owed him a favour.

"Isn't she in grade ten?" Yumi asked.

"Sort of. She got held back in a couple of classes — like music and math." October really knew way too much about Ashlie Salmons's life and class schedule.

"Good luck with all that," Yumi said, absent-mindedly juggling her nectarine. The cast had recently been taken off Yumi's arm, and she was keen to demonstrate that she could use both arms with ease. "Let us know if you need backup."

A kind offer on Yumi's part, no doubt, but October noted that only Stacey had been able to embarrass or repel Ashlie so far. He was Perseus's shield to the Medusa's head that was the most popular girl in (sort of) grade ten.

☠ ☠ ☠

After dinner with her dad (Mr. Schwartz, to you and to the students at Sticksville High), October worked in the living room on *Two Knives, One Thousand Demons* while he marked tests to a background soundtrack provided by Fleetwood Mac. October was in the midst of writing a fast-paced action sequence in which protagonist Olivia de Kellerman was being pursued through narrow streets by demonic killers on bicycles. So rapid was this bicycle chase that October's hand was having a difficult time keeping up with her brain to take down all the relevant words. It was so engrossing, she completely lost track of time and before too long, her dad was yawning intensely and making his way — big pile of tests in hand — up to his bedroom.

This was ideal. Soon, her dad — far too trusting for the father of a girl who'd snuck out of the house almost nightly and had nearly been killed twice in the past four months — would be dreaming, and October could enter the Sticksville Cemetery, just paces from her back door, to raise the dead kids again.

She continued writing until she reached the end of a bloodbath of a bicycle chase (that featured many creative uses of chains and tire pumps), before quietly tiptoeing to her room. She pushed open the door and the hallway light made the antique phone on her bedside table gleam. Luckily, her dad hadn't noticed her sudden new interest in early twentieth-century telecommunications. Mr. Schwartz was a private man and generally believed in personal privacy. He stayed clear of October's room.

Since October had stolen the phone from the Crooked Arms, she had tested a variety of methods to reach the person she imagined was her mother, but every attempt had the same disappointing result: total silence. Recently, with some help from Percy — a goth hardware store clerk who'd helped her figure out who was harassing Yumi — she'd jerry-rigged a cord connector to the old phone that, in theory, would allow her to use it with the modern phone jack in her bedroom wall. Sadly, the theory fell apart in practice, but October held out hope. She had first spoken to her maybe-mother on this very phone in a building that had been without telephone service for decades. Clearly the phone had some sort of supernatural power and didn't require a telephone repairperson.

As she did every night, she lifted the receiver to her left ear and held the horn close to her mouth. No dial tone could be heard, but that wasn't unusual or even a concern. Magic phone, remember?

"Hello? Is anybody there?" October spoke quietly. Her dad was in the next room and she didn't want to concern him more than she already did. In general, October tried her best not to be trouble for her dad. Loyal readers will remember that Mr. Schwartz struggles with clinical depression, and October always feared — though she knew depression wasn't like a mousetrap triggered by the slightest problem — that her misbehaviour would trigger one of his depressive episodes. But when you're running a detective agency with a bunch of dead kids, unbeknownst to your father and the public, it's hard to stay on the straight and narrow.

October asked the same question a few more times before giving up for the night. While she had no regrets about stealing the phone, the phone was really being annoying! Noticing that the midnight hour was, as the witches say, close at hand, October packed her composition book into her bag, laced her black boots, and donned her black peacoat before making that familiar journey out the kitchen's sliding-glass door and down the steps of her back deck.

October pushed through the iron fence at the end of her backyard and cut a furrow through the snow. Given the grim winter weather, it had been a while since she'd visited the cemetery. Writing outdoors beside a gravestone just didn't have the same appeal when you were sitting in a snowbank, your jeans slowly sopping up the slush. She trudged through the snow — apparently the cemetery caretakers had also been absent this winter — until she reached the large stone mausoleum near the cemetery's centre. Reluctant to just plunk down in a patch of cold snow, October leaned back into the tomb's wall and whipped out her composition book. This being the third time she'd tried this, she had the drill down. Uncapping her Bic pen (not a product placement), she began to write.

> As Nature turns twisted and dark,
> To this dread graveyard I donate my spark,
> And as tears begin to blind mine eyes,
> The innocent young and the dead shall rise.

Once that was done, she read the words out loud. Authoritatively. No pussyfooting around this time, readers. But there was no hot, blue lightning bolt, no unearthly drone, no sign that October's originally accidental spell had succeeded at all. One would expect something dramatic or momentous to happen, but no sight or sound altered the grey, chilled landscape. October worried that she'd messed up the spell once again.

But then, one by one, as if central performers in a rousing musical production, five dead kids appeared from the dark wood at the far end of the cemetery.

Tabetha Scott, former American slave who journeyed to Sticksville via the Underground Railroad, arrived first, stomping through the snow in shiny black boots that seemed out of place with her ratty plaid dress. (She was grunge before her time.)

Second, Derek Running Water, a Mohawk boy who met his

end in the early 1990s, ambled out. Being dead meant you didn't feel the harsh elements, so he was comfortable in his black T-shirt and baggy jeans.

Kirby LaFlamme came next, hitching up the belt of his khaki shorts. (You wouldn't catch anyone living in short pants.) The first to die of the LaFlamme quintuplets, he'd left his four minor-celebrity brothers in 1954. Despite losing his life, he never lost that feeling that he was better than everyone else.

From behind a smattering of short bushes came Morna MacIsaac, an appearance that filled October with relief. Since October had uncovered Morna's murderer, she half-expected to never see her again. The rules the dead kids had described suggested as much. But when Morna didn't disappear or anything when October closed the case, they all realized she must still have some unfinished business. Either that, or all the dead kids' business was her business.

"It's nice t'see ye'!" Morna said, her face splitting into a big smile. "And nice that there's so much snow!"

October found it rather strange how much Morna loved snow, considering her dead body was found partially buried in the stuff. One would think she'd associate snow with some particularly bad memories.

Finally, the man (or thirteen-year-old boy) of the hour arrived. Taking long strides out of the shadows, Loyalist Cyril Cooper tilted back his tricorn hat and waved to October. His small drum, slung over one shoulder, bumped against his side. He was October's longest-dead friend — quite an accomplishment — and he knew that with October's help, he might soon have the answers to his longest-held questions.

The dead kids had returned, and October had their supernatural assistance until the next full moon. And, almost more importantly, she had their companionship. Seeing their sallow, bluish white faces again, October Schwartz realized how much she had missed her dead chums. Her heart just about burst like an overworked water main.

"October!" Derek yelled.

"Come on," Kirby growled, throwing his round arms wide

open. The other dead kids mirrored him for a big group hug, as if they were camp counselors, seeing each other for the first time since last summer.

October spread her arms wide, full wingspan, and waded into the mass of dead-kid love, at which point her dead so-called friends became suddenly very intangible. October wobbled and fell through them, stomach first, into the snow. Brushing ice from her upper lip, she turned back to the ghost children.

"And here I was, thinking it was nice to have you back."

That set the dead kids off on a massive belly laugh. Nothing had ever seemed as funny to them as October going in for the hug and getting a face full of snow. Despite October's somewhat injured dignity and much colder face, she was pleasantly surprised with how simple the necromancy had been.

"Ready t'get started?" Tabetha asked, tangible once again and pulling the heavier and much more alive October to her feet.

"Cyril," October replied, "let's find out how you died."

☠   ☠   ☠

Hangin' with Master Cooper

My dad was on a date the following night with Crown Attorney Salmons, a.k.a. the incubator that hatched the devil child who had been tormenting me since I first walked through the doors of Sticksville Central. So rather than spend the evening dry-heaving into the toilet as I imagined Dad romantically feeding Ashlie's mom popcorn shrimp at Red Lobster, I invited the dead kids over to discuss our whole strategy. It wasn't the first time the dead kids had been in my room, but I felt their presence was going to be more frequent, given I had no real desire to have a bunch of outdoor planning sessions in the sub-zero Sticksville Cemetery.

So, yeah, with Dad and my hopefully-not-future-stepmom off at Lobster Fest or whatever, I thought it would be the ideal time to have my dead friends over, but I couldn't help worry that they'd get a little *too* familiar with the house. I didn't want them dropping by like they were Jazz and this was my Bel-Air estate. Already, they'd rooted through a storage closet to find the board game Sorry! and had carried it to my room.

Derek was shaking the top of the Sorry! game box open.

"Hold on," I said. "We can play that later. First, I want to talk to Cyril about his death."

My young, dead Mohawk friend pouted and folded his arms across his black shirt. Tabetha Scott threw me some serious stink-eye.

"I'm serious. This is the Dead Kid Detective Agency, not the . . . Dead Kid Board Game Enthusiasts' Society, or whatever."

"Understood," Cyril said, crouching down while trying to find a spot on my floor where he wouldn't crush a pile of CDs or books or get dust all over his pantaloons.

"What's been happening in the world of the livin'?" Tabetha asked.

"Nothing." Sticksville really shut down in January. Everyone kind of just hibernated. And aside from semi-regular visits with Dr. Lagostina, the school therapist — owing to my dual traumas of a kidnapping and an attack by a baseball-bat-wielding assailant — not much had changed in the past month.

"None of your friends are at the centre of some conspiracy?" Kirby cracked. What a goon.

"You certainly haven't spent the past month cleaning." Kirby waded intangibly through a dusty stack of Anne Rice novels. "How do you even move around in this room?"

"It's gonna be hard t' find enough space to play this game," Tabetha agreed.

"Wait," Derek said, his dark eyes drawn to something on my nightstand. "Is that the phone?"

"The *magic* phone," Kirby scoffed.

"Cyril, that's a —" Morna began to explain.

"Oh, I remember. You talk to people far away."

Morna showed even more teeth than usual. "That's right!"

"So why do you have Morna's old phone?" Derek asked.

At that point, I was forced to admit what *had* happened in January. Namely, that I was almost sure that my long-lost mom, who I hadn't seen or heard from since I was three, was the voice at the other end of the Crooked Arms' telephone who'd helped us solve the mystery of Morna's death. And that I'd stolen the phone from the Crooked Arms before the rickety building was demolished.

"But how would your mom even use that phone?" Derek asked. "Was it even hooked up to anything?"

"An' how did she know so much about m'death?" Morna added.

All good questions. All ones that had kept me from a decent night's sleep since the start of the year. I rubbed the heel of my palms into my eye sockets, probably giving myself the most serious case of raccoon face ever, knowing my eyeliner. "I don't know."

"Have ya tried it?" Tabetha asked. "Tried callin' 7-3-5 again?"

"Of course."

"Here, let *me* try," Kirby said, marching over to the nightstand. As if he were so charming that the phone would work only for him. In truth, Kirby had a personality that could make lettuce wilt. He pulled down on the hook at the base a few times as if he were sending Morse code. "Seven-three-five," he said into the horn.

Obviously, it didn't work. Did he think I was an amateur?

"We can all try the phone later," I said. "But it's definitely not going to work. Can we please just talk about Cyril's case?"

"Can we please jes' play Sorry!?" Tabetha tilted her head as if her right ear had suddenly turned to lead. Cyril stared at her.

"After. There will be plenty of time for that stupid game later, but right now I need Cyril to tell me about the days leading up to his death."

The most annoying thing about the dead kids — it wasn't even Kirby, as you might expect — was that none of them remembered much about their mysterious and tragic deaths. And given that we had made a deal whereby I was supposed to solve the mystery of each dead kid's death — a deal I made, I should point out, before I knew this fact — I was less than impressed by this whole memory loss situation. As a result, I had to be like some kind of lady Indiana Jones or short, chubby Tomb Raider and do, like, historical research that had never been done in Sticksville before. Though the dead kids had, technically, saved me from being stabbed to death by a bayonet, I still felt like this was a lot to ask.

"Okay, I'm jes' gonna set up the pieces," Tabetha said. She and Derek were kneeling on October's dark carpet, arranging the little skinny pawn-shaped pieces onto the old game board.

"Cyril," I said, moving the Loyalist in front of me by his shoulders. (He made the mistake of resting in a tangible state.) "Tell me everything you remember."

"Everything?" he swallowed nervously. I couldn't remember Cyril ever being nervous. He was always like the Bruce Willis of the group. No matter what asteroids might be hurtling toward Earth, he'd keep his head.

"Ye know the rules, October," Morna reminded.

"Rules?"

"Truth or Dare!" they all shouted. (I really hate when they do stuff in unison.)

"Ugh." The ridiculous dead kids really only enjoyed answering questions in Truth or Dare format, so I either had to tell them something embarrassing or, like, eat an old sock before they'd tell me anything. This wasn't really a "rule," but the dead kids were pretty adamant about it. *Très* unfair. "Fine, truth."

"Are ye going to ask anyone to be yer Valentine?" Morna asked, nearly blushing as she did. Blushing on a corpse looked like a very pale mauve.

"Such a stupid question!" Tabetha complained.

Kirby thought so, too. "Come on."

"Cyril, do you know what Valentine's Day is?" I wasn't sure how long the stupid holiday had been around. I mean, I imagine a thing like Arbor Day was pretty new.

"Is that that Catholic holiday about love?" he asked.

"Basically, but now most people in Canada celebrate it," I said.

"Ye give a Valentine's card t'the person ye love!" Morna beamed.

I guess I lucked out with an easy question. And an easy "no." It's not that I thought boys were gross or anything. But right now, in my life at Sticksville Central High School? Boys were gross. They were either trying to kill me — literally — or were endlessly insulting me. No, thanks. If I were to have a Valentine, it'd more likely be Yumi. At least we liked a ton of the same things like My Bloody Valentine and garlic cheese fries, plus she was super cute. I put a little laugh into my answer.

"Aha. No," I said, with just the right amount of disdain.

"No?" Cyril said.

"Everyone at my school is awful."

"What about Stacey?" Morna said, asking about the distant male relative of hers who also happened to be one of my two living friends.

"He doesn't count," I said. "Though do you think you can keep *your* hands off him, Morna? Given he's, like, your descendant?"

"Oooh," the other dead kids howled. Derek stroked his index finger in the shame-shame-everybody-knows-your-name gesture. I had to admit it was a pretty sick burn, if out of line. In December, Morna developed a bit of a weird crush on my tall, silent, oddly dressed friend, which made things super awkward when we learned they were branches of the same family tree.

Morna, in keeping with the colour palette, turned dark lavender. "How should I have known? We're barely even related, y'know!"

The other dead kids doubled — even tripled — over in laughter. I guess it was mean of me to bring it up, especially since Morna had always been really nice to me, just a little boy crazy. But whatever. It was difficult enough explaining to Stacey what that Christmas card "from his big sister" meant. I didn't want to have to deal with a Valentine from beyond the grave, so I'm just glad that whole infatuation was over.

"Sorry," I said, putting my hand on the shoulder of Morna's polka-dotted dress.

"It's okay," she said, slowly losing some of the purple in her face.

"Did somebody say Sorry!?" Derek said, jangling dice in his hand and gesturing toward the game board.

"Not yet! Cyril, I need you to say 'truth.'"

"Truth," he obliged. Trusty, 250-year-old Cyril.

"Cyril," I said, locking into his clear blue eyes. "What do you remember about the days leading up to your death?"

I gave Cyril a more difficult question than the one Morna gave me. Slightly.

"Well, I came to Sticksville when they were still *building* a Sticksville. The town was still being settled. And we didn't call it — what do you call it now? Ontario? Maybe the natives called it that."

"Were there natives in Sticksville when you white folks started settling things?" Derek pointedly asked.

"Probably."

"Typical," Derek muttered.

"It was my parents," Cyril protested. "What was I supposed to do?"

"Okay, okay," I said. Was I going to have to referee a fight between Derek and Cyril? They'd never bickered before. "Let's not get sidetracked just yet. Cyril, tell me more about proto-Sticksville, please. It might help us figure out what to investigate."

"Well, my mother, father, and I moved to Sticksville in 1779. Before that, we had lived in Nova Scotia for a year, but my parents hated it. I guess I should backtrack and tell you why we were in Canada in the first place."

"Yes, please make this story even *longer*," Kirby said, a Sorry! piece dangling between his lips like a toothpick.

"I was born in one of the British colonies, in New York. But in 1775, the troubles started. People in some of the other colonies didn't like being ruled by a king. Or maybe just the king we had in particular, King George III. Or they didn't like paying taxes to an overseas government. In any event, they started a revolution. First there were protests. Then, when British soldiers arrived to disarm and arrest the rebels, it turned into a full-scale war.

"My parents were Loyalists, loyal to the king. They had come to the New World from England and my father was a shipbuilder, building ships to go along Lake Ontario and up the St. Lawrence. But with the outbreak of war, the American patriots confiscated our land in New York and our shipbuilding business. We had heard that those loyal to the British crown were being arrested or hanged. Father wasn't going to wait for that to happen. We fled one night by horse and carriage with most of our possessions. Father knew he could get shipbuilding work in Nova Scotia. The colony was still loyal to England and even assisting in the war effort."

"Then how'd y'get t'Sticksville?" Tabetha asked an important question. Nova Scotia was over a thousand miles from Sticksville. By horse and carriage, I have no idea how long a trip it would have been. Two months?

"After one harsh winter in Nova Scotia, my parents decided we had to move. We'd never been so cold and damp in our lives! My father knew they needed shipbuilders in the Niagara area, too. It was just across the river from American rebels and an important nautical position, so we packed up the coach again in the spring of 1779 and headed west into Quebec."

"You mean Ontario?" I said.

"No, it was all Quebec then. I guess it became Ontario later. Anyway, our journey there was long and difficult. Very different from how we'd been living in New York or even Nova Scotia. It was frontier living: hunting for food while avoiding wild animals and Indian raids."

"Like the Oregon Trail," Derek said.

"What?" I asked.

"It's an old video game. And don't think I didn't hear that 'Indian raid' crack."

"It was a real danger," he protested. "When we arrived in the very new town of Sticksville, we first had to build a house."

"And that's the Sticksville Museum?" I asked.

"Sort of. I think my parents made some improvements after I died. But there weren't many buildings or structures when we first arrived. Maybe three dozen residences? Many of the militia lived in barracks. My father worked not far away, along the Niagara River, building ships for the British war effort."

"And what did you do while he was off building ships? Drum?" I asked, gesturing toward the small leather drum slung over his side.

"Yes. In a sense," Cyril said. "Because we were near Niagara, there was quite a large British military presence. We always felt safe from the American soldiers. I wasn't old enough to be a soldier, but I could join the local militia. I played drum in the colour guard."

"Oh," I said. "How many of you were there in the militia?"

"I don't know. About a hundred."

"Do you think one of them might have been responsible for this?" I said, waving my arms up and down, around his body, indicating his general deadness.

"Hmm." Kirby's eyebrow snapped up like a jackknife.

"I suppose that would be possible," Cyril admitted. "Though there were many dangers around Sticksville. Whenever I wasn't needed at the militia, I'd hunt for food: beavers, wild turkey, deer."

"Poor deer," Morna said.

"Who's to say I wasn't mauled by a bear while out hunting one afternoon?"

"I am," I said. "When we first met, you told me it happened one night after manoeuvres with your militia. You went over to the harbour to see your dad. I don't think there are any bears down at the harbour."

"They *do* like fish," Morna helpfully suggested.

Derek added, "Bears make good navigators. They're always able to find their *bear*ings."

That was, like, probably the worst animal joke I'd ever heard, but it didn't stop the dead kids from laughing like the audience at a taping of *Def Comedy Jam*.

"Seriously, guys," I interjected. "Cyril, what happened during manoeuvres? Or did anything happen earlier that day?"

"I went hunting earlier that week, but I don't remember catching anything."

"Do you remember anythin'? Did ya go huntin' *with* anyone?" Tabetha asked.

"No, I always hunted alone, unless I was with my father," Cyril said. "Though I think that was the day I discovered that narrow little shack."

"Shack?"

Apparently Cyril had stumbled across an unusual shack deep in the woods shortly before he died, and instead of telling me this *first*, he decided to front-load his story with a recap of the American Revolution and other junk. The dead kids were their own worst enemies sometimes.

"There was a shack?" I repeated. "What was in this shack?"

"I don't remember. I'm certain I looked inside, but I can't remember what I saw." Cyril

removed his tricorn hat and held it to his chest with his left hand while his right vigorously scratched the golden hair atop his rotten skull.

"Far be it from me to jump to conclusions, Cyril," I said. "But I think whatever was in that secret shack in the woods got you killed."

"Sorry," Derek said, though whether he was expressing his condolences over Cyril's early death or just reminding us all of the board game he wanted to play, I can't be sure.

History
Comes Alive!

After a rather late night of lessons about the American Revolution, frontier life in early Sticksville, and the rules and regulations of Sorry!, October Schwartz's eyes were ringed with darkish circles that even the pint of liquid eyeliner she typically wore couldn't hide. Our heroine attempted to make her eyes focus on the blackboard before her as Mr. Santuzzi, everyone's least favourite math teacher, hastily marked it up with various quadratic equations.

Santuzzi, once he'd covered nearly the entire board with white chalk, turned to face the assembled students, whom he viewed more as cadets in some sort of mathematic army.

"Which of you brave soldiers would like to solve the first problem for me?" he asked, swaying back and forth on his heels a bit. A variation on his usual fashion theme, his vest and pants were a light purple, and no matter how much he rocked on his heels, his perfect Lego-like hair never moved a stitch. Most of the school was in agreement that whatever his hairpiece was, it was not of this earth. As one might expect, his question produced no volunteers. Like a military drone, he started to patrol the aisles of desks, seeking one unlucky individual in particular.

"Miss Schwartz," he said, placing the cylinder of chalk in October's palm. "Why don't you give this a whirl?"

October already felt the shame-heat and sweat developing under her arms and along the back of her neck. She was certain she could solve the equation without much trouble, but she tried to avoid standing in front of the entire class. When you're known as the Zombie Tramp, you tend to shun the limelight.

"Knock knock!" said a voice from behind the barely open classroom door. October's unlikely rescuers were representatives of the Sticksville Central student council, again interrupting class with an announcement regarding what was sure to be yet another inane holiday-themed initiative. The boy at school with the only name more unusual than October herself — Zogon — and one of Ashlie's friends (Goose Neck) strode into the room and quietly said something to Mr. Santuzzi while the rest of the students started murmuring amongst themselves. Santuzzi's facial expression slowly morphed from one of confusion to one that looked like he'd just been patted on the bum by one of the council members.

"Okay, settle down, everyone. Attention!" he shouted, palms outward. "Your student council has an announcement. It will just take two minutes," he said, shooting the council members a penetrating stare. "And then we'll return to math."

Ashlie's friend moved up and down the aisles, handing out what looked suspiciously like tests. Two papers landed on October's desk: they were unmistakably a computer-generated multiple-choice answer form and its accompanying sheet of questions.

"As I hope you all know," Zogon began, slapping his hands together as if he were about to lead a Zumba class, "the student council is hosting a big Valentine's Day dance, and we'd love to see you all there."

October seriously doubted the Z-boy would love to see her, Yumi, and Stacey at his trash-fest dance.

"To make things a *bit* more interesting, we want to set you up with your love match."

A few girls clapped. One of the burnouts who sat in the back, Jesse, groaned audibly.

"All you have to do is answer the Love Match quiz: use the questions on the one sheet, then complete the Scantron form and return it to the student council office before February 12. The following day, you'll receive your top Love Match of the opposite sex.

If you bring your Love Match to the dance, you can both take two dollars off your admission."

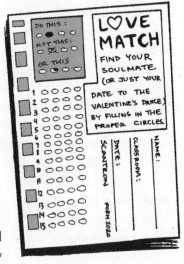

A bit more applause ensued from the overly enthusiastic girls. To October, this seemed like an extremely small discount for so much personal humiliation. More immediately, October's natural inclination to disappear in class was overwhelmed by her even more natural sense of injustice. (After all, she dressed up like a streetwise vampire every day for school. How great was that inclination to blend in, really?) That Spidey-sense of injustice started tingling something fierce.

October's spotty black nail polish gleamed as her hand shot up. Zogon looked like he was trying to rapidly figure out a way to *not* answer her question. Reluctantly, he gestured toward October.

"Uh, yes? The girl in black?"

"Why are the love matches only between people of the opposite sex?" she asked. "Isn't that kind of discriminatory?"

Zogon looked like he'd just lost control of his bladder at a state dinner.

"Schwartz wants to be paired up with a chick!" shouted some joker at the back.

"Lesbian," muttered burnout Jesse.

"Hey, hey," Mr. Santuzzi shouted, taking control of the room in ways Zogon and Goose Neck could only dream of. "Enough of that garbage talk. You two want to go to the office? Miss Schwartz, if you have a genuine concern, I'd recommend you bring it to the principal. But do so *after* class."

More tittering came from the students.

"Council members? May I get back to teaching now?" Santuzzi asked, or rather, told.

Zogon, who still looked like he'd just been shaken awake from a long nap, said, "Yes. Just remember: return your forms by February 12."

Perhaps the worst part of that morning was that after all that, when October could still feel the sweat on her black shirt and the heat in her face, Mr. Santuzzi still expected her to go to the board and solve that stupid quadratic equation in front of the whole class, who now not only thought of October as a Zombie Tramp, but as a Gay Zombie Tramp. Maybe they'd already thought that.

Whatever. October was of a similar mind to your narrator, dear readers. Let people think what they want to think; it's not like there's anything wrong with liking people the same sex as you. And shame on anyone who would say otherwise.

October marched to the front of the class as if there were a guillotine awaiting her there. She solved the problem, handily, demonstrating all her work to boot. It turns out there was a reason that Mr. Santuzzi was making her tutor Ashlie Salmons. October felt a small glimmer of pride that at least now her classmates would think of her as the Gay Zombie Tramp who was really good at math.

☠   ☠   ☠

Yumi and Stacey, who always seemed to get out of class before October, could be found in their usual cafeteria corner. As soon as October took her seat, Yumi volleyed a question at her: "Did student council get all OkCupid in your classes this morning, too?"

Yumi held the Scantron form in front of her like it was the first ten dollars her business had ever made.

"Yeah, it's terrible," October said.

"Super bad," Yumi agreed. "I'm still going to do it, probably."

"Even though your real love match has been arrested?"

Yumi Takeshi briefly had a thing (let's call it) for Devin McGriff's older and totally age-inappropriate brother, Skyler, which was made all the more inappropriate when we discovered he was the person committing hate crimes against her. Yumi pulled a grape from Stacey's lunch and launched it at October's face. Stacey was so busy doing the jumble in a newspaper he'd brought, he didn't even notice the theft of his grapes.

"Don't worry," October said. "I hear tell there are plenty of fish in the sea. Ones not in jail, even. What about you, Stacey?"

"Dunno. We'll see."

"Look at some of these questions, Schwartz," Yumi interrupted. She flattened the quiz on the table between their two lunches.

Your ideal date would be:

a. Dinner and a movie.

b. Baseball game.

c. Beach picnic.

d. Art gallery stroll.

"E," Yumi said. "Making out on a pinball machine in the corner at a Misfits concert."

"Write-in!" October said.

Your friends would describe you as:

a. Caring.

b. Smart.

c. The life of the party.

d. Funny.

"Why is *morose* not a choice?" October asked.

"I'd describe you more as *Zombie Trampish*," Yumi said.

"A total killjoy," Stacey said, joining in what was sure to be the only fun aspect of this Love Match business.

As if summoned by a vague sense that someone other than her was having fun, Ashlie Salmons sidled up to their cafeteria table with her resting-face sneer in full effect.

"I can save you losers some trouble with that form," Ashlie said, starting with Stacey. "Your perfect match is a well-used prison Swiffer. Yours, little one, is a wet border collie. And Zombie Tramp — original recipe — will be paired up with a brain-damaged hippopotamus in a Korn T-shirt. Hope you all have fun at the dance."

Yumi narrowed her eyes. "Why are you here, Ashlie? Shouldn't you be guarding the Golden Fleece?"

"I almost forgot," she said, jutting out her left hipbone to prominently display her thick, lacquered red belt. "I need to sort out with Zombie Tramp when we're meeting for our first tutoring session."

"Ugh," October said, glancing quickly back and forth between her friends and her future student. "I guess your place? Sunday afternoon? Like, three?"

"Perfect," she said. "Get the address from your dad. He certainly visits enough. Should I make sure I have anything? Holy water? A seat cover so our house doesn't pick up any diseases?"

"Your brain, if you can find it," Stacey muttered through his fifth tuna sandwich of the week.

"See you then." Ashlie Salmons tapped the cafeteria table twice with her delicate palm, then spritely crossed the room to her usual spot. Every so often, something would happen that made October wonder if maybe — deep down, somewhere — there was a vestige of humanity in her greatest enemy. And, inevitably, that thought would be completely eradicated in less than a day's time.

"Mr. Santuzzi is forcing me to do this, guys," October sighed and stirred her instant ramen.

"I was only following orders," Yumi squeaked in mock disapproval. "You know what they say: you shake hands with the devil, you wake up with fleas."

"Or something like that," Stacey added as he choked down the last of his sandwich.

☠ ☠ ☠

Friday, January 31, was a momentous day in October's high school career. Not only did it mark the introduction of the Love Match Scantron form, and forever brand her as a strident lesbian in the mind of her fellow math students (not a bad brand, really), it was also the day that Ms. Fenstermacher, her mostly helpful, lawful-good history teacher, gave her a monster assignment. And provided that October was a little busy solving a centuries' old murder after classes, an overly involved history project was something she really didn't need at the moment.

Ms. Fenstermacher removed her boxy eyeglasses and buffed them on her royal blue plaid shirt. To the horror-stricken faces of her

grade nine history students, she again explained the assignment.

"Trust me, it's not going to be that difficult. Once you start, you'll find the material just flows out of you like a faucet," she said, rather optimistically. "All you have to do is pick a historical figure — anyone who lived before 1960 — and write one thousand words on that figure. You'll also need to do an oral presentation — a shortened version of your written assignment — for the class. But the catch is: I want these to be lesser-known historical figures. No Abraham Lincolns or Laura Secords. No Genghis Khans. This project is going to test your researching skills. The more obscure your subject, the better. Feel free to pick someone local, if you'd like. As a volunteer at the Sticksville Museum, I can tell you there's a lot of history to your town . . . and a wealth of resources at the museum."

Almost the moment it was announced, Ms. Fenstermacher's history project weighed October down like a concrete pendant around her neck. Was it better, she wondered, to figure out how her dead chum Cyril died or to not flunk her history assignment? The two seemed mutually exclusive. The only bright point of Ms. Fenstermacher's whole lesson that day was that it reminded October that there was a Sticksville Museum, and even if that museum hadn't once been the home of Cyril Cooper's family (which it had), it was bound to have some information about the town in 1779 — maybe even information connected to Cyril's death. She remained silent for the rest of Ms. Fenstermacher's lecture on Canada in World War II, then bounced as soon as the final bell sounded.

"Remember, these history projects are important. We're at the end of the semester," Fenstermacher shouted over the cacophony of kids shifting their desks and stuffing their backpacks. "Presentations will start February 21, the week after the Valentine's dance."

October remained unsettled by how vigilantly the universe was asking her to pay attention to this Valentine's dance. It was as if all her fellow students and her teachers had a significant sum of money riding on the outcome of this school-sanctioned grope-fest. She wedged her way between students and their desks to reach Ms. Fenstermacher. The history teacher was engrossed in placing papers into an accordion file.

"Ms. Fenstermacher?" October asked.

"Yes, October?" She looked up from behind her thick glasses and swoop of chestnut hair.

"I have a question about the museum."

"Well, I can probably help you with that," she said. "Were you thinking of profiling a local Sticksvillian for your end-of-term project?"

"Maybe." It suddenly struck October that she could kill two birds with one stone, if one were being violently metaphorical about it. Cyril Cooper *was* a local Sticksvillian. "I was curious if the museum had, like, information or files or something on the late 1700s. Like when the town was founded."

Ms. Fenstermacher rolled up her sleeves in a real elbow-grease way and wound the string of the accordion file around its tab. "The museum is the house of the Cooper family who first settled in Sticksville around that time — during the Revolutionary War. There's actually a fairly extensive collection of material from that family, including letters and correspondence."

"Really," October said. She hoped — we all did, really — that the Coopers had written a bit about how their son Cyril died in that correspondence. It would make her life so much easier. "Will you be at the museum this weekend?"

"I'll be there on Sunday."

"Maybe I'll see you there," October said with a tiny wave and heaved her massive backpack onto her shoulders. One would think she were about to leave for a trek through the Alaskan wilderness.

And while it was true that October Schwartz would (maybe) see Ms. Fenstermacher at the Sticksville Museum on Sunday, she had clandestine plans to visit much earlier.

☠   ☠   ☠

On Saturday night, less than twenty-four hours before her first dreaded tutoring session with Ashlie Salmons, October Schwartz bounded into the middle of the Sticksville Cemetery with an announcement:

"We're going to the Sticksville Museum!"

Since Cyril once lived there, it was only a matter of time before they'd be visiting the museum, but the dead kids hadn't expected October's invitation to be so gosh-darn enthusiastic. The dead kids themselves were always eager to participate in something that involved breaking and entering (which going to the museum late on a Saturday night certainly did), so within moments, they were all en route to Cyril's old house.

As per usual, October walked closest to the road, while the dead kids stayed close to the hedges and shadows wherever possible. Sticksville was largely asleep past midnight — even on a Saturday — and most living people couldn't see the dead kids (or any ghosts, for that matter) unless they'd experienced some sort of untimely death in their immediate family. But if people knew about October's team of secret super sleuths, the dead kids would become a lot less effective at detection and stuff. That creeptastic real estate agent who always seemed to be everywhere, Alyosha Diamandas, could practically see dead people better than he could see living ones, and he always seemed to arrive at the exact right moment to mess up an ongoing investigation. Because the museum wasn't for sale (as far as she knew), October was cautiously optimistic her night would be Diamandas-free.

October and the dead kids arrived at the museum without incident. Or, at least, no incidents occurred on their journey *to* the museum. They skulked across the shadowy green of the lawn bowling club next door like they were panthers and the museum itself were some sort of delicious wildebeest.

"There it is," Cyril said, pointing.

"Not a moment too soon," October said, hot steam spewing from her mouth. "It is *way* too cold to be solving mysteries. Think we can reconvene in May, Cyril?"

"No."

The dead kids, being nothing more than desiccated, unfeeling flesh, were unsympathetic to October's chilly plight.

"And you still don't remember anything more about that shack you found in the woods?" October asked.

"I'm afraid not."

"Well," she said, "let's hope your parents wrote something about it in their decades of correspondence."

The museum was a two-storey house with a gabled roof, surrounded on each side by skeletal bushes and trees. Numerous changes had been made to the building since Cyril and his parents had lived there — such as the long entrance hallway with glass windows on every side — but the basic framework from 1779 was still in place. And as the dead kids and October stalked closer to that entrance hallway, they noticed one of those windows had been broken wide open. Glass littered the lawn below the window like glittering costume jewelry.

"Wait," October said, holding an arm up to block Tabetha and Derek from going any further. "Do you see that?"

"Someone's broken in!" Morna whispered with far too much concern for someone who was just about to break into the museum herself.

"Do you think they're still there?" The last time October had trespassed — into the McGriff household — she nearly found herself on the receiving end of a Louisville Slugger, and she kind of wanted to keep her face, more or less, as it was.

"Who cares?" Tabetha said. "Let's go in and see."

"I don't want my head bashed in by a baseball bat," October whispered.

"Then let's do some reconnaissance," Kirby suggested.

With that, he leapt up and gave Derek Running Water's head a massive bear hug and twisted.

"What are you doing, idiot?" Derek shouted as Kirby struggled to keep hold of his head.

"Someone take his body and pull the other way," Kirby shouted.

Tabetha grabbed Derek around the waist and started to roll him in the opposite direction.

"Stop it, ye two!" Morna yelled.

Derek was about to complain as well, but then, with a satisfying wet rip, like an X-Acto blade cutting through a damp swimsuit, Kirby sheared Derek's head clean off his body and pitched it through the broken window.

"Ow!" Kirby's horrifying three-point throw failed to sail harmlessly through the window. Instead, a few shards of the remaining glass grazed Derek's face as it sailed through the window.

"That's one way of doing things," Cyril said.

"Derek, can you see anyone inside?" Kirby shouted.

"They'd have definitely heard all this," Tabetha drily noted.

"No!" came Derek's voice from inside the hallway. "All the lights are out. Come here and bring my body."

The other dead kids followed, passing through the wall, with Cyril dragging Derek's shuffling body behind him. They unlocked the front door for October, and she opened it and immediately flipped the light switch. In addition to the broken window, the lights revealed a whole catalogue of broken things: smashed display cases, overturned desks, missing artifacts. The area by the front welcome desk (which was itself upside down) looked like a diorama of the aftermath of a tornado. Someone had been to the museum already and taken nearly everything!

"The museum's been robbed!" October shouted.

And that's when the burglar alarm went off.

Fighting back outrage that the alarm went off *now* and *not* when some thief was emptying the place of valuables, October and the dead kids ran for her life. Derek followed last, kicking his severed head along like a soccer ball until October made him pick it up.

Grand Theft Archaeology

I was woken up at the inhuman hour of ten o'clock that Sunday by my dad, as he pounded on my bedroom door. Through the sleep dirt covering my eyes, I could see the *Heathers* movie poster on my door shaking like there was a localized 2.2 earthquake on the Richter scale or something. My Saturday night ended with a two o'clock run from the museum's surprisingly piercing burglar alarm, so I wasn't totally ready for my wake-up call.

"October!" Dad called. "Phone for you!"

This was a surprise. Yumi and Stacey were the only people who ever called me. And neither of them were what I'd call early risers. They'd be entirely nocturnal if they didn't have to go to school. I shuffled out of my bedroom in my Rancid shirt and plaid pajama pants to see Dad — fully dressed like the adult keener he was — cradling the cordless phone in his shoulder.

"Your history teacher," he mouthed and handed me the phone. I was confused (and kind of outraged). I thought teachers were, like, forbidden from contacting students on the weekend. Propping the cordless phone up to my face, I tried to find a slightly more private place to speak. Like the bathroom.

"Hello?" I asked. Honestly, I felt more prepared to talk to the ghost voice on the old Crooked Arms phone.

"October? This is Ms. Fenstermacher," she started. "Sorry to call so early on a Sunday, but there was a break-in at the Sticksville Museum last night."

"Oh," I said, sounding — I'm sure — suitably surprised. "That's terrible. Are you okay? Was anything stolen?"

I should have realized that Ms. Fenstermacher would have to deal with the aftermath of last night's attempted *Ocean's Eleven* heist at the museum, but I didn't really see what that had to do with me. And I told her as much.

"Well, I know you were planning on coming by today to research your history project, but we won't be open due to the burglary. We have to clean up and figure out what was taken."

Remembering the scene in the museum lobby last night, I couldn't imagine all that much was left.

"Thanks for letting me know, Ms. Fenstermacher," I said, not really understanding why she'd called so early. Did she really think I'd be leaving for the museum at ten? "I'm really sorry to hear about the robbery."

"One more thing, October," she said. Just as I was about to hang up, too. "Even though we're closed today, I still think you should come by."

"You sound like you'll be really busy . . ."

"I saw you were here last night, October. There are security cameras at the museum."

Suddenly, the early morning call made a lot more sense. They had video of me (and maybe the dead kids!) breaking into the Sticksville Museum. I was thankful I was already in the washroom because I was liable to pee my pants.

"The police have already been here," Ms. Fenstermacher continued. "But I can call them back. So, I'll see you in an hour?"

"Oh . . ." I said, not really able to form words yet, more concerned about what I'd look like in an orange prison jumpsuit. "All right."

"We'll talk then," she concluded, then hung up the phone. Why did I ever think Ms. Fenstermacher was so cool? Those glasses? Former American Secretary of State Henry Kissinger wore glasses like that and he ordered an illegal bombing of Cambodia! I was in *so* much trouble. I exited the bathroom, trying desperately to will the nervous sweat back into my body so Dad wouldn't catch on to the crisis that was currently swallowing my life whole, the way a German shepherd swallows an ice cream cone.

"What was that all about?" Dad asked, taking the 1992 model telephone from me.

"Oh, Ms. Fenstermacher wanted to see if I was still coming by the museum to research my history project," I said, which, technically, wasn't a lie.

"Do you want a ride? It's cold out."

"I'd prefer to walk."

My dad was definitely going to find out about the museum robbery at some point — this *was* Sticksville after all — but I was hoping to avoid him having to deliver me personally into the back of a police cruiser. I locked myself away in my room to get dressed.

☠   ☠   ☠

The museum looked significantly worse in the day. In the late morning light, I could see the one window we'd found last night wasn't the only one that had been broken, and through the front vestibule I could see almost nothing was left in the lobby. After rapping on the front door a few times — I suppose I could have just entered through a busted window — Ms. Fenstermacher, still bundled up in her puffy down jacket, unlocked the front door for me.

"If it isn't our little Catwoman," she said.

Okay, Catwoman is pretty cool, but I think Ms. Fenstermacher was only calling me that because she's a famous thief I would know.

"I swear it wasn't me," I said, unbuttoning my black peacoat until Ms. Fenstermacher stopped me.

"You might want to keep your coat on," she said, pointing to some of the smashed-in windows. "We had a new ventilation system installed last night."

Leaving my coat, scarf, and mittens on, I followed Ms. Fenstermacher through room after room that had been picked

nearly clean until we arrived at the museum's office. It was like there was a hurricane coming, and instead of stocking up on food, water, and batteries, people had hoarded all the local history they could carry. The computers were untouched in the museum office, but I noticed a lot of other things were missing. Ms. Fenstermacher's co-worker — the woman who looked kind of like her, but *way* older . . . maybe in her forties — was waiting at the printer. She seemed perplexed that I was with Ms. Fenstermacher, but not so perplexed that she asked about it. Being her basic self, she asked, "Going to *The Rocky Horror Picture Show* tonight?" Given the dire circumstances, I couldn't even form a decent comeback, which is one of the most tragic things about the whole situation.

"Roberta, is that the museum inventory?" my history teacher asked as the other woman (Roberta, I gathered) collected a short stack of papers from the printer.

She nodded.

"Can you start in the kitchen with that and I'll join you in a second?"

Fenstermacher's museum co-worker picked up a pen and carried it and the sheaf of papers down the stairs. Ms. Fenstermacher quietly closed the office door behind her.

44

"So what were you doing here, October?" she asked, turning to me and lowering those glasses again.

"Listen, Ms. Fenstermacher," I said. "It was stupid. I'll never do it again. But I didn't rob the museum!"

She nestled the glasses more snugly on her face and softened her eyes. "I know."

"You know?" She knew and still wanted to watch me squirm like a piece of bacon on a sizzling frying pan.

"We saw the security tape — it saves the last twenty-four hours onto the office computers and to an online server — and you broke in a couple hours after the robbery . . . and it looks like you left a minute after you arrived. As soon as the alarm went off."

A wave of relief rode up my body, feet first, like I'd been submerged into a kiddie pool of apple pie. And Ms. Fenstermacher was under the belief that I'd been alone. Apparently, the dead kids didn't show up on video, which was ideal.

"Besides, you didn't even cover your face. Not much of a master criminal. But you still broke into the museum. Why?"

Luckily, I'd anticipated that I'd need to explain myself and had rehearsed an excuse on the walk over. My alibi was that Stacey, Yumi, and I were walking home from a late movie at the Sticksville Mews and wandered by the museum so we could stroll along the river. That's when we noticed the broken windows and thought we should check out what had happened. Not the most convincing story on paper, but I'd daubed the story with intricate detail, like how Stacey's laces were undone and how I'd seen a grey cat, to make it seem more plausible. Plus, Ms. Fenstermacher was aware that I had a penchant for wandering the streets of Sticksville at night and sneaking into places I didn't belong.

"I only saw *you* on the security tape," said Ms. Fenstermacher. "Yumi and Stacey were here, as well?"

Again, the confirmation of no weird, pale kids dressed in old-timey clothes. At least I didn't have to explain who the dead kids were. But I might have to coach Yumi and Stacey on this fake story, if Ms. Fenstermacher ever wanted to check it. Luckily she didn't teach either of them this semester.

"Yeah. But maybe they didn't come in before the alarm went off?"

"That could have been very dangerous, October," Ms. Fenstermacher admonished. "You had no idea whether the burglar was still here or not. Next time, call the police if you see something like that."

I nodded my head, maybe a bit too enthusiastically. Still, I think Ms. Fenstermacher could tell I was definitely not ever going to do that.

"What got stolen?" I asked.

Ms. Fenstermacher pursed her lips, as if she'd already said too much to her grade nine student about the robbery, but continued anyway. "Frak," she sighed, spouting her favourite *Battlestar Galactica* slang. "Almost everything. Whoever it was must have had a truck waiting. They took a ton of artifacts and historical pieces, letters and documents, the Roxy Wotherspoon diary you found — even all the stuff from the 1700s you were asking about. The Cooper family correspondence is missing."

"Ugh," I said, feeling legitimately upset. And not just for historical legacy reasons. Figuring out Cyril's mystery without any help from the museum was going to be a proverbial night-mare on whatever street the museum was on.

"The robbery couldn't have had worse timing either. We were getting things ready for the annual spring Sticks-ebration."

"The what?" I said. Whatever Ms. Fenstermacher said, it sounded way made up.

"Sticks-ebration. It's the annual spring festival to celebrate the town's founding in 1779. People dress up in costume, there's music, games, a cake walk . . . This year, they were going to launch the restored *Kingfisher*, a ship built during the found-ing year, on the river."

All this was news to me. "I just arrived in town last August. I must have missed last year's."

"Well, it's a big thing for the Sticksville Historical Society, and the fact that we've had our entire history basically stolen is going to put a real damper on things."

"Why didn't the alarm go off when the burglar broke in?" I asked. "It totally went off as soon as I set foot in the building."

"I don't know," Ms. Fenstermacher said, chewing on her index finger. "It should have. It's an old system, so it can be a bit spotty, but it obviously worked last night on you. Also, I'd tagged some of the special items in our collection, like the Wotherspoon diary, with electronic chips. As soon as they're taken off the property, they're supposed to send me a text message and email. But nothing. Frustrating isn't the frakking word for it."

Ms. Fenstermacher loomed over her computer and refreshed her email to check that her second theft prevention method hadn't sent a late email.

"But your computer didn't get taken," I said. The thief had hauled off some large-sized pieces of Sticksville history; why not the very resaleable computers?

"The cash box was untouched, too," she said, tapping on the space bar. "Just stuff of historical value was stolen."

"And do you have any suspects?"

I didn't want to sound *too* interested in this robbery, but given this thief had really stuck a banana in the tailpipe of the car that was my investigation, I wanted to know all I could. Ms. Fenstermacher slowly raised an eyebrow and glanced sideways at me. Her weird goth student was getting weirder all the time, I suppose.

"I probably shouldn't show you this, but the news will be out in the *Sticksville Loon* soon enough," she said, opening a movie file on her desktop. "It would appear that we were robbed by a pirate."

The security video started and — sure enough — someone in a very elaborate pirate costume was grabbing pieces of history — books, silverware, an old telephone, posters — and hauling them all off-screen. Most distressingly, he seemed to be glowing. Clearly, he wasn't a real pirate — not that that had ever been a possibility — but someone in an elaborate costume, complete with a rubber mask. The mask was pale yellow, framed with an impressive black beard, with its mouth open in

a predatory grin. The thief stalked around the lobby, where I'd show up just a couple hours later according to the timestamp of the video, in black boots and a faded orange and navy blue coat, with matching tricorn hat. Light seemed to emanate from within the coat, though it was hard to see on the low-resolution video. Really, he looked like a grown-up version of Cyril if he'd gone on to make a few bad life choices.

"If you know anyone with a glowing pirate costume like that," Ms. Fenstermacher said, her face taking on a bluish tint from the full-screen video, "you may want to tell the police."

"What's that?" I said, pointing to a triangle of fabric spilling over the pirate thief's prodigious belt buckle.

"Probably the thief's shirt," Ms. Fenstermacher said. "I doubt he was naked under that pirate suit."

"But it's floral," I said. "Like a Hawaiian shirt." To me, it seemed like Ms. Fenstermacher wasn't even interested in solving this mystery. Like she was totally content to have the police figure it out or whatever. "That's a clue. Not everyone just wears loud Hawaiian shirts like that. Did you find any other clues?"

Ms. Fenstermacher's eyes goggled behind her thick glasses. Goggled behind her goggles, basically.

"Any clues?" she said, seemingly offended. She closed the movie file window. "Let's leave this to the police, October. What do you think this is, *Scooby-Doo* and you're Velma?"

"*Thanks*," I said, not overly happy that my teacher immediately associated me with the awkward nerd with glasses.

"Hey, no offence intended. I'm Velma, too," she said. And she was, if you thought about it. "October, I think I've probably involved you too much in this already. Go home, let the police handle this, and try to stay out of trouble, okay?"

That's when Ms. Fenstermacher unceremoniously shooed

me out of the crime scene and locked the museum front door. Staying out of trouble in Sticksville was, as I was finding, easier said than done. And though Ms. Fenstermacher didn't think we were all living in an episode of *Scooby-Doo*, I couldn't help but think last night's robbery was seemingly committed by a ghost pirate.

☠   ☠   ☠

The worst thing about Sunday wasn't waking up early. It wasn't even that the Sticksville Museum was ransacked. But that after that miserable start to the day, I was now expected to visit the Salmons residence and tutor Ashlie in math. This insult to the day's injuries was the reason I was pressing my thumb into the doorbell of a two-storey house on Lippincott Lane, standing outside a blue front door decorated with a wreath of pink and red Valentine's hearts.

Just as I was about to ring the doorbell a second time, the door swung open to reveal the unimpressed, scowling face of my one-and-only nemesis, Ashlie Salmons. For a Sunday, she was really dressed up, in a cream collared shirt, grey plaid skirt, and matchy-matchy grey tights.

"Zombie Tramp," she said. "I was hoping you wouldn't show up."

"Mr. Santuzzi is very convincing," I explained. "You're dressed up. Do you have a job interview later?"

"Church" was her one-word explanation.

"You go to church?" For some reason, I couldn't imagine the person I considered to be compelling evidence for the existence of the devil to be a regular churchgoer.

"Yeah. I know you're more into sacrificing babies and drinking blood and stuff, but some of us go to regular church."

Ignoring whatever she meant by the troubling phrase "regular church," I soldiered on with the task at hand.

"Okay, let's get this over with," I said. "Where do you want to study?"

"In the kitchen," Ashlie answered without hesitation. "Ground floor, in case I need to make a sudden escape. Closer to witnesses, too."

Ashlie guided me through the first floor of her house, which had — I felt — an inordinate number of doilies for a house occupied by a Crown attorney. She sat down at the plain wooden table in the brightly lit kitchen, where she'd already left her math text and binder open. Mr. Santuzzi had informed me, as if I were a Navy Seal and improving Ashlie Salmons's grade average were, like, creating stability in the Crimean, that Ashlie was currently having trouble with trigonometry, so I'd tried to brush up on some of that earlier in the week. I plopped down in an arch-backed chair beside Ashlie.

"So, what do you know about triangles?" she said, idly flipping back and forth between a few pages of her textbook. Her nails were really nice compared to mine, which were speckled with chipped black nail polish. She blew the front swoop of her auburn hair from her face with a sigh.

"Well . . . what do *you* know about triangles," I countered.

"They've got three sides," she said.

We were off to a pretty great start.

"Maybe we should do some math now?"

And math we did. For about two full hours. I won't bore you with all the ins and outs of what difficulties my enemy (who, I hate to admit, was quickly becoming my frenemy) had with sine functions, cosine functions, and tangents, no less their reciprocals. But by the end of the afternoon, she was already starting to solve some problems on her own. I would have felt proud if it didn't feel so much like I was helping an assassin improve his golf swing.

"Zombie Tramp, what would you normally be doing right now?" she asked, locking eyes with me in a Gorgon-like stare. "Like, if you hadn't been forced to teach me about triangles today. What do you and your loser friends do with yourselves?"

"I don't know. Probably the same stuff you and your friends do. We just watch better movies and listen to better music."

"Hmm," she said, unimpressed.

"Are you a brain in all your classes, or just math?" Somehow Ashlie managed to make even the most innocuous of compliments sound like an insult.

How do you answer that question, really? "Not really. I'm okay, I guess. I'm kind of worried because they just assigned a big project in my history class."

"Yeah?"

"Yeah, you have to do a presentation on someone, like, *not* famous in history," I (sort of) explained.

"Too bad the Sticksville Museum got robbed," Ashlie said, pushing her books forward as if they were a meal she'd just finished. "There's information on lots of not-famous people in there."

Considering the museum had been robbed overnight, and it wasn't exactly trending online, I was suspicious that Ashlie already knew all about it.

"How did you hear about that?" I asked.

"My mom, genius. You forget? We've basically got the police band on the radio non-stop," she said. Then, a sly smile on her face, "How did you?"

No point in lying about it. "Um, I stumbled across the break-in late last night. I saw the broken windows and went to check it out and set off the alarm."

Ashlie started laughing her Maleficent laugh. "Now I know what you do for fun!"

While having a Crown attorney for a mom certainly could explain Ashlie's knowledge of the robbery, I couldn't quell my desire to raid her closet and look for a Hawaiian shirt. But given her fashion sense, I highly doubted I'd find one.

"Well, good luck on your history project," she scoffed. "Maybe you can just interview someone super old. You can get out of my house now."

Interviews with the Dead

Though Ashlie had been typically condescending most of that afternoon, her comment about the super old did inspire one idea: if the museum was closed (and now devoid of any actual historical material), October could still do research through first-person interviews. After all, she had a direct line to her chosen Sticksville resident from the 1700s: Cyril Cooper.

October's epiphany, if you want to call something so obvious an epiphany, led directly to the scene that followed on Monday night: Cyril Cooper, sitting on a lone stool in October Schwartz's filthy bedroom, facing the worst inquisition this side of *Marathon Man*'s dentist chair. Maybe it wasn't so bad, but October was really expecting him to spill the United Empire beans on everything he could remember about the summer of '79. (Not to be confused with that Bryan Adams hit single, which is about the summer of '69.)

Monday night marked another date for October's dad and Crown Attorney Salmons, so October figured it was the perfect time to interview her oldest dead friend. Her dad would be out of the house for hours, talking to his new girlfriend about doilies. October stopped by the cemetery not too long after dark and invited the dead kids up to her room. Which is why Cyril was seated on the stool by the drafting table that once, long ago, was purchased with the vague notion that October might one day take up illustration. October sat across from him on her bed, like Michelle Pfeiffer interrogating Coolio in the video for "Gangsta's

Paradise," with Kirby, Morna, and Derek beside her. Tabetha was rifling through October's dresser.

"How come yer interviewin' Cyril?" Tabetha asked, digging through a drawer of black sweatshirts. "We all got stories more interestin' than ol' Cyril."

"Yes, and some of us can tell them better than he can," Kirby piped up from behind October, jamming his — for whatever reason — very tangible knee into her back.

"You know the deal." October elbowed Kirby back.

"But this is for a school project, too," Derek pointed out. "You're going to tell your whole class all about Cyril and not about the rest of us."

"How come he gets to be the golden boy of our group?" Tabetha asked.

This was something October, though usually quite the planner, had not anticipated: the other dead kids were envious of the presentation she was writing on Cyril. For the others, she was merely solving the mysteries of their untimely deaths; Cyril would be talked about before dozens of disinterested teenagers.

"Don't be jealous," October said, popping off the cap of her pen with her teeth. "It's just how the timing worked out."

"I would gladly trade places with any of you," Cyril said from his stool, idly nudging a pile of CDs underfoot with his buckled shoe. He didn't like being put on the spot.

"Just relax," October said, but she was leaning over her notepad like a peregrine falcon on a rock cliff. "All you need to do is tell me everything you can remember about what life was like in Sticksville, back in 1779."

"I've already told you what I remember."

"October," Tabetha interrupted, now elbow-deep in her living friend's clothing. "Do you own any shirts that aren't black?"

"I think there's a red one," she said, not taking her eyes from the corpse of the United Empire Loyalist seated on her stool. "Now shhhh. Tell me more about that shack."

And so, Cyril Cooper began his story.

☠   ☠   ☠

"Sticksville did not look anything like it does today," Cyril said. "Mostly, this was a wilderness outpost. Or rather, a spot of some military significance because we were so close to the border with New York. As you know, I was something of a soldier myself."

This was sort of true. Though the Cooper family had fled what is now known as the United States of America, future home of game shows and rap music and corn dogs, at the outbreak of the revolution, by the time they arrived in Sticksville, it was a full-fledged war, with the British trying to suppress American patriots who hoped to establish an independent nation. In 1779, Sticksville was mostly a military settlement of soldiers and their families, established to protect the area west of the Niagara River for England. The town had a local militia, and while Cyril was a bit too young to be a militiaman himself, he tried to get involved. They let him participate in manoeuvres and training, and he played drum for their little marching band, but the militia in Sticksville never would have let him see combat . . . probably. Basically, he was like the bat boy in a baseball game. Part of the team, but not really.

But we should back up a bit for those of you who might not be overly familiar with North American history. What was this American Revolution and why was there a war going on in 1779? Cyril had somewhat explained this to October earlier but left out a few key details. Originally what's now the United States was inhabited by a number of indigenous tribes — Cherokee, Cayuga, Mohican — but in the late 1400s, European explorers started arriving by ship, and by the 1600s, groups of Europeans, largely from England, started moving to the United States and claiming land, settling European-style villages, towns, and cities (and displacing — often violently — the people who were already there). By 1775, the eastern seaboard of America was thirteen British colonies. This meant that although these places were located in America, with families living and working there, they were actually ruled over by the King of England, way over on the other side of the Atlantic Ocean. And that king made the American settlers pay taxes, as members of the British Empire. After a series of events too numerous to mention here, many of the American settlers got fed up — fed up with paying taxes to a government they had no say in, fed up with the rule of a king who had absolute authority. So they revolted. Obviously, their British rulers didn't like that one bit, so that's how a war developed. And it was in the midst of this turmoil that the Coopers came to Sticksville, part of British territory that later became known as Canada.

"And your dad was a shipbuilder. Did he build your house, too?" October asked.

"Yes, of course."

"Did it look like a boat?" Tabetha asked.

Cyril just stared at her.

"But it wasn't easy with Father out at the harbour almost all the time. There was a lot of work to do at home. There were no real general stores or anything like that. There was firewood to chop, food to hunt and gather, clothing to make . . . there were scores and scores of chores to do, and my mother did almost all of them. I assisted. And did some of the hunting, as well."

Yes, it was true. When not doing formations or learning how to quickly load a musket, then shoot in a military line with the

Sticksville militia, thirteen-year-old Cyril Cooper was often out in the wilderness, shooting rabbits and deer and other such critters. This may seem unpleasant to many of you — vegetarians or people who buy their meat prepackaged or frozen at the supermarket — but it was what people did in 1779. Compare this to the life of October Schwartz, who, though the same age as Cyril Cooper, had never seen a gun in her life before her old history teacher had threatened her with a bayonet on Halloween. The land all around Sticksville had not been endless fields of Walmart, Staples, and pita restaurants, as it was in October Schwartz's day. Instead, it was a deep, dark wood, filled with all sorts of potentially edible animals.

"I was a pretty good shot, too, so it's really their loss they wouldn't allow me to do anything besides play the drum in the militia," Cyril said, brushing some imaginary dust off his shoulder.

"I've never heard ye play yer drum, Cyril," Morna said.

"They forgot to bury the sticks with me," he said, mournfully. "Anyway, the other boys in the militia and I didn't really get along. A lot of them teased me for being the drum boy."

"Was that kind of like being the water boy?" Derek asked, referring to that unheralded football position made famous by Adam Sandler.

"I don't know what that is," Cyril said. "But I'm going to say yes."

Cyril Cooper was the youngest in the militia, and all the others — boys of sixteen and seventeen — would often mock him for being the drummer boy. No one had yet written a Christmas carol to outline the many virtues of drummer boys. The older boys, while cleaning their muskets, would make disparaging remarks like, "Where does the gunpowder go in that drum?" or "I've heard the American patriots are helpless against a good rhythm." (The American revolutionary soldiers were called patriots.) The ringleader of these militia tormentors was a red-haired boy named Patrick Burton. The amusing part — in an ironic sort of way — was that Burton wasn't even that good a solider. He was far from the best shot and not even that physically adept. But he was — by far — the best at insulting the drummer boy.

"So, one day — it seems ridiculous now — but I decided to

get even." Cyril's face darkened as he wedged his tricorn hat back on his head.

For a second, the faces of all the listeners in October's room grew tense with this revelation. All faces, that is, except Tabetha's, whose face had broken into a smile wider than the Niagara River. October, while kind of terrified by what Cyril might say next — how he achieved his revenge — also realized this Patrick Burton seemed like a definite suspect in Cyril Cooper's death.

"Are you familiar with poison ivy?" he grinned.

Almost instantly, everyone's eyebrows popped in disbelief.

"Really?" Kirby said, unimpressed.

"I found a patch while hunting one morning," Cyril continued. "I carefully gathered it in a burlap sack, then left a bunch of it in Patrick's britches when we went swimming one day." Cyril barked out a few laughs before silently shuddering in hilarity atop his stool, but no one else was laughing.

"That's it?" Tabetha said.

Cyril abruptly stopped laughing. "I think it's pretty clear that Patrick Burton found out it was I who left the poison ivy and is responsible for my death."

"I don't know . . ." October said.

"I thought ya were gonna shoot 'im an' make it look like a huntin' accident," Tabetha shouted. "Poison ivy?"

"I would never shoot a fellow soldier," Cyril said, offended.

"Cyril," October said diplomatically. "That seems more like a harmless prank than a motive for murder . . . no offence. It was a good prank."

"He couldn't sit down for five days," Cyril argued.

"Still . . . maybe something else . . . unusual . . . happened in the days leading up to your death. What about that shack? Or the harbour?" October felt like she was missing something important.

"Yes, I'd go often to the harbour to see if Father needed help," Cyril explained. "I really wanted to learn shipbuilding, and I'd just as well skip militia training, with all the teasing, but my father often didn't appreciate the distraction. He was working on a ship, the *Kingfisher*, and I suppose it was fairly complicated."

The *Kingfisher* sounded familiar to October, and the little rats that ran the wheel in her mind started jogging.

"I still think we should try to find out more about Patrick Burton, though, especially after what I discovered in that shack," said Cyril.

"Yes, the shack!" The rats in October's mind ground to a halt. "Do you remember more about it now?"

"The shack in the woods?" Kirby asked.

"Yes, I'm starting to remember what was inside," Cyril said.

As he'd mentioned earlier, less than a week before his death, Cyril was in the woods north of Sticksville, hunting. He stopped suddenly when he'd heard a few twigs snap and hunched behind some nearby bushes, musket at the ready. However, it wasn't a deer (which would have been nice) or a bear (which would have been *not* very nice) — it was Patrick Burton.

The red-haired militia bully was walking, dressed in a full uniform that matched his hair, away from a narrow wooden shack in the middle of the woods. Cyril didn't think anyone lived out there. And especially not Patrick Burton; he had seen the Burtons' house in Sticksville. He counted slowly to twenty after Patrick was out of sight before standing up and approaching the dark shack.

The windows (which were just empty square holes cut into the shack) were darkened, but to be safe, he stood just outside the door frame and knocked. No one answered. Glancing all around him, like a spy in a movie that wouldn't be produced for 200 years, Cyril crept into the shack and was astonished by what he found.

"You remember?" October shouted. "What was in the shack?"

"Gunpowder and rifles, for one," he said, counting off two things on his greyish fingers. "There was a book filled with secret writing and what looked like a map of Sticksville."

"What do you mean 'looked like'?" Kirby asked.

"I can't read," Cyril said.

"So this secret writing in the book could have just been . . . writing," October said.

"I suppose. But it *looked* secret! There was also a spyglass. And our commanding officer had just had his spyglass stolen!"

"And ya thought the poison ivy was more important?" Tabetha said in disbelief.

"I had a difficult time remembering, Tabetha," Cyril protested. "I suppose you remember your death perfectly?"

Tabetha responded with a face like she'd just chugged a glass of sour milk.

"What did you think?" October said.

"I thought Patrick must have stolen all this . . . and he must have been plotting something . . . sinister!"

"Did you tell anyone?" Derek asked, raising himself up on his elbows in excitement.

"Of course I told someone!" Cyril shouted, standing up suddenly. "I thought we had an American spy in our midst. I told my parents right away."

"What about yer militia? Did ye tell them?" Morna asked.

"Well, no," he admitted. "I couldn't. Patrick Burton was always around. My dad said he'd tell the commanding officer, but I'm not sure if he did before I . . . well . . ."

"Died?" Kirby finished his thought.

"Yes," he said. "It had only been a couple days."

"What did you do once you found the book and spyglass in the shack? You left?" October asked. This interview, though probably entirely useless for her history project, was going to be beyond helpful in the mystery-solving.

"No," Cyril explained. "If it was the secret hideout of some patriot spy, I couldn't just leave it. I took some things — the spyglass, a necklace that looked valuable — and I drew some pictures of what I saw. For later."

"What is this, art class?" Kirby said.

"I already told you, I can't read or write. This was the next best thing!" Cyril said. "I also took the book of secret writing and threw it into our fire when I got home. I was sure it was some sort of American military plan."

"What did you do with the other stuff?" October asked.

"I don't remember. I don't remember much after that day."

All the dead kids sat around looking at one another, their mouths open like marionettes at rest, almost on the verge of asking another question, but no one knew quite what to say. Even Tabetha had stopped cataloguing October's wardrobe.

"Is the interview over?" Cyril asked.

"Sure," October said. Already, she had more than enough cryptic colonial conundrums (conundra?) to sort through.

"There's no way the shack is still around. It's too bad someone stole all the Cooper correspondence from the museum," Derek said, chewing on the collar of his moth-eaten T-shirt. "We could have seen what Cyril's parents had to say about Patrick and this shack. I mean, what do we do now?"

Some criminal mastermind *had* ruined October's best and simplest method of research, true, but there were other options.

"Tomorrow, we go to the library," October announced. "We need to find out more about this Patrick Burton. But for now, you dead people have to scoot."

Mr. Schwartz was liable to walk in the front door at any minute. It was nearly midnight, and, when he was out, he didn't like his daughter having guests over, dead or alive.

Pirates of the Dewey Decimal System

Stacey and I had music class together just after lunch, and as we walked to class we were busy complaining about the current songs in Mrs. Tischmann's repertoire. While we'd played some fun — or relatively fun . . . "Under the Sea" wasn't exactly my idea of a club banger — songs at the start of the year, and December had been filled with holiday carols, now all the songs we played were, like, Symphony no. 9 by some old guy in B-flat minor or "The Insert-Name-Here March." I don't have to tell you, the trombone and drum parts weren't the most exciting.

"Yumi told me you've got a pretty cool history project in Ms. Fenstermacher's class," Stacey said. The fact he said more than five words in a row meant he was more than a little interested in the subject.

"Cool is pretty generous, Stacey," I said. "More like elaborate or complicated. We have to do a project on somebody in history that no one knows much about."

"Could be fun."

In response, I just moved the bangs around on my face.

"That Ms. Fenstermacher is always coming up with great ideas," he added.

See, I had almost forgotten that Stacey had this gross obsession with my keener history teacher.

"Stacey, you know you're not going to be matched up with my history teacher on these Top Match Valentine things," I said.

"It's okay," he said. "I can wait until next semester when I have history class."

"Yeah, then you'll figure out she's not that amazing," I said. Stupid hip-glasses-wearing Fenstermacher. "She's not Veronica Lodge."

"I'm more of a Josie and the Pussycats fan." He smiled.

"Which one?"

"Doesn't matter."

"Well, she's not any of them, either."

Mrs. Tischmann arrived, wearing a truly bonkers necklace adorned with what looked like a variety of sea creatures — starfish, sea horses, crabs — and rapped her baton on the music stand at the front of the classroom, which meant class was about to start. Ms. Fenstermacher's biggest fan took his usual position behind the snare drum while I screwed the mouthpiece into my trombone.

One overly tedious rehearsal later, I jammed the separate trombone components into my case and tossed it into the instrument room as fast as I could manage, then wove my way through groups of people chatting in the hallway. I wanted to get to history class early to ask Ms. Fenstermacher a few pertinent questions that I'd *pretend* were about my presentation, but that were *really* about Cyril's mystery.

Suffice it to say, Ms. Fenstermacher was suitably creeped out when I tapped her on the shoulder as she faced the wall, unpacking her briefcase of files and books.

"Frak!" she shouted, nearly jumping out of her polka-dot shirt. "Oh, October. It's just you. You scared me."

"I get that a lot," I admitted.

"I was just setting up for class," she said, adjusting her glasses. "I didn't expect any students to be here so early. Is there something I can help you with?"

In retrospect, I imagine Ms. Fenstermacher regretted every time she asked me that.

"Yes. Have you heard anything more about the museum robbery?" I asked.

"Unfortunately, no," she said, flipping through her history

text to a Post-it note. "The police asked a lot of questions and took a lot of photos on Sunday, but it's only been two days. And to be honest, it's possible they'll never find anything unless this ghost pirate guy shows up again."

"That sucks," I groaned, maybe a bit more forcefully than I'd planned. "I was going to do my project on the Coopers and now all their stuff is gone."

"The robbery does make that a bit difficult," Ms. Fenstermacher said. "All the Cooper letters were stolen, but to be perfectly honest, the letters stop between 1792 and 1812. You'd have had a hard time fully researching the Coopers anyway. It's actually a very strange thing about Sticksville — there are almost no documents or records of that time."

I didn't want to correct my history teacher, but *that* was far from the strangest thing about Sticksville, Ontario.

"If you're dead set on presenting on a member of the Cooper family," she continued, "there are other ways you could research. Outside of the museum, that is. Have you tried the library? Or you could talk to the organizers of the Sticks-ebration."

"What does the Sticks-ebration have to do with the Coopers?" I asked. My classmates were beginning to enter and were already giving me the eyes. Zombie Tramp couldn't do anything without managing to be totally weird.

"The Coopers were shipbuilders, and this year, they've refurbished the *Kingfisher*, a battle clipper that Eustace Cooper built in 1779. The other Sticks-ebration organizers must have lots of information about the Cooper patriarch — at least in terms of his profession."

So *that's* why the *Kingfisher* had rung a bell. Eustace Cooper must have been Cyril's dad. And one of his ships was going to set sail in Sticksville again this spring — over 200 years after its initial voyage.

"But don't feel anchored to the Coopers," Ms. Fenstermacher advised. "There are *many* interesting characters in Sticksville's past. Just think of that witch guy I told you about, Fairfax Crisparkle. Some of the historical documents have a few bizarre things to say about that guy. People viewed him as some kind of sorcerer or something, though I imagine he was just an odd old guy who lived on the edge of town. That was usually the case with witches in history."

Looking into the mystery of Fairfax Crisparkle seemed inevitable, given there hung a German needlepoint in my house that indicated we were under his protection (lucky us?), and that Skyler McGriff was ranting an awful lot about him when he was threatening me with a baseball bat around Christmas. Fairfax Crisparkle also seemed to be connected to the "Asphodel Meadows" graffiti found in the Crooked Arms, so there was certainly more to him than just being a kooky old guy who nobody liked. But investigating his past and how he connected to Skyler McGriff and the needlepoint in my house seemed like something that should wait until I was done with Cyril's mystery.

"Okay, thanks," I said, heading over to my seat. The classroom was nearly full and the bell would ring any second.

"Any time, October."

A row across from me sat Victor Breen, a friend of the band members in Phantom Moustache, high school band ordinaire.

"Butt kisser," he hissed, then handed me a picture he'd drawn of me kissing a big hairy butt.

Super mature.

KISS!
KISS!

☠   ☠   ☠

My dad had no plans with Ashlie's mom that night, so I was forced to wait until he'd fallen asleep on the couch to the sounds of the radio before I edged open our sliding-glass door and crept through the snow in our backyard, directly to the centre of the Sticksville Cemetery. The dead kids and I had one secret operation tonight: to discover whatever happened to Mr. Patrick Burton, he of the itchy bum, by searching the library's copies of the U.K. military rolls.

After school, I'd dropped by the library to ask how one might find out about a super-long dead person's military service during the Revolutionary War. Having this history project was like a magical blessing, as none of the librarians thought this was a really unusual thing for a teenager to ask — like, *How do I get on the internet?* and *Where do you keep your military records?* Apparently some *real* buttkissers from my history class had already asked about the same thing yesterday. Well, Jolly Olde England kept an online database of their soldiers' records, but it started in 1793, so I was just going to have to hope that Private Burton lived through the war . . . and remained a soldier for a decade afterward. Luckily, the library had also printed out records of any Sticksvillians who'd served in the British — or, later, Canadian — army and collected them in plastic sheets in a white binder in their local history alcove.

This, however, had to wait until I had my ghost companions with me. I wanted the dead kids — Cyril, especially — to be on hand when and if I found any mention of Patrick Burton. If he'd lasted until 1793 and hadn't been arrested for treason or owning a weird shack (whatever the actual criminal offence was), that made it much less likely he had anything to do with Cyril's death.

When I arrived, the dead kids were leaving grim messages in the blanket of snow covering the cemetery grounds.

"October," Derek said, while digging the words *VISIT ME* in front of one tombstone. "Are you ready to go?"

Ready to break into the public library? It's like my entire life was leading up to this point.

"Yeah, almost," I said. Tabetha was busy scratching the phrase

I'LL BE BACK in the snow before one stone crucifix. "I need to put this stuff on, though."

The incident at the museum had pretty much proven that security cameras couldn't record the dead kids, but I was a different matter, which was why I was dressed all in black — not an overly challenging task for me. But to be extra careful, I'd wrapped black electrical tape over the white rubber of my Chuck Taylors, worn black leather "strangler issue" gloves instead of my black-and-white striped mittens, and brought a black ski mask. As Ms. Fenstermacher had said before, I wasn't much of a master criminal if I didn't even cover my face. I pulled the black balaclava over my head and tried to move hanks of black hair out of my face.

"*Now* I'm ready."

The library wasn't all that far from school, so it didn't take us long to get there. And this time, I was navigating instead of Derek, who seemed to have a sense of anti-direction. Once at the doors of the library entrance, Derek turned to me and asked, "How are you going to get in without setting off an alarm?"

"I'm not," I said. "You are."

Really, I had no idea whether the library even had an alarm. I wasn't even sure if they had security cameras (despite the signage saying they did), so I could have been dressed up like a shadow for no reason at all.

"You dead kids walk through the wall and stay intangible," I instructed. "Until you find the power box or whatever. Then turn tangible and shut it off. You should have a little while before the burglar alarm goes off."

Cyril raised his hand in confusion. "Power box?"

I'd forgotten most of these dead kids had been working with kerosene, if that, when they were alive.

"Oh, uh . . . Derek and Kirby, do you think you can find it?"

The two most recently deceased of my dead friends nodded and ghosted through the walls of the Sticksville Library. One day, I was going to have to give the dead kids a crash course in modern technology, so I didn't have to explain myself every time I needed them to find a calculator or whatever.

Just as I was beginning to assemble my mental list of important technology that had happened since, say, the 1800s — that was almost *all* of it, for the record — Cyril appeared at the other side of the library doors to unlock them.

"Your library awaits," he said, bowing and removing his hat as he held the door, all gentlemanly like.

The downside of cutting the power was that things were darker than a family reunion in a V.C. Andrews novel. Sure, it was great to not have an alarm blaring — or perhaps silently alerting police — but snooping around was all the more difficult. To our advantage, though, was that this was one of the few times in my illustrious B & E career when I'd remembered to bring flashlights. Plural. I handed them out to Cyril, Tabetha, Morna, and Derek like they were Christmas crackers. They just had one switch, so I figured they'd be easy enough for the older dead kids to use.

"We need to go to the local history nook," I said, secretly ashamed I'd used the word "nook" unironically. "It's just a bit past all the computer work stations." I paused, adding for the pre-PC dead folks, "They're like grey boxes with typewriters in front of them."

Bright circles dancing around us like a light bulb had been caught inside a clothes dryer, we rushed to the desk, two chairs, and cabinet that comprised Sticksville's local history section. Maybe the museum got all the good stuff. I pulled open the cabinet and tossed the white binder marked *U.K. Military Rolls, 1793–1949* onto the desk.

"Kirby, start speed-reading," I ordered. "Look for Burton, Patrick." For some reason, it felt really good to boss Kirby LaFlamme around. Instantly, Kirby started flipping through the plastic pages as fast as his chubby little fingers would let him.

"But this binder only goes back to 1793," said Derek, who was apparently more observant than I gave him credit for.

"I know, I know. But that's as far back as the records go," I said, pulling down the hole in the balaclava from my mouth. I felt fuzzballs from the ski mask all over my tongue.

"So, we just have t'hope Patrick was still in the army, fourteen years later," Morna said, giving Derek an encouraging pat on the back. I felt like it was the first time I'd seen one of the dead kids physically interact with another in a way that wasn't, like, sawing off the other's head. Was it unsettling or heartwarming? I usually have a hard time differentiating between the two. I was still pawing the black lint from the balaclava off my tongue when Kirby found something.

"Patrick Burton! Look here!" he said, laying the printout from the military rolls' database across the desk.

"What does it say?" Cyril said, leaning over the desk. He and Tabetha were supposed to be keeping watch.

"Whoa, he became a colonel?" Derek marvelled.

70

"Yeah," I added, reading along. "He even served in the War of 1812 and died at the age of fifty."

"Patrick Burton was awarded a Military General Service Medal," Derek read.

Cyril, as anyone would be, was unimpressed his childhood tormentor had gone on to military fame and accolades. Imagine if Ashlie Salmons went on to become, like, Commissioner of the Toronto Police one day. I'd be pretty miffed. "He was probably a crummy colonel."

"Don't get your pantaloons in a twist," Kirby said.

"Well, all this suggests that it's pretty doubtful buddy was a traitor," I said.

"But the shack," Cyril almost whispered. "I thought he was a spy."

"The guy fought against the Americans in two major conflicts," Kirby said. "If he was a spy, that was over thirty years of deep cover."

"Cyril!" Tabetha shout-whispered from around the corner. "Where'd ya go, ya stupid pirate? Yer supposed t'be keepin' watch with me!"

Cyril was, however, a little too dumbfounded to keep watch at the moment. Our sole lead in his colonial death had been erased by a record of unimpeachable military service.

"But . . . didn't my father tell them . . . about what I'd found in the shack?" Cyril always seemed to have a plan in mind or method of approach, no matter what the situation, but now he just seemed lost.

"Maybe it wasn't his, Cyril," Morna suggested.

"Bet you feel pretty bad about that poison ivy right now," Kirby said. He could probably stand a bit of poison ivy down his shorts himself.

"Don't despair, guys," I said, though as far as cheerleaders or morale boosters went, I was about as good as a goat mascot that had been kidnapped by the opposing team. "Maybe there's something else we can discover in this local history nook that can help with Cyril's mystery."

There was that pesky word *nook* again.

"Forget it, October," Kirby said, picking up the white binder of military records and snapping it closed. "With the red-headed kid exonerated and everything of use stolen from the museum, Cyril has to remain unknowing forever, so let's move onto another mystery, shall we? Might I humbly suggest my own, which happened a mere half century ago and is, therefore, likely linked to ample historical records — maybe even living witnesses? Something more concrete?"

A large cinder block then loudly entered the library followed by a comet trail of broken glass, sparkling in the twilight, and punched a toaster-sized hole through Kirby LaFlamme's belly. As Kirby fell to the brown carpet below, Tabetha — a bit tardy for a lookout — announced, "We've got company!"

☠ ☠ ☠

Battle of the Books

Company was indeed what October and her dead friends had, dear readers, and it was company in the guise of — you guessed it — a ghost pirate.

But before the ghost pirate made his appearance, the dead kids and young October Schwartz were sent scrambling. Following the violent entrance of the cinder block through both the library window and Kirby's poor stomach, the dead kids all ran to hide behind the closest row of bookcases they could find, with Cyril pausing to scoop up the newly perforated Kirby from where he was rolling around on the floor. October flipped off her flashlight and the dead kids followed suit.

October was huddled in the mystery section — identifiable by spine after spine of books adorned with red skull labels — alongside Morna, Cyril, and the donut-shaped Kirby, when the sound of two heavy boots hit the ground. Derek and Tabetha were trapped on the other side of the bookcase with cookbooks and crafting books.

"Are you okay, Kirby?" October whispered to her friend, whose tie kept catching in the large square hole in his middle as he tried to sit down.

"That hurt," he said, "but I'll be fine. My belly should grow back, unfortunately. Who is throwing cinder blocks at us?"

"I liked it better when it was just quarters we were attacked with," Morna whispered.

"Shhh!" October insisted. She could hear the cinder-block-tossing intruder on the move. He must have had cinder blocks affixed to the soles of his shoes, too, given the heavy thuds he made as he crept closer. (This is why it's always a good idea to wear running shoes when breaking and entering, readers. They call them sneakers for a reason.)

"Cyril!" October whispered. Cyril was experimentally pushing his left hand through Kirby's vacant middle. "Cyril, peek over the shelf. See if you can spot the intruder."

"What if he sees me?" he asked, removing his hat.

"He probably won't. It's dark. And you're a ghost."

Two solid points, but never a guarantee with the dead kids.

Moving some P.D. James and Sue Grafton books out of the way to make handholds, Cyril slowly stood on his toes and carefully peered over the library stacks. He crouched down much more rapidly about a second later.

"Um . . . it's a pirate."

"A pirate?" Morna said.

"A ghost pirate."

"Oh no," October said. "It's the same pirate who robbed the museum."

Despite the danger, October Schwartz had to see this for herself. Her eyes had begun to adjust to the dark, so she shuffled over beside her Loyalist friend. She was a bit shorter than Cyril, but using a stack of Ellery Queen novels, she managed to get high enough to see that same ghost pirate she had seen on video this past Sunday, making a slow beeline for the local history nook. (Nook, incidentally, is a *fine* word.) The familiar grinning, bearded face bobbed above the orange and blue coat. A realistic-looking cutlass was tucked into the pirate's belt. And though October's eyes had adjusted to the low light, she needn't have worried, as — just as in the security footage — the pirate generated his own light. Like one of those terrifying fish that evolution forgot somewhere near the bottom of the ocean, the pirate robber (perhaps a redundant phrase, I'll admit) emanated an unearthly glow.

As October stared at the bioluminescent sailor, attempting to figure out where the light was coming from, the pirate turned its smiling head in her direction. October ducked down as fast as she could manage and whispered to the three assembled dead kids: "I think he saw me!"

"Let me look," Cyril said. He stretched to see and came back shaking his head. "No. He's ducked into that corner we were in before."

"October, you told us about the museum robbery, but you neglected to tell us that the thief was a *ghost pirate*," Kirby said, propped on one elbow.

"Shhhh."

"You remember we're ghosts, right?" he continued. "Don't you think this information could have been relevant?"

"He's right," Morna said. "Ghost pirate is a pretty big deal."

"Of course, I'm right."

"But he's not a real ghost, right? You guys can tell," October insisted via whisper.

October's question was answered only by the sunken stark white eyes of the three dead kids ping-ponging back and forth between each other.

"Right?!"

"We don't know, October. We can't tell from here," Morna said, craning her neck around the corner to take a second look.

"Aren't you dead kids like dogs or something? So you can tell when you see another dog and not a cat or fox or whatever?"

"I don't think so," Kirby said.

"But you don't glow. He's glowing!" I insisted.

"Listen," Kirby said. "He doesn't *seem* like a real ghost."

Exasperated, October stood on her stack of mystery novels once again. "I'm going to see if Derek and Tabetha are okay."

Looking past the glowing ghost pirate, who was busy raiding

the local history section of all its contents, October could see Derek and Tabetha, backed against nearby bookshelves, their arms in an exaggerated shrug. October had no idea what to do. The safest thing would be to simply wait the pirate out until he left, but if she were to do that, it was possible he'd clean out the library of all its historical records. She could see the white binder she'd recently looked at atop a stack of crumbling historical atlases. If she didn't act quickly, Sticksville might not have any history left.

"Cover me," she whispered to her three dead friends. "I'm going to put the power back on so the alarm starts. Kirby, where's the electrical box?"

"In the staff room," he said, pointing with his outstretched left hand.

"I thought ye said there were cameras!" Morna protested.

"That's why I'm putting this back on," October said, donning the balaclava. "If I don't sound the alarm, this pirate's going to take everything, just like he did at the museum."

October teetered on her stack of books and looked over the library: four aisles of bookshelves separated her from the staff room and the circuit breaker. Of course, there was also the ghost pirate to consider — but if she remained silent and wove in and out of those bookshelves, treating it like a big game of Frogger with the rummaging pirate in the place of highway traffic, she could make it. When the pirate crouched down to pull some books from the lowest shelf of the local history cabinet, October sprinted for the next aisle. Once there, she looked around the corner to see the pirate with his big head and hat still in the cabinet. She ran for the next aisle. That's when she heard the yelling.

"October!" Derek yelled.

The pirate had clearly noticed October and was chasing after her, leaving the hodgepodge of historical junk at the desk behind him. October took off like an antelope or one of those more exotic African deer things — an oryx? — only not nearly as fast. Apparently even a heavy-booted ghost pirate could outrun her.

With the door to the staff room in clear sight, October felt a tug at her backpack, and before she could slide out from the straps, she'd been turned around and was face-to-rubber-face with the pirate. Real ghost or not, the thief was certainly wearing a mask. October could barely breathe from the powerful odour of fresh latex. And his hands were pretty tight around October's upper arms, so if he *was* a ghost, he could do that same tangibility trick that her dead friends could.

"What do you want?" October shouted into the pirate's too-close face. "Why are you stealing these things?"

"October, duck!" Cyril shouted.

A heavy mystery hardcover came sailing through the air, its spine landing squarely on the pirate's left temple. The ghost made its first noise yet — a high-pitched squeal that was somewhere between unholy banshee and teenaged boy going through puberty — and loosened his grip on October's arms. Not being one to let a golden opportunity pass, she grabbed the pirate's cheeks and twisted the face around ninety degrees. (At that point, October was pretty convinced it wasn't a real face.)

The pirate, still glowing in the centre of the library like a tile in Michael Jackson's video for "Billie Jean," staggered back and grasped at his sword handle.

"October, y'idjit. Get out of there!" came the encouraging words of Tabetha Scott from across the foyer.

Derek had other ideas: "Kirby, jump on that guy and encircle him with your body. Like a tire!"

"I'm not doing that!" Kirby shouted. He wasn't about to be reduced to a restraining device.

"I think I can unmask —" October started, approaching the temporarily blinded intruder. Her confidence rapidly diminished, however, when the pirate produced his sword and began brandishing it wildly. Though it seemed likely the sword was merely a spray-painted bit of wood, even getting that smacked against your leg or face could smart. October defensively pulled a Where's Waldo? book from the nearest shelf. Imagine her horror when the sword came down on the book, which was protecting her face at the time, and cleaved it neatly in two. October fell backwards onto her bum, holding the halves of Where's Waldo? like paper sandwiches at her sides.

"I think that sword is real, October!" Cyril shouted, gathering a few more books and hurling them in the pirate's general direction. (Due to ghost rules, he couldn't just run up and punch the ghost pirate . . . a clear sign the ghost pirate was an actual living person.)

The minor bookstorm was enough of a distraction — well, it *and* the pirate's still-sideways rubber mask — for October to struggle again to her feet and rush through the staff door. If she'd known detective work would involve so much running, she'd probably never have taken it up as a hobby.

Spotting the circuit box immediately upon entry — the dead kids had left it hanging open, bless them — October ran to it and started mashing her palm against the various switches, flipping each one from its down to its up position. Fluorescent lights sputtered on and digital displays in microwave ovens and clocks began to flash aquamarine. The library was going to look like a massive power outage hit it tomorrow morning. Finally, October heard the whooping sound of the alarm. Spinning around on her heel, she saw the red glow of an emergency exit sign just beside the staff room's stove. Not waiting for the dead kids, she bolted through the door. The dead kids could walk through the wall whenever they wanted, she figured, and they didn't have to worry as much about being sliced into bacon by the angry pirate.

Once outside in the cold February night, October tried to catch her breath while bent over by the dumpster behind the library. Certainly, the garbage stench wasn't helping in the matter. Just when her normal heart rate had almost returned, Derek leapt into view, putting her back to square one, heart-wise.

. "You scared me!" October shouted.

"Still got it," Derek said.

"Did ye think we were the ghost pirate?" Morna joined Derek, along with the others.

Not a totally unreasonable question, given what had just happened.

"Let's get out of here," October huffed.

Ghost pirate or just very homicidal person in a convincing costume, October felt this was a mystery for another night. She'd been as close to a tempered blade as she'd ever wanted to be. The dead kids and October fled to the Sticksville Cemetery, the wind whistling through Kirby like he was an empty Coke bottle.

☠   ☠   ☠

We Hate It When Our Friends Become Unlawful

8

You'd think I'd be allowed a little time to recover from the terror of nearly being sliced in two like some of the less fortunate babies brought to wise King Solomon, but no such luck. Apparently, I had to go to school, as my dad reminded me by rapping on the door when I slept through my alarm on Wednesday morning. He couldn't figure out why I slept in so often, but then he didn't know I was fighting with ghost pirates until two in the morning. And it was probably best to keep it that way.

I emerged from my bedroom, face creased with so many red lines from my pillow, it looked like a grammatically challenged student's English essay, and greeted my dad, who seemed to be dressing better since he started dating Ashlie Salmons's mom. His black patent leather shoes were certainly new, as was his belt. I guess attention to one's belt must be paid when one is dating a Salmons.

"What's the deal, October?" my dad asked, doing an exaggerated double take at his wrist. "It's getting harder and harder to wake you up."

"Been having nightmares," I yawned. "About your dates with Crown Attorney Salmons."

"Ha ha," he mumbled.

"Does her head turn completely around?"

"October," he said, "are you sure you're okay with me dating the mother of your school friend?"

"Friend" was not a term I'd use, but Dad definitely wasn't one to use "mortal enemy" in polite conversation. "Yeah, I was just being a brat. Go, be happy. Date and stuff."

"Well, that's a relief," he said, sliding the new edition of the *Sticksville Loon*, still in its plastic bag, into my hands. "You know, I'm really glad you've stopped sneaking out every night. Especially with this clown running around town. I already worry myself sick about you." I think that sort of observation is called dramatic irony.

I peeked at the headline of the *Loon*, which screamed LONG JOHN PILFER: *"Ghost" Pirate Baffles Sticksville Police*. The news was just about the museum, not the library. Hopefully, my super-ninja black outfit would keep me out of the papers. My eyes scanned the story frantically, all the while trying to maintain a studied air of disinterest in front of my suspicious dad.

"Huh. Pirates," I coughed, as if I was like, "Huh. Milk's on sale." Not at all like I was living a real-life episode of *Are You Afraid of the Dark?*

"One more thing to watch out for," Dad said, getting his coat and briefcase ready.

"Good thing I don't go to the cemetery at night anymore." Real casual-like. Real smooth. "Because that's totally where a ghost pirate would hang out."

Before school, I really needed to (a) shower, and (b) figure out how human beings lie . . . or just talk, in general. I took the *Sticksville Loon* with me and slid it into my backpack, because I had some questions — both for Ms. Fenstermacher and (gulp!) Mr. Santuzzi.

☠ ☠ ☠

On my arctic trudge to school, I thought about how good things had been since Dad started seeing Ashlie's mom — despite how cryptic he had been this morning. I know a romantic relationship can't prevent depression. That's like deranged romantic-comedy logic. But for the moment, the old sea-witch seemed to be doing him good. Personally, I wanted to stay away from Ashlie as much as possible, so I wouldn't shed a tear — well, not multiple ones — if their relationship fell apart, but my dad really seemed to like Crown Attorney Salmons.

Needless to say, my mind was also pretty occupied with the very recent and vivid memory of nearly being chopped up by a ghost pirate. True, I was no stranger to mortal danger. Every couple of months, it seemed some malefactor was trying to stab or maim me. But seeing how close that blade came to my face, and watching that book cleave neatly in two, had really shaken me. I couldn't stop thinking about it; the memory interrupted every other thought I had. Maybe this was something I needed to talk to Dr. Lagostina about, but I wasn't sure I wanted the school therapist to know about my late-night confrontations with random pirates in the public library.

After some cursory morning remarks with my besties Yumi and Stacey, and a dullsville French class with Mr. Martz, I decided to ask Mr. Santuzzi the question I probably couldn't ask Dr. Lagostina: that is, how did he deal with life-threatening events? I mean, the other students and I had always kind of made fun of his military service, but that wasn't entirely (or at all) fair. After all, as far as we knew, Mr. Santuzzi had seen some truly heinous stuff while he was in the military. And ever since my near dicing last night, I'd felt constantly on the edge of panic. More so than I had been after being kidnapped and almost skewered on a bayonet; more so than I had been after entrapment in a phone booth; more so than I had been after an attack by the Baseball Furies. Maybe this stuff was cumulative. My dad's mental health issues made me wonder about this type of thing, and whether Mr. Santuzzi, who I naturally assumed was some kind of war vet, struggled with similar things.

Before Mr. Santuzzi was able to launch into all the latest and greatest in the world of math, I ambushed him (bad choice of words) at the blackboard.

"Miss Schwartz," he said, peering down over his, admittedly, massive shoulder. "We'll be starting class in just a few

minutes if you'll take your seat."

"Sure, Mr. Santuzzi. But before that, can I ask you a question? You were in the military, right?"

"Protocol prohibits me from either confirming or denying that statement." He put down his stick of chalk and folded his arms across his broad chest, covered in a teal vest.

"Okay, well . . . if you *had* been in the military, might you have seen some, like, really horrible and unpleasant stuff? Like, people falling on grenades or getting shot in the face . . ."

Mr. Santuzzi started to look worried. "What are you getting at, Miss Schwartz?"

"Mr. Santuzzi," I asked, "did you ever have, like, nightmares or flashbacks or feel horrible after those terrible experiences?"

"I'm not sure what you're asking," he said.

"Like, that unsettled feeling goes away, right?"

He thought about this for a second, then glanced at me. "Miss Schwartz, do you need to talk to someone? I'm afraid I can only help you with your math problems."

Okay, so Mr. Santuzzi was going to stonewall me, which meant I probably shouldn't continue this line of questioning. He was going to be no help regarding my new-found fear of swords. Maybe I really did need to schedule another meeting with Dr. Lagostina.

☠   ☠   ☠

During lunch, I brought out the *Sticksville Loon* front page (well, actually, the whole paper) nearly as soon as I'd sat down with Yumi and Stacey. It wasn't that I thought they could help me figure out who or what this ghost pirate was, but I thought they might be able to help me speculate where the diabolical thief might strike next. He seemed to be going from spot to spot, cleaning buildings out of whatever historical material was contained inside. Being relatively new to Sticksville, I wasn't sure if there were any more storehouses of history to be robbed.

"Long John Pilfer," Yumi said, smoothening the paper against the table.

"I would have gone with 'Captain Crook,'" Stacey commented, stuffing another chunk of tuna sandwich into his mouth and turning up his Walkman.

"Why'd you bring this? I usually bring the paper," Yumi said. "You really into pirates?"

"No, I just thought it was kind of strange," I said. "Sticksville in a crime wave. With a costumed criminal, to boot. I feel like I'm in Gotham City."

"Good luck finding Batman," Yumi said, nudging Stacey with her elbow for no apparent reason.

"Apparently the pirate guy is only taking stuff of historical value. That's weird, right?" I said. "I mean, what does he have left after the museum and the library?"

"Who said anything about the library?" Yumi asked, way too sharp for the current situation.

Caught in revealing I knew too much about this pirate thief, I scrambled. "I mean, I *assume* the pirate will target it, too. But what else?"

Yumi shrugged. "The school? The hockey arena has some old stuff, too."

"What about people who have private collections?" Stacey asked. He was still somewhat paying attention.

The options weren't extensive or encouraging. There was no way I could track down which people in Sticksville had collections of historic stuff in their houses, but maybe the dead kids and I could stake out the school or the arena.

"Never mind the pirates, Schwartz," Yumi said, reaching

over the cafeteria table to steal a Triscuit. "Can you come dress shopping with me after school today?"

"Dress shopping? For what?"

"Schwartz, have you just emerged from a cocoon?" she said, biting down with a crunch that highlighted her vampire-like canine teeth. "You *do* know there's a Valentine's dance coming up, right?"

"Yeah, I just didn't figure *you'd* want to go." Yumi Takeshi didn't seem like much of a joiner when it came to school stuff.

"Schwartz, it's an opportunity to dress up. Of course I'm going. I'd go to a stranger's funeral should I have the chance to wear some crinoline."

I eyed my friend, decked out in a plaid skirt with a monster safety pin and skull-bedecked nylons. I should have realized this would be the case. Turning to her platonic male companion, I asked, "You, too?"

He swallowed with some effort. "There is a red tuxedo at Value Village that I've had my eye on."

"I'd ask Stacey to come with me dress shopping, but he's always got drum practice. And look at how *he* dresses."

"Drumming nine to five," he sang. "Or three to five, more accurately."

"I'm going over to his house after dress shopping to eat dinner and watch *Switchblade Romance*. You want to join in?"

Though I'd wanted to puke every time someone mentioned the Valentine's dance or showed me one of those question-naires, spending the afternoon with Yumi and Stacey would probably be more fun than staying home alone . . . or trying to protect more historical records from theft. And if I *did* go to the dance, I'd need a dress or something anyway.

"I'll have to tell my dad, but sure."

"Yes!" Yumi hissed through her teeth. "This is going to be great. You need to help me find a dress that's total murder."

"Murder?"

"Yeah," Yumi said. "Like, super amazing. It's my new slang."

"I don't think you get to make up new slang," Stacey chewed.

"Sure I do," Yumi said. "That's how new slang happens."

"No, I mean *you*, personally," he said.

Her eyes contracted into mail slots as she regarded her tablemate and gathered her garbage.

"I have to go," she said, rising from the table. "Schwartz, meet me at my locker after school."

Stacey and I hadn't spent that much time together alone, so sitting across from each other in the cafeteria felt really awkward. We decided to head to music class early, where at least we could both sit facing the blackboard with instruments in our hands, to distract us during the duller moments of our conversation.

☠   ☠   ☠

Shopping for a Valentine's dance dress was important — I'm not going to lie to you — but it wasn't even in the same neighbourhood as this ghost pirate crime wave, which was making it pretty much impossible to solve the mystery of Cyril's death (not to mention future mysteries of Sticksville's past). So before I caught Yumi at her locker, I pumped poor Ms. Fenstermacher for information. My history teacher, however, was not overly impressed when I asked her why someone was going around stealing our town's few historical treasures.

"October, I know you love history and I know this pirate guy has really thrown a wrench, or peg leg, or something into your plans for the history project, but I still think it'd be best if you didn't get involved," she said, wiping down the blackboards. Sometimes I'm amazed our school still has blackboards, because the school doesn't look that old. "These things are better handled by the police. Promise me you'll stay away from all this."

I promised, because, unlike Benjamin Franklin, a historical figure who we weren't allowed to profile for the project, I didn't think honesty was that great a policy. Ms. Fenstermacher wasn't going to help me with a motive, and it was probably too, like, self-absorbed to assume someone was stealing all of Sticksville's history so I'd fail her class. The dead kids and I were just going to have to stake out some of the town's more important build-ings. But first, I'd have to help Yumi find a dress.

Our fashion-finding mission took us, by the 19 bus, to the Sticksville Galleria. At first, we went to Hot Topic, but then we realized there wasn't anything there worthy of a fancy ball, which is what Yumi was kind of going for. Like, a fancy Halloween ball at Criss Angel's house. Finally, we found a store named Vanity Foul that seemed like it might have some prom-ising options.

"You're going to the dance, too, right?" Yumi asked me as she emerged from the dressing room. She was dressed in this black-and-white striped thing that was kind of making my head hurt — not that it was a bad thing — and looked like a World War II–era goth girl out on the town after a rough day at a munitions factory.

"I guess," I said. "That looks really good."

"You'll need a dress, too, won't you?" she asked, then reassessed herself in the mirror. "There's a lot of white. I'm worried I'll spill something on it."

"What are you going to spill? It's a dance."

The spillage debate was a nice diversion from talking about my personal dress shopping. I was still getting an allowance from my dad, but I wasn't totally sure I could afford to buy a dress. But picturing my closet at home, I didn't have anything I could wear to the dance other than my band uniform.

"There'll be pop," Yumi explained. "Maybe chips, too. Chip dust! Doritos. Ugh. I'll have to be careful. Let me try this other one on."

Yumi disappeared behind the heavy velvet curtain of the

dressing room while I continued to sit in one of the chairs just outside. Beside me sat a terminally bored adult playing Fruit Ninja on his phone.

"Do you think you'll bring anyone to the dance?" Yumi had always been more into dating and stuff than me, as demonstrated by her poor choice of crush, Skyler McGriff. I was only interested in boys if they'd killed someone or stolen something. I guess you could say I was into bad boys.

"Doubtful," I shouted to the curtain, though it was weird shouting with the Fruit Ninja right beside me. "Maybe I'll fill out that quiz and get paired with, like, Stacey and we can each save a couple bucks."

Yumi's little hand shot out and dragged the curtain back just to show her face. "OMG, do you *like* Stacey, October?"

Yumi's face was hard to read — the coordination of her angled eyebrows and wide eyes and open mouth did nothing to help me sort out whether it was confusion, anger, betrayal, or surprise that I was witnessing.

"Stacey?" I nearly spat. "No. Gross. And weird. I just meant to save some money . . . Since we're all going anyway."

"Oh, yeah," she said, disappearing behind the curtain again.

"What about you? Who are you trying to impress now that your crush is in jail? Or will be soon."

Yumi emerged from the curtain again, this time dressed in a red plaid dress that poofed out at the bottom, just above the knee.

"I don't know. Someone weird would be ideal."

"I just filled in identical answers without reading the questions. All Bs," I said, displaying the Scantron love test that I'd already completed. "I'll probably get paired up with an overhead projector."

"Could be worse," Yumi said.

Yumi used her dad's credit card to buy the plaid dress, and we left for the bus stop. Barring any real traffic problems, we'd be back at Stacey's for the movie fifteen minutes after his drum lesson ended.

Stacey's parents provided us each with a bowl of instant ramen noodles and we went upstairs to watch *Switchblade Romance* in his room. So, yeah, *newsflash*: Stacey MacIsaac has a television in his room, and a DVD player, so that was pretty choice. But his parents were pretty adamant about him leaving the door open, as he was having not one, but *two*, girls in his bedroom after hours. As *if* either Yumi or I would ever make out with Stacey. Especially with two of us there. And *especially* especially when we were full of beef ramen.

Anyway, *Switchblade Romance* is a French movie, but, despite that, it's pretty gruesomely amazing. Probably because it's rated NC-17. Given my French skills, I could even understand a lot of it without the subtitles. Yumi was perched on Stacey's bed while he and I sat on the floor below her. I was halfway into my Mr. Pibb by the time the guy in the gas station got killed with an axe. That's when, mid-movie, Stacey scrambled to his feet and announced, "We should do this next week, too. Same day. Wednesday night movies."

"What, watch *Switchblade Romance* again?" Yumi said through a mouthful of noodles.

"No," he scoffed. He reached into his closet and was halfway swallowed by a pile of bowling shirts and other junk. "This close to Valentine's Day, we've got to watch *My Bloody Valentine*. It's Canadian, too."

"Isn't that the night of the dance?" I asked, searching for the remote, because if we were going to discuss movie plans, I'd rather not miss a whole lot of important bloodletting *en français*.

"No, it's on Friday. Actual Valentine's Day," Yumi explained. "Stacey, what are you doing in your closet?"

"Just making sure I still had it," he mumbled, then he fully emerged, holding out the DVD of *My Bloody Valentine* in his outstretched hand like he was in a Mentos commercial.

And that's when I saw it. In the closet, behind my friend, wedged just to the left of a rainbow spectrum of vertically striped shirts, atop a white wire shelf: a navy and orange tricorn hat. A hat just like Cyril might have worn — or, more accurately, just like a ghost pirate *did* wear. My mouth was left hanging open like an ejected DVD tray that someone had neglected to push back in, but my friends couldn't have known the reason.

"It's just a DVD, Schwartz," Yumi said. "Don't be so amazed. I'm sure Stace's closet is jam-packed with them."

Yeah, them, and all those stupid Hawaiian shirts he was always wearing. That was what was so troubling. I closed my mouth. Stacey had both a pirate hat and a plethora of Hawaiian shirts; he could basically wardrobe a full luau. I was almost too terrified to ask.

"Stacey, why do you own a pirate hat?" He hadn't been a pirate on Halloween; he went as Lois Lane, and Yumi was Clark Kent.

"Oh, this?" he said, plunking it on top of his rat's nest of light-brown hair. "It's for that history project. I'm going to be a pirate."

"Stacey," Yumi said, pointing out the obvious, "you don't even have history this semester."

"I know," he said. "But I will *next* semester, and it's not like Ms. Fenstermacher is going to change her class. We're definitely going to do the same project. I'm going to dress the part for the oral presentation."

Given Stacey's obsession with all things Ms. Fenstermacher, this was nearly a plausible explanation, as incredible as Stacey preparing months — or even hours — in advance of a project's due date seemed.

"Who . . . who are you doing your project on?" I managed to ask.

"Anne Bonny," he said, tilting the hat at what I assumed he thought was a jaunty angle. It was more upsetting than anything.

"Who?"

"Exactly. The projects are supposed to be about people in history that no one knows," he said, tossing the hat back into the closet. "Anne Bonny was one of the only *female* pirate captains."

"So you're dressing up as a woman again," Yumi said.

"That's a pretty good subject, actually," I said, realizing with some disappointment that it was probably a friendship breaker to steal Stacey's idea.

"Whatever," Yumi said, flattening out on Stacey's bed like an Olympic skeleton athlete. "I'm happy to watch MBV next Wednesday, but can we get back to *this* movie? There's still a post wrapped in barbed wire that we need to see in action."

We settled back into our usual horror-movie viewing positions, but nothing that was happening on-screen was as unsettling as the nagging feeling that Stacey could be the ghost pirate. He wore Hawaiian shirts; he had a pirate hat just like the ghost pirate's. Someone like Ashlie's mom might deem that circumstantial evidence, but at this point I had nothing else. Why would Stacey have any interest in stealing the historical artifacts of Sticksville? Unless he was so far gone for Ms. Fenstermacher that he'd stolen stuff from the museum only to "find" the material later, save the day, win his history teacher's heart, etc. *That* old story. The idea was a bit far-fetched, and I had a hard time believing Stacey really liked Ms. Fenstermacher that much. It seemed more like a thing he said to annoy Yumi and me. So it was difficult to believe he'd prepare so far in advance for a presentation in her class.

The most troubling aspect was that Stacey, if he was the ghost pirate, tried to kill — or, at the very least, maim — me. I thought we were friends; friends don't mutilate one another. I think that's in the Bible. Then again, he wouldn't have known the intruder in black was me. Was Stacey capable of killing anyone at all, though?

As it was, just sitting beside him in his bedroom — even though Yumi was there and the door was open — left me quivering with nerves and uncertainty.

☠ ☠ ☠

Later that night, the dead kids and I snuck out . . . well, the dead kids didn't really have to *sneak* out of the cemetery. There was no dead dad or mom who'd given them a curfew. Nonetheless, we had decided to stake out the O'Dare Sticksville Arena, named after some hockey guy I didn't know named (obvi) O'Dare. I'd never been inside the arena before, but Yumi was right: there was a lot of historical memorabilia on display. Notably some very old hockey and curling equipment and photographs in the front lobby, but also, in a locked glass case, a peach basket that was used in the first-ever basketball game by Canadian basketball inventor James Naismith. Since that famous game happened in Springfield, Massachusetts (I Googled it), and since a basketball hall of fame, like, exists, I was highly dubious this was the genuine article. I mean, how hard is it to take an old peach basket, cut out the bottom, and say it was a Naismith original? If it was the real deal, I'm sure the ghost pirate and history enthusiast would have struck the arena first. Maybe he was only interested in Sticksville history, and maybe that was a clue. My detective mind was working on overdrive.

After breaking in and loitering by the trophy cases for about an hour, with no sign of the pirate, the dead kids and I fell quickly into dire boredom, so we moved over to the actual rink. Derek made the mistake of telling Cyril about the Zamboni, which he described as a "slow-moving automobile that made the ice smooth," and that was all Cyril needed to hear. He loved anything related to automobiles, so before long, he was erratically steering the Zamboni in maze-like curls around the rink. I'd said it was okay as long as (a) he took Derek along for the ride (so he could keep an eye on him), and (b) he kept it slow. Not really an issue with a Zamboni, I suppose.

While Cyril and Derek sat perched atop that combination of go-kart and steamroller, Tabetha, Morna, and Kirby took the opportunity to grill me all about Valentine's Day as we waited on the bleachers for something to happen.

"Look at me, October!" Cyril yelled, turning the Zamboni in tight circles as he waved his hat in the air like a rodeo cowboy. Derek sat beside him doing a champion job of not looking totally embarrassed.

I waved back. It was only polite.

Tabetha kicked at my shin with her tall boot. "You takin' someone t'yer Valentine's dance?"

"No. I'm going with friends."

"But are ye askin' anyone t'be yer Valentine?" Morna asked.

"No. Valentine's Day is stupid, you guys."

"Yer no fun!" Tabetha said. "I had dozens of boyfriends."

"Dozens?" Kirby said.

"I've bet you've never even kissed a boy," Tabetha continued.

"No, I've never kissed anyone," I said. "So what? I'm thirteen."

"Tabetha, don't expect much from October," Kirby said, lolling his feet over the bleachers. "I mean, look at her. You've got a better chance at finding a Valentine, and you've been dead for one hundred and fifty years."

"Watch it," I warned Kirby. "You're not exactly a dreamboat, either."

Talking with the three dead kids was what I imagined it must feel like to have a mom to bug you around Valentine's Day. But thinking about that only made me disappointed that I never knew my mom, and that the woman on the Crooked Arms' telephone (who may or may not have been my mom) wouldn't talk to me anymore. A few minutes of increasingly depressing Valentine's talk, and I slid out onto the ice to follow Cyril and Derek around. We lasted until about three in the morning before we accepted that no one — alive or dead — was coming to rob the place and headed back to the cemetery.

All my recent nighttime excursions must have created a false sense of security. I quietly slid the back door open, trying to make the least noise possible, but it didn't matter. Dad was sitting at the kitchen table in his pajamas, his arms folded in a pose he must have learned from Mr. Santuzzi.

"Forget something at Stacey's?" he asked.

Unprepared as I was to see him sitting in the dark, like some middle-aged vampire in flannel pajamas, I could only manage "Uhhhh" in return.

"Looks like I was wrong about you," he said, standing from his place at the table and turning his back to me. "You realize there's a costumed criminal on the loose, don't you?"

"Dad, I was just in the cemetery . . ."

"Please don't insult my intelligence, October," he said, his back still turned. "I can see most of the cemetery from this seat at the kitchen table. It's only a matter of time before that weird real estate agent shows up with you at our door again."

We hadn't run into Alyosha Diamandas, Sticksville's most diligent realtor and frequent target of the dead kids' pranks, in a while; I guess because he wasn't selling the museum or hockey arena. At least Dad thought he was strange, too.

"Dad, I'm so sorry," I pleaded. If he'd just turn around and face me and *see* how sorry I was attempting to be. Really, speaking to his back was painful. He must have been truly disappointed. "I won't do it again, I promise. Tell me how I can make things up to you."

"I know you won't do it again," he said, finally looking over his shoulder. "Because from now on, you're only leaving the house for school and to tutor Ashlie. Otherwise, you're under house arrest."

My mind ran through all the things I had to do within the next month that involved me leaving the house: the Valentine's dance, movies at Stacey's, not to mention all the Cyril Cooper detective work I had planned to do. If Dad was going to be truly vigilant about this, I was in a lot of trouble.

"But Dad . . ." I started to moan, but he was already on his way out of the room.

"I'm going to bed."

With dread, I realized that maybe the Dead Kid Detective Agency was going to have to operate without a living agent for a spell. I felt the prison bars (figuratively, of course) close shut on my bedroom door as I resigned myself to a few hours rest.

☠   ☠   ☠

Stacey Fought the Law and ... the Law Won

If you've been an observant reader of the exploits of the Dead Kid Detective Agency, and I know that you have, you will have noticed that October Schwartz has the unfortunate and sloppy habit of using her *Two Knives, One Thousand Demons* composition book to record notes about whatever mystery she happens to be working on at the moment. Even worse, she had recently been leaving her notes for Ashlie Salmons's tutoring sessions in that very same composition book. She wasn't so stupid to actually write them on the pages of the notebook — no, she wouldn't sully Olivia de Kellerman's adventures with some math problems designed to improve Ashlie's algebraic comprehension — but she was writing her notes on loose-leaf paper, then folding them in half and tucking them into *Two Knives, One Thousand Demons*. And that's where her most recent troubles began.

October was at the Salmons residence on Thursday night, again tutoring her arch-nemesis in the way of basic trigonometry. All was going relatively well — they were both seated at the kitchen table, working on some problems involving triangles that Mr. Santuzzi assigned, and enjoying refreshing glasses of iced tea.

"Okay," October sighed, then began pointing to various parts of a triangle illustration as she continued. "If we know this side is twelve and this side is seven, and, also, that this angle is fifty-eight degrees . . . what is the length of this side?"

Ashlie stared at the diagram intently, as if she were about to move the notes with her mind. "I don't know . . . twelve? Eleven?"

"No," October said. "It's not *The Price Is Right*. You can figure it out by writing some numbers down."

"But I don't know *what* I should be writing down!" Ashlie's auburn head fell into her folded arms in exasperation.

"This is just like the last problem," October insisted, trying fairly hard not to let the aggravation cut through her voice *too* much. "Ugh. I'll walk you through it . . . just as soon as I get back from the washroom. Where is it again?"

The iced teas were having an effect on October.

"Upstairs, first door on the left," Ashlie said, her head still buried in her hands.

That was when mistake number two happened.

We won't dwell on the details and specifics of October's brief washroom visit, but when she came back downstairs only minutes later, she discovered her tutee — her math protégé — reading *Two Knives, One Thousand Demons*. October's mind went into a blind panic. Had she actually left her composition book wide open? Had Ashlie opened it and started reading from the very beginning? What pages was she reading and did they have any incriminating notes about, say, hanging out with ghosts?

When she noticed October cross the threshold of the kitchen, a cruel smile opened up on Ashlie's face like the belly wound of the tauntaun Han Solo cuts open in *The Empire Strikes Back*. "It's really too bad you don't have my mom as your mom, Zombie Tramp. She'd *love* you. You're quite the little crime-solver."

Really, it's too bad that October had no mom at all, but that's not what concerned her at the moment.

"Why are you reading my book?" she asked.

"Zombie Tramp, you left it open and my eyes just sort of . . . *drifted over*." She made her dainty fingers skip over the table.

"Don't call me that."

"Never mind that. You've been busy — not just with school work and tutoring but . . . look at this! You think Stacey MacIsaac might be the ghost pirate that's robbing everyone?" Ashlie's large green eyes bulged in mock surprise.

October could feel the heat rising in her cheeks.

"Who is that again? Stacey MacIsaac?" she asked.

"He's my friend," October said. Absolutely no one could remember who Stacey was.

"Oh, the tall, goony one?" she said, scrunching up her nose and raising her shoulders unconsciously. "I should probably tell my mother about this evidence you've found."

October stood a few paces from the kitchen table, literally vibrating with rage. She had no clue how to act. What could she do that wouldn't make things worse? But she stopped worrying about that when Ashlie picked up the composition book again and began to skim through its pages.

"Okay, so if that's Stacey, who is this Cyril guy?" Ashlie asked.

In reply, October lunged across the table and wrenched her book from Ashlie's hands.

"I can't believe you read my journal, you stupid pig!" October yelled. "What kind of *monster* are you?!" She backed up and was nearly in the front foyer of the house now.

"I didn't know it was a journal," Ashlie shouted, rising from her chair. "It looked like one of your stupid stories about demons and whatever! Was I supposed to guess a book called *Of Knives and Demons* was your innermost thoughts on notable Sticksville crimes?"

"*Two Knives, One Thousand Demons!*" October corrected.

"Whatever!"

"Ashlie, if I can't even trust you to not read my stuff while I'm on the toilet, I can't be your math tutor," October shouted. Like Lainey in *She's All That*, she was trying her darndest to never let them see her cry. She jammed the book in her bag and ripped open the closet to retrieve her peacoat.

"You *have* to tutor me!" Ashlie shouted. "Mr. Santuzzi said."

"Mr. Santuzzi," October insisted, shoving her left hand

through the coat sleeve, "will understand when I explain what a sneak you are."

"Mr. Santuzzi likes me, so I really doubt that," Ashlie pouted, hands on hips.

"Oh, Mr. Santuzzi doesn't like *anyone*!"

October had a very solid point there.

"Ashlie, if you tell anyone about Stacey, I promise you, I will kick your stupid, pretty face *right* off," October warned, yanking open the front door. "Good luck understanding triangles without me."

The door slammed shut and October slogged home through twenty-degree-below weather, but even that couldn't cool the incredible heat coursing through her body or calm the terrible rumble in her stomach.

☠   ☠   ☠

The most tragic aspect of that tragic tutoring session is that Ashlie Salmons was correct. Apparently, Mr. Santuzzi *did* like her more than he liked October. Following math class, she approached her teacher and explained she couldn't tutor Ashlie anymore because she didn't trust her, and the result of this distrust was much more fighting than tutoring. Mr. Santuzzi was unmoved.

"If the two of you are having some sort of interpersonal problem, you'll need to sort that out yourselves or take it up with Dr. Lagostina," he said, combing his impressive Fu Manchu with his thumb and forefinger. "You've only completed two tutoring sessions. I'm not letting you off *that* easy."

"But she went into my *personal belongings*," October pleaded, her pale hands out like a street panhandler. "She read my journal, Mr. Santuzzi!"

"Miss Salmons came by first thing this morning and explained the misunderstanding."

"Misunderstanding?"

"If it was your personal diary, Miss Schwartz," he said, beginning to pack up for lunch, "maybe you shouldn't have brought it to a math tutoring session. Maybe you leave those things at home."

Mr. Santuzzi was completely unreasonable! Or so October

thought. Ashlie Salmons must have been blackmailing him or something. Why else would he continue to force her to tutor Ashlie in math? This was like asking Jean Valjean to tutor Javert in civil rights. October made a mental note to consciously be as bad a math tutor as possible during their next session.

In music class that afternoon, October, likewise, made a very conscious effort to be overly nice to Stacey. After all, she had kind of, inadvertently, betrayed him to Ashlie Salmons, and though October really doubted Ashlie would do anything with the information, the fact that she had it still made October very uncomfortable. During an extended period of rest in the middle of one of the marches they were mauling, October looked over at Stacey, entirely focused on crashing the cymbals together at the correct time. Who could ever think he was a sword-wielding master thief? October felt ashamed that she had ever entertained the thought. He looked so happy behind the wall of drums at the back of the music room. So goofy in his green and yellow Hawaiian shirt. And, most importantly, he looked like he was threading a needle with some boiled angel-hair pasta — that's how difficult it was for him to keep time. Hawaiian shirt and pirate hat aside, Stacey just didn't have the temperament for being a burglar. Did he?

Maybe October was gazing a bit too intently at Stacey MacIsaac, because he glanced back, caught her staring, and hit his cymbals a beat too late, throwing off the timing of the entire band. Mrs. Tischmann had to stop them all.

"Sorry," Stacey shouted over the laughter and complaints. "Sorry, that was my fault."

None of the other music students were paying attention, but Mrs. Tischmann, in all her frizzy-haired glory at the front of the class, mouthed, "It's okay."

"Don't worry, Stacey," October said, fully realizing this is not a thing she would normally say and weirding herself out a little. "You'll get it next time."

Stacey smiled or grimaced or puffed out his cheeks — his facial expressions were all very similar — and picked up his cymbals again.

Mrs. Tischmann was counting in the class again. She was already on the three, raising her arms in a dramatic bird-of-prey-like way, when the class telephone rang.

"Keep your instruments up," she instructed. "This will just take a second." After some nodding and furtive glances toward the rear of the room, Mrs. Tischmann hung up and said, "Stacey, would you please go to the office? The rest of you, we're going to run it through from the top. Just without any cymbal crashes for now."

Shrugging his Hawaiian shirt a bit higher onto his shoulders, Stacey loped toward the back door, then was gone. October, keeping a stiff upper lip — as much as one can maintain lip stiffness while blowing into a trombone — played along with the rest of the band, but her mind was somewhere else entirely. Stacey *never* got into trouble. He was just so amicable. October got called to the office. Ashlie Salmons got called to the office. Not Stacey. So she was extremely concerned the sudden phone call had something to do with Ashlie and last night's math-tutoring revelation. As soon as Mrs. Tischmann closed her little fists to cut off the band, October's hand rocketed into the air.

"Mrs. Tischmann, may I please go to the washroom?"

Her music teacher motioned yes with a quick little hula movement of her hands, and October dropped her trombone at bit more carelessly than she should have and jogged out the classroom door. She didn't have long — rehearsing the song had taken over two minutes and Stacey, almost a full foot taller than October, would have beaten her to the office even if they'd left at the same time. She cursed his long, graceful strides! Despite her better judgment, October ran through the halls and atrium to get to the office. Sure, some of the kids loitering in the atrium might have laughed, and one comedian definitely yelled something about Usain Bolt, but October ignored them.

As she swerved closer to the office doors, she noticed her other living friend, Yumi Taskeshi, standing just outside the corner of the door. October crept up beside her.

"Yumi, what are you doing here?" October loudly whispered.

"Stacey's in the office," she pointed to the tall figure sitting in a swivel chair behind the front desk. "I saw him go by the library windows and I knew something was up. He has music class now. He wouldn't leave his drums unless he really had to."

"What do you mean, something's up?" October whispered.

"Look who's there," she said, pointing through the other door where Crown Attorney Salmons was standing, arms crossed, tremendous red belt on display, right in front of Stacey. She was accompanied by a police officer who looked like he'd been roughly hewn out of canned ham.

"Why are the police here?" October whispered, though she most certainly knew the answer.

"Beats me," Yumi shrugged, making her many chain-link necklaces jingle. "And you don't have to whisper. They can't hear us in the office."

"Oh," October said, returning to her normal volume and rubbing the back of her hand across her oily forehead. "I might have an idea why . . ."

"Shhh," Yumi interrupted, bringing a black nail to her lips. "Here they come."

Ashlie's mom led the way, holding open the door for Stacey and the tinned-meat-like police officer who followed.

"Stacey, where are they taking you?" Yumi called after them when they didn't stop to say hello or acknowledge the two of them and their general existence.

"Police station," he said, rather matter-of-factly.

"What?!" Yumi's eyes shrunk to pinholes. "This is so wrong! You didn't do anything!"

"Miss," the policeman said, assuming no further words were needed. Then he held Yumi by the shoulder and walked her backward a few paces.

"This is an outrage!" Yumi yelled, but she didn't struggle with the officer.

"An outrage!" October yelled in solidarity.

Soon, all three — Crown Attorney Salmons, the police officer, and their friend, Stacey MacIsaac — were outside and far from view. Yumi, rather dramatically, was now hunched over as if in a dry-heave, her eyes locked on the tiled floor, her hands nervously wiping up and down the knees of her black-and-white striped nylons.

"I don't understand," she told the floor in confidence. "Why would they arrest Stacey? What do they think he did?"

"They didn't arrest him," October said, patting Yumi's shoulder, now at waist height. "Probably they didn't. I think they just took him in for questioning."

"Questioning about what?" Yumi asked, hoisting herself up to full height again.

"Probably the ghost pirate stuff . . . all those robberies."

"What does Stacey have to do with any of that?"

And, at that point, October felt compelled to explain herself. Which, in hindsight, was probably not a brilliant idea. It was no secret that she didn't always think honesty was the best of all policies, so why she opted to tell her friend Yumi the awful truth, we may never know. Friendship, probably, or something useless like that.

"You did what?!" Yumi shouted, predictably. All the lolly-gaggers cutting class in the atrium ratcheted their heads to the side like a gunshot had just gone off.

"Calm down," October pleaded, smoothing an invisible tablecloth with her hands. "I didn't *do* anything. Not really. I just wrote in my notebook that Stacey had a pirate hat and wondered if he could be, like, the ghost pirate thief."

"That's the *stupidest* thing you've ever said, October. And you've said some amazingly stupid things. You said that Good Charlotte was a 'pretty good band,' you traitor."

"No one was supposed to see it, Yumi! You have to believe me. It was in my journal and Ashlie totally invaded my privacy — NSA style — and went through it while I was tutoring her."

"And now my best friend is going to jail. Thanks, Schwartz!" Yumi spat, yanking on both toggles of her hoodie.

That statement, more than any other, hurt October. Not the part about going to jail — unless October was wrong about Stacey's abilities as a master criminal, he wasn't going to be held by police for long — but the part about Stacey being Yumi's best friend. She realized they had known each other longer, and October was the new kid, but she'd kind of hoped she and Yumi had rapidly become closer, due to them both having ovaries and that sort of thing.

"Stacey will be fine," October said. "It's not like he's actually the ghost pirate."

"This is your fault," Yumi said, her eyes ablaze with the hatred of a hundred thousand suns.

"No!" October shouted, clearly offended. "It's Ashlie's! It's all her!"

"Ashlie is our enemy," Yumi said, jabbing her little index finger in the air. "You're supposed to be Stacey's friend."

Whatever October might have attempted to say to defend herself, Yumi gave her no time to say it, as she turned on her boot heel and stomped down the linoleum hallway, not bothering to glance back at October even once.

10

The Not-So-Great Depression

Bad news: my friends were either under arrest, hated me, or dead. The dead thing wasn't *so* bad, but they also expected me to solve their murders. So, even dead friendships came with a few complications. My life over the past six months had its share of low points, but never before had both Yumi and Stacey (probably, if he found out why he was being questioned by the police) despised me so earnestly, or had the trail of one of my mysteries gone quite so cold. It seemed impossible, but things were about to get worse.

When Friday night rolled around, I was in a writing mood. Plus, I didn't think my friends really wanted to speak to me. My confrontation with the Cruella de Vil of Sticksville Central, Ashlie Salmons (she was so bad in math, I'm not sure she could count to 101), had reminded me that I used to be a writer, not just a solver of really unpleasant mysteries. Olivia de Kellerman had been neglected for far too long; I had to dream up some more demons for her to stab. Unfortunately, I was just not feeling it. Just writing about knives and blades — even sharp edges — made my hands shaky. I guess I still wasn't over my brush with death in the library. And, in unrelated matters, I seemed to be using the word "ghastly" more frequently than was necessary.

I had promised to make an appointment to see Dr. Lagostina, the school therapist, first thing on Monday. My overall feeling of looming dread explained why, when my dad came home very early from his date with Crown Attorney Salmons, I was watching random episodes of *Kolchak: The Night Stalker* on the family computer. Dad liked to reserve the computer for official business (and not for watching headless motorcycle riders do their thing), so I was sure he was about to punish me, but something was off. I barely noticed as he slipped in the front door and shut it with a nearly inaudible click. It felt almost like an homage to my attempts to slip in undetected. Friday night – date night – and he was home before nine.

"Dad?" I called, pausing *Kolchak* for a second. It was just getting good, too.

He didn't answer, so I padded over to the front door. What seemed like the ghost of my dad was already making its way to his room. I followed until I was just about five paces behind his stooped figure.

"Dad?"

"Oh, October." He turned around with a sheepish smile. When he swiveled, he revealed his crisp white shirt had been rumpled and bore a faint burgundy stain. "I didn't hear you. I thought you'd be reading in bed."

"It's only nine, Dad. I was just trying to write."

"Sorry to hear about your friend Stacey," he said.

"Thanks. Have you heard anything about him from Ms. Salmons? Weren't you on a date tonight?"

"I was. Maybe the final date of my life, pumpkin," he sighed, then added. "I need a coffee."

What followed was a grim post-mortem (def-o the best term for it) of my dad and Ashlie's mom's date, which sounded like it ranked right up there (or down there) with a romantic dredging of a garbage-strewn pond in terms of misery. I guess they got around to talking about work, and Crown Attorney Salmons mentioned that they'd brought in this MacIsaac boy, and wasn't he a friend of his daughter's? In fact, she'd received a tip from Ashlie that October found some clues that led her to believe the MacIsaac boy might be involved with the string of historical robberies recently. All this was total lies, and I told my dad as much — about how I didn't think Stacey was really a criminal and how Ashlie had stolen my journal.

"I know," he said, sipping the coffee, which must have still been scalding hot, since our coffee maker was still percolating. "When I asked how Ashlie had heard this from you, she said she'd read it in your book. And that's how our fight started."

"Fight?" My dad had made a scene in a local restaurant.

"I might have mentioned that her daughter shouldn't be reading other people's books without their permission, and that given *my* daughter was doing *her* daughter a favour by tutoring her in math, the least she could do was keep out of *my* daughter's stuff. Well, the Crown attorney didn't like that."

Wow. Go Dad, I thought. Under that science teacher's pocket protector beat the heart of a mama lion.

"She continued to defend Ashlie's actions, noting the unusual circumstance of there being a Sticksville crime wave, and I countered by pointing out that this was not the first time her daughter had caused hardship for you. I definitely said something about her daughter's behaviour . . . and how it was very bad."

"How did that go over?" I asked, though I already knew the answer. The stain on his shirt was starting to make a lot more sense now.

"Could have been better," he said, doing a pretty decent impression of a frog. "There was a lot of yelling. She tossed her drink at my face, then stormed out."

"Oh, gosh, Dad. I'm so sorry."

"In good news, you'll never have to worry about being stepsisters with Ashlie Salmons."

Dad tipped the last of his coffee back into his distraught face and shuffled to his room. The door shut with a big huff of air, and I was left to tend the coffee maker and think about the latest way in which I'd ruined my dad's life. On the positive side of things, my dad was no longer dating the birthing canal of pure evil. But the downside was that the terrible mother of the more-terrible girl — for some reason — had made my dad happy.

So . . . maybe he wasn't going to be so happy for a while. Or ever. Only time would tell just how damaging their lover's spat would be. Pushing that from my brain for a minute, I curled up again on the folding chair in front of our computer and unpaused *Kolchak*.

☠   ☠   ☠

Update: my dad's lover's spat was basically worse than the apocalypse. Like, if life were a series of movies, his date last night would have been *Armageddon* — both because the world almost explodes and because it was so heinously bad. I figured I should ask my dad out for breakfast on Saturday — get him out of the house, remind him that not all meals ended in heartbreak and wine to the face; some ended with home fries. But Dad never emerged from his room all day. I'd periodically knock on the door and make him tell me he was okay, and I'd occasionally bring such provisions as a mug of coffee or a plate of peanut-butter toast to his door, but I didn't see his face for a full twenty-four hours. For all I knew, he'd set up a voice recording on his cell phone to say, "Don't worry, October, I'll be fine in a little bit," whenever I knocked. He *was* a science teacher. How difficult would it be to set something like that up?

Whatever. Someone was drinking the coffee and eating the toast.

Though it was past Dad's usual bedtime on Saturday, I knocked on his bedroom door again. Really, this would have been the perfect time to sneak out of the house to visit the dead kids. It wasn't like he was going to wonder where I was. He was more than preoccupied. But I felt low even thinking that way, taking advantage of my dad's mental illness. It really *wasn't* the perfect time to do some undead sleuthing; I should have stayed home to watch over him. Being a good detective sometimes meant being an awful daughter.

"Dad," I stuttered. "Is it okay if I go over to Yumi's?"

In a surprise move, the door opened. I had worried he'd be in there all week. "I guess it's not too much fun to hang around here," he said.

"I know you said I'm grounded and —"

"Well, you can forget that!" Dad said, making a beeline to the kitchen sink and filling his cupped palms with water. "You're un-grounded now, pumpkin. We'll show Crown Attorney Salmons what a trustworthy young woman you are!" Dad splashed cold water onto his unshaven face and rubbed so hard I thought he was reshaping it.

"Are you okay?" It was like, after a depressive episode, Dad's fight with Ashlie's mom had energized him.

"I'm good, October," he said. "I think I'll give Mr. Santuzzi a call and see if he'd like to grab a coffee."

What had I done? I'd worried about leaving Dad home alone, but now I'd led him straight into the burly arms of Sticksville's most dangerous math teacher! Still, he'd probably be fine. Much better my dad spending an hour over coffee with Mr. Santuzzi than me. I didn't dare look this gift horse in the mouth, and instead rode it straight to the Sticksville Cemetery (after making it look like I was walking to Yumi's first, natch).

I arrived in the middle of the cemetery with my peacoat on and black toque screwed tight onto my head. The dead kids were scratching tic-tac-toe games into the snow and dirt with cane-sized sticks they'd sharpened. Though only a few days had passed since we'd broken into the arena, it felt like I hadn't seen the dead kids in weeks. So much had happened.

"Kirby," I said. "Your stomach grew back." The dead boy from Canada's post-war era was no longer an open wound.

"Amazing what a few days rest will do," he said, patting his not-inconsiderable gut.

"Few days is right," Tabetha said. "Where you been, October?"

"We thought you'd given up after what happened at the library, then the no-show at the arena," Cyril said, scratching an X into the snow.

"Scared of a ghost pirate, huh?" Tabetha shouted. "I shoulda known."

"That's not it," I shouted right back. Maybe I was a little touchy about my sword panic still. The dead kids could be so aggravating. I'm not sure why I bothered trying to explain *anything*. "There's been a lot going on . . . with my dad, with Stacey."

"There's something wrong w'Stacey?" Morna asked.

"The police thought he might be the ghost pirate," I said.

"But he's not!" came Morna's predictable response. "He's a MacIsaac; we're no pirates."

"I know, I know." I said. "And they must know that, too. It's all stupid and out of control. And I wish, Cyril, I wish we could stake out the arena again or do something to solve your mystery, but I have no idea what to do next and my dad is in a really bad place now."

Nothing was going right — not just for me, or my dad, but for the whole Dead Kid Detective Agency operation.

"My dad needs me," I said, trying to make the point. "I think. He's out with my math teacher right now, but I know the symptoms of his depressive episodes when I see them."

The dead kids were not impressed, I could tell. Tabetha had that penetrating scowl on her face that sliced deep into my belly like a boning knife . . . or some kind of knife. (I have very little training in butchery.) Kirby was working overtime on his eye-rolling, and even Derek was about to wear grooves into his arm, given how much he was drumming his fingers along it. (And I guess the fact that he was kind of decomposing didn't help any.) Only Morna and Cyril seemed to possess some semblance of empathy, because they made their way to the front of the group to let me know it was okay.

"October, it will be okay." See what I'm saying? "We'll reconvene in, what, three nights?"

"That should be fine."

"In three nights, refreshed and with a new plan of attack," Cyril decided.

"Oh, we have a plan now?" Kirby heckled from behind.

Kirby, while invariably annoying, typically had a point. Staking out all the spots in Sticksville that might contain items of historical value didn't make for much of a plan. And even if we did, by pure coincidence, run into the ghost pirate mid-robbery again, what exactly would we do? Last time we encountered him, we'd run for our lives, despite the fact that most of us didn't even have lives to lose. And I was certainly not looking forward to facing his sword again. I was beginning to think that I wasn't projecting the type of confidence needed in a leader.

"I'll think of something. Don't worry," I said. But already, I was worrying. "Will you be all right if I take care of my dad for a few days?"

Derek nodded. "You can take all the time you need. We'll try to think of a plan in the meantime."

Then I left the snowy cemetery, to let the dead kids continue their tic-tac-toe game. Honestly, I felt pretty rotten to just ditch them in the graveyard, but not nearly as rotten as my dad must have felt. And, really, as much as the ghostly sleuthing has become so important to me, family comes first. I mean, not in regards to telling the truth or obeying my dad's rules or anything like that. But for the important stuff.

☠ ☠ ☠

By Monday, Stacey was back in school, but my dad was not. As I left my bedroom that morning, I noticed Dad was in the kitchen, clad in sweatpants and a ratty old T-shirt. I felt obliged to remind him that he had a job and was a teacher and all that, but all that emitted from his unshaven face was a muffled response: "I called in sick."

So that was that. Either his little kaffeeklatsch with Mr. Santuzzi didn't do the trick, or he backslid over the course of Sunday. Now that I thought about it, he hadn't left the house since his man-date with Mr. Santuzzi. But since he hadn't locked himself in his bedroom, I had to trust that Dad would manage on his own all day, because, unfairly, substitute *students* were not yet a thing.

"I may take a few days away from work, October," he admitted, stirring some sugar into a mug of coffee. "I'll be okay, but I'm not sure if I'm up to teaching just yet. My students are my priority, and I don't want to go in when I'm . . . well . . . not at my best."

"I thought *I* was your priority," I joked.

"You are," he said, taking a long sip and following me to the front hallway. "Just not when I'm at school."

"Take care, Dad," I said, heading out the door. "And take all the time you need."

"I'll make us dinner tonight," he called after me.

When I reached my locker bay, Stacey was waiting nearby to tell me he was no longer under suspicion for, like, grand larceny.

"Next time you suspect me of being a master criminal," he said, listlessly spinning a nearby combination lock, "you could always ask me first."

"I didn't actually suspect you — no one was supposed to see that," I said. Besides, whenever I had asked criminals if they were criminals in the past, I wound up being tied to the modern equivalent of a railroad track.

"I'm joking," he said. "It's no big deal. Like, no harm done. I missed half a day of school and now most of the school thinks I'm a renegade."

"No one thinks that. No one uses that word, Stacey. How's Yumi?" I asked, knowing she'd have been the first person to spot Stacey as he walked through the school's front doors.

"She might have cried a little bit," he said, looking embarrassed. "But pretend I didn't tell you that."

"Does she still hate me?"

"Your name and Judas Iscariot were referenced in the same sentence. But I'll smooth things over with her; make her see it wasn't your fault."

"Good luck," I said, slamming my locker shut.

"She can't stay mad at you if I'm not mad at you, right?"

Sometimes, it was like Stacey was new to this universe or something.

The P.A. system crackled like a half-finished firework, then the morning announcements commenced with a reminder for all students to submit those stupid Love Match cards (they didn't put it quite that way), followed by an a cappella rendition of the William Tell Overture.

"Our cue to leave," I whispered.

"See you at lunch," Stacey mouthed, but I wasn't so sure. Yumi, I suspected, might need another day free from me.

After making an appointment with Dr. Lagostina about my sword-based fears — or "anxiety issues," as I put it — I made my way to lunch. I sat on my own in the cafeteria, just like old times, to be safe. Aside from the early morning conversation with Stacey and the therapy appointment, I couldn't tell you what else happened at Sticksville Central that day. My mind was mostly preoccupied with worry over my dad. I worried that if he missed too many days of school, he wouldn't be a teacher at Sticksville Central for much longer. Even though he was diagnosed with clinical depression and the school board supposedly knew that, he'd already missed a few days this school year and there could only be so many absences that they'd excuse. Or so I imagined. So after the bleakest day at school ever, I went straight home, not even attempting to say goodbye to Yumi or Stacey, to check on my dad. He was lying on the couch, staring at some soap opera playing on the television. Unwilling to get much closer until I was sure he'd showered, I asked about dinner.

"So what's for dinner, Dad?"

"Oh," he said, snapping out of his television trance. "Honey, I totally forgot to pick something up for dinner. I've just been . . . thinking."

"It's okay, Dad," I said. "Luckily, we live in a world of Kraft Dinner."

I made the cheesy macaroni for the both of us and I ate mine in my room, listening to Joy Division, since Dad seemed absorbed with anything and everything that was on the television. Originally, I'd hoped to visit the cemetery, since it seemed safe enough to leave my dad unattended for a few hours, and get back on track to solving Cyril's mystery. But lightning had failed to strike, bright-idea wise; I still had no idea what to do. Scraping hash marks into the orange cheese left on my plate, I assessed my dead kid dilemma.

Normally, I'd try to read up more on Sticksville in 1779, but all the information from that era had been stolen by a ghost pirate. There was always the option of trying to catch this ghost pirate and retrieve the material I needed, but I had no idea where (or even if) the ghost pirate would strike again. And I'd probably just freak out when I saw his sword again. The dead kids and I could split up — each of us stake out some site of historical importance for the next few nights — but what was one of us going to do to stop the ghost pirate on our own? I was tempted to just give up for the moment, let the dead kids disappear, and try again in the spring when it wasn't so cold and my dad (I hoped) wasn't quite so depressed.

Maybe, I thought, I shouldn't visit the dead kids in the cemetery tonight. Maybe I should just play hooky, keep my dad company, and watch more *Kolchak*. And so, I did.

Then Tuesday arrived and Dad didn't make it into school again. I sat in classes and answered questions and pretended like I wasn't worried sick. Tuesday night, after another lack-lustre meal prepared by yours truly, I was plagued by the same doubts: could I really spend the night hunting ghost pirates with the dead kids with my dad in his current state? As I rose from my bed to return my dishes to the kitchen sink, the phone rang. And by phone, I don't mean our cordless landline, the one we have a number listed for in the phone book (if those still exist). And I don't mean my cell phone, because that definitely doesn't exist. (When and if I could have one was the subject of a constant battle with my dad.) The ringing phone was the super-old antique I'd stolen from the now-demolished Crooked Arms. The plate and fork slid off my lap and collapsed on the floor and all I could do was stare at the candlestick telephone.

On the fourth ring, Dad shouted

out from across the house, "October! Can you pick up the phone?" I guess he was too out of it to notice that it wasn't our usual ringtone. I crawled across my bed, belly-down, like a soldier ducking under barbed wire. I gathered the covers around myself in a cocoon and lifted the receiver.

"Hello? Schwartz residence?"

Okay, but what was I supposed to say, really?

The voice at the other end, the same voice that seemed so familiar, said four words: "Dig up his body."

"Mom?" I called, but the line, like most of my friends, was already dead.

☠   ☠   ☠

11

Cops and Graverobbers

And so, it was decided that October Schwartz would dig up Cyril Cooper's corpse. Obviously, she hoped the dead kids would chip in and do a little digging, but there was no guarantee of that. She felt she'd landed on her dead friends' bad side with all the time she'd been spending at home with her dad lately. This chain of reasoning was how October found herself alone in her garage that night, searching for a suitable grave-digging tool.

Though Mr. Schwartz's depths of depression certainly worried October, and were more cause for concern than celebration, the un-grounding remained in effect, which allowed October a bit more freedom to roam at night. Her father had encouraged October to come and go as she pleased — almost like a hotel resident whom he was very fond of — possibly because Mr. Schwartz himself seemed unwilling to leave the house, and he knew October would have to be a bit more self-reliant for the immediate future. Which was all for the best, really.

October Schwartz wedged her body between her dad's car and the wall in their almost-but-not-quite-two-car garage. A selection of long-handled garden tools were hanging along this wall, like swords in an arsenal, and she had to squeeze past the rake, the chainsaw, and the snow shovel, before she reached the other shovel — the one, ostensibly, intended for digging ditches and the like. She pulled it down and dragged it with her as she extracted herself from the tight crevice, and then noticed the car had left salt and dust all over her black jeans. But given that she planned to spend the night digging down six feet into an old grave, her pants were only going to get messier. She had just the one shovel, which meant it would be a long night. Not that she'd ever dug up a grave before. For all she knew, it might be a breeze. Still, additional shovels, she reasoned, might be handy.

Putting on her black coat and winter gear, October set the shovel beside the cemetery gate in her backyard. She then returned indoors to take all the available cash out of her dad's wallet, which was conveniently resting on the kitchen counter. She felt bad about stealing from her dad, but she reasoned that he'd probably never notice. Plus, he'd only been eating toast and coffee (with an occasional contribution from the fake dairy food group, Kraft Dinner) for three days straight, so even though their monthly budget hadn't accounted for any surprise shovel purchases, it probably wouldn't be an issue. She gathered up the many coloured bills and counted seventy-five dollars. She hoped that could get her two shovels at Beaver Hardware. If not, she'd have to settle for one.

After stuffing the bills into her coat pocket, she moved as quickly as she could to the hardware store without actually running or jogging. It was already seven thirty and she wasn't sure how late Beaver Hardware stayed open. The cold night air cut across her cheeks like a dull razor blade. At ten minutes before eight, she opened the door of the hardware store and sounded the jangling bell overhead.

"We close in ten minutes, little lady," the gruff man behind the counter warned. He wore the same style of glasses as Ms. Fenstermacher, but on him they looked more utilitarian.

"Shovels?" October said, either as an explanation or a question. Her breath formed steam that curled upward in a lazy question mark.

"Aisle twelve," he said from beneath his push-broom moustache.

Her black boots squeaked along the aisles as she strode to the back. Melting snow trapped in the tread of her Doc Martens seeped out behind her, like a really ineffective trail of bread crumbs. She found the shovels in a back corner. There were only a few varieties. There's not all *that* much to a shovel, after all. And she discovered the cheapest kind was twenty-seven dollars. If you know your math, you'll realize October had more than enough money (even with tax), so she lifted two from their hooks and tucked them horizontally under her armpits. All this eleventh-hour shovel purchasing did not go unnoticed by October's old acquaintance, the Goth Hardware Clerk.

"Buying shovels?" he said, though it seemed fairly obvious that she was.

"Oh . . . Percy," October said, succeeding against the odds to remember the clerk's real (and ridiculous) name.

Goth Hardware Clerk, also known as Percy, looked nearly identical to how October remembered him: long mop of jet-black hair, shorn closely on the one side; fishnet sleeves beneath his green uniform golf shirt; black boots with the shoelaces carelessly left undone. The only new addition to his wardrobe were black racing gloves that he was presumably wearing to protect his hands as he restocked the larger tools. (Unless he was part of some goth *Fast and the Furious* street racing team, though that seemed highly unlikely.)

"What do you need two shovels for?" he grinned and lowered his left eyebrow in a way that probably read as charming in his brain, but actually looked painful. "Burying a body?"

"Actually, kind of the opposite," October answered and wedged the shovel handles further up into her armpits.

"Good luck," he scoffed, completely committing to what he most definitely assumed was a really hilarious joke. "It's February. Probably about a foot of frozen soil. You can't dig anything outside without heating the ground first."

October hadn't thought of this. Was she supposed to be a geological expert at thirteen?

"Then could you direct me to where you keep the charcoal?"

It's tough to imagine a hardware store employee who wears fishnets and racing gloves to work being flustered or taken aback by anything, but he appeared a bit fazed by that. At the very least, he had no response and silently led her to the proper aisle. Which was fine by October. As pleasant as a tête-à-tête with Goth Hardware Clerk could sometimes be, the store was closing and

Cyril Cooper's body remained buried in the ground behind her house, so she didn't have a lot of time for chit-chat. Her maybe-mom-on-the-phone had given her a directive and she aimed to follow it. For some reason, the voice always came up with a great idea when October was most lost and confused. Leaving Percy puzzled beside the heating supplies, she returned to the front cash register and paid for the two shovels and a small bag of briquettes. She held onto the receipt, too, as she figured if the dead kids were gentle with the shovels, she might be able to return them tomorrow and her dad wouldn't be out the money. Not that the dead kids were ever gentle about anything.

☠ ☠ ☠

When she returned home, October left the two new shovels and charcoal bag by the old one, at the entrance to the cemetery from their backyard. Nine was likely too early to start the secret, highly *illegal* gravedigging, so she sat doing her math and French homework at her dad's side in the living room, until it was nearly midnight and he'd gone to bed. Then she suited up in her almost exclusively black winter gear once again, took the camping lantern from the garage, and retrieved the shovels.

She greeted the dead kids in the usual cemetery clearing, carrying three shovels in her arms, a lantern, and a bag of charcoal like they were the firewood that would last them the remainder of the winter. October dumped everything onto the ground, where they thudded over numerous tic-tac-toe matches cut into the snow by the dead kids that had been played to cat's games.

"You're back!" Morna said.

"How's your dad?" Derek asked, hopping off the tombstone he was seated on.

"Um, not great," October said. "But I had an idea I wanted to try."

"What's with the shovels?" Kirby chimed in with the most popular question of the night. It's almost like you couldn't walk around with a shovel without getting the third degree.

"I want us to dig up Cyril's grave."

"And why the bag of charcoal?" Derek asked.

"Are we roasting marshmallows?" Morna yipped.

"We need to heat the ground up before we dig, guys," October said, wielding her newly acquired wisdom like a blowtorch. "It's February."

"So we're just going to create a bonfire on top of Cyril's grave?" Kirby was dubious.

"I guess."

The dead kids laughed and laughed and laughed. Finally, Tabetha spoke, but only to say, "Perfect." The dead kids did not take much convincing.

"Are you sure about this, Cyril?" October asked. She wondered if it would be trying for him — or, at least, strange — to see his skeleton or whatever remained of Cyril's body, but then she realized it wouldn't be the first time Cyril had an out-of-body experience.

"Oh, yes, October," he replied, picking up one of the shovels and heading toward his gravesite. "I'm not squeamish about the sight of my own dead body, and this could be really helpful."

October and Derek picked up the other shovels and they all followed him to Cyril Cooper's grave.

"Do you really think there will be a clue hidden in Cyril's coffin?" Kirby hollered, bringing up the rear of our troop. "If there's even a coffin left at this point. I mean, fine, let's dig him up. It'll be good for a laugh. But what do you think we'll find, October?"

"I don't know. Something," she answered over her shoulder. "We can't just wait around for the ghost pirate to strike again, because we don't know if that will ever happen. And without any historical information, this is, like, the one concrete thing we can do."

October emptied out the entire bag of charcoal briquettes in front of Cyril's tombstone.

"Can you spread them around?" she asked.

"Why don't you do it?" Kirby insisted.

"I don't want to get charcoal all over myself."

Considering October was wearing literally no non-black clothing that evening, her concerns were puzzling. After the dead kids laid the charcoal out in a misshapen rectangle, October produced a matchbook from her pocket.

"What if the fire gets out of control?" Derek asked.

"It won't. It's February," October replied.

Fire safety tip: that's not how fire works, readers. Cold air and snow do not affect the spread of open flame very much. As it is, it's almost a miracle the Dead Kid Detective Agency wasn't ended in a conflagration right then and there.

The five dead kids and October watched the bonfire crackle and pulse as the snow gave way to a puddle under their feet.

"This is going t'be messy," Morna said.

October had other concerns. "I really hope no one walks past the cemetery tonight," she said, watching a thick plume of smoke rise into the starry sky.

"Good luck explaining this," Kirby chuckled.

"How long is this gonna take?" Tabetha asked, her foot impatiently tapping the now-muddy ground.

October shrugged her shoulders and looked at her Swatch. "Maybe an hour? Someone should fetch a bucket of water and maybe a blanket from the garden shed so we can put this bonfire out when we need to."

Luckily for October and the dead kids, no one noticed the late-night funeral pyre in the Sticksville Cemetery. As the smoke dissipated, October set the camping lantern atop the tombstone of Cyril's nearest cemetery neighbour (a "Silas Alwood") to shed some light on their clandestine dig. Cyril Cooper broke ground on his grave first, with Derek and October joining him soon after.

"We'll take shifts," Cyril said. "In a half hour, Tabetha will take my spot, Morna can take October's, and Kirby, you replace Derek."

"I don't do manual labour," Kirby said, watching the chunks of the still-kind-of-frozen earth fly in an arc before his face.

"You do tonight, pal," Tabetha said, putting Kirby in a headlock.

"Over my dead body," he gasped, trying to wrench free from Tabetha's elbow crook.

"No, over mine," Cyril said. (Pretty clever.) "You know, October, February is probably the least ideal time to dig a grave. Even with the heated soil."

"Why do I feel like this isn't your first gravedigging experience, Cyril?"

The way Cyril had strode over to his own gravestone, the way he took charge of the situation, started delegating responsibilities — it seemed like the young master Cooper had done his fair share of gravedigging in his time. He just looked at October without saying a word.

"Well, we need to dig up your grave," October explained, her face harshly lit by the lantern. "So we had to light your grave on fire, and the ground's *still* going to be hard, and I'm going to freeze to death, not that any of you care about that. But we can wait to do this in April, if you'd prefer."

"No, thank you," Cyril said, taking off his hat and resting it on top of a nearby grave marker.

"We'll stop complaining," Derek added, and he continued to dig.

"Can you remember anything else about the week you died?"

October asked, hauling a big chunk of grass and dirt over her shoulder.

"Well, there were a few strange . . . phenomena, I guess," he said, face pointed toward the dirt. "They happened just after I'd found the spy's secret hideout."

"I hate to interrupt," said Kirby, who loved to interrupt, "but won't someone notice that Cyril's grave has been disturbed tomorrow morning?"

"We'll worry about that later," October said, sweat already starting to bead on her forehead. "What happened next, Cyril?"

Cyril grunted, then continued. "Well, I already mentioned that I was certain that Patrick was a revolutionary spy, given what I found in the shack. I took my commanding officer's spyglass, and the large book I tossed on the fire immediately upon arriving home."

"Just because you can't read, doesn't mean you have to treat books so roughly," Kirby mocked.

"Ha ha," Cyril said. "The book was evil. I didn't need to read it to tell."

October, Cyril, and Derek were now standing in a rectangular trench about six inches deep. October wondered how they'd even finish tonight.

"What did you do with the spyglass?" Derek asked.

"The spyglass I returned to our commanding officer when he wasn't looking," Cyril said. "I wanted Patrick to realize his scheme had been discovered, but I didn't want him to know it had been me who discovered it."

"Do you remember if he reacted? When the officer found the spyglass?" October asked.

"Keep diggin'," Tabetha shouted from a few feet away.

"No, I don't remember," Cyril said, "but . . ."

"But what?"

"The commanding officer, Whitmore . . . I remember he lost his voice later that day."

"Lost his voice? Like, he got laryngitis?"

"I don't know what that is," Cyril said. "But probably not. More like he couldn't speak at all."

"He was really hoarse?" Morna asked.

"The words just wouldn't come."

A mysterious silence befalling a soldier was intriguing, no doubt, but October wasn't sure how this would help her find Cyril's murderer, unless his commanding officer killed him in some weird revenge over a lost voice. The trio of hard-working shovellers was now approaching the one-foot mark.

"I guess that's interesting," October said. "But I have no idea what it means. Do you remember anything else, Cyril?"

"One day that week — it might have been the same day, in fact — a lightning bolt struck out of the clear sky and set a bush beside the Tylers' barn afire."

"That sounds very symbolic and would probably look great in a music video, but I'm not really seeing a clue here," October said. Cyril's "phenomena" sounded like the kind of superstitious nonsense that Ms. Fenstermacher had regaled October with about that old Fairfax Crisparkle guy. Not, in her humble opinion, overly helpful to the case.

Cyril shrugged and leaned into his shovel again.

"Did you just have three shovels lying around?" Derek asked.

"Um, no. I had to buy a couple at the hardware store."

"You do realize they *have* shovels in a cemetery, right?" Kirby asked, appearing taller all the time as the hole October stood in got deeper and deeper. "We saw about a dozen of them in the garden shed when we retrieved that bucket."

October felt like a dolt. She should have realized a cemetery would be lousier with shovels than a university campus is with hacky sacks.

"I didn't," she said. "But now that you mention it, why don't you, Morna, and Tabetha rustle up a few more shovels? With six of us digging, we should reach Cyril in no time."

Kirby's face? The dictionary illustration of unimpressed. He stomped off with Morna and Tabetha toward the caretaker's shed.

"So, Cyril," October continued, "you took the spyglass and the book. Is that it?"

"No, I took a weird necklace, too, as I wasn't sure what it was for . . . and it seemed like it would be valuable."

127

"You were going to sell it?"

"No!" he blurted out. "I was just going to hide it. And once we were sure that Patrick Burton was a spy — once he'd been tried and proven guilty — then . . . I was going to sell it."

"So you *did* hide it?"

"Yes."

"Where?" Derek asked. "Maybe it's still there, if you hid it really well. Maybe it's a clue. Right, October?"

October nodded.

"That's the thing. I can't remember where I put it."

Kirby, Morna, and Tabetha returned with three more shovels.

"Start diggin', LaFlamme," Tabetha ordered. "You, too, crazy Scotch girl."

"Somebody should make sure the lantern doesn't fall," Kirby said.

"Ye can't remember where ye put wha'?" Morna asked, having caught the tail end of Cyril's story.

"The spy's necklace," Derek said.

"Oh, great."

"I wrote it down!" Cyril insisted. "I wrote it down!"

"Fat lot of good that does us," Kirby said. "You wrote it down where? On some scrap of paper two hundred years ago?"

"What if ye put it in yer pocket?" Morna said quietly.

Morna had barely spoken for most of the evening. Even when she did speak, she was often so quiet, she was hard to hear. But it would have been truly tragic if October and the dead kids missed the words she had just uttered, because they were sheer genius.

"What did you just say, Morna?" October asked.

"I said maybe the note is in Cyril's pocket."

"Morna!" Cyril shouted, grabbing the small Scottish girl by the shoulders. "You wizard! I could kiss you!"

That, readers, was kind of mean, because, like Drew Barrymore in that 2002 movie classic, Morna MacIsaac had never been kissed, so it was unfair for Cyril to make such empty threats or promises.

"Well, check your pockets," Kirby said.

Cyril began to pat down all the pockets in his waistcoat. His pantaloons, sadly, left no room for pockets, and, troublingly, little room for imagination.

"Just 'cause the note isn't in his pocket," Derek said, "doesn't mean it's not in *his* pocket." He pointed to the disturbed grave below them.

"Why not?" October asked.

"It just doesn't."

"Guys," October whined, resting her head on the handle of her shovel. "I don't understand your ghost rules. Can we just finish digging Cyril up?"

"Then we'll know for sure," Derek said.

Cyril searched his pockets again, down his shirt, in each of his shoes, and then finally gave up and resumed digging.

A few hours later, around three in the morning, the six of them had made an impressive crater in the graveyard. The lower they went, the easier the dirt was to dig. Which would have been great if October's arms hadn't turned to jelly about two hours ago.

"What kind of note did you even write to yourself?" Kirby asked, shoulder-to-shoulder with Cyril. "You can't read or write."

"I think it was a picture," he answered. "Like a diagram or a map."

"I'm sure it'll be a very helpful clue, Cyril," Morna said.

"Oh, brother," Tabetha moaned.

"*If* we ever find his body," Derek said. "And *if* there's a note —"

A metallic clang that shuddered up his arms stopped him from finishing his thought. He drove downward with the shovel again and it hit the same resistance.

"I think we've found Cyril," Derek said.

Cyril swallowed hard and everyone scrambled to clear the dirt away from the coffin. As they did, it became clear there still was a coffin, crudely made from pine, though it had largely rotted through. Once they'd cleared the top of the old coffin, Cyril shoved the spade of his shovel into the space just below the coffin's flat lid.

"Somebody help me," he said, as he stepped down on the shovel handle. He hoped to pry it open with leverage. "Get a few more shovels in here."

Using three shovels, they were able to pry open the lid. Shooting out from the open coffin, like a cork from a champagne bottle, popped an unholy stench of pre-Confederation death. Not that it bothered anyone but October. The odour of burnt animal fur rolled in the excrement of a goat that survived only on diapers for food gave her an uppercut to her throat; October had to reel backward and vomit behind some other poor United Empire Loyalist's grave. Once she recovered, she walked back to the open pit to see — just barely lit by the camping lantern — a withered brown skeleton, dressed in a more tattered version of the outfit Cyril was wearing. The same drum — a little more beat up, for sure — rested beside him in the coffin.

The dead kids wasted no time and started pawing through Cyril's corpse's clothing, feeling in the pockets like they were wounds and they were five Doubting Thomases. Even Cyril barely hesitated to go through his old apparel like a vulture-pickpocket hybrid. In truth, it was pretty revolting, and October was kind of glad she'd already puked out everything she'd eaten that day.

"Search every piece a' clothin'," Tabetha ordered.

"This is useless," Derek sighed, already resigned to the initiative's (if you can call the morbid endeavour an "initiative") failure. "We've searched all his pockets three times already; we've looked through the drum. There aren't any clues here."

Derek was right — there were only so many places you could hide something in a coffin. Unless it was one of those trick coffins, like a magician might use. But this cut-rate, budget-conscious wooden version certainly wasn't that. The dead kids wiped off their hands on their pants (or dresses) and stood back to survey the desecrated corpse.

"Wait a second," Kirby said. "What about *this*?"

That's when Kirby leaned over — in a sudden move no one was expecting — and tore open Cyril's pants. A button rocketed out of the open pit and Morna gasped as Kirby tore the two halves of Cyril's pantaloons from one another.

"What are you — ?" Derek began, but Kirby wasn't quite done. He dug into Cyril's actual skeleton, fitting his hand into the cavity of his pelvis. When he turned around to face October and his dead friends, he held a brass locket the size of a flattened chicken's egg in his right hand.

"Is that the spy's weird necklace?" October asked.

"No," Cyril said. "That's my mother's locket."

"Great," Tabetha grumbled. "Your ma's locket. So what's it doin' inside yer body? An' where's the note you wrote about the spy's necklace?"

Digging a thumbnail into the locket, Kirby flipped it open like he was shucking an oyster. Fluttering to the dirt below came a folded and yellow piece of paper.

The dead kids all turned to Cyril.

"I guess I swallowed it."

☠   ☠   ☠

12

Shipping Hard

Cyril, like some sort of reverse Christopher Walken in *Pulp Fiction*, had swallowed a locket to protect its contents before he died. This was a surprise to me, because I didn't even know they had lockets in the late 1700s. They didn't have photographs. I knew *that* much. So what were they putting in their lockets?

"Oh, yes, we had lockets," Cyril insisted, turning the locket over in his hand. "Usually people put their lover's hair in it or what have you. I took this from my mother and tossed a lock of my father's old hair into the river."

"That's sad," Morna said, looking at the unfolded drawing that he'd just retrieved from the locket.

"And gross," I added. "So you swallowed this whole locket? You must have thought you were in danger."

The locket was about the size of an Oreo cookie, which I think I'd have a hard time swallowing whole. (It sounded like a delicious experiment to test later at home.) In my estimation, old Cyril would have had to figure himself in some very immediate danger to swallow a chunk of metal that size.

"Didja worry you were gonna die before ya could tell anyone?" Tabetha asked. "About the spy?"

"I'm not sure," he said. "Certainly I must have believed that I was in trouble."

"Yeah," she continued. "I mean, how would ya know ya

weren't gonna ... y'know ... pass it?" Tabetha asked the horrible questions the rest of us couldn't bear to ask.

"I guess I would have just swallowed it again if I did."

"Disgusting," Kirby croaked.

"I would have washed it first!"

As gross and amusing — mostly gross — as that conversation was, I really wanted to know what the drawing meant and who Cyril was so deathly afraid of.

"But *who* was this immediate danger from, Cyril? If you were scared enough to swallow a locket, you must have some memory of *who* you thought was, like, out to get you."

"I wasn't *scared*," Cyril insisted, putting down his foot. Quite literally. He had removed his corpse's foot and had been inspecting the buckled shoe.

I glared at him, like, *Loyalist, please.*

"Okay, maybe there was a certain level of fear. Perhaps because I knew an American spy was in our midst."

"Patrick Burton doesn't sound all that scary," Derek said.

"Let me see that drawing, Morna."

Morna passed me the limp paper that appeared to have been folded fifty-seven times before its insertion into the locket. Here's what it looked like:

Though the ship illustration was pretty basic, I thought it was safe to assume the crude boat was supposed to be the

Kingfisher, since that was the ship Cyril's dad had been building and I didn't know of any others in Sticksville around 1779. I mean, I guess it had been a naval yard of sorts, so there were, conceivably, dozens of ships around Sticksville then. But thanks to the ghost pirate, I wouldn't be able to find out anything about them. I flipped the paper over and held it up to Cyril's sunken eyes.

"Is this the *Kingfisher?*" I asked.

"I would imagine so."

"You know, the ship is back," I said.

"What do you mean?"

So I had to explain that, usually, 200-something-year-old ships weren't still in use. Or existence, even. But as Ms. Fenstermacher had told me, because this particular ship had particular importance to Sticksville history, it had been re-stored and was going to be put back on the river for the weird annual Sticksville tradition known as the Sticks-ebration.

"Do you think it has its original steering wheel?" Derek asked, taking the paper scrap from me.

"It does look like somethin's hidden in th' wheel," Tabetha said.

"I don't know. I mean, it's possible. A steering wheel would be more likely to last that long than, say, the sails," I guessed. "But I don't know where the ship is."

"Can you find out?" Kirby asked.

"Probably," I said. I took my Swatch watch out of my pocket. (I hadn't wanted to damage it while in the midst of so much serious gravedigging.) It was just after three. "We need to clean up Cyril's grave, though. In a few hours, it will be light. Maybe if we re-bury him and cover the grave with snow, no one will notice its been disturbed until the spring. I can look into the *Kingfisher* tomorrow." Or, technically, later today.

"Let's get movin'," Tabetha shouted. "Cyril, you want a final look at yer skeleton?"

Cyril thrust his shovel into the hill of dirt we'd made and tossed some of the soil onto his old self's skull. "Sleep tight, little buddy."

"Uh, let's put the coffin lid back on first," I suggested.

My arms were so sore, it felt like invisible clamps had tightened around them, but I had to fill in Cyril's grave, then, hopefully, get in an hour or two of sleep before school. Why did I ever decide to go graverobbing on a school night?

☠   ☠   ☠

The next morning I was so tired, the town of Sticksville seemed like a hazy, half-remembered dream. I had the ingenious idea to stop off at Luke's Coffee, which was sort of on my route to school, purchase an extra-large coffee using my allowance — I would have felt bad if I used the leftover ill-gotten shovel money — and chug it like I'd been poisoned by a cobra and Luke's greasy coffee was the antivenom. That I even managed to secure a coffee was a minor miracle, as I'm sure I wasn't able to form English words for the first few hours of my day. Just moan vague vowel sounds like a sea lion, and tramp through the snow like an early-rising zombie. Lukewarm coffee was dribbling down my chin (side effect of chugging it too quickly) as I stepped into the warmth of Sticksville Central from the tundra outside. Dad had been up and about by the time I walked out the front door, but he wasn't dressed for work, so I figured some random substitute would cover his science classes again. I started to worry if he'd ever go back to work. This was the third day he'd been on leave. And while Dad didn't show up for school again, I was incorrect about the randomness of his replacement.

Appearing totally out of place — like a zebra at the Kentucky Derby — was that little old lady who sometimes worked the front desk at the Sticksville Museum, standing just outside the school's office doors. Spotting someone she recognized — me, tragically — she flagged me down and walked over.

"Little vampire girl," she said, as if this was an okay way to address any human being, "I didn't know you went to this school. Can you show me to room 205?"

"Yeah, that's upstairs. Follow me," I said, ignoring that vampire crack. Like, a vampire wouldn't go to school during the day, old lady. What did she think this was, *Twilight?* We trudged up the stairs just behind the atrium, and since she wasn't talking, I figured I probably had to.

"Are you guest-speaking in a class or something? About history or whatever?" Probably not doing a guest lecture about tact, I assumed.

"Oh no," she said, walking behind me like I was her security detail. "I'll be teaching here for a little while. One of the science teachers is out on a personal matter, so I'm covering his classes until he returns. I'm a retired teacher. Being docent at the museum is how I spend my retirement."

Room 205. I should have recognized it immediately! The museum lady was taking over my dad's classes. Ms. Fenstermacher passed us on her way downstairs and I suddenly felt like the entire Sticksville Museum had been transported to my school. I left the museum woman, who was apparently named Mrs. Crookshanks, at room 205 and continued on toward French class, all the more worried — or *préoccupé* — about my dad. The school was already looking into a semi-permanent replacement for him. He was going to have to will himself out of his depression and *fast.* The only trouble was, that wasn't really how depression worked.

The school day — other than the strange and troubling (only to me) arrival of Mrs. Crookshanks — was otherwise uneventful. The only thing of note, really, was that we all had to submit our stupid Valentine's Scantron forms because, apparently, public high schools are now responsible for finding students companionship as well as teaching them the periodic table or whatever.

When the student council goons showed up in Mr. Santuzzi's class — an arrival that made my math teacher significantly *less* than happy — to collect the Valentine's forms, I dug my all-B edition of the form out of my bag. I'd be lucky if I were paired up with a really neat vacuum cleaner. One with a good personality. Mr. Santuzzi shot beams of flame from his eyes until the student council people left, then turned his frustration onto us. Lucky us.

Actually, I guess there were really *two* significant events that day, because lunchtime was when Yumi and I spoke again for the first time since our fight, and that felt so much better than basically anything else in the world. Even just to sit with Yumi in the cafeteria, to sit across from her and not feel hate coming from her eyes, was the absolute best. We even joked about the stupid Valentine's dance and the match forms.

"I can't believe you just filled it all out with one letter," Yumi said. "You missed out on some genius-level questions."

"You'll probably be paired up with Stacey. You two are like twins," I said.

Stacey nearly choked to death on his tuna sandwich because of that.

"Right," she said. "Here comes your boyfriend. I'm sure you got matched up with this hunk."

Mr. Santuzzi glided past us on one of his daily patrols of the cafeteria. It was absolute torture attempting not to laugh while he did.

"Yumi!" I burst out, once the moustached one was out of earshot. "You're a monster! Even if I were fifty years old, I'd rather date a wet bag of raccoons."

Yumi seemed pretty willing to pretend our fight last week had never happened, and since she was talking to me again, I was more than happy to play along. It was nice that some things were back to normal.

☠   ☠   ☠

The last thing I did during the school day was ask Ms. Fenstermacher the current location of the *Kingfisher*. As luck would have it, she passed along the info without any follow-up questions, which worked out well as I was already almost late to my after-school appointment with Dr. Lagostina.

I'd become quite familiar with the school therapist since moving to Sticksville, given my many traumatic adventures. He was also, coincidentally, the school physician, which explained why he was bandaging up a skater kid's palm as I entered his office.

"Art class accident," he explained as the injured boy left his office. "They're doing woodcuts and a knife slipped."

To be fair, Dr. Lagostina couldn't have known I had come to talk about my new anxiety around blades, so I forgave him for mentioning that. Still, the phrase "a knife slipped" set my teeth on edge.

"Have a seat," he said, gesturing to one of the burgundy armchairs. "It's been a while since I've seen you sans Ashlie, your compatriot."

Ashlie and *compatriot* were not words I liked hearing together. But it was true we'd been visiting Dr. Lagostina together ever since our fairly vicious fight in the cafeteria this October.

"I hear you've started tutoring her in math?" he half-said, half-asked.

"Wasn't my idea," I answered.

"And how is it going?" he asked, finally taking a seat in his own chair. His chair was a swivel office chair, which never failed to unsettle me. I felt like a thera-pist should have a more serious chair. I could only laugh in response. Given that so far, our math tutoring sessions had led to at least one of my friends nearly being arrested for theft, it wasn't go-ing overly well, but I wasn't here to talk about that.

"Okay, I get it," he said, laying both palms flat on his desk. "You're not here to talk about tutoring Ashlie." Dr. Lagostina was more intuitive than I gave him credit for. "What *are* you here to talk about, October?"

"Um, I think I've been experiencing . . . anxiety?" I started. I had forgotten how awkward it was to talk about these things to him. "Not panic attacks, really, but anxiety."

"Anxiety about . . . school work?" he said, scratching his curly, black hair.

Man, I wish it were that easy. To *just* be anxious about school work, what a dream! My real dilemma is that my anxiety seemed to be connected to nearly being killed by a fake ghost pirate's sword. But I probably shouldn't let Dr. Lagostina know I had any interactions with Stickville's current celebrity thief at all. Luckily, I had at least two other brushes with doom that were on the public record that I could pretend this was about.

"No," I admitted. "More anxiety about, like, death."

Dr. Lagostina sighed heavily. "October, that's nothing to be ashamed of. After all, just months ago, you were attacked by a teaching assistant with a baseball bat. And a month or so before that, one of our former teachers threatened you with a bayonet. That's a lot for a thirteen-year-old to deal with."

"I guess."

"Mr. Page taught you history before he kidnapped you at bayonet point," he reminded me. "Does that make history class difficult for you? Do you feel anxious or panicked around Ms. Fenstermacher? Do you feel like you can't trust her?"

"No," I said. "I've never had a problem with Ms. Fenstermacher. She's cool."

I couldn't believe I just said that. But compared to Dr. Lagostina, she was basically Patti Smith.

"And Mr. Santuzzi was — correct me if I have this wrong — quite instrumental in rescuing you from your baseball-bat attacker," he continued. "Has that helped you at all? Or do you still feel anxious around your teachers?"

I nodded my head slightly to quiet Lagostina, but my mind was still catching up with something he'd just said. About trusting Ms. Fenstermacher. Who else would be interested in stolen historical goods save a history teacher? Is there a chance I'd overlooked her as a suspect for the fake ghost pirate? Did I really have to worry about my history teacher trying to kill me again?

"I'd recommend looking toward those teacher-helpers in moments of anxiety," Dr. Lagostina said, with a suggestion I barely registered. "Do you think that might help?"

"Absolutely," I nearly shouted. "This has been a huge help. Thank you, doctor."

Dr. Lagostina was taken aback as I nearly leapt to my feet and shook his hand vigorously. I was positive he hadn't helped my anxiety at all, but he did give me a new lead to pursue, which was even better. "I really appreciate all your advice."

Lagostina wore a stunned look on his face as I zipped out into the hallway and headed to my locker to retrieve my coat. He'd barely had a chance to settle into his swivel chair.

☠ ☠ ☠

Despite my new doubts about Ms. Fenstermacher, she had been very open with information about the exact location of the newly restored *Kingfisher*, but she probably assumed I just wanted to take some photographs, not break, enter, and commit some form of robbery. The ship was anchored down at the Sticksville Marina — kind of an obvious place, I guess. It's probably pretty tough to hide a ship that size in Sticksville. So, after my session with Dr. Lagostina, I headed down to the marina, a place I'd never thought to visit before in my life. But then I'd only lived in Sticksville for less than a year, and most of that time hadn't exactly been boating season.

It turned out that the marina wasn't all that far from the Sticksville Museum. I knew I'd probably need to take the dead kids to see the ship at some point, but I wanted to make an initial visit to get a vague lay of the land. Or water. Whatever.

Built out into the Niagara River, which had not frozen over even a bit but was still not a body of water I wanted to take a swim in, was Sticksville's largely unimpressive marina. A narrow little dock had been built out from the shore, just making the tiniest reach out into the Niagara's width. The river was so wide across, some blurry buildings and the flashing lights of America were all I could really make out on the other side in the dreary weather.

(Later on, I read it was a little less than a kilometre across.) Along the dock bobbed about a dozen smaller boats, with the *Kingfisher* given a spot of honour all its own on the far side of that dock, butted up against the shore and park that led into the marina.

Turned out there were two security guards stationed by the wooden gangplank to the ship like bouncers outside a nightclub. Dressed in big black parkas, both the large one with a black goatee and the skinnier one with glasses sipped slowly from steaming coffee cups and followed my approach with their eyes, like two cats watching a pigeon with a broken leg limp closer and closer to their window ledge. Behind them, almost disappearing into an overcast grey sky, was the *Kingfisher*. Now, I don't know anything about ships. I couldn't tell you if it was a clipper or a schooner or a sloop, but it definitely had sails. Like, a couple big ones. The ship was made of wood, too. And I don't think I've ever used the word majestic before, but I wouldn't hesitate to use it here. The *Kingfisher* was majestic.

The two guards, however, didn't care for me appreciating its majesty.

"What are you doing here, girl?" the bigger guy with the goatee asked.

"Uh, I just wanted to see the boat."

"That's far enough, then," he said, mostly into his coffee cup, so it got a bit echoey. "You can appreciate it from *that* distance."

"Not a boat," said the reedy guy with glasses. "It's a clipper."

Clearly, I was talking to a boat aficionado. Sorry, *clipper* aficionado.

"Are you guys here all night?" I asked. Not my most subtle question.

"Yessss," said the bigger one, his eyes narrowing with malice.

"What's your name?" the clipper friend asked, moving toward me and producing a pen and notebook from his jacket.

So that, naturally, is when I ran away. As fast as I could, given the snow.

☠   ☠   ☠

Dad seemed in higher spirits when I returned home, so that was a plus. But he still hadn't changed out of the dirty old clothes he usually wore while doing yardwork. After making him something resembling a dinner, doing my homework, and then cleaning up the dishes, I went to visit the dead kids. Unfortunately, my plan for searching the ship — the clipper — meant that they'd be doing a lot more waiting to see action than usual. As expected, they weren't pleased.

"It's a valuable ship," I explained. "They've got security guards watching it around the clock."

"So?" Tabetha pouted, kicking some snow in a high arc into the air. "We're ghosts, remember? No living people are gonna stop us."

"I want to be there, too," I said.

"And I would have liked to *not* die at age thirteen," Kirby said. "We don't always get what we want."

"I think we should wait until Friday," I said.

"An' why?" Tabetha asked.

"Okay, so Friday is our Valentine's dance, right?" I said, though the dead kids really had no way of knowing that. "It's a big deal. Almost the entire school will be going. Even me. Even though I've already had my grounding revoked, I can stay out a little later because my dad will think I'm at the dance."

"But wait," Derek said, rising from his seat on a raised tomb. "*Won't* you still be at the dance?"

"Yeah," Tabetha added. "Are ya goin' or aren't ya? Make up yer mind."

"I'm going because Yumi wants to go," I said. "But first chance I get — maybe the first slow dance — I'm going to sneak out and head over to the marina and then we can *all* figure out how to get past the guards and search around the *Kingfisher*. How does that sound?"

"Can we have a moment?" Cyril asked.

While I stood beside the one large mausoleum in the cemetery — the one we often used as a sort of conference room — the dead kids huddled to discuss . . . something. I'm not totally sure what. If they wanted to investigate the ship on their own, there was really no way I could stop them. How do you stop a ghost? It's like truly enjoying a meal in the school cafeteria: impossible. But I was the leader and founder of the Dead Kid Detective Agency, so I was a bit cheesed off that my plans were up for debate. Their huddle broke, and the dead kids approached me once again, with Cyril at the forefront.

"We agree to this plan on one condition," he said, removing his tricorn hat in a gesture of weird formality. It's not like I was his mom. "You take us to this Valentine's dance."

"What?! No!" My answer was immediate and visceral. I somehow prevented myself from throwing up all down my shirt.

"But we never get t'go anywhere!" Tabetha complained.

"Because you guys are menaces! I took you to the movies and Yumi nearly lost her mind. I took you ice skating and the whole school couldn't stop talking about the 'weird Finns' they never saw again."

"I want t'dance, October," Morna said. "Please."

"Morna, this isn't what you think it is. It's not like some fancy ball where boys will be in suits and girls will be in gowns and everyone will be waltzing or however they danced a hundred years ago. This is going to be sweaty kids in Angry Birds T-shirts and Uggs awkwardly pawing each other over slow jams."

"What is this . . . *slow jams?*" Cyril asked.

"It's . . . never mind," Derek said, defeated.

"Yer gonna take us to this dance," Tabetha insisted.

"You said yourself, we won't be there long," Kirby reminded.

"Oh, *fine!*" I groaned. Arguing with the dead kids was like raging against the wind. "But you'd better be on your best behavior."

"Are ye goin' t'the dance with anyone?" Morna asked, getting that loopy boy-crazy look in her eyes whenever anyone male was mentioned in passing.

"No, I already told you. It's not like that, Morna."

"It's Valentine's Day!" she said.

"I'm just going with my friends." And if I wasn't matched up, via Scantron sheet, with someone too objectionable, maybe I would go with some virtual stranger to save a couple dollars.

The answer to that question — how objectionable my Valentine's match, as determined by Sticksville Central's student council, was — would be answered the following day during Mr. Santuzzi's math class. But before that, something even stranger happened: I received a Valentine's Day card. I mean, objectively, it wasn't that strange. It *was* Valentine's Day in two days. It was the *me* in the equation that was weird. I didn't really know any boys who didn't despise me as a Zombie Tramp, and a chubby one at that. Or any girls for that matter. The only fellow students who could have been accused of liking me were Yumi, Stacey, and maybe Tricia MacKenzie, my old curling partner. Could one of them have been in love with me? Not that it wasn't flattering; just that having someone think of me that way, in secret, made me a little uncomfortable. Besides, I was a detective and a writer. Two jobs that kind of required solitude.

The card featured a hand-drawn cartoon goth girl on the front. The interior was blank, but my secret admirer had written:

> *Roses are red.*
> *Your hair is black.*
> *You make my pulse race.*
> *Like I'm having a heart attack.*

Not the most romantic notion I'd ever heard, nor the best rhythm or metre, but I guess it was a cute sentiment. Plus, whoever it was had taken the time to make the card him- or herself. This wasn't something bought at a Hallmark store. I had found the little black envelope at the bottom of my locker first thing that morning and remained confused for the rest of the school day.

The more I thought about it, the more I considered the real possibility it was a cruel prank from Ashlie Salmons or one of her friends. There was no immediate humiliating situation that the card led to, but it was possible my tormentor was working the long game.

The worldwide conspiracy toward romantic love continued in math class. Mr. Santuzzi was outlining a question about triangles that used revolutionary insurgents as its theme.

"If you have one platoon of insurgents here, at Tikrit, moving at twenty-six miles per day, and a second platoon moving from Fallujah at twenty-one miles per day, which platoon will be first to reach Baghdad?"

All our blank stares slowly drifted over to the door where student council president, Zogon, appeared with a stack of printouts. Mr. Santuzzi let out a dejected sigh.

"You again."

"This is the last interruption for months, sir. I promise," Zogon promised.

He and his student council assistants went up and down the rows of desks, calling out last names and leaving printouts in red ink on each of our desks. The content of these print outs? Our perfect matches. Or, more realistically, our ticket to a discount for the V-Day dance. I raised my studded bracelet wrist into the air when he called "Schwartz" and a red printout landed on my desk.

Henry Khan.

I had no idea who Henry Khan was. But he was my perfect match. Or rather, the perfect match of someone who'd chosen all Bs. Since I hadn't the slightest idea who Henry Khan was, it looked unlikely I could save two bucks on a dance ticket. But given he was a perfect match for an arbitrarily chosen series of Bs, maybe it was best I didn't know who he was. He was probably a sociopath.

"Who's Henry Khan?" I asked Yumi and Stacey, once they arrived at our usual cafeteria table.

"I'm stumped, Schwartz," Yumi said, throwing her hands in the air. "Who is he?"

"Is he related to Genghis Khan?" Stacey asked.

"Or Chaka Khan?" Yumi pointed.

"I read somewhere that, like, ten percent of East Asians are related to Genghis Khan," Stacey said.

"Where do you get this stuff?" Yumi asked, then sheared the top of her canned peas off. "Why do you want to know about Henry Khan? You think he's the ghost pirate?"

It was a low blow but also a deserved one, I suppose. "*No.* He's my perfect match."

I tossed the printout onto the table. Right beside the pixelated red hearts was Mr. Khan's name.

"I see . . ." Yumi said, waving her fingers like she was casting a spell or was Stevie Nicks. "Mr. Khan's warm for October's form. Going to make his move at the Valentine's dance."

"Doubtful. Who did you guys get?"

"Guess," Yumi mumbled.

My two friends produced their printouts, and, as I could have predicted — *did* predict, even — they got each other.

"Awkward," I said. "But at least you both get to save two dollars. We were all going to go together anyway, right?"

Like clockwork, Ashlie Salmons appeared, very holiday appropriate in a pink gingham dress, pink headband, and wide pink belt.

"Disappointed in your love match, Zombie Tramp?" she asked, rhetorically, and fanned her pink nails out on the cafeteria table. I quickly snatched my form up so she couldn't read it. "But it'd be *so* cute if you arrived at the dance with an extra-large diaper filled with dead cats. I didn't even realize the cat-filled diaper *went* to our school."

"That's funny," I said, stuffing the form into my bag, as discretely as possible. "I thought he was your ex. Who'd you get paired with?"

"Ugh." She stuck out her tongue, which matched her ensemble. "Our student council president. He probably rigged it so he was matched with all the pretty girls."

"I didn't get him as my match," Yumi said.

"Exactly."

"Ashlie, have you met Stacey MacIsaac before?" I gestured to the lanky boy holding down the Y chromosome at our cafeteria party. "He's the one you tried to get incarcerated."

My nemesis didn't have an answer for that. Or didn't feel it deserved an answer. Either way, she skulked off, leaving my friends and I alone to plan that night's screening of *My Bloody Valentine* at Stacey's.

☠ ☠ ☠

Just after the film's evil coal miner murdered his first victim and the less-than-impressive movie title dripped in blood down the TV screen, Yumi turned into my shoulder and whispered, "Do you have a dress for the dance?"

"Why are you whispering?" I asked. "It's just you, me, and Stacey."

We were in one of our typical movie-screening configurations in Stacey's bedroom: two girls on the floor, tall boy on the bed above, door left open.

"Okay, do you have a dress?" she asked again, using her usual high volume.

"No, I was going to go to Value Village tomorrow to see if I could find something."

"Can I come?" she asked, gripping my arm with her black-nailed claws.

"I guess."

"Guys," Stacey droned, "you're talking over all the slashing. Or the reasons for the slashing, at the very least."

The plot of *My Bloody Valentine* may have been too close to the bone. After all, it does feature a deranged killer who is set off by the town's Valentine's dance, so it wasn't totally irrelevant. In the film, the mayor was just explaining to Mabel, the laundromat owner, the very valid reason the town no longer held dances around Valentine's Day when Stacey's dad started bellowing from below. We couldn't make out what he was saying — Stacey's dad is pretty evenly matched for Stacey in terms of mumbliness, and he was a floor below us. Stacey rose from the bed and went to the door frame, then had to scurry downstairs to discuss something with his dad. I never discovered what his dad wanted, because I was so distracted by what Yumi told me next.

Yumi paused the movie with the remote and leaned into my shoulder again. "I'm going to ask Stacey to the dance," she whispered.

"Yeah, I know," I said, shrugging her off me. "And save two dollars. You don't have to gloat."

"No," she said. "I mean, like, once we're there, I'm going to ask him to slow dance."

"Yumi," I whispered back, "do you *like* Stacey?" My mind was now in the process of being fully blown.

"I don't know," she whispered, then laughed, then turned completely red. I thought she had a fever for a second. "But I figure if we have a slow dance, maybe I can figure some things out."

Too many thoughts were happening at once. On the one hand, it's nice when anyone — and your best friend, especially — finds love. No one wants to be alone and all that other nonsense you might find expressed in a hit song by Jewel. But on the other hand — the other, very real hand — if Yumi and Stacey started being a duo, we could no longer truly be the trio we currently were. They'd spend all their time making out while I went increasingly mad having only five dead kids to talk to. That's all just a long way of saying my emotions were conflicted, and my face probably showed that to Yumi. Or showed that I didn't know how to express human emotion, but she must have kind of known that already, if she'd been paying attention.

"But —" I started.

"Shhh!" She slapped my shoulder. "He's coming back!"

And after that, even as the mine-based murders and '70s fashion became increasingly more elaborate, I found I couldn't focus on the movie. All because I was leaning against the bedframe of Yumi's secret crush.

☠   ☠   ☠

There was a lot of circumstantial evidence accumulating that my dad was on the upswing: he'd actually started helping to make dinner, and he was watching far fewer soap operas than he had been. But a week had elapsed since Dad had crossed the threshold of our front door. For the past seven days, I was, for all intents and purposes, an orphan. Which is why I did something that Friday evening that I'm not overly proud of. Being a detective — a great one, like the Great Mouse Detective and so forth — involves a fair amount of emotional manipulation. And though Dad's situation and the high school dance had very little to do with my case, it was a chance to practice that acquired skill.

Around seven on Friday evening, I approached his post on the living room couch ready for the dance. I'd found a dress for sale at Value Village. Being entirely black, it was probably more suited for a wake. But I'd also found some black evening gloves, which clearly elevated my whole look to fun, flirty wake territory. You know the kind. Careful not to accidentally kick the freshly used plate at the foot of the sofa, I tapped Dad on the shoulder.

"Dad?" I said, but I didn't necessarily expect him to turn around. He sometimes went in a television trance at times like this. "Uh, Dad?"

"October," he answered, in a real twist. Maybe he was at the respond-to-your-concerned-daughter stage. "I'm sorry, but I don't want to talk now. I'm sorry. I'm a terrible father."

"No, Dad. Don't be ridiculous."

"I'm . . . dealing with some stuff right now," he said. That was clearly the understatement of the year, but I sympathized with my dad, so I felt a bit mean with the trick I pulled next.

"That's okay, Dad. I just wanted to let you know I'm going to the school dance tonight . . . my *first* dance . . . and I might not be home until late."

"School dance?"

"Yeah. I understand you need to be by yourself right now. I just thought you might want to drive your only daughter to her very first . . . maybe *only* . . . school dance."

"*Only* school dance?" He turned to face me, eyebrow raised.

"You never know." I smirked. "Modern life is just, like, fraught with various dangers."

Full disclosure: my black (death) party dress didn't totally fit, so I felt a bit like a mini-baguette that had been crammed into a sausage casing. And I'd probably overdone it on the eyeshadow, as usual, but I guess Dad didn't notice, because as soon as he saw me in the dress, he started to tear up.

"You look great, October."

"Thanks," I said. "Do you think you might be able to get dressed and drive me to the dance?"

Dad frowned. "I see what you did there."

"Me?"

"I'll try, pumpkin."

"I don't have any other ride . . . and there *is* a ghost pirate on the loose in this town," I said, my eyes widening in mock fear.

"Okay," he sighed. "You've tricked me into leaving the house. Give me a half hour to shower and get ready."

"Thank you, Dad. Do you think you might come back to school next week, too?"

"Honey," he sighed more heavily than usual. An Olympic-level sigh. "We'll see."

"Dad, you have to get back to school," I said. "This museum lady, Mrs. Crookshanks, took your place, and she's awful. I'm pretty sure she told her class that the sun revolves around the Earth. You *have* to come back."

In truth, I had no idea what sort of teacher Mrs. Crookshanks was. I didn't take my dad's science classes; I hadn't interviewed any of the kids who had. But seriously, who could be better at teaching science than my dad?

"I said I'll try, October," he repeated, then pulled me into a sneaky hug.

"Dad, you stink!" I shouted.

He glared at me and returned to his room. "Do you want a ride to the dance or not?"

I apologized without hesitation, because I had an increasingly crucial Valentine's dance to get to.

☠   ☠   ☠

Little did October realize that the Valentine's dance, rather than being filled with fun and frivolity, would be filled . . . with *terror*.

13

They Shoot Zombie Tramps, Don't They?

Sorry, friends. Narrator here. I had to interrupt the last chapter there. I suppose October was doing a passable job outlining the most pedestrian of details and happenings, but she was about to end the chapter with a moment resembling human warmth or emotion, and that's just not the kind of thing that happens in *The Dead Kid Detective Agency*. You'll be happy to know what follows is more of the expected minor thrills and pratfalls and abject horror.

But, yes, it was Friday night: dance night! And October was all gussied up in a black dress and black gloves and even blacker eyeliner and a blacker mood, because her dead friends were tagging along, and it was almost certain they'd destroy something or other. They were all about busting stuff up. To minimize property damage and ghost sightings, after her dad dropped her off in the school parking lot, October met with her dead friends to go over some basic guidelines. This was annoying for two main reasons: 1) she'd have much rather walked into the school dance with her friends Yumi and Stacey, like a regular person; and 2) it was February, you might recall, and standing outside in a dress, even with a heavy black peacoat over top, was unpleasant. October had also dragged along her backpack, which — while not appropriate dance attire — did contain most of her post-dance ship exploration supplies, like flashlights, Cyril's note, and her trusty *Two Knives, One Thousand Demons* notebook.

"We need to go over the rules," October insisted.

"Rules?" Kirby said.

They'd decided to meet behind Sticksville Central, as it was fairly close to the entrance to the gym, where the Valentine's dance was taking place, but it was also close to the dumpster, where the incredible stench of a school's worth of garbage made it a very unpopular teen hangout.

"Yeah, rules," October said. "You're dead. You can't just walk in there and start doing the robot or whatever."

"I don't know what that means."

"Besides, none of you are really dressed for a dance," she added. "I guess Kirby's got a dress shirt and tie. And you girls are wearing dresses, though they're pretty . . . out of style. I suppose some kids will dress casual like Derek, too. But Cyril's going to be an issue."

"What is this issue?" he asked, generally curious both about the definition of the word and how it applied to this situation.

"Nobody wears tricorn hats anymore, Cyril . . . or whatever your pants are. This isn't a *Halloween* dance. It's going to be way hard for you guys to blend in for those people who can see ghosts."

Cyril, looking very disappointed, took off his hat to examine it further, to see, perhaps, what had caused it to fall out of fashion.

"The rest of you can come into the dance — but *only* if you stick to the shadows. Luckily, it should be dark in there. And *only* if you behave. But Cyril, I think you're going to look too out of place."

"What if I take off my hat?" he asked.

"Behave *how*, exactly?" Tabetha asked.

"Sorry, Cyril. I hate to ruin your fun, but it's just too weird."

"Maybe if we get you a tricorn hat, as well, it won't look so strange," Morna offered.

"Sorry, but no. Cyril has to stay out here. The rest of you can come in, but don't walk in with me. That'd be weird, too."

October rushed over to the gym entrance, escaping the cold as fast as she could, leaving poor, 200-year-old Cyril Cooper outside like some wet dog. As she crossed the gym doors' threshold, she was warmed not only by the heightened temperature of the room, but also by how dark it was inside. Few lights remained on inside the expansive gym, and those that still shone had a red filter over them. The dead kids would barely be noticed. Red, pink, and white balloons had been placed alongside the walls of the gym with shimmering ribbons. Two student council members sat behind an old wooden folding table right at the front doors, where they were checking people's romantic matches and collecting money for tickets. In one corner, some other student councillors sat at a table with soft drinks and bags of chips for sale, and the other corner featured the DJ and his booth of sound tech. The less said about the DJ, the better. Suffice it to say, he had chinstraps for facial hair and wore a black bowling shirt with decorative flames along the bottom. So, yeah, that's a look.

What was most notable, aside from the truly innovative red, pink, and white decorating scheme someone had applied to the usually quite stuffy and foul-smelling gymnasium, was that nobody was dancing. The boys were lined up along one wall, like they were awaiting inspection for a military physical, and the girls were lined up on the opposite side, like contestants in a sad, badly lit version of Miss Teen Sticksville. Absolutely no one ventured into the basketball court proper, which was serving as the dance floor, despite the fact that one of P!nk's more danceable songs was blasting through the speakers.

After October disappointed the student council table by informing them she hadn't arrived with Henry Khan, and paid full price for entry, she dumped her peacoat and knapsack across the closest folding chair. The first person to welcome her to the dance was Mr. Santuzzi, of all people. Though he frequently dressed like a background actor from *Saturday Night Fever*, a school dance is not the place you'd expect to find October's math teacher.

"Miss Schwartz," he said, hands looped around the top of his pale pink vest. "I'm surprised to see you."

While unsurprised, October was a bit disappointed that even her math teacher thought of her as an irredeemable loser.

"Well, y'know . . ." She trailed off. "Dance is my life."

"You didn't participate in that disgusting electronic mating ritual the student council was pushing, did you?"

"What, the Valentine's matching thing? No. I'm just hanging out with Yumi and Stace—"

October cut herself short, realizing she was in the middle of naming two students who had, only months ago, dedicated an hour-long radio show to mocking her math teacher.

"Good. That's not something you have to worry about now. But it's good to spend time with friends."

Mr. Santuzzi's general dismissiveness of romance made October wonder: was there a *Mrs.* Santuzzi? Hard to imagine. Maybe Santuzzi was a lifelong bachelor. It would be difficult for him *not* to be, given his general style and personality.

"Speaking of friends," Mr. Santuzzi said, "I thought I'd drop by your house tomorrow and give your dad a visit. I know he's having a difficult time, so maybe I'll bring by a coffee and see how he is. Just thought I'd forewarn you. I know students don't typically appreciate weekend visits from teachers. Ha ha."

Did Mr. Santuzzi just laugh? And why was he being so kind to October when almost every other day of the school year, he was only a few Zombie Tramps short of being her worst enemy. Was October dreaming? Some song by Sean Paul started playing.

"Uh, thanks, Mr. Santuzzi," October said, looking around for Yumi and Stacey fairly desperately. "That would be really nice."

"I'll let you go dance," Mr. Santuzzi said, gesturing to the still-empty dance floor. "I'm going to find my fellow chaperone, Ms. Fenstermacher."

October then spied Yumi and Stacey huddled in the corner across the way. Yumi was in the plaid dress she'd bought last week and Stacey was wearing an honest-to-goodness suit. It was probably a size or two too large, but it was an actual suit. He looked like Funky Winkerbean cast in a remake of *Reservoir Dogs*. October tried to look inconspicuous as she crossed the empty gym floor, all alone.

"October!" Yumi cried over the Sean Paul. "You're a mega-babe! Look at that dress!"

She forcefully spun October around like they were playing pin the tail on the donkey while Stacey gave a solid thumbs-up.

"Uh, thanks. You guys look good, too. Look good *together*," she added, remembering Yumi's ulterior motive at this Valentine's dance. (She might as well have winked.) "How does it feel to attend the dance as a couple?"

"We're each two dollars richer than you," Yumi said, digging her hands into her hips.

"I guess," October said, but she couldn't continue, given that she spied four of her dead friends enter the dance and snake unnoticed past the student council.

Tabetha led the dead kids with a beckoning of her hand and they made a beeline along the darkened wall for the refreshments table. As the girl working the table chatted with a friend, Tabetha carefully crouched beside the folding table and passed cans of pop to the other dead kids, who shook them vigorously and returned them to Tabetha for restocking on the table. Several unfortunate classmates at the dance were going to spray Coca-Cola all over their nice clothes, thanks to the dead kids. She'd have to remind Yumi and Stacey not to buy any pop.

"You see that?" Yumi asked.

October, distracted by the dead kids' juvenile hijinks, hadn't heard anything Yumi had said. "What?"

"I said the Love Match software or whatever matched Becky Coyne up with her younger brother. Did you see that?"

"You'd think they'd have an algorithm to prevent that. Did they actually come together?"

"Two bucks is two bucks," Stacey said.

"Who'd Ashlie Salmons show up with? The student council guy?" October asked.

"Some guy I don't know. The recipient of a handsomeness scholarship?" Yumi pointed. "Over there."

Yumi was right. *Could nothing bad ever happen to Ashlie Salmons*, October wondered. *Or even solidly mediocre?* While she was observing her enemy with her arm around Joe Hollywood, October also noticed the dead kids had moved on to the DJ booth, taking the disc jockey's records (for he had a few milk crates of actual vinyl records with him) and sliding them into the wrong sleeves while he was looking the other way, or had his eyes closed as he passionately grooved to the music. The prank led him to accidentally play a song that accomplished the impossible: the students of Sticksville Central started dancing.

"You guys ready to dance?" Yumi asked, bouncing her eyebrows like a ventriloquist's dummy. "Let's hit the basketball court."

Dancing was not an activity that October naturally did, given that she was both out of shape and uncoordinated. She'd never be discovered on a street corner and given a shot on *So You Think You Can Dance*. Still, with Yumi and Stacey at her side, she felt a bit safer demonstrating her clumsiness to her classmates. Stacey started off just bobbing his head, like one of those drinking bird toys, but Yumi was a fair deal more expressive, a dirty bomb of arms and legs shooting out like shrapnel in every direction. October, having never really danced outside the comfort of her bedroom before, decided to take her lead from Stacey, as it seemed less dangerous.

Midway into the song — maybe at the bridge, if that means anything to you readers — the record scratched and was replaced by "Time Warp" from *The Rocky Horror Picture Show*. Confused, the students on the dance floor quickly adjusted, making jumps to the left and pulling their knees in tight and going in-say-ay-ay-ane (due to the pelvic thrust). And as relieved as October was to hear a song with actual dance instructions, she knew the abrupt change in song probably had a supernatural cause. She excused herself from her two friends and headed toward the disc jockey's table. Sure enough, the flame-shirted DJ was looking over his equipment in total befuddlement while Tabetha, Kirby, Derek, and Morna huddled in the darkened corner, convulsing with laughter. October slid over to them, behind the preoccupied DJ, and hissed at Tabetha.

"What are you doing?" October whispered.

"We're just having a li'l fun at the dance," Tabetha answered.

"Why can't you just dance like everyone else?" October asked, flinging her arm out to show people having fun via the power of dance.

"Pfft," Kirby said, raspberrying with his tongue. It's an unsolved mystery how the dead kids manage to generate saliva. "Boring, October. Leave that stuff to you living folks."

From the corner of her eye, October could see that Morna, however, did not believe dancing was so boring. In fact, her eyes were following Yumi and Stacey across the gym floor.

"Stacey looks so smart, all dressed up," she said, scratching her little upturned nose. Morna sounded genuinely proud, not unlike a mother seeing her son selected as the next contestant on *The Bachelor*. "Who's the Chinese girl dancing w'him?"

"She's Japanese . . . Japanese-Canadian," October corrected herself. "And Yumi's the best, Morna."

"Ye think he likes her?" Morna asked.

"Maybe? I really have no idea," October said, though she knew a bit more than she was willing to reveal to her dead Scottish pal. "Besides, they're, like, fast-dancing. It's hard to tell."

Just as October was about to expand on the relative meaninglessness of fast-dancing with someone, Led Zeppelin's slow-dance classic, "Stairway to Heaven," started to play. October and Morna and all the dead kids — save for Cyril, who was still banished to the outside — watched as Yumi shrugged her shoulders, then Stacey shrugged his, then they held each other's shoulders timidly, like a teenaged boy holding an infant for the first time, and shuffled around in a small circle. They were slow dancing. Together.

"Hmm," October said to Morna. Slow dancing was much more serious business. "Maybe they *do* like each other."

Derek Running Water strode over to interrupt our creepy spy mission on the Yumi-Stacey dance situation. He presented his palm like he had just made a coin disappear and said, "Morna, would you care to dance?"

"I have t'go," Morna said, flushing a very muted colour, then ran to the gym entrance, out the main doors.

"Morna, come back!" Derek shouted.

"Derek, what are you doing?" October whispered, attempting to slug him but pitching forward through his intangible shoulder. To the other students assembled for the Valentine's dance, it merely looked like she was a terribly ungraceful dancer. (Which wasn't incorrect.) "You know what Morna is like with boys and stuff. You can't just *ask* her for a dance."

"What? I like this song," he said.

"Where's that crazy Scotch girl goin'?" Tabetha called out.

"I'll get her, guys. You stay here and don't make any more trouble."

October jogged past the DJ booth and wove in and out between slow-dancing couples in the spinning coloured lights that reflected off a massive disco ball dangling from the high gymnasium ceiling. Some were holding each other like they were handling a venomous snake, others were embraced so tight, you'd need a letter opener to separate them. She picked up her coat and backpack from a folding chair and looped it over her shoulders. Once October had reached the gym doors, she was surprised by Cyril Cooper, who'd removed his hat and taken off his stockings in an attempt to look almost normal.

"Cyril!" October said, out of breath. "I thought you were going to stay outside."

"Yes, well . . ." he coughed. "I heard a slower song start playing and, well, I thought I'd inquire if you'd like to dance."

He presented his right hand, palm upward, while October's mind reeled with one thousand bits of problematic news at once. Why were all these dead boys so keen on dancing?

"Where is the band?" Cyril asked, looking around the room. He was unfamiliar with recording devices. The wax record hadn't been invented until the 1880s, a full hundred years after he'd died.

"Oh" was all October could manage.

"So," Cyril said again, undaunted by the considerable pause. "Might you honour me with a dance?"

"Cyril," October asked, "did you write me a Valentine's card?" It was as if October had found a few missing puzzle pieces under the living-room couch after tripping and falling to the carpet.

Cyril turned a pale peach. "Derek helped. He did the actual writing."

"And the cartoon?"

"Oh, Derek did that, too," Cyril admitted. "I'm not much for illustration. But the poem was mine!"

Derek. Were all the dead kids trying to complicate October's life? She could see how, perhaps, a milkmaid in rural Upper Canada could have found Cyril Cooper a real catch, but this was just too strange for her.

"Listen, Cyril. I'm really flattered," she said, watching the dead boy's half smile drop, "but I have to find Morna right now. I think she's really embarrassed."

Before October could learn just how heartbroken (or not) Cyril was by the polite brush-off, an excruciating bang cut through the noise of Led Zeppelin's epic eight-minute-long song. Everyone's eyes turned to the source of the sound, an ancient blunderbuss (that's an old-timey pistol, friends) in the hand of a pirate. And not just *any* pirate, but that ghost pirate who'd been robbing Sticksville of its historical treasures for the past few weeks. Though the other students may not have realized it at that moment, October recognized the grinning rubber mask and blue-orange outfit immediately.

Incredible panic ensued, with slow dancers suddenly pushing their partners out of the way as they searched for an exit or hid behind the few folding tables or chairs. The glowing pirate was blocking the main entrance and screaming something while waving the cocked blunderbuss at the DJ. The DJ got the general idea and shut off the music. To a chorus of screams, the pirate stalked over to the student council table and lifted the cash box, depositing it in a satchel looped over his shoulder. Then, with the gun still trained on the entire school gymnasium, he extracted a cutlass from his belt and shouted in a gravelly but high-pitched voice: "Where is October Schwartz?"

October watched in horror, but without too much surprise,

as a full two-thirds of the kids assembled in the gym — with no hesitation — pointed directly at her, just a few yards from where the pirate was standing. Apparently, October had not made many allies in her first six months at school.

The pirate laughed and stomped over to October, who was slowly backing up as fast as possible without startling the pirate. Perhaps she was under the mistaken impression that ghost pirates were like black bears. In any event, she found it hard to remain calm, as her greatest source of anxiety had just singled her out for special attention. When the ghost pirate was about three or four sword-lengths from his target, our very own October Schwartz, Stacey lunged into the eerily lit pirate's path. But as tall as her friend was, Stacey was no brick wall, and the pirate tossed the lanky boy aside with little struggle. At the very least, Stacey's act of misguided heroism definitively proved to October he couldn't be the ghost pirate. The momentary distraction also gave October the opportunity to turn and make a break for it.

She was so happy she'd worn flats to the dance, but she regretted not wearing sneakers, which would have been even better for her getaway. October sprinted and the gathered students, who had been trying to appear motionless or unthreatening, began to cheer. They'd ratted her out moments ago, and now they were all cheering on the chase. High school has few differences from the Roman Colosseum. October promised herself, should she survive this Valentine's dance — a possibility that seemed less likely with each passing minute — she'd look into transferring schools. She scrambled to take a wide arc around the advancing ghost pirate to dash for the gym doors, but she wasn't as fast as her nautical stalker. Also, the fact she was carrying her backpack proved to be a detriment, as the pirate managed to grab hold of a little bungee loop hanging off the knapsack and pulled October closer. The pirate drew back his sword, and October felt her heart nearly explode with panic. Lucky for her, that was exactly when three of the dead kids opened pop cans in the pirate's face, sending a tri-coloured geyser of soft drinks everywhere. The general rule was the dead kids couldn't harm the living — even if they happened to be in the middle of killing their best living friend — but spraying living people with soda pop seemed kosher.

Still, the fountain of soft drinks didn't faze the pirate for long, and if it hadn't been for Yumi Takeshi pulling on his sword arm, October would have been chopped up like so much ham on a chef salad. While Yumi pulled back the pirate's arm, October turned to face her attacker and swiftly kicked him squarely in the groin. The kick seemed to have little effect — less than the pop in the face — so October tried to worm herself out of her backpack. The pirate, off balance from being kicked and pulled in different directions, swung wildly with his sword.

"October! Look out!" Derek yelled.

October closed her eyes and jumped back as far as the straps of the backpack would let her. The sword cut through the backpack's left strap, severing it, and sending October butt-first onto the gym floor. She could have cried. Her sword-based anxieties had kicked into hyperdrive. The pirate kicked Yumi in the stomach, then hoisted the backpack over his free (non-sword) shoulder. The dead kids and all the living students started to shout, "Run! Run!" But as much as October wanted to make them all happy, she could barely stand, given the combination of pain and paralyzing fear.

The ghost pirate slashed at October once again, but the thick wooden handle of a straw broom stopped it a foot from October's legs. At the other end of the broom — typically the business end, but not during a sword fight — was October's math teacher. October had no idea where he'd been two minutes earlier when the gun went off, but she'd never been happier to see the grim face under his bad toupée.

"Where's Ms. Fenstermacher?!" he shouted to no one and everyone at once. "Someone find Fenstermacher and have her call 911!"

Mr. Santuzzi took the broom in both hands and pushed the pirate back. The pirate reeled, off guard for a second, and Mr. Santuzzi jabbed forward with the broom, poking the pirate in the solar plexus.

"Or just call 911 yourself!" he shouted again, sweat spritzing off his forehead and the edges of his handlebar moustache. "Get help!"

Dozens of the students went in all directions as Sticksville Central's most-feared math teacher and a pirate launched into a full-on, swashbuckling, Errol Flynn–style swordfight. Santuzzi had the size advantage on the mysterious pirate, but he was wielding a cleaning tool, so that evened the playing field a bit. As chaos once again reigned in the gym, the four dead kids — Morna was still AWOL — helped October to her feet.

"You have to run!" Cyril insisted. "Get out of here!"

"But Santuzzi!" October protested. As much as she loathed her math teacher, he'd saved her life, literally, twice now, and she didn't want him to fight this battle alone.

"We'll help him out," Tabetha said.

"Just go!" Derek said and shoved October toward the doors.

Even though the quickest route of escape would have been the main entrance — the one the ghost pirate had so recently barricaded — October fled through the other gym double doors, the ones that led to the rest of her school. With the clacking of metal on wood behind her, she raced through the darkened corridor of the school to the building's front entrance. If she left through this side of the school, she figured, there was less chance of the pirate finding and pursuing her if or when he subdued Mr. Santuzzi. October swallowed heavily and tasted bile. She couldn't bring herself to consider that the fake pirate might kill her math teacher. She didn't want Mr. Santuzzi to die.

But tragically, when she reached the school's front doors, she found they were all locked from the inside. The school must have taken safety measures to prevent anyone from entering and exiting the school during the dance, save through the outside gym doors. And, ironically, those safety measures were going to get October murdered. She ran back to the gymnasium.

Just outside the gym, the ghost pirate was waiting for her, standing beside the school trophy case. He was breathing like an angry minotaur and his rubber mask had been knocked sideways, but otherwise, it appeared his battle with Mr. Santuzzi hadn't had much of a negative impact on him. October feared that Mr. Santuzzi was lying somewhere in the gym, criss-crossed like a butcher shop's cutting board.

"Had trouble finding your way out?" the pirate rasped.

The dead kids, whom Morna had rejoined, could do nothing but stand around the threatening pirate and shrug their shoulders.

"Ah, *this* is what I was looking for," the pirate said. He aimed his blunderbuss at the trophy case, pulled the trigger, and watched as the case exploded into a blizzard of glass. As October desperately tried to figure out how to get around the pirate and, you know, not bawl uncontrollably, her assailant calmly collected the photos and trophies and placed them in his satchel. Though rather menacing, the pirate's calm actions gave October time to devise an escape strategy, though the dead kids were *definitely* not going to like it.

"Spirits, protect me in my escape," she said, sounding more like some kind of video-game sorceress than she'd planned. She bulged her eyes at the dead kids, hoping they'd catch on. Kirby, first to figure it out, shook his head aggressively.

"What's this now?" the pirate said, now focused on October and her apparent conversion to religiosity.

"I said *spirits*" — she stomped her foot and looked at the dead kids again — "*please* protect me."

Finally understanding what was going on, Morna MacIsaac, brave soul that she was, stood directly between the ghost pirate, who clearly could not see the ghosts, and October. Once Morna landed in place, October ran. The ghost pirate, seeing October dash for it, brought his sword down, but the sword embedded deep into Morna's shoulder and got stuck.

"Thank you, spirits!" October shouted and ran like she'd never run before, leaving the pirate to free his sword from Morna's body, or — in his view — from where it had inexplicably paused in mid-air. The pirate swore and continued to struggle with his sword as October passed the gym doors and ran into the cold night air in only her party dress. As soon as she reached the outdoors, she heard sirens and saw the red lights of newly arrived police cruisers, but she didn't stop running or turn around until she reached her home on Riverside Drive. More than anything, she feared for Mr. Santuzzi, possibly cut up and bloodied, or worse, after his attempt to stop the pirate. Mr. Santuzzi may have been a math-class menace, but October really hoped he was okay.

14

Sail of the Century

Normally, answering my doorbell on a Saturday morning and finding Mr. Santuzzi on our doorstep would have been an unsettling, if not outright horrible, thing. But given that just a few hours ago, I'd thought he'd been stabbed multiple times and left for dead by a ghost pirate, I nearly hugged him. He probably wouldn't have liked that. I already knew he hadn't been killed by the ghost pirate after a police officer visited our house late at night to get a statement from me about the disturbance at the Valentine's dance. According to him, Santuzzi hadn't suffered any serious injuries. Still, I was so relieved to see Santuzzi alive and without any massive scars across his face that I barely noticed that he appeared to be wearing a knee-length fur coat. Possibly a ladies' fur coat.

"Miss Schwartz," he boomed. His voice was too much for a Saturday morning. "Are you feeling okay? I lost track of you during the fracas at the dance."

"Yes, and you're not dead!" I blurted. "I mean, that's good."

"We're agreed on that," he said. "May I?"

"Oh, yeah. Come in," I said, betraying every fibre of my being.

"Police took statements from everyone who hadn't already fled the school about the pirate attack," Mr. Santuzzi said, sliding off his pelt, as if both his fur coat and the phrase *pirate attack* were totes normal. "But you'd already left."

"They visited us last night. Did they catch the pirate?" I asked, opening the closet for him.

"Unfortunately, no," he answered. "He escaped. Do you have any idea why he was targeting you, Miss Schwartz?"

"No." And that's what I'd told the police. My only guess was the pirate was after me for interrupting his library break-in, but that wasn't something I really wanted to disclose to the police or old Ironsides. (I guess that could be a military nickname.) "Did you ever find Ms. Fenstermacher?"

"Yes," he said, shorn of his coat and adjusting his shirt cuff. "My co-chaperone was in the ladies' washroom during most of the excitement. She emerged as the police arrived, to not much help."

"I guess when she agreed to chaperone the dance, she probably figured she'd be dealing with kids dancing too closely, not pirates trying to, like, decapitate everyone." I snorted.

"A chaperone should be prepared for all scenarios."

As I stood there, mentally grappling with the facts that (a) Mr. Santuzzi had possibly anticipated a deranged pirate attacking the school dance, (b) Ms. Fenstermacher, who could very well be the fake ghost pirate, was missing when said pirate arrived at the dance, and (c) I was currently in the midst of the longest conversation I'd ever had with my menacing math teacher, I realized Mr. Santuzzi was just standing there, purposeless, in our front hallway, looking out of place in his peach waistcoat. He knew I had escaped the Valentine's dance, so why was he at our front door on a Saturday morning?

"I came by to check on you," he said, as if reading my thoughts. "It's not every day one of my students is nearly murdered."

That was actually nice. And it's true. For me, it only happened every couple months.

"Also, I wanted to talk to your father."

My *dad.* Now I remembered how, before all the dance chaos, Santuzzi mentioned he'd be dropping by today. While Dad was alarmed, though probably used to police arriving at the house in the middle of the night, he wasn't fully aware that the celeb criminal pirate came to the dance looking for *me*. He knew the Valentine's dance had become, like so many Sticksville Central school events before it, a potential death-trap, but he didn't know I had personally been targeted. The police had interviewed me privately in the kitchen while Dad sat, head in hands, in the living room. All they mentioned to him was that his daughter should stay at home in the evenings, just in case. (He was probably halfway to that conclusion himself.) If Dad had been depressed before, a ghost pirate with a vendetta on his only daughter wasn't going to help matters. I had to throw myself on the mercy of the court.

"Mr. Santuzzi, can I ask you a favour?" I asked.

Mr. Santuzzi just raised an eyebrow. I thought it safe to assume he gets asked for favours as often as he gets asked for beauty tips.

"I haven't talked to my dad about last night's dance yet," I said, eyes cast downward. "Do you think you could leave out the part about how the pirate was specifically looking for me?"

"Miss Schwartz, I —"

"Please? I think he might return to school on Monday, but I don't think that will happen if he finds out."

My math teacher stared at me for a long time. "Fine. I'll leave it out for now," he conceded. "But you need to tell him in the next few days."

"Deal," I agreed. "I'll go get my dad."

I ran to Dad's door and knocked loudly to tell him Mr. Santuzzi was paying a visit. At the same time, I also informed him I was going out to meet Yumi. I didn't really want to hang around while my dad and my math teacher had a little male bonding, and he seemed okay with me leaving the house during daylight hours.

☠ ☠ ☠

While I gathered my stuff up to visit Yumi, I realized I had one major issue — not just for visiting Yumi but for the remainder of my life — my bag was stolen. That terrible ghost pirate had taken my backpack. The locket Cyril had swallowed was in the backpack, so if the ghost pirate was looking for Sticksvillian historical gems, he'd lucked out. And I was heartbroken when I realized the first 150 pages of Olivia de Kellerman's battle against the demons of hell might be lost forever, as the backpack also contained my *Two Knives, One Thousand Demons* composition book. How would I ever remember what I'd written? The book also contained a bunch of notes on all the mysteries the dead kids and I had investigated. My only hope was that either the dead kids and I — or, less likely, the police — would bring this fake pirate to justice and recover his stolen booty. But time was of the essence. Once the pirate figured out my notebook wasn't from 1800 or, like, written by the first mayor of Sticksville, it was probably going to end up in a landfill somewhere.

Feeling somewhat unclothed and unprepared without my backpack over my shoulders, I suited up in my coat and winter boots and headed over to the Takeshi residence. Yumi wasn't really expecting me to show up at her door on Saturday morning — she wasn't fully made up like when I'd see her at school — but she was glad to see me after last night's rumpus.

"Schwartz! After the pirate left, I was so worried you'd died! Sorry if I woke your dad up by calling you after midnight."

"It's okay. I couldn't have gone to sleep without talking to you first," I said. "I was really worried about you, too!"

Really, I didn't think Yumi would have been killed by the mystery pirate, but she took a pretty sharp kick in the stomach. I really owed her and Stacey, who — aside from Mr. Santuzzi — were the only ones who tried to defend me at last night's Valentine's Day Near-Massacre.

"Nah, I'm fine," she said, bundling me up in a hug on her doorstep. "I feel like I did three-hundred sit-ups, but I'm okay."

"And Stacey?"

"Pfft," she said, waving her hand. "Stacey's Stacey. He called last night to see if you were okay. Does he really not have your phone number? Anyway, come in. It's cold outside."

While I took off my boots and coat, Yumi explained that

after I ran away from the dance, the police came and questioned a number of the students who were still there. I told her the police visited me at home around the same time she'd called.

"Someone must have told them that the pirate was looking for you," she said. "Why *was* the pirate looking for you?"

I could only shrug.

"In a way, I'm kind of glad the crazy pirate showed up when he did," she said, hugging herself and sitting down on her steps. "Slow dancing with Stacey kind of freaked me out."

I knew all too well how she felt. The pirate's entrance also allowed me to briefly escape some awkwardness with my eighteenth-century suitor, Cyril Cooper.

"But I thought you liked him," I said.

"So did I, but making it real . . . I'm really confused."

"Do you think he knows?" I asked.

"Stacey? Pfft."

That seemed to be the answer to most questions about Stacey.

"What do you want to do?" she asked.

"Anything," I said. "Mr. Santuzzi is at my house right now talking to my dad, so as long as I'm away from home, I'm happy."

☠   ☠   ☠

As much help as the ghost pirate was in escaping uncomfortable romantic entanglements, he did cause me a pile of other problems. For one, if, while going through my backpack, he found Cyril's locket and the diagram hidden inside, he could find whatever we were looking for in the *Kingfisher* before the dead kids and I did. That is, if the pirate were smart enough. That meant we had to investigate the old ship as soon as possible, even without the distraction of a Valentine's dance to aid us. There was no time left to waste. Even if things were going to be awkward with Cyril, now that I knew he was — for whatever bizarre reason — into me, it was a bridge we'd have to cross or burn or something later. We had to get onto the *Kingfisher* this weekend.

For two, the pirate was trying to kill me, it seemed, so I'd have to be extra careful and watch my back at all times. That is, unless I could figure out who he was and somehow get him arrested. I'd done it before, but solving two mysteries at once was not among my top ten favourite ways to kill time. At least last night had ruled out a few suspects, like Stacey and Ashlie Salmons and Mr. Santuzzi (none of whom were ever really suspects, as much as I really wanted them to be). Still, that left me little idea who he could be. Unless *he* wasn't a *he* at all. As cool as she usually seemed, Ms. Fenstermacher was conspicuously absent when the pirate attacked, and she loved history. Dr. Lagostina reminded me that I had been unwise to trust history teachers in the past. Likewise, I also remembered the alarm never went off when the pirate first robbed the Sticksville Museum, and as one of the museum's only employees, Ms. Fenstermacher could certainly arrange such a thing. As much as it made me feel like someone had dropped a package of Pop Rocks directly into my stomach, I had to entertain the thought that Ms. Fenstermacher was trying to kill me. She seemed nice, but so had Mr. Page before he bound me to a chair in his laundry room.

Dad had a good weekend and we even had a nice dinner on Sunday, half-joking about the pirate at the dance. (Mr. Santuzzi must have really downplayed the personal danger.) He was pretty sure he'd return to school Monday and had called the office to say so. Things seemed so relaxed and back to normal — who knew how effective a little chat with Mr. Santuzzi could be for the chronically depressed? — that I didn't think too much about sneaking outside about an hour after Dad retired to his bedroom on Sunday night. Cyril's mystery couldn't wait. A crazed fake seaman was on the loose and every free night had to be used for mystery-solving, as each could easily be my last. Also, technically I was still un-grounded.

Entering the Sticksville Cemetery, I was both weirded out and pleased to see Cyril before anyone else, loitering just beyond the iron gates. As awkward as it was going to be, I'd rather discuss last night's dance debacle with him alone.

"Cyril, hi!"

"October," he nodded, removing his tricorn hat. "I want to apologize for last night."

"No, listen," I said. "You don't need to apologize for, like, how you feel."

"I don't?"

"No, but can we . . ." I really hadn't thought about how to phrase this. "Can we delay any discussion of how . . . difficult . . . any sort of relationship would be until *after* we figured out how you died?"

Words, I'm sure, few girls imagine they'd ever have to say.

"I think that would be a prudent idea," he said. "And, if possible, bring this pirate to justice, as he seems bent on killing you."

"Yes." I exhaled. Cyril was taking things much better than I'd expected. Much better than I would have, were I in his buckled shoes. "That would be a huge bonus."

Derek Running Water then arrived from behind the nearest bushes with the greeting, "What's up, party animals?"

"That was a *wild* scene last night!" Tabetha shouted, following close behind Derek. "Your school dances always get so out of control?"

"We should go more often," Kirby added.

"Thanks for the backup," I said. "It feels nice to still be alive."

"You'd do the same for us," Derek said. "If that were possible."

"Where did you go after the dance?" I asked. "I ran all the way home and figured you'd catch up with me at some point."

"We followed the ghost pirate," Cyril said.

"Wait, what?" October said. She hadn't even thought to ask them to tail the pirate. Her dead friends were becoming bonafide detectives. "This is amazing!"

"Don't get too stimulated," Kirby warned. "We followed him, but we couldn't tell you where he hangs his little pirate hat."

The pirate hat was actually quite broad.

"What happened?"

"We lost him in the marina," Derek confessed. "We tracked

him across the city to the dock, but then he seemed to just dis-appear."

"We waited for some time, but the pirate didn't emerge," Cyril added.

"So, it looks like your interest in the marina is more than justified," Derek said.

Was it possible the ghost pirate really *was* a ghost? One that haunted the ancient *Kingfisher*?

Morna sidled up to my left and tugged at my sleeve, which made her look all of six years old. She pulled me away from the other dead kids. "Is Derek angry with me?"

"No, I don't think so," I said. "He just wanted to dance. You could have just said *no*. You didn't have to run away."

"I didn't know what t'do," Morna whispered. "I'm not good wi' boys."

"So, we gonna hunt down that fake ghost pirate?" Tabetha interrupted, rubbing her palms together with verve. "Or are you an' Morna gonna girl talk all night?"

"Well, we *are* going to a marina."

☠   ☠   ☠

I don't know what images come to your mind when you hear the word *marina*. Prior to moving to Sticksville, it was a word that described something I figured I'd never see, like a *grotto* or *fjord*. And I figured if I ever did see one, it would be epic — a sprawling network of masts and sails. I mean, Sticksville's not huge, but it's also not tiny, yet only a few of our residents are boat owners. The *Kingfisher*, probably thirty feet high at the top of its mast, towered over the other smaller pleasure craft nearby, all of which had cringeworthy names like *Summer Breeze* or *Buoys Will Be Buoys*. The old wooden *Kingfisher* still featured two conspicuous security guards posted outside its gangplank. If the dead kids and I were to search inside the ship, we were go-ing to have to get past them. We all huddled behind an electri-cal transformer in the park across from the marina, just out of

view (we hoped) of the two guards. Step one, in my mind, was to determine if either of our guards could see the dead kids.

"We need to figure out if those guards can see you," I whispered to my dead friends. "Derek, you look the most normal, clothes-wise. Don't walk right up to the guards, but kind of walk *by* them. Think you can do that?"

Derek gave me the thumbs-up.

"Most normal," Kirby scoffed.

"You know a lot of other kids wearing shorts in February?" I said.

Kirby just glared because he knew I was right.

Derek then left the safety of the transformer and started whistling as he walked close, but not *too* close, to the ship.

"You!" the skinny guard with glasses yelled. "What are you doing?"

Derek just kept on walking as the guard tried to call him over.

"Who are you talking to?" the thicker, goateed guard asked.

"Him!" Skinny Guard shouted, pointing at the receding figure of Derek Running Water. "That Native kid in the T-shirt!"

"I don't see any kid," Goatee Guard said, confused. He moved closer to where his co-worker was pointing, but still couldn't see anything.

And that made things awkward. Having two guards, one who could see my friends, and one who couldn't, was the worst of both worlds. Derek returned to our huddle as I struggled to formulate a plan.

"You can't just sneak by them because the one guy can see you," I reasoned.

"We could jes' scare 'em," Tabetha said.

"But the other guy can't see you . . . and that might be more trouble than it's worth."

"We could sneak onto another boat," Derek said.

"But we need to get onto the *Kingfisher*," I said.

"Just watch."

Derek took Kirby by the hand and they went two boats over, to a yacht named *Garage Sail*. A minute later, loud music blasted from underneath its deck, accompanied by breaking glass and loud bangs. Immediately, I realized Derek's genius.

"What is happening?" the four-eyed guard asked his fellow guard.

"Sounds like a keg party."

"In Sticksville? Sounds like trouble. Go check it out," he said.

Goatee Guard left to investigate the *Garage Sail*. As genius as Derek's idea was, it had drawn the wrong guard away from the *Kingfisher*. If only the big guy had been the more assertive one! My back slid down the transformer again until I was seated in the snow.

"The one who can see us is still there," Morna said.

"I know . . . We're going to have to scare him."

"I can do it," Cyril asserted.

"Cyril, no," Morna said.

"Morna, it's my mystery," he said, loosening his neck scarf. "Besides, it's been a while since I've given someone a good scare."

Cyril marched directly toward the remaining guard, who noticed him almost at once.

"You. Stop right there," he said, holding a black baton in front of him like a lightsabre. He adjusted his glasses and rubbed his eyes. "What are you dressed as? Wait, are you that pirate guy?!"

Cyril, now just a few yards from the poor guard, answered, "You tell me." He dug his fingers under his chin and, in the most disgusting action I've ever seen in real life, peeled his face off like it was an adhesive sticker. It was way, way grosser than that movie with John Travolta and Nicolas Cage where they switch faces. I nearly threw up on the snow; the skinny guard *did* puke, right into the water, then ran toward the music-playing *Garage Sail* as the skull-headed boy continued moving toward him.

"Cyril!" I shouted, bounding out from behind the transformer. "You horrible genius! Let's get inside that ship!"

Cyril (sans face), Morna, Tabetha, and I ran up the gangplank and onto the ship and started looking around.

"Captain's quarters!" the skull of Cyril Cooper said, as his hand pointed to a wooden door at the back of the ship. Or stern, whatever. We quickly went inside and closed the door, just in case the guards decided to come back and confront the faceless boy. We'd have to be quiet while snooping around — unless Cyril had somehow miraculously scared them away for good. There wasn't much to be seen in the captain's quarters — a replica of an old map of the Sticksville area and its waterways, a plain wooden table, an astrolabe, which was admittedly pretty cool but of little use in solving Cyril's mystery. I realized we'd have to check the ship's deck to find what we were looking for. After all, the crude picture that Cyril had drawn in 1779 indicated he hid . . . something . . . in the ship's steering wheel. If the ship even had its original wheel.

"We're going to have to look outside," I whispered.

We heard approaching footsteps, so Tabetha opened the door a crack.

"It's jes' Kirby an' Derek," she said, and waved the two of them inside.

"Did the guards follow you?" I whispered, vapour shooting out of my mouth like I was a ready tea kettle.

"I think we scared them off for good," Derek said, overjoyed. "Whatever you guys did really spooked them."

Morna pointed to the faceless Cyril.

"That'd do it."

"They've probably gone to get reinforcements," Kirby noted, always with the negativity. "So we should find what we're looking for quickly."

We left the captain's quarters to find the steering wheel, typically near the stern of the ship, Cyril told us. (I don't pretend to be a ship expert.)

"It's the necklace," Cyril said. "Obviously, I must have hidden the necklace I took from the spy's house in the ship's helm."

"In the steering wheel?" Tabetha asked.

"Yes," he turned to her. It was *very* unsettling carrying on a whole conversation with a talking skull. Beyond the necklace, Cyril had a much larger realization. "And I think I died here."

"What? On the ship?" I asked.

"Yes, just being here . . . I'm remembering more."

"Finally," Kirby snarked.

"Shhh," I said. "What else do you remember, Cyril?"

Cyril looked skyward (not a ship direction) and held the sides of his skull (very literally) as if in the grip of the world's worst brain freeze.

"I can remember the man who attacked me," he said. "He was older — a man with arched eyebrows and a pinched face."

"So, not Patrick Burton," Derek concluded.

"No, he was older. He attacked me on this ship."

"What happened?" I asked. The dead kids and I paced around Cyril as he called out his revelations. It was like the grimmest square dance ever.

"I don't remember."

"Okay," I said, undaunted. It was still more information

that we'd had two minutes ago. "Let's find the necklace. Maybe seeing it will jog your memory more."

Morna pointed just above us to the steering wheel; it was mounted a level up, just above the captain's quarters. We almost fell over ourselves running up the wooden stairs to reach the upper deck. The upper deck, by the way, was splattered with red painted letters that read "Asphodel Meadows." Something told me that wasn't part of the ship's restoration.

"Asphodel Meadows again?" Tabetha cried.

"What does that *mean?*" Derek said.

Inside, I panicked just as much as Tabetha and Derek. The two words appeared at the murder site of each of my dead friends, and it was a phrase that Skyler McGriff referenced a few times while chasing me with a baseball bat. And maybe it had something to do with my mom, too, if the needlepoint in my living room was any indication. Whatever or whoever Asphodel Meadows was, it seemed connected to everything unseemly — save, say, Ashlie Salmons and Alyosha Diamandas — in town. My hands were shaking, but I tried to remain calm and hide my anxiety from the dead kids.

"Never mind that. We'll figure it out later," I ordered. "Let's find the necklace before the guards return."

The dead kids turned the massive wooden steering wheel over and over, checking each component for a place where one might squirrel away a necklace. The wheel itself was like a very large and ornate (but wooden) funnel cake with a dozen handles the size of table legs protruding from the centre. And it was on one of those handles where I noticed a small cut.

"Look at that handle!" I spat. Tabetha stopped turning the wheel. "I think that handle is a secret container."

Tabetha began pulling on the handle.

"I think it unscrews," Cyril said.

I just couldn't believe it was the original ship's helm, 200 years old. Thank goodness for the Sticks-ebration or the Sticksville Historic Society or whoever was responsible. Unfortunately, our own miniature Sticks-ebration was short-lived.

"There's no necklace," Tabetha said, having successfully unscrewed the trick handle. "Just this."

In her outstretched palm was a rolled-up little slip of paper. And new paper, too. This wasn't the tattered, decaying parchment that Cyril's drawing had been scribbled on. This paper had been ripped out of a Hilroy notebook, probably purchased at a local Shoppers Drug Mart or something.

"Not dredging up any memories, is it?" I asked Cyril.

If it was possible for a skull's hollow eye sockets to express confusion, Cyril's lack-of-face was emoting that right then. With some trepidation, I unrolled the little paper. There was a single sentence printed on it: *Too late, October.*

"I think our ghost pirate is working on the same mystery as we are, guys."

As unbelievable as that sounded, there was no other explanation. The ghost pirate had my bag, which contained Cyril's locket, and somehow knew my name. Even more unbelievably, the ground beneath my feet seemed to be shifting as we excitedly ranted about this pirate and his many unforgivable faults. The shoreline was moving. The *Kingfisher* had set sail.

"Are we moving?" I asked, though the answer was obvious. The marina's docks were receding into the night's darkness. The *Garage Sail* was about the size of a Lego tugboat now. Someone had cut the thick rope that was mooring the vintage ship to Sticksville's marina, and we were coasting off into the middle of the river.

"We have other problems," Cyril said, his jawbone clacking open and shut as he gestured toward the curls of smoke coming from the front of the ship. "This ship is on fire."

Rolling on a River (While on Fire)

The *Kingfisher*, the eighteenth-century ship refinished for Sticksville historic celebrations and the like, was ablaze. Bright orange flames licked along both sides of the boat and began to engulf the bottom of the stairs, trapping young October on the upper deck at the helm. The ship's sails had begun to catch fire, too, as the marina receded from the port side of the boat. (Here's a fun way to tell "port" from "starboard." Port has four letters, just like left, which is the port side of the boat if you're facing the bow. Just in case you get trapped on a ship that's on fire yourself. In fact, this whole chapter may prove handy in such a situation, or will, if October survives it.)

As blistering flames swallowed more and more of the ship's deck, everybody scrambled as much as they could in such a confined area — the fire was seriously restricting their options. No one had a clue how the fire had started, but it seemed clear that this ship arson was the work of a dastardly ghost pirate and not the security guards. The pirate must have beaten October and her friends to the *Kingfisher*, stolen the necklace that Cyril had hidden there over 200 years ago (and left that smug little note for October in the process), and set the ship on fire as soon as October had set foot on its creaky boards. She'd walked right into a trap.

"Where's the lifeboat?" October yelled to Cyril, since he had been somewhat involved in the shipbuilding.

"Probably on fire, too," groaned Kirby as he looked over the ship's sides.

The dead kids, being corpses and intangible at will, leapt through various walls of fire to search around the ship for some sort of raft or rescue craft. Cyril, in the meantime, put his hands on October's shoulders to deliver some very unfortunate news. All the more troubling as it was delivered by a boy without a face.

"October, there is no lifeboat."

"What do you mean?" October started to panic . . . more.

"We never built ships with lifeboats," he explained. "I'm not even certain what that word means, though I can sort of figure it out."

Unluckily for October Schwartz and every sailor who lived before its invention, the first ever lifeboat used on a sailing vessel was built in 1784, a full five years after the *Kingfisher*. That's not something that comes up in most history books.

October's eyes bulged. "No lifeboat? What are we going to do?"

"I'm sure we'll come up with a solution," Cyril said, doffing his tricorn hat and fanning it in the flames' general direction.

"Are we just going to *die*? Or am *I*?"

"No, uh . . . we'll . . ." he said, continuing to wave his hat.

"What are you doing?! That's a *ghost hat*. It's not putting out any fires."

October probably would have continued to rant about how ridiculous Cyril was in his attempts to put out a burgeoning nautical inferno with one measly ghost hat, but the smoke caused her to hack and cough uncontrollably. Smoke inhalation is often the primary cause of death in fires, after all. The other dead kids, unable to find a lifeboat, returned to their living friend at the helm.

"You okay?" Derek asked, slapping October's bent-over form on the back.

"There's no lifeboat," Morna reported.

"I know," October croaked and glared at Cyril, as if it had been his decision to build ships without lifeboats until the later 1700s.

"What are ye gonna do?" Morna asked.

"Ya should swim fer it!" Tabetha said.

"It's February," October said. "Maybe if I'd jumped into the water as soon as we'd seen the flames, I'd have made it to shore without dying of hypothermia, but we're too far along the river now. It's about a half kilometre. I'd never make it."

October briefly entertained the thought of lashing all her dead friends together with a strong rope and using their bodies as a makeshift raft to paddle to safety, but figured that should be Plan B.

"We need," she wheezed, "to find something that floats . . . and is big enough . . . to carry me."

"An' it looks like we need t'find it fast, as the only girl w'workin' lungs is about t'bust 'em," Tabetha added.

"The captain's table!" the grinning skull of Cyril Cooper shouted. "It's made of cedar!"

"Beautiful," Kirby said. "I'm sure it's a lovely piece."

"No," Cyril continued. "It's one of the lightest woods there is. We could use the captain's table as a raft."

"Are you sure?" Kirby asked.

"I used to make boats."

"Your *dad* did."

"We're already trashing this boat," Derek shrugged. "It's worth a shot."

"The captain's quarters are on fire," October said from below. She had remembered the school instructional fire safety videos and, as such, was staying very close to the ground — or in this case, the deck of the ship — to avoid as much smoke as possible.

"I'll retrieve the captain's table from the burning cabin," Cyril insisted. "The rest of you, rip up some boards so we can use them as paddles."

"You're going to get burned," October protested from her supine position on the ground.

"So? I'm already dead. And currently missing a face. It doesn't matter if I catch fire," he said. "Besides, it's because of my mystery that we're in this mess."

"Okay," October said. "Just don't let the table catch fire, too."

Cyril hurried down the wooden steps, through a corridor of angry flames. The fire blackened him as he continued to the lower deck, like he was the meat cooked on a shish kebab. In the meantime, Tabetha, Morna, Kirby, and Derek started to kick at loose boards and the spokes of the steering wheel, gathering any wood oblong enough to use as a paddle. October, kneeling, face down to the ship's floor, tried to recall if she should be breathing quickly or slowly. She decided slowly seemed more sensible and tried, through sheer willpower alone, to slow her heart rate, which currently had the tempo of *The Green Hornet*'s theme song.

When Cyril returned, hauling the four-by-four cedar captain's table up the steps to the ship's upper deck, he looked like he'd arrived straight out of a medieval engraving of the most commonly experienced nightmares, should such a thing have ever existed. Most of his clothing had burned away, and it was as though a flaming skeleton was dragging the table out of hell. Somehow, he'd managed to avoid setting the table aflame, but once he dumped it right in front of October, one of the table legs started to spark and a yellow spill of fire shot up the table's side. October, thinking quickly, removed her coat (one of the few articles of clothing on board that wasn't part of the spirit world) and smothered the leg with its heavy folds.

"Well, that ruined my coat," she mused.

"Someone help me dump the table into the water," the skeleton that used to be Cyril said. "I don't have much muscle left!"

October, getting a full view of Cyril's new-and-not-so-improved look, vomited on the deck.

"Stop vomiting. We have to move quickly," Cyril shouted. "There's not much left of the ship that's not on fire!"

"October, get those oars ready," Derek said, helping Cyril and Tabetha to lift the table over the side of the *Kingfisher*.

By oars, he meant the irregular pieces of wood piled behind the ship's now-desecrated steering wheel. With a final, hippo-like grunt, the three dead kids hoisted the table over the side of the ship. A massive sploosh followed, and, at first, October feared the table had sunk like a stone to the bottom of the river. She raced to the lip of the boat and was relieved to see it bobbing up and down on the black water.

"Hurry!" Derek shouted. "Jump, October. We won't have much time before the table floats away!"

"You go first," she coughed. "I need your . . . um . . . bodies . . . to cushion my fall."

Unfeeling as she may have sounded, October Schwartz was correct. There was about a twenty-foot drop from the ship to the captain's table in the water below, and the dead kids' soft bodies — the skeletal Cyril notwithstanding — would help her survive the jump.

Tabetha leapt first, carrying a plank with her. "Everyone grab an oar!" she shouted on her way down.

The dead kids tumbled over the side of the mighty ship, one by one, each carrying an oar (of sorts) with him or her. Cyril was the last of the dead kids to jump, and instead of aiming for the fairly small table, he fell directly into the water, hoping to extinguish some of the flames that clung to him like a spiderweb that just won't come off your face. He emerged from the deep and frigid water moments later, free of fire, and clung to the side of the table raft, like some undead Jack Dawson. He steadied the table, swimming it closer to the slowly burning *Kingfisher*.

"Jump, October!" shouted the drenched skeleton below.

"Get closer together," she shouted, waving her shaking hands together and ignoring the flames at her back, as if she were a super-cool action hero not noticing an automobile exploding behind her. She waited and tried to wave the kids closer together. This scene, minus the burning frigate, will be familiar to anyone seeing a nervous concert-goer about to embark on his or her first crowd-surfing experience. And, like all first-time crowd surfers, October finally jumped, landing on Kirby's back, just bruising herself a bit on contact. The table tipped and rolled, but all five of them managed to stay out of the water.

"Get October in the middle," Derek said. "Keep her away from the water."

"Here, take my spot," Morna said, trading places with her.

The dead kids took their steering wheel spokes and ragged wooden boards and started to paddle back to shore. Cyril trailed behind, holding on to the table like a dog that had been mistakenly leashed to its owner's boat.

"No," October said. "Go further along the far shore. Look!"

At the marina, visible beyond the *Kingfisher* (which was now almost completely engulfed in flames), the two security guards were back, their flashlights bouncing around like a malfunctioning game of Pong on the night sky. Behind them flashed the red lights of the Sticksville Fire Department, who had arrived on the scene but had nothing to do, not being in the possession of any sort of water vessel. The firefighters, decked out in their heavy reflective coats, stood at the edge of the dock with the security guards who had been scared away earlier.

"We'll have to avoid them," October said, her teeth beginning to chatter on the open water. "I d-don't think I can answer their questions about why I, f-four dead kids, and a sk-sk-skeleton are fleeing from a b-burning historical boat."

Though it took longer than it would have to paddle to the part of the shore occupied by a gaggle of firefighters, security, and, now, police, the dead kids finally got October to a secure spot a kilometre and a bit down from the marina. October threw on her coat, which now smelled like cat hair dropped into a furnace, said her hasty goodbyes and thank yous to her ghost saviours, then ran all the way home, hoping the exertion from the run would warm her up. She snuck back into her house via the back door, dove into her bed, and swaddled herself in as many blankets and blanket-like fabrics she could find. Her dad — thank goodness for small miracles — hadn't been awakened by the unusual number of sirens in Sticksville that evening. October Schwartz, bundled in her bed, imagined herself as the spinach in a particularly warm lasagna. She wondered if she'd ever truly be warm again. And, just as importantly, she wondered how she was going to deal with the fallout: what was possibly Sticksville's most important historic relic had been torched.

☠ ☠ ☠

October was awakened by her father knocking at her bedroom door. Considering he had barely left his own bedroom over the past week, this was unexpected.

"Dad?" October said groggily. "Are you going to school?" She opened her door to find Mr. Schwartz, smiling, shaved, briefcase in hand.

"Yes, and I hope you are, too. You'd better hurry up."

There was really no good way to tell one's dad that you slept in because the process of escaping a burning ship is much more tiring than one might expect.

"I'll be quick," she promised.

"You smell like smoke," her dad noted. "Were you out smoking last night?"

Stupid burning ship.

"No, that's fireplace smoke. Can't you tell fireplace smoke from cigarette smoke?"

"We don't have a fireplace!" Mr. Schwartz said. His smile had mutated into a great scowl of disbelief (not to be confused with the Great Owl of Disbelief, a wise and magical creature) within a minute.

"But the Takeshis do," October said, hoping her dad wouldn't fact-check this statement. "When you and Mr. Santuzzi had coffee, Yumi and I were sitting by her fireplace." She couldn't determine which was worse; if her dad suspected her of smoking or if he suspected her of setting fire to a historic ship.

Mr. Schwartz seemed still unimpressed. "That was nearly two days ago. I don't have time to argue this any further. But if I find out you've been smoking, I might have to ship you off to a military academy." He glanced at his watch. "Now get your butt ready for school. You don't have much time."

☠ ☠ ☠

What ensued was a bit of a mad dash to arrive at school before the morning bell, like an episode of *The Amazing Race*, but with no partner and where the only prize at the end is a full day of school. Walking — or power-walking, in this instance — to school also takes more time in the winter, with the snow and ice and partially obstructed sidewalks, so October Schwartz didn't even have time to toss her backpack into her locker before her first class, French. This was just as well, since she no longer had a backpack. It was now in the possession of a devious ghost pirate and who knew what he (or she) was doing with it.

And speaking of devious ghost pirates, the one person October ran into that Monday morning before French was a possible ghost pirate candidate, Ms. Fenstermacher. Though

October, running late, was prepared to just wave to her history teacher and continue her run toward French class, Ms. Fenstermacher's face was contorted with such dismay, it stopped October in mid-hustle.

"Are you okay, Ms. Fenstermacher?"

"Oh, I'll be fine," she said, waving her hand in front of her face as if Windexing an imaginary face window. "But last night someone set the *Kingfisher* on fire. One of the oldest surviving ships in Canadian history was burned to the ground . . . or to the river. This year's Sticks-ebration is ruined."

October Schwartz hadn't realized quite how important the ship was to her history teacher. That sort of information eluded you when you're fighting for oxygen in the middle of its burning hull. Ms. Fenstermacher did seem distraught over the loss of the *Kingfisher* — much more so than someone who started the fire would be — so maybe October had been wrong to mentally accuse her of being the ghost pirate. By the same token, the fire had happened at about two or three in the morning, too late to appear in today's *Sticksville Loon*. And it was unlikely anything that happened in Sticksville, short of an atomic explosion, would make the Toronto media. News travelled quickly in a small town, but Ms. Fenstermacher seemed to have scored this inside arson info before anyone else. Though in some way, October's morning encounter with Ms. Fenstermacher partially exonerated the teacher from the ghost pirate crimes, in another way, it was the proverbial straw that broke the camel's back. (In this scenario, the straw was circumstantial evidence, and the camel's serious back injury was Ms. Fenstermacher being the now notorious ghost pirate.)

Just as confused as ever — not often the sign of a great detective — October Schwartz extracted herself from her conversation with the history teacher by offering a few condolences and hurrying toward her awaiting French class.

October hadn't even had the chance to check in with Yumi and Stacey to see if there was further fallout from their awkward slow dance to "Stairway to Heaven" before lunch. She had to wait until midday to see how weird things were or weren't between them, and that didn't happen until after math with Mr. Santuzzi. And math with Mr. Santuzzi, typically a harrowing experience for even the most hard-bitten student, ended on a surprisingly pleasant note. As October left the classroom to join her two friends in the cafeteria, Mr. Santuzzi stopped her. It seemed she couldn't travel anywhere in Sticksville Central High School anymore without some teacher or other stopping her for a brief conversation.

"Miss Schwartz," he said, his meaty forearm blocking her exit. "I see your father returned to teaching this week."

October nodded.

"I'm glad to hear it," he said.

"Whatever you said to him must have had an effect," October said. "Thanks."

October had, in the past few months, thanked Mr. Santuzzi more than she would have ever thought possible upon first meeting the tough but unfair and slightly unhinged math teacher months ago. She supposed one couldn't judge a book by its moustachioed and tightly leisure-suited cover.

October entered the cafeteria searching for Yumi and Stacey, and nearly every other student seated at a table averted his or her eyes. The weekend had been so incident-filled, she'd forgotten how the entire school had betrayed her to the ghost pirate at the Valentine's dance. So, it was with some twisted pleasure that she attempted to catch the eyes of as many of her fellow students as she could. People were way more interested in their meatloaf and mashed potatoes than October could ever remember them being. The only people looking back at her were Yumi Takeshi and Stacey MacIsaac, who waved her over to their corner of the table.

On her journey there, though, she did encounter one other student unafraid to lock eyes with her: Ashlie Salmons. She sat at the edge of a table, dangling one little boot into the centre aisle like a fisherman angling for a flying fish. She twirled around a celery stick near her mouth, like an old-timey villain waxing his moustache. The cool green of her newly done nails matched the vegetable in her hand.

"How did your date with the crazy ghost pirate go?" she asked. "Was it love at first one-eyed sight, or is he going to give you the heave-ho?"

"He almost killed me, so I'm glad you managed to find the humour in the situation, Ash," October said.

"Just helping you work through the pain, doll."

October may have mumbled something then about helping Ashlie work through some pain herself. When she finally sat down across from Yumi and Stacey, Yumi did one of her all-time favourite things: slap the newest edition of the *Sticksville Loon* on the table and express her shock. Seriously, she must have been the only high school student in the world to take such an avid interest in their local paper.

"Look at this!" she said.

October had surmised correctly. The *Loon* didn't have any information about last night's burning ship. Instead, the front-page story was the attack and tense standoff at Friday night's Valentine's dance.

HEART-BREAKING AND ENTERING! screamed the headline, clearly written by someone who went to the same terrible pun seminar as the person who dreams up this book's chapter titles.

"I didn't think anyone at the *Loon* could be so clever," October said.

"If I ever find out who came up with that headline, I'll probably marry them," Yumi decided.

Or slow dance with them to "Stairway to Heaven," October thought. "Still, why are you showing me this? We lived it."

"Not quite," Stacey said, chewing his tuna like a Holstein with a wad of cud.

"There's no mention of you, no mention of me trying to come to your rescue, or Stace here getting tossed aside like an old banana peel," Yumi shouted, swiping her hand across the paper. "And look who they quote!"

October's heavily lined eyes followed Yumi's black nails to the paragraph she was pointing at: *Honour student Ashlie Salmons says she was afraid for her life. "I just kept thinking, I'm too young to die," the fifteen-year-old sobbed.*

195

"Come on!" Yumi said.

"Honour student?" October said.

"That's a shame," Stacey agreed. He chugged a carton of chocolate milk, then said,. "I'm going to get another. Do either of you want anything?"

The two girls shook their heads and their lanky male friend left.

"Now that he's gone, you have to tell me if anything new has happened," October said. "Are things super awkward between you two?"

"I almost wish they were," Yumi exhaled. "I'd kill for awkward. It's like we never even danced at all. He hasn't said a thing."

"Maybe he just thought it was a friendly dance," October said. "Besides, you said you didn't even know if you still liked him."

"I know," she said, burying her face in her hands. "But it would be nice if there were *any* indication from him about how he felt. I just don't think he likes me like that."

"What's not to like?" October asked, feeling weird that she was now at that stage of life where she had to talk about feelings over lunch.

"I'm no tuna sandwich."

Stacey then reappeared with another carton of chocolate milk and the conversation quickly drew to a close, reopening on the ghost pirate and his (or her) identity.

Talking (some) things about the case over with her friends, it became clearer than ever to October that not only was the ghost pirate stealing Sticksville's history, he also had some sort of connection to Cyril. Why else would he take the Coopers' letters (among other things) from the Sticksville Museum first? Why else try to murder October and steal her bag? Then take the necklace Cyril had hidden and set fire to the ship he helped build? The evidence suggested that the ghost pirate was Ms. Fenstermacher. After all, reasoned October, who else knew that the dead Loyalist ever existed, aside from October herself and Ms. Fenstermacher, the teacher who (a) knew October was planning an assignment on his family and (b) worked part-time in the Coopers' old house? But something told October Ms. Fenstermacher's plot was motivated by something darker (and less petty) than making sure October received a failing grade in history. And given that the alarm never went off during the initial break-in at the Sticksville Museum, October had a hunch about where she could find the Coopers' missing historic letters.

☠   ☠   ☠

Night at the Museum

I realize I've been wrong in the past, but I was, really and truly, ninety-six percent sure that Ms. Fenstermacher was the ghost pirate. And that she was trying to kill me, which, I'll be honest, made me less inclined to finish my history assignment on Cyril Cooper. The ghost pirate had made my homework pretty much impossible, anyway, by stealing everything that had ever been written about or owned by Cyril Cooper.

My ninety-six percent surety ratcheted up to a ninety-seven on Tuesday, when the *Kingfisher* fire news appeared in the paper. Ms. Fenstermacher knew a lot about the incident a full twenty-four hours before anyone else in town did, though I couldn't rule out some sort of Sticksville History news wire or listserv that my history-mad teacher was privy to. Assuming I was right (something I like to do), the missing Cooper correspondence was likely in one of two places.

For one, it was very possible that the letters, and, in fact, all the missing museum artifacts, were still *in* the museum, just in a hidden location. It would easily explain why the alarm never sounded, and would be the easiest way to hide the material if the main goal of the break-in was to prevent me, October Schwartz, teen detective (sort of) extraordinare, from finding out anything regarding Cyril Cooper's life and death. After all, Ms. Fenstermacher's little email tracker didn't work. Most likely because the stolen property never left the premises. The other possibility was that it was hidden somewhere in Ms. Fenstermacher's house, and if the dead kids' and my search of the museum didn't reveal anything, her house would be our next stop. I was going to have to go there, anyway, to prove she was the ghost pirate. (I figured I would probably find a rubber mask or pirate's cutlass in her crawl space or something.)

But before any of that could happen, I needed to make it through another day of school. Another February day of school. We were getting near the end of the semester — final exams loomed and projects were nearing their deadlines — but every evening of mine recently had been devoted to solving horrible murders and break-ins, so I didn't have high hopes for my report card. With the distraction of Valentine's Day and computer Love Matches gone, most of the school day was devoted to exam review. The only break was lunch, where Yumi again revealed details from the cover story of the *Sticksville Loon*. (*FIRE SAIL!* Yumi's future husband had written.) While Yumi pretended she wasn't still crushing on Stacey, I likewise pretended I knew nothing about the ship fire.

For a minute, I worried there might be security cameras at the marina, because it seemed like the kind of people who could afford pleasure craft were the same kind of people who would buy and install security cameras. But the paper, as read to me by Yumi, confirmed there was no security footage, which was a major relief.

☠ ☠ ☠

That evening, I informed the dead kids we were going to break into the museum again and explained how we'd have to be careful, as security was sure to be high after the recent string of pirate-related robberies. There was no hesitation from the dead kids; I'm sure they would have been content to break into any structure, really. Ghosts have such lax ethics when it comes to property rights.

Just after midnight, the dead kids and I made our way to the Sticksville Museum, Cyril Cooper's old house. Cyril himself had thankfully grown back his face and skin, so I didn't have to spend all night trying not to look directly at his rotting skeleton. The windows of the old house had yet to be repaired from the previous break-in, so all that stood between us and the interior of the museum was some flimsy cardboard taped to the window frames. Actually, that was all that stood between *me* and the museum's interior. Walls were no match for the dead kids, so nothing prevented them from walking in and taking a stroll around.

"Last time we were at the museum, the cameras didn't pick up you dead kids," I said. "So maybe you can go in first, shut off the cameras and alarms, and let me in?"

"We'd be happy to," Cyril said, brushing some graveyard dirt off his shoulder. "If you'll just remind me what a camera is."

"I can explain when we get inside," Derek said, dragging Cyril through the walls of the house with him. The other dead kids followed. Morna MacIsaac, the last to enter, told October, "I'll come t'get ye when it's safe."

While I waited outside in the February night, I wondered why mysteries ever needed to be solved in February. I could never be a police officer in the Northwest Territories. I also noticed that not all the broken glass from the earlier break-in had been cleared. A pile of shattered glass shimmered in the moonlight in the grass just under one of the boarded up windows. The broken glass was *outside* the museum. What a fool I was! It should have been obvious the break-in was an inside job: the windows had been broken from the inside. It was the oldest TV mystery clue in the book, a book that was probably written by Jessica Fletcher from *Murder, She Wrote*. (I knew what that was now, thanks to Goth Hardware Clerk.) I cursed myself for not realizing earlier that the ghost pirate must have been a museum employee, namely one Ms. Fenstermacher.

As I tried to warm my hands, I imagined Derek showing Cyril and Tabetha and Kirby where the security cameras were, how the wires connected the cameras to a video recorder, and where to switch off the alarm. I didn't quiz them on it afterward, but I assume they disconnected everything because nobody arrested me in the day that followed. (That came a bit later.) When Morna half-ghosted through the wall of the museum house and called out to me, I popped out one of the cardboard windows and hoisted myself into the old Cooper House.

Once inside and alarm-free, the immediate problem was finding the Cooper family correspondence, which could have been hidden anywhere inside the museum. We stood on the stone floor of the museum in front of the black cauldron in the fireplace and, like, strategized.

"What I want to find is those old letters your parents wrote," I told Cyril. "They're probably our best chance at finding out who killed you."

"But where do we start?" Tabetha said, jamming her knuckles into her hips.

"Do you have any idea, Cyril? This was your house."

"It's changed so much," he said. "This kitchen looks the same, but there are rooms that didn't even exist when I lived here."

"Why don't we split into two teams of three and each take a floor?" Kirby suggested.

Kirby, Derek, and Tabetha planned to search the ground floor while Cyril, Morna, and I snooped around upstairs. As weird as I felt about being paired up with Cyril — what with him being my secret (but no-longer-secret) admirer and all — having recently seen him skinless certainly made things feel a lot less romantic.

"Remember, I want to find those letters, but any museum stuff you can find that's been stashed away will help prove that my history teacher is the ghost pirate."

"Cyril here found his face again," Kirby said, elbowing the taller dead boy in his stomach. "So a few letters shouldn't pose him any trouble at all."

"Ha ha," Cyril said. "Let's go."

My first idea was to look through the museum's administrative offices, as they were hidden from the public and Ms. Fenstermacher would be familiar with all the little nooks, crannies, and various hidey-holes in the vicinity. But a thorough search of the cabinets and closets revealed nothing. I even stood on a precarious and somewhat broken wheelie chair to pop open the foam ceiling tiles to see if anything had been hidden above. Then I followed a hunch based purely on too many viewings of TV police procedurals. I turned the light on in the staff bathroom and opened the white porcelain toilet tank.

As soon as I lifted the heavy porcelain block, I saw them, stuffed in a large Ziploc bag, crammed behind the rubber plunger: the Coopers' letters. Television, for once, had steered me right! Ms. Fenstermacher watched too much television, too, if her *BSG* consumption was any indication, so she had no choice but to live out the detective show cliché and hide her "stash" in the toilet. I couldn't believe it!

"Morna! Cyril! Everybody!" I shouted. "I think I found them!"

I gave the dead kids time to gather in the museum offices while I toweled off the bag. Once the outside had been dried, I opened the bag and spilled its contents onto Ms. Fenstermacher's desk. I felt like that kid in *Miracle on 34th Street*, but instead of restoring a jaded public's sense of hope and wonder, these letters were going to help prove who killed a thirteen-year-old boy and, maybe, convict my history teacher of grand larceny and assault with a deadly weapon. This "miracle" was decidedly darker.

"What do they say?" Tabetha pawed through the various envelopes, impatient. "Come on! Open 'em up an' read 'em!"

"I can't just *rip* into these, Tabetha," I explained. "These are two-hundred-year-old artifacts, not a magazine subscription letter."

"Yeah, Tabby," Kirby said, using Tabetha's least favourite nickname. She stuck her purple tongue out in response.

"Cyril, when did you die? Can you remember that?" I asked, shuffling through the pile of opened envelopes. "I know it's 1779, but the month, day?"

"It was in the later summer . . . before the harvest."

"Okay, that should help," I said.

Over about eight decades, the Cooper family must have written close to a hundred letters that had been preserved here at the museum, most recently in a Ziploc bag in the staff toilet. Flipping through a batch, I found one from September 1779. Knowing the paper was as old as the ship that had been torched last night, and made of less sturdy material (although still technically a tree, I guess), I carefully pulled the letter from the envelope, unfolded it, and began to read it aloud for the benefit of the dead kids assembled around Ms. Fenstermacher's desk. Their sunken eyes shone with curiosity.

September 17, 1779

Dear Mother,

Greetings once again from the New World. I wish, as in our previous letters, I could say all was well here in Quebec, but I write to you in great sorrow. Recent events in our life in the colonies have been marred by tragedy. Our son, Cyril, was found dead just days ago, drowned near the ship Eustace was building. Eustace and I have been inconsolable. For the past few months, Eustace has overseen construction of the Kingfisher, a new clipper commissioned by the British Navy. Cyril himself sometimes went to help his father with the shipbuilding whenever his duties with the militia would allow.

However, your grandson will not see a fourteenth year, Mother. His lungs filled with water from the Niagara River, and my husband and I have no idea how it happened. Just days ago, our boy was telling us something about a strange shack in the middle of the forest, but there's so much forest (and so little anything else), it was impossible for Eustace to discover what he was talking about. Cyril claimed the little building contained a number of books, but he didn't know what they were. Our life has been in such tumult, moving from New York to Nova Scotia, and now to the Niagara River, and Cyril often had to work. As a result, he never received proper schooling — I don't know where one would receive proper schooling in Sticksville — and so, the poor dear never learned how to read. But he feared the books were those of an American spy! I realize that south of us, a fierce revolution is being fought, but we fled north to avoid all that. I dread to think the American revolution is following us. Or worse, that it might have something to do with our darling son's drowning. Eustace fears that if Cyril did stumble across a spy's hideout, that could have certainly led to foul play.

But that's the strangest part, mother. Cyril drowned. Cyril, who has been helping his father build ships since age seven and is more at home in the water than most eels, drowned. I have no idea how such a thing would occur, unless he'd been knocked unconscious or forcefully held underwater. But the soldiers who found Cyril said he showed no signs of trauma. There was, however, one bit of strangeness. They said Cyril's arms were held flat to his sides, and his legs held together perfectly, as if he'd been bound by invisible ropes or tied to a spit. They said it was the most unnatural pose of death they'd ever seen.

Listen to me! Going on like a ghoul with all these gruesome details. You don't want to hear all the grim facts of how your grandson met his early end. It is simply sad enough that this happened at all. Eustace and I don't know what to do with ourselves without our little Cyril. I promise to you that we shall write more in happier times. Until then, I remain,

Yours in tragedy,
Elizabeth Cooper

"Um," Cyril said, a bit taken aback by the letter. I suppose it's not every day you more or less hear your coroner's report recited aloud.

"Man, you British people are prim," Tabetha commented, and I had to admit, I'd heard more sorrowful letters written about the cancellation of television shows. "Sorry, Cyril."

"But on the positive side," Kirby said, taking the letter from me, "Cyril's mother did include an unusual amount of detail about her son's death."

"Yeah," Derek said. "What was that about being bound by invisible ropes? That was weird, right?"

Cyril stood up and started pacing around the museum office, passing harmlessly through chairs and cardboard boxes.

"I'm remembering something," he said, taking off his hat, like that was going to help air get to his brain or whatever. "I think I'm remembering something."

"Think, Cyril," Morna encouraged. She was kneeling on the ground and patted her knees like she was goading a dog to bring her a Frisbee.

Meanwhile, Kirby had taken the rest of the letters from me and was skimming their contents. "Maybe his mother or father said something about their son's death later. Maybe they provide more details."

I took half the stack from Kirby and attempted to help, but when I scanned the letters, there was nothing new. Cyril's death was mentioned, as was how strange it was that he drowned, but no further clues came up, no possible suspects revealed. There was, however-er, something else strange about the Cooper correspondence.

"Kirby," I asked, "do you have any letters dated after 1792?"

Kirby shuffled through the pile, then rummaged through a few more scattered across Ms. Fenstermacher's desk. "Yeah. This one from 1812. 1814. Another 1812."

"But do you have any between 1792 and 1812?"

He looked around some more, then shook his head.

"Me neither. Why did the Coopers stop writing letters to each other for twenty years?"

"Bored?" Kirby suggested.

"If they were bored, they'd probably have written *more* letters," I argued. "Besides, why start writing again once the War of 1812 started? They'd probably be busier than ever."

"Maybe the ghost pirate hid the letters from that time elsewhere," Derek said.

"But why?" I asked. It didn't make any sense. "Although . . . wait, Ms. Fenstermacher said something about almost no documents existing from a couple decades in Sticksville's history."

"Why would everything from that era go missing?" Kirby asked.

"I don't know. Ms. Fenstermacher told me about the gap," I said, "and I kind of don't entirely trust her."

That's when Cyril kind of yelled at us.

"Be quiet! Be quiet, all of you. I'm remembering something."

"About how ye died?" Morna asked.

"Yes. And about why my body was found in such a strange pose."

"Well?"

"Remember how I said it wasn't Patrick Burton, but a man who jumped me near the ship. That it was *he* who killed me?"

"Do you remember who he is?" Derek asked.

"No."

"And how did he kill you?" Kirby asked. "Your mother just said in her letter you drowned without any signs of trauma."

"The man used magic."

I was dumbfounded. I wasn't sure how the other dead kids felt, but Cyril telling us that magic caused his death was, to me, about as believable as if he'd said that he'd been impaled by a unicorn. I mean, I realize I've spent a lot of my time since the fall hanging out with dead kids, so there's a supernatural world out there, but this was Sticksville, not Narnia. The only thing magical about suburban Ontario was that the Wendy's drive-thru was open twenty-four hours a day.

"Magic?" Kirby scoffed.

"I know how it sounds," Cyril said.

"It sounds like ya've gone off yer rocker." Tabetha said the one thing we all kind of thought.

"Maybe we've been working too hard," Derek said.

"Guys, let's let him finish," I said. Even if I doubted the involvement of any magic — and more so the involvement of a magical American patriot spy — whatever Cyril remembered was bound to be of use.

"Thank you," Cyril said, and nodded. "As I was saying, the man found me by the docks, at the *Kingfisher*. He must have followed me there. I can't remember what he said, but I do remember him waving his arms and, after that, I couldn't move. I stood stiff as a board, like somebody was measuring my height or I was awaiting inspection during morning routine at the militia. So there I was, perched at the edge of the water, standing like a flagpole, frozen on the spot. That man came up right behind me, just gently pushed me square in the back, and sent me face-first into the river. I couldn't move my arms or legs, so I floated to the bottom like a lead weight. I drowned in what was no more than five feet of water."

Magic or no magic, the image was a terrifying one. Imagine knowing that if you stood to full height, you could prevent yourself from drowning, but being totally unable to.

"So, you're saying this man was some kind of wizard?" Kirby said.

"I guess so."

"An' why would he wanna kill you?"

"Maybe the Americans had a wizard spy working for them." As outlandish as Cyril's suggestion was, I had no better ideas. Though I figured if the American Revolution had a little help from a wizard spy, it definitely would have been made into a movie by now.

"Listen," I said, hoping the dead kids would listen. "Spy

wizard or no spy wizard, we found all these Cooper letters *inside* the museum, which means my history teacher, Ms. Fenstermacher, is the ghost pirate!'"

"What?" Derek said.

"Think about it. The ghost pirate hid the stuff stolen from the museum *inside* the museum. Only a museum employee would do that. Add that to the fact that Ms. Fenstermacher was nowhere to be found when the pirate showed up at the dance, she *knows* I was trying to do my project on the Coopers, and she knew about the *Kingfisher* burning way before anyone else. She's got to be the ghost pirate."

"So what do we do?" asked Morna.

"It's only a matter of time before she tries to kill me again," I said, as a shiver ran down my spine at the thought of her sword. "So we don't have much time. Before too long, it'll be the full moon again, and you dead kids will disappear. As soon as possible, we have to search her house. I'm thinking tomorrow night."

"What about right now?" Derek asked.

"Right now, I have to work on my history project. It's due Friday."

"The history project for the teacher who's trying to kill you?" Kirby asked.

"Just in case I'm wrong."

I sealed the bag of Cooper letters and placed them back inside the toilet tank, just so Ms. Fenstermacher wouldn't know we'd found them. As the dead kids and I walked back down the stairs of the Sticksville Museum, Cyril asked, "Are you still using me as the subject for your history project?"

"Yes," I said. "So we need to solve this mystery by Friday, because I'm definitely going to fail if I tell the class you were killed by an American spy wizard."

☠ ☠ ☠

Still Just a
Rat in a Cage

And so it was that October Schwartz and her five dead friends set a snare for Sticksville's most notorious (and probably only) ghost pirate, like an Arctic trapper out for ermine (or some Arctic animal prized for its pelts or whatnot). October determined that they needed to search Ms. Fenstermacher's place of residence to find airtight (rather than circumstantial) evidence that she was, in fact, this villain plaguing Sticksville's historical and ghost detective communities. But first, they needed to find out where she lived. And the only way October knew how to find her address was by searching through the personnel files stored somewhere at her school.

The night after they found the Coopers' letters, October and the dead kids walked to Sticksville Central High School around midnight, practicing their usual method of keeping far from the road and hiding the dead kids whenever a car passed. Last time the dead kids had visited October's school after hours, they had to scare away a pesky — or rather, unfortunate — custodian by sawing off Kirby's head. And the dead kids were prepared to do something similar tonight, though Cyril was still recovering from pulling off his face, so he was going to abstain from any gross-out or scare tactics. What they didn't know was that, after the string of strange events, the school now had all custodial staff leave the premises by eight at the latest. Not that the school administrators were superstitious or anything. They would just rather avoid as many ghost- or pirate-induced sick days as possible. And/or a lawsuit.

October and her dead friends waited out of sight, behind a big sign at the school entrance, identifying it as Sticksville Central High School, and in smaller letters underneath, declaring that *February Is Black History Month*. October was lucky Tabetha couldn't read, or she'd have surely berated October to solve her mystery next.

"Okay, who wants to see if the coast is clear?" October asked, her breath rising like a white ribbon into the clear night sky.

"I'll go," Tabetha said.

"Don't scare anyone away without the rest of us!" Kirby admonished.

Tabetha trudged through the snow and through the locked front doors of the high school, returning about five minutes later, shaking her head.

"Nobody's home," she said.

"Good," October said, though the dead kids looked like Christmas had been cancelled. "Now cover any security cameras — Derek will help you find them — and turn off the alarm system."

October dropped a roll of black electrical tape into Derek's open palm and let her dead friends go . . . do their thing. Their thing, such as it was, involved standing on plastic chairs and taping over the camera lenses while Kirby sat in the office and slowly taught himself to learn how to use the school's rather straightforward alarm system. Within ten minutes — enough time for October Schwartz to sing the song "Bullet with Butterfly Wings" twice in her head — the dead kids returned to let October know it was safe to enter the school.

"Great! Open up the office!"

If there were records of the teachers' addresses, October figured, they had to be in the office's filing cabinets. Perhaps they had separate files on each of the school's teachers, just like they had the much-ballyhooed permanent records of all the students. At the very least, they'd have pay stubs for the teachers somewhere, which — in addition to their monthly salaries — should list where they lived. But first, they had to overcome one minor obstacle: the filing cabinets were locked. Or rather, all except two were locked, which contained nothing but office supplies like ballpoint pens and paper clips and a baseball-sized collection of rubber bands.

"All these stupid cabinets are locked!" October shouted, exasperated.

"Don't sweat it," Derek said. "We can use our ghost-lockpicking skills. Which cabinet do you want opened?"

October jogged around to the five filing cabinets placed around the front office to see what the little labels, clearly made by one of those label makers, said.

"This one," she gestured wildly. It read *finance*, so, in her mind, it was sure to contain some teacher addresses.

Derek knelt down in front of the taupe filing cabinet and ghosted his hand through the front, just under the little keyhole, and pushed his hand upwards. His eyebrows pushed together like two caterpillars doing a chest-bump as his fingers fiddled with the tumblers on the other side of the cabinet. The four other dead kids crouched around their friend as he continued to play with the lock.

"This is ghost-lockpicking?" October asked, folding her hands in front of her.

"Yes," Kirby said. "Inside the lock are a bunch of pins at different depths. The notches on a key make those pins push up, simultaneously, so they're flush with a cylinder, and then you can turn the lock, and open the drawer. But Derek's trying to do that now with his fingers . . . without looking at the inside of the lock."

So now, readers, you sort of know how a basic pin-and-tumbler lock works. Who said these books aren't educational?

"Why don't you stick your face in there, Derek?" October asked. "So you can see what you're doing?"

"Too dark inside the cabinet," he answered, and he dug his other hand into the drawer.

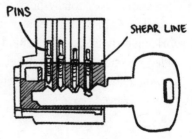

While October waited for the ghost-lockpicking to work, she thought about her history project, which, despite her big talk, she had barely started. Assuming Ms. Fenstermacher wasn't led away in handcuffs before Friday, she'd have to deliver her project. And she was doubtful that solving the mystery of Cyril Cooper's death and/or the ghost pirate's identity would be counted for equivalent credit. She either had to get her history teacher arrested by Friday morning, or pull an all-nighter tomorrow night to finish her stupid project on Cyril Cooper. Typical high school problems, you know?

October's introspection was interrupted by a satisfying click, followed by the thundering sound of metal as Derek rolled the finance cabinet open.

"Derek! You're brilliant!" October shouted and dug into the newly revealed files.

"Yes, a very skilled juvenile delinquent," Kirby said.

Derek smiled broadly, and when he turned to Morna, she quickly averted her eyes.

"What're ye looking for?" she asked, looking at the floor.

October's fingers were flipping through file folders so fast it sound like a colony of bats had flown into the school's offices.

"This," October said, extracting a folder of payment records for all the teachers. She opened it up and found Ms. Fenstermacher's stubs, paper-clipped into a short stack, then wrote down her address on a piece of scrap paper that she'd brought in her coat pocket. "Let's get out of here. Once I'm through the front doors, reset the alarm, and take the tape off the cameras. I want it to look like we were never here."

October strode through the front doors of the school. Dressed in her peacoat, and barking orders like a staff sergeant, she felt more like a totally boss thief or spy than ever before. Kind of like Carmen Sandiego, if she travelled only as far as New Hammersmith. She hid behind the entrance sign again and unfolded the scrap of paper that listed an address on Spindlewood Lane, which she remembered was just a few blocks from where Yumi's family lived.

☠   ☠   ☠

Sticksville is, in general, a town with a lot of houses that appear similar. Variations on a theme. There are a few older houses near the museum and on Turnbull Lane (though those are being demolished one by one), but, in general, they are rectangular houses with triangular roofs, and a number of front-facing windows, the kind of house a child draws when she first learns to draw a house. One of the few exceptions to this rule was the house on Spindlewood Lane where records showed that Ms. Fenstermacher lived. The theme of this house, it seemed, was *how much like a Rubik's cube can we make a house?* The boxy building, missing any sort of real roof, stood out on Spindlewood Lane like a Great Dane standing in a police lineup. However, October Schwartz was not so much concerned about architectural fit as she was in finding evidence of her teacher's ghost piracy.

The distance from the high school to Spindlewood was not inconsiderable, so it was a long walk for October and the dead kids, and it was nearly two o'clock in the morning before they arrived at the house's front door. October almost regretted not taking up Cyril on his offer to take a car from the school's now-infamous auto shop and drive them there, though she'd probably have regretted it more when Cyril's inexpert driving led to an inevitable car accident. The dead kids walked through the front door and unlocked the house from the inside to let October in.

"Be quiet, everyone," October whispered. "Ms. Fenstermacher's probably sleeping and we don't want to wake her."

This was a first. Though October, with the help of her dead friends, had often broken into and entered homes in the course of their investigations they'd never done so when the occupants were inside. This elevated their crime from breaking and entering to the more troubling category of home invasion, which sounded more sinister and likely resulted in stiffer legal penalties. Despite often breaking the law (for only the most pure-hearted reasons), October Schwartz wasn't overly familiar with its ins and outs. If her father ever went on a date with Crown Attorney Salmons again (which was unlikely), perhaps October could make conversation with her by asking about the differences between various crimes and their punishments.

Cyril, Morna, and Tabetha offered to go upstairs, and October asked them to be careful. In essence, to *not* be their usual loud and careless selves. Basically, she wanted the dead kids to do the complete opposite of everything they would normally do in such a situation, so they wouldn't disturb Ms. Fenstermacher. As the three of them tiptoed up the staircase, October, Kirby, and Derek searched around the living room, looking under the couch, in some steamer trunks in the corners. They found nothing. And not just "nothing" as in "stuff that had no connection to the ghost pirate" but as in "absolutely nothing."

"Does this house seem unusually clean to you?" October whispered.

"We live in a graveyard," Kirby said. "Most places seem unusually clean to me."

"There are no magazines or bills strewn around," October said, slowly opening the front hall closet. "There's not even a coat in the front closet."

"Let's check the kitchen," Derek suggested.

The kitchen was also spotless. October couldn't have imagined someone had cooked on the stovetop in two years. The blue countertop of the kitchen island, running down the centre of the room, was also free of clutter, save for a ceramic bowl containing some perfect-looking apples and oranges.

"What kind of evidence are you looking for?" Derek asked, opening a nearly empty fridge.

"Ghost pirate stuff," October whispered, confused by the ultra-clean kitchen. "But first, any evidence that a human being lives here would be good."

"We'll start small," said Kirby.

Something was definitely off in Ms. Fenstermacher's humble (though boxy) abode. Like when you visit a friend's house and it all looks totally normal, but then you realize they have no bookshelves, and also no books, and then you realize your friends are inhuman monsters and have to be shunned. Like that, but spookier because it was the dead of night. Footsteps thundered down the stairs and the remaining three dead kids bounded into the kitchen.

"October," Cyril said, breathless (though he was, strictly speaking, *always* breathless). "The bed upstairs is empty. Your history teacher isn't here. Is it possible she's out for the night?"

October felt like she was in some sort of immersive theatrical production of *Goldilocks and the Three Bears*.

"It's two in the morning on a Wednesday," October said in disbelief.

"I guess we can turn on some lights, then," Kirby said, flipping on the kitchen lights. It only served to highlight how bare it was.

"Yer teacher don't own a lot of stuff," Tabetha mentioned.

"Did you search her closet?" October asked. "Was there a pirate costume or anything?"

"There was almost nothing," Morna said, biting her blue lower lip.

"Check it," Derek said, tossing her an apple from the bowl. It landed in October's combined palms with unbelievable lightness. "This fruit is fake."

October's mind raced like a greyhound on a doggie treadmill. She and the dead kids were searching for evidence to, ideally, put Ms. Fenstermacher in jail, so why did the pit in October's stomach make her feel like she was the one who had walked into a cage?

"Cyril, take me to her bedroom," she said, grabbing the young Loyalist by his neckerchief. "I want to see the closet for myself."

Cyril led her to Ms. Fenstermacher's bedroom, the other dead kids trailing behind. October, first thing, turned on the light and dramatically threw open the closet. It was bare, save for a couple pillows and a folded blanket on a shelf. Bare coat hangers hung like sneakers dangling from telephone wires. She immediately turned to the bedside table and held up the framed photo of an overly attractive blond family.

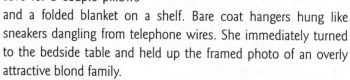

"Ms. Fenstermacher doesn't live here," she announced, tossing

217

the store-bought photo frame onto the bedspread. "No one does. Fake fruit, fake family photos, overly clean. I think someone is trying to sell this house."

Disappointment crawled onto October's shoulders like a short girlfriend attempting to see Limp Bizkit's set at a summer music festival.

"But didn't her file say . . ." Morna started.

"They must be fake. Or wrong," October said.

"I just hope this isn't one of the properties that Alyosha Diamandas is selling," Derek laughed, sitting down on the bed.

The front doorknob rattled, and a whoosh of cold air entered from downstairs.

"Yes? Who is here?" called a voice downstairs, familiar to both October and the dead kids. Like Bloody Mary or Candyman or Beetlejuice before him, Alyosha Diamandas, Sticksville's most sleep-deprived real estate agent, appeared at the mention of his name. He didn't even require it repeated or said into a mirror in the dark. "I saw the lights on from the street, so you should make yourselves known. I have already called the authorities."

"Oh God," October gulped. Diamandas's voice was rimmed with a harsher tone than it usually had. And she'd already been found trespassing on his properties more than once before.

"Hide!" Kirby whispered, and the five dead kids shoved October backward into the bedroom closet and closed the door. "Stay here! We'll get rid of Alyosha."

"Who is there?" the realtor shouted downstairs. "I can hear you, you know. Is it you ghost children?"

If you haven't read the first two books in this series, you might not know that Alyosha Diamandas is one of the few living beings other than October who is pretty certain the dead kids exist. And he kind of despises them, what with them having a multi-year history of breaking into houses he was selling and messing stuff up, making life generally miserable for him. While October was trapped in the closet of not-Ms.-Fenstermacher's room, the dead kids devised a quick scheme to scare Alyosha Diamandas out of the house, being unable (ghost rules and all) to forcibly eject him.

Tabetha and Morna pulled the bedsheet from the bed and draped it over Kirby's body, traditional ghost costume-style, and ripped a couple of holes in the fabric near his face. They guided him to the stairs, around the foot of which Mr. Diamandas was already skulking, with what looked like a flashlight in one hand. Curiously, it was not turned on, perhaps because so many lights had been left on by the dead kids.

Tabetha slapped Kirby hard on the back and said, "Go get him!"

Kirby charged down the stairs toward Alyosha, arms outstretched, doing the best rendition of a demonic growl that he could muster. The dead kids on the second floor hooted and shouted. Diamandas turned to see the anthropomorphic bedsheet barreling toward him and sprayed his flashlight in Kirby's eyeslits. Because it wasn't actually a flashlight. It was a canister of pepper spray. And the spooked realtor unloaded about a shot glass full of spray into Kirby's face.

Though he was dead, and he couldn't quite feel pain the way we living folks do, getting a face full of pepper spray did cause Kirby to cry out in pain as he tripped on the sheet and tumbled down to the bottom of the stairs. Diamandas, sensing other dead kids on the second-floor landing, ran up the stairs after them.

"Ghosts!" he shouted. "I knew they were real!"

The other dead kids abandoned Kirby, crumpled up in a bedsheet below and exited the house through the various walls as Alyosha raced in and out of the rooms on the second floor. Kirby, meanwhile, staggered to his feet and limped out the front door.

October Schwartz, however, waiting in the darkness of the bedroom closet, was unaware of all of this, hearing only shouts and growls and being too afraid of being discovered to open the closet to take a peek. Moments after the most recent and fevered round of shouts, she heard someone enter the bedroom. She hoped it was Cyril or Morna or anyone dead. Anyone dead would be appreciated.

But you readers, having knowledge of the situation that October did not, realize that was not the case. Instead, it was Alyosha Diamandas who entered the master bedroom and, seeing the bed unmade and a framed photo abandoned on the floor, decided to investigate further.

The closet doors opened, and instead of the pale and gaunt faces of the dead kids, the sweaty, balding head of Alyosha Diamandas greeted her. The thin moustache above his mouth twitched as his jaw dropped involuntarily.

"You again?" he said, confused. "But you're not a ghost."

October didn't know what to say. She saw the pepper spray clutched in one of his unusually hairy fists and figured running was a bad choice, so she just shrugged.

"I am afraid I will have to ask you to stay here until the police arrive," he said, then closed the closet doors again.

October didn't have to wait long; she could already hear the cherry top of a police car in the distance.

18

October Is the New Black

No one can ever claim I'm *not* a prodigy, because I had my first arrest and first night in jail at thirteen. So, take that, Doogie Howser, M.D., and, like, current spelling bee champions everywhere. I spent the rest of Wednesday night in the Sticksville police station's jail cell, all by myself. I suppose one bright spot about living in a relatively small town like Sticksville is that I didn't have to share my cell with, like, an angry biker or suspected baseball-bat murderer or something.

Just like in the movies and on TV, the police allowed me a telephone call when I arrived at the station — or, rather, they called my dad because I was a minor, to let him know his only daughter was under arrest. As general life advice, you want to prevent your parents from ever getting a call like that. This was especially true in my case. I often worried that my dad would have to struggle *that* much more with his mental illness due to my, let's say, unpredictable actions. But I also blame that ludicrously unreasonable Alyosha Diamandas who put me behind bars in the first place. He could have easily dropped me off at home like he had those few other times I'd trespassed. Right?

Anyway, I was fingering the scrap of paper that held Ms. Fenstermacher's address, hating myself for being so gullible, when Dad eventually entered the police station around half-past three. Happy was not an emotion that his facial expression could be mistaken for. But before I get to that, I should tell you what had happened with Ms. Fenstermacher's address.

While we both waited for the police to arrive — Mr. Diamandas outside the closet, me inside it — I tried to explain why I was at the house. So I made up some story about pulling a prank on my history teacher, Ms. Fenstermacher, as that sounded a bit less criminal and a bit more believable than that I was going to accuse my history teacher of being a murderous pirate thief.

Diamandas, who was strangely even-keeled for someone who'd stumbled upon a girl and coven of ghosts (or at least one angry sheet) ransacking a house, asked, "What is this teacher's name again?"

"Oh, um, Fenstermacher," I said from the other side of the closet door.

"Yes, this Fenstermacher," he said, "she was part of the couple that was going to buy this house. I had drawn up the contract and the entire thing. I am sorry it didn't work out."

That explained some things. I guess Ms. Fenstermacher must have given the office her address before she moved to Sticksville, and it never got updated.

"Once she and her fiancé split, she decided she didn't need . . . or I guess couldn't afford such a large house. I wish I had not found out it was haunted . . . now. I might have to lower the asking price."

Despite the fact that Ms. Fenstermacher was maybe a terrible ghost pirate, breaking off your engagement just as you start a new job and move to a new town would be rough, no matter who you were. I almost felt bad for her, but then I remembered the multiple times she'd attempted to kill me.

"You know those ghost children?" he asked.

I didn't answer. So Diamandas started knocking on the closet door.

"You still awake in there? You know those ghosts, hey?"

"Ghosts?" I asked, trying to sound as innocent as possible. I figured this would be good practice for my inevitable trial.

"Yes, yes. The ghosts! The one in the sheet. And the other

ones I heard." He started to rant. "The ones who are always breaking in, slowly and surely ruining Alyosha Diamandas's real estate empire."

"I don't know what you're talking about."

That he had started talking about himself in the third person and referring to his Sticksville-based realty company as an "empire" were probably troubling signs. He harrumphed, and then we waited in silence until the police walked in.

Ms. Fenstermacher's heartbreaking romantic life aside, nothing was quite so disheartening as when I thought about the remainder of my life following my dad's arrival at the police station. I knew my detective work was in jeopardy, and it was most likely I would spend the rest of my teen years training to be a nun or air cadet, maybe, once the visual of his goth daughter in the local lock-up sunk into my dad's brain.

"October!" he said, running up to the bars, where I joined him. He took my hands in his, which were a little cold. It was February, and it looked like he'd left the house in too much of a hurry to bring along his gloves or a hat.

"Dad," I said, "I'm really sorry."

Ever since the police placed me in the backseat of a cruiser, I had determined I was going to be tough and not get all emotional about being in jail, but with my dad there, holding my hands, his face wavering between disappointment and total confusion, I couldn't hold it together. My chest started to spasm and I felt my cheeks go clammy with moisture.

"I'm so sorry, Dad," I sobbed.

"Don't cry, pumpkin. Okay?" he said, still holding onto my sweaty hands. "We'll get you out of here."

I noticed with some relief that my dad was not yelling at me about breaking into the house. He never yelled at me that much, but it's not like I had been arrested for no reason whatsoever. Perhaps he was saving the anger for when we got home, away from police officers' judgey eyes and faces.

"You will?" I said, freeing one of my hands to wipe my nose.

"Yes, of course," he said, making a crooked little smile. "At some point tomorrow."

Tomorrow?

"Tomorrow?" I said. Apparently I was going to become even more familiar with my jail cell. My sobbing abruptly stopped. "But what about tonight?"

"The real estate agent, Mr. Diamandas, told the police about your previous break-ins. They view you as a repeat offender," he explained.

This was true, but *I* was the repeatedly offended one, because the police had no proof of my past break-ins, just the creeper Alyosha's word!

"They also said they have security footage of you at the museum on the night of the robbery, and they've yet to apprehend anyone." Dad sighed. "October, I know you didn't rob the museum, but what were you even doing there?"

Disappointing my dad was the worst. I didn't know what to say. "I can explain when we get home, Dad. So pay the bail and let's get out of here."

"Yeah, honey," he said, dropping my hands and turning his attention to the far wall for some reason. "That's a definite problem, because I don't have that much in the bank account right now."

"Dad?"

"I'm going to have to visit the bank tomorrow after work and arrange a loan," he said, now looking toward the ground. "It shouldn't be a problem. I may also talk to . . . um . . . Ms. Salmons to see if there's a way to get the bail amount lowered."

I was a little shocked. Wasn't this what credit cards were for? How could Dad not have enough money to bail me out? I mean, I know he hadn't worked for a little while before we moved to Sticksville because of his breakdown in Markham and whatever, but I didn't think we were in *that* much trouble.

Not so much trouble that he'd have to turn to Crown Attorney Salmons, his partner in a very recent, very bad recent, breakup, for help.

"Oh, uh, I should be fine until then," I said, taking a quick glance at the open toilet at the back wall and feeling appreciative, once again, that I had no cell partner. "Just don't leave me here to rot, Dad."

"Of course not, pumpkin," he said, and he kissed my cheek through the metal bars. "Can I get you anything?"

"I feel like my jailers might frown upon that sort of thing."

"Oh, right," he smiled. "Okay, then stay strong. I'll see you tomorrow afternoon."

Dad left and I started to get paranoid. Of course, it was very possible — likely, even — that we Schwartzes were poorer than I realized, and Dad *couldn't* bail me out tonight. But I also couldn't help wondering if my dad was just really mad at me. Was he trying to punish me by making me spend the night in jail? If that were the case, he probably wouldn't go begging for assistance from Ashlie's mom. Whatever was going on, I felt somehow betrayed or unfairly punished, even if I *did* technically break into somewhere I shouldn't have been. And since I was trapped in this bare cell for another twelve hours at least, I had nothing to do but worry and obsess over what my dad had said and what it *really* meant.

"Why am I even here?" I asked, loud enough so the one police officer on duty, a woman in her thirties whose brown hair was pulled back in a tight bun, could hear me from her desk. "Is this even legal?"

"Probably not," she sneered.

Realizing that I probably wouldn't be able to talk my way out of my dubious incarceration, I asked my not-so-chatty jailer for a pen and some paper. The officer looked suspicious but eventually relented.

"I suppose that would be okay," she said, and handed me a lined pad of paper and one of those black plastic Bic numbers. I mean, it's not like I was arrested for stabbing someone with a writing implement or crafting really incendiary manifestoes,

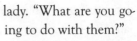

lady. "What are you going to do with them?"

"My history homework."

Since I'd be spending a night in the police station, it was looking unlikely I'd get Ms. Fenstermacher arrested before Friday. That meant I needed a history project and presentation on Cyril Cooper. Unfortunately, doing anything elaborate, like Stacey was planning with his pirate costume, seemed out of the question as I was behind bars. But at least I could write down everything I knew about Cyril. And maybe I could do it in a somewhat interesting way.

TOP TEN THINGS ABOUT CYRIL COOPER:

10) Cyril Cooper shows how Canada's and America's histories are intertwined.

Cyril Cooper and his family fled what is now the United States to what is now Canada during the American Revolution. A number (some even say majority) of residents of the newly formed British colonies decided they didn't like paying taxes to a government in which they had no say. This was just one of the many grievances they held that led to violent revolution to make those thirteen colonies an independent nation. Cyril's parents, hoping to remain British subjects and fearing the wrath of the revolutionaries, ran from their homes in New York to what is now Canada (which was not directly involved in the revolution). Their story is similar to that of many of the British settlers who came to Canada during the Revolutionary War, from 1776 to 1783, and after the war, once the revolutionaries had won. These "Loyalists" came to Canada – especially what is now Ontario and Nova Scotia – in droves as refugees and created English settlements where none had been before. Loyalists who best understood the temper of the times left the thirteen colonies at once, some historians have said, with American revolutionaries like George Washington saying, "Loyalists are only fit for suicide." So, it's safe to say the Coopers were Loyalists who understood the times.

The last bit I remembered from one of the books on Loyalists I'd actually read and researched, but I might have misremembered the quotation.

9) Cyril Cooper is part of Canada's naval history.
The Coopers were shipbuilders. Or, at least, Eustace Cooper, Cyril's father, was. When they first left New York, they travelled immediately to Nova Scotia to continue their work on building ships for the British.

"Psst" came a hiss from the barred window of my cell.

Before even looking to the window, where I assumed one or more of the dead kids would be waiting, I looked to the officer on duty. I could barely see her from where I was, but she was seated at her desk, her face trained on either her computer or her phone screen, playing online poker or something as engaging as that (I hoped), so it seemed safe to talk to the dead kids. I left my pad and pen on the concrete floor and sat on the toilet, just a few paces from the barred window.

"October!" Cyril whispered. "It's us. We are here to break you out of prison."

"I don't want to break out of prison," I whispered, barely believing the words as I spoke them. "I have to do my history project. Besides, this isn't *prison*."

"What?" Tabetha shouted. "We're comin' in."

"No, don't!" I whispered.

It was too late, though, the dead kids walked through the police station wall. My jailer didn't budge, so I guess it was okay the dead kids were with me, as long as I didn't speak too loudly.

"Why don't you want to be broken out of here?" Tabetha demanded.

"I can't just escape from jail," I explained. "That will cause more problems than I have now. Besides, my dad is going to get me out tomorrow. Until then, I'm going to finish this history presentation."

A dead-kid jailbreak would have been awesome, I admit. But it would just lead to a million questions I'd have no idea how to answer once the authorities finally caught me. At my house. Where my dad lives.

"Boooring," Kirby yawned.

"Do you mean the history presentation or me?" Cyril asked.

"Both."

"Let's see what you've done so far," Derek said, getting down on all fours to read the notepad. "I hope you mention how white settlers like Cyril's family displaced the indigenous population who were already living in the United States and Canada."

"Oh," I said, embarrassed. "I was just about to add that." So, I did some editing:

A number (some even say majority) of [white] residents of the newly formed British colonies [stolen from Native Americans] decided they didn't like paying taxes to a government in which they had no say.

"If you really want to help me out," I whispered, "you can help me finish this history report. Especially you, Cyril, since you lived it."

For the next hour and a half, the dead kids sat beside me and helped me frantically write my report. Around 5 a.m., they returned to the cemetery and shortly after that, I nodded off and napped on the cot in the far corner of the cell. But not before using the super-scary toilet. I reasoned it was better to use it with only one very distracted female police officer in attendance, rather than a whole squadron.

☠ ☠ ☠

Around eight thirty, police staff started to arrive at the station and ask questions about me. I spent the day alternating between edits on the Cyril Cooper presentation, which contained more information about witchcraft than I'd have liked, and napping on the cot in the cell. My dad arrived with Crown Attorney Salmons at about four, and my heart flipped up nearly into my windpipe. I might finally get to leave!

My dad, looking even more hangdog and disheveled than usual, stood beside the perfectly put-together Crown attorney (clearly the victor in their breakup), and the two of them discussed a few things that I couldn't hear with two police officers, who began looking more and more worried. I stood right up against the bars, looking for all the world like a puppy in a pet store. A few minutes later, all four adults walked over to my cell and the police officers unlocked the door. I jumped out and swallowed my dad in a hug.

"You're free to go," the police officer said. Without much enthusiasm, I thought.

"Thanks, Dad!" I yelled into his chest. Then, much more professionally, "And thank you, Ms. Salmons. Do I have to appear in court or something in a few weeks?" I'd seen enough *Law & Order* while at home sick to have a general idea of how this all worked.

"Actually, no," my dad interrupted. "And you can thank Cecilia — I mean, *Ms. Salmons* — for that."

"The police had no authority to hold you in the first place. I'll need to have a serious talk with the police chief," she said, holding her briefcase in front of her like it was a barbell. "Additionally, Mr. Diamandas has agreed to drop all charges. And because you're a minor, this incident will not appear on your permanent record."

"Wow, thanks," I said. Either Ashlie's mom still had feelings for my dad, or he had pleaded and promised her his second-born or something. She certainly wouldn't have had any fondness for me, given our past.

"You'll have to thank your math teacher, too," my dad added. "He suspected there was something fishy about keeping you in jail overnight, so he contacted Ms. Salmons as soon as I told him about your situation."

"Mr. Santuzzi?"

Santuzzi's random acts of kindness continued and were some cause for alarm. Was this a debt to be collected by some future favour? Would I be forced, a year from now, to dispose of a body for him or something more sinister: volunteer for the mathletics department?

"School's out for the day, so we should go home," Dad suggested, and I was very amenable to that suggestion. If I never had to spend another minute in a police station again in my life, that would be fine by me. Still, before we left, I decided now was a good time not to be a brat, as I'm sure my legal entanglements were only beginning. It seemed appropriate to show my appreciation to my saviour.

"Ms. — Crown Attorney Salmons." I took her hand and shook it, like we'd just closed some major business merger. "I really, really appreciate this. I know your daughter and I haven't always gotten along and that's caused you some problems, so I'm going to do my best to make it all better. Make it *all* better. Really, thank you."

She looked really confused, like she was shaking hands with a goat that'd been trained to shake a hoof, but I was already out the door and on my way home with Dad. For the first time in months, I was genuinely looking forward to a quiet night at home.

☠   ☠   ☠

In fact, the night *was* spent at home, and not in a cemetery (as per usual), but it wasn't quiet. The main reason for that is that my dad left after dinner, explaining that he was meeting up with Crown Attorney Salmons and Mr. Santuzzi — to take them out for a thank-you coffee. I was sort of offended he didn't want to spend the night helping his only daughter recover from a harrowing night in jail, but part of me was pleased that he'd been spending time with Ashlie's mom. Maybe this intense situation had kindled feelings — just like with Keanu Reeves and Sandra Bullock in *Speed* — or maybe the three of them were plotting a really diabolical punishment for me. Either way, I was happy he felt comfortable to freely leave the house. As a bonus, I was home alone, so I visited the cemetery to invite the dead kids over to help me put the finishing touches on the Cyril Cooper project.

"But what about the *other* Cyril Cooper project?" Cyril Cooper himself asked. "What about finding out how I died?"

The dead kids and I were in the living room, the effect of which was kind of unsettling. The dead kids had been in my bedroom before, and at my school, but not on my couch or easy chair, in the room where Dad and I played Scrabble. Seeing their dead bodies lounging there filled me with unease.

"You guys aren't going to stain the couch, are you? Should I get some Febreze?"

"What's that?" Derek asked.

"It's a spray that, uh, covers terrible odours," I explained.

"Seriously," Kirby sighed. "Have we ever stained anything before? Do we even smell?"

"Actually . . . no."

I hadn't thought about that before. If the dead kids *had* smelled like your typical dead body, I don't think I could have stood being near them long enough to form a detective agency.

"Back to the important question," Cyril said. "What about my mystery?"

"I'm getting to that, Cyril. But this presentation is due to-morrow, and I still have you dead kids around to help me solve this mystery for nearly a week after that."

"How did your dad feel about yer time in jail?" Morna asked. Finally, someone interested in *my* feelings.

"He was strangely relaxed," I said, "but I'm worried. He seems okay about it now, but I feel within days, he's going to ship me off to a boarding school or something. Or he would if we had any money. Which means we should solve Cyril's mystery ASAP . . . after my presentation. This must be the calm before the storm. Once Dad's brain recovers, I'm dead."

"Like us?"

"Not quite."

"And what do you suggest?" Kirby asked, perched between pillows on the couch like a Roman emperor. (They liked pillows, didn't they?)

"We can start Friday just as night falls. We should confront Ms. Fenstermacher at the Sticksville Museum," I said. "Show her we found the letters, that we know she's the ghost pirate — make her confess."

"Your dad's going to let you go out after school?" Derek asked.

"He's kind of limited me to just school and home after what happened," I said. "But I'm already fried. Jumping curfew one more night is like putting a drop of water into the ocean of disobedience."

"What if she doesn't confess?" Tabetha asked.

"We have to try."

"Okay, what else?" Kirby said.

"I could really use something extra for this history presentation."

The dead kids groaned and fell back where they were seated. "Come on!"

"Some of the other students are getting *way* elaborate," I complained. "They're making costumes . . . One girl wrote a song about Marilyn Bell, the first person to swim across Lake Ontario, to the tune of 'Highway to Hell.'"

"What do you want us t'do about it?" Tabetha said, driving her fist into a puffed-out cheek.

"Ye could do a seance with Cyril," Morna said. "Ask him questions wi'that Ouija board in class an' get him t'answer."

"No," I sighed. "Class is during the daytime, and what if someone in my class can actually see ghosts?"

"I could draw a picture of Cyril!" Derek said.

"What do you mean?"

"I'm pretty good at drawing. I mean, I drew the cartoon on your —" Derek shut his mouth abruptly.

"She is aware of your work on the card, Derek," Cyril confessed.

"So then you know I'm pretty good," Derek said. "Give me a pencil and a big sheet of paper, then you'll have at least one visual aid for your presentation."

"Okay!"

As far as value-adds to school projects go, a drawing of the subject wasn't much, but in this eleventh hour, it would have to do. At the very least, it would separate me from the herd of kids who'd just paraphrased Wikipedia and increased the font size to fill out their report. I just hoped Derek was as good an illustrator as he boasted. I ran to my room to retrieve a pencil, pencil sharpener, and the biggest sheet of paper I could find. When I returned to the living room, Derek was posing Cyril in the easy chair.

"Hat on or off?" he asked me.

"On."

"Okay," Derek said, "now tilt your head slightly to the right, Cyril."

I passed the supplies to Derek and noticed Tabetha studying the weird German needlepoint on the wall.

"Too bad y'don't know how ta do this," she said, thumbing at the sewn sampler. "A needlepoint portrait of ol' Cyril would be pretty impressive."

"What is that, anyway?" Derek asked, putting pencil to paper.

I started to explain how I wasn't really sure, how it was in German and had been a family heirloom of my mom's, and how, a while ago, Ms. Fenstermacher helped me translate it and —

"Holy smokes!" I said. "Fairfax Crisparkle!"

"Who?" Derek asked.

"Why did you say that name?" Cyril asked.

"Don't move," Derek admonished.

"You know that name?" I asked Cyril.

Cyril, under strict orders not to move while being drawn, nodded vigorously in the tiniest way possible.

I started for my room again until I remembered that my *Two Knives, One Thousand Demons* book, along with my back-pack and everything else of relevance to this mystery, had been stolen by some stupid pirate. That included, now, the transla-tion of this needlepoint.

"I forget the *exact* translation, but this weird needlepoint basically says this house belongs to a member of Asphodel Meadows and pal of Fairfax Crisparkle."

"An' who is that?" Morna asked.

"According to Ms. Fenstermacher, a Sticksvillian who lived a long time ago and was thought to be a witch. And someone that Skyler McGriff kept mentioning when he was trying to kill me with a baseball bat."

Cyril's face had gone pale — well, *paler* — and his mouth swerved downward into a terrible frown.

"Try to smile a little," Derek said, obviously not cottoning on to what the rest of us had moments ago. "What?"

"I remember Fairfax Crisparkle now," Cyril said, his face gravely serious.

"Wait," I said, having a horrible realization that I could have solved this mystery a whole lot earlier if I'd only believed in magic. "Were you and Fairfax Crisparkle alive at the same time?"

Everyone was looking at Cyril, and Cyril wasn't looking in any one direction. He seemed to be staring through the house's walls, to his tombstone in the cemetery beyond.

"I think I know who killed you, Cyril, and for some reason, my history teacher is trying to protect him. Though he must have died hundreds of years ago."

"Must he have?" Cyril said. "He is a witch! He bound my arms and legs with invisible forces. What's to say he couldn't live for hundreds of years?"

"That's not possible," I said.

"Isn't it?" he stood up, no longer content to stand for the portrait.

"We have seen that 'Asphodel Meadows' everywhere," Derek said. "They must be connected, right?"

"This is getting ridiculous," Kirby said. "Magic? Immortal witches?"

But before the argument could heat any further, bright lights flooded the living room and an engine growled outside.

"That's my dad," I shouted. "Scoot! This conversation is to be continued. Meet me at the museum at seven tomorrow."

The dead kids ghosted through the back wall, leaving behind a mostly finished (and pretty accurate) portrait of Cyril Cooper, victim of Sticksville witch Fairfax Crisparkle.

Stand and Deliver

One would think, having determined the identity of both Cyril's eighteenth-century killer and the dread ghost pirate, that this mystery was almost completely solved, but rest assured that solving mysteries, like life and crossword puzzles, is never as easy as one would hope. And before October could enact her proverbial *Scooby-Doo* finale of unmasking the pirate and revealing a crotchety not-that-old history teacher who would have got away with it if it hadn't have been for those meddling dead kids, she still had to deliver her final presentation.

But first, she had to (a) get to school and (b) survive just one more day of school. Action (a) was managed without much difficulty. Despite her now public penchant for breaking into homes, October was allowed to walk unescorted to the high school that Friday morning. There was a minor hiccup when small snow flurries threatened the dryness of the rolled-up paper that held Cyril Cooper's portraiture, so October spent much of her stroll wiping snowflakes off the drawing with her mitten. Action (b), however, remained in question. Surviving a day of school in Sticksville should have been relatively easy. It's not like October went to that high school in *Battle Royale* or even the one in *Dangerous Minds*. But she was convinced her history teacher was trying to kill her. And that homicidal impulse of hers would probably only heighten once she heard October's presentation.

Any question October had about whether her classmates knew she'd been temporarily incarcerated was answered the moment she entered Sticksville Central's front doors.

"What's up, jailbird?" asked some guy with massive headphones she'd never seen before.

"Um, nothing," October said, probably because *too much*, really, was up.

Seconds later, she did encounter someone she knew, but also someone she really didn't want to see: Ashlie Salmons.

"Zombie Tramp, hardened criminal," Ashlie announced, her books under one arm. For this grey winter day, she wore a muted black dress and grey leggings. "I never thought I'd see the day. What were you in for?"

"Shot a man in Reno. Wanted to watch him die. That kind of thing."

"I'm sure," she said. "As much as it would have been good to have you in jail for the rest of the semester, I did miss seeing your ugly moon face around here. It's no fun tormenting some of these other wastebots. They mostly just cry and run away."

October tried to remember her promise — more like vague offer — to Crown Attorney Salmons to try to get along with Ashlie. In a perverse way, that was Ashlie paying her a compliment.

"Thank you, Ashlie," she said through clenched teeth. "Your mother is a good woman and was instrumental in my release."

"Uh, okay, *freak*," she said, clearly disoriented by October's overly earnest response. Not wanting to subject herself to any further gratitude from her usual tormentee, Ashlie hurried down the English hall.

October Schwartz's pre-class morning journey also took her past Yumi Takeshi's locker, where she and Stacey were holding, of all things, a peanut-butter jar full of money. Change, mostly, but a few five-dollar bills and even one or two tens filled the plastic container.

"You've been freed!" Yumi shouted, handing the jar off to Stacey and attacking October with a bear hug. Somehow, she managed to actually lift October off the floor.

"Nice to see you back," Stacey said, then awkwardly smiled

and looked at the jar. Stacey never quite got the hang of human emotions.

"What's that?" October asked, freeing one hand from Yumi's death-grip embrace to point at the jar.

"This is the October Schwartz get-out-of-jail fund," Stacey said, jingling the loonies and toonies inside the plastic jar.

"We held a miniature drive to pay for your bail yesterday," Yumi said, letting October loose. "We didn't raise nearly enough, but I guess you can keep it now."

"That's so sweet."

"We're way sweet," Stacey said.

"People other than you and Stacey donated money to get me out of jail?" October asked. The Valentine's dance hadn't been so long ago. She remembered how nearly everyone had sold her out.

"Well, not quite . . ." Stacey said.

"We made up a girl and said she had lupus," Yumi admitted. "We figured we'd get more donations that way."

Depressing as this was, you had to admire October's friends' marketing savvy.

"What was the girl's name?" October asked.

"Lucy."

"We thought the alliteration was catchy," Yumi added. "*Help Lucy Fight Lupus* made a good sign."

"Thanks . . . I guess."

October wondered about the ethics of taking this money, when a boy wearing a grey sweater vest over a blue gingham shirt jogged up to them, holding his wallet out.

"You're the ones raising money for Lucy, right?" he asked, adjusting his glasses with his free hand. "I couldn't find you yesterday. Here's five dollars."

He held the blue bill in front of him like a soccer referee presenting a yellow card. Or red card. Referees present the two cards in much the same way.

"Help Lucy fight lupus, right?" he said, confused by the silence and interminable pause since he'd offered his five dollars.

"Listen," October said. "You seem like a nice guy, but you

239

should know that there is no Lucy with lupus. At least, not at this school. My friends here were trying to raise money to bail me out of jail, and they figured the school would be more keen to help out a completely fictional lupus victim than me."

Her friends, upon revelation of the hoax, turned to look deeply into Yumi's open locker. They'd do anything not to face this new donor.

"Oh, well, that's fine," the boy said, still holding out Mr. Wilfrid Laurier. "Anyway, you can still have the five dollars, if you had to be bailed out of jail."

"Really?" October said.

"Yeah. You're the girl that pirate was trying to kill, right?"

"That's me," October answered, a stupid grin across her face.

"Enjoy life outside the joint," he insisted, pressing the folded five into October's palm, then retreating down the hallway in the direction he'd come.

"Thanks . . ."

"Henry," he said, anticipating her question. "Henry Khan."

October put the five into the jar, leaving Henry Khan — generous donor and the love match to an all-B answer set — as a mystery to investigate at a later date (which may or may not be a euphemism).

"Here, you hold onto this," October said, handing the jar back to Yumi. "I don't know what to do with it. And I have to drop my stuff off in my locker before French class."

A little bit ungrateful, one would think, October left her enterprising friends to visit her locker. While French was her first class of the day, all she was really thinking about was her history presentation. Nothing else mattered at school — nothing else mattered that day — but history class.

☠   ☠   ☠

The arms of every single wall clock in Sticksville Central moved as if encased in rust or operated by tree sloths that hid behind the wall, turning the gears of the clockworks. Obviously, neither was the case, as the clocks were plastic, which doesn't rust, and tree sloths are notoriously difficult to train. What we're getting at is the day moved quite slowly for October, who was wired by a lack of sleep and a nervous energy about her history presentation in front of Ms. Fenstermacher. So her classes with Mr. Martz, her sometime-ally Mr. Santuzzi, and Mrs. Tischmann felt about as long and unnecessary as the extended cuts of the Lord of the Rings movies.

Finally, history class arrived, and Ms. Fenstermacher started announcing presentation order immediately after the bell sounded.

"All right, who's frakking excited about these final history presentations?" she shouted, rolling up the sleeves of yet another plaid cowboy shirt. Now that October was fully convinced Ms. Fenstermacher was the ghost pirate who made her life so difficult, she was irritated by her every single character trait: her hip thick-frammed glasses, her anachronistic obsession with *Battlestar Galactica* (which had almost nothing to do with history), her shirts.

The class let out a smattering of applause. They were *almost* frakking excited, it would seem.

"We won't get to all of your presentations today, I'm afraid," she said. "But you all need to hand in your written reports at the end of the class." Ms. Fenstermacher said Ahmal Wheaton would go first, then listed a few more names. October's name was the fourth one she'd listed. She would undoubtedly present this afternoon.

Midway through Ahmal's presentation on Fred "Cyclone" Taylor, October's father, known to some of the other kids in class as science teacher and volleyball coach Mr. Schwartz, quietly entered and snuck into an empty chair at the back of the room. Fred "Cyclone" Taylor was — history time! — the first immigration officer to meet the *Komagata Maru*, a ship of Hindu, Muslim, and Sikh immigrants who were not allowed to land in Vancouver back in 1914. He also happened to be one of the first hockey stars. But that's a story for another book. October, realizing she should probably be appreciative that her dad cared enough to see her presentation, was instead mortified. Having her dad as a spectator was going to make her subtle confrontation-through-oral-report with Ms. Fenstermacher all the more awkward. October was slowly adjusting to the notion that nothing ever, ever went right in her investigations. She took deep breaths and avoided looking behind her at her father.

When applause had died down for the third presenter and Ms. Fenstermacher called "October Schwartz," October walked to the front of the room with a rolled-up paper under one arm, and her other hand clutching a series of index cards. She stood in front of the blackboard and brushed away a hank of black hair from her eyes with an index card.

"Ex-con!" someone coughed. At which her father frowned.

"Settle down, settle down," Ms. Fenstermacher said, as if people were just getting way too excited about October's presentation. "October, you can begin."

"Sure," October said. One more deep breath. "I'd like to tell you all about one of Sticksville's first residents. Uh, first *white* residents," she corrected, remembering Derek's words. "Cyril Cooper."

With a flourish worthy of a Las Vegas magician, she unfurled Derek's portrait. The class audibly *ooohed*. (It was a very good portrait. Derek was not prevaricating when he claimed he could draw.)

"Cyril Cooper was not only one of the original residents of British background to live in Sticksville, he was also probably Sticksville's first murder victim."

The class sucked in oxygen in unison. October was actually, awkwardness aside, quite good at this. She held the class, Fenstermacher seemingly included, wrapped around her stubby, black-nail-polished finger.

"What will follow are ten fascinating things about the life and times of Cyril Cooper, the final such thing being his mysterious and unsolved death."

You could practically hear the theme song of *Unsolved Mysteries*, hosted by Robert Stack, begin.

"And if that final entry about Cyril's untimely death seems a bit thin or poorly researched, it's only because my research was blocked at every turn by a . . . wait for it . . . *ghost pirate*."

That was it. Everyone in the history class was on board now. Murder? Ghost pirates? If October could somehow manage to fit in something about dinosaurs with machine guns mounted on their skulls, she probably could have been unanimously elected valedictorian.

"For this ghost pirate stole valuable historical information from the Sticksville Museum and the library, as well as, I strongly suspect, set fire to the *Kingfisher*, a ship that Cyril Cooper's father helped to build. But despite the ghost pirate's efforts, I am confident I have managed to solve Cyril Cooper's murder."

Chatter arose in the classroom. Clearly, this was no pedestrian report on some historic nobody. October continued her report, going through her "Top Ten Things About Cyril Cooper." But as she cycled closer and closer to Thing #1, the presentation verged closer and closer to a court case. At times, it felt like October was a Crown attorney herself, presenting the case against Fairfax Crisparkle, Sticksville witch and (maybe?) American spy, though

October wasn't overly clear on that part. Ten minutes later, once she'd finished her presentation, the class actually applauded. And real, genuine applause, too, like the kind found in the final scene of a teen movie. Spontaneous and heartfelt.

October didn't really know how to feel. Nobody had ever applauded anything she'd done before, except Yumi and Stacey, or facetiously, like when she dropped her tray in the cafeteria that one time. Everyone seemed to really enjoy the presentation. Even Ms. Fenstermacher, who October thought would have hated it because it exposed her dark puppet master (or whatever), Fairfax Crisparkle. Somehow, October was going to ace history with a final project largely written on the floor of a police holding cell.

Ms. Fenstermacher did, however, have one significant misgiving. "That was an excellent presentation, October. However, do you really feel you can blame Cyril Cooper's death on witchcraft? Throughout North America's early colonial period, reported cases of witchcraft have largely — almost universally — been dismissed and disproven as mass hysteria, fed by prejudice against outsiders and women. Do you really think this Crisparkle was an actual witch with magical powers?"

October wanted to scream. It was Ms. Fenstermacher who told her about Crisparkle's witchy reputation in the first place! She also wanted to tell her how Cyril himself had said he'd been bound by invisible ropes or chains, but she doubted that would be a good idea. Was this just the ghost pirate's clever way of undermining her after that big ovation?

"I don't know, but with all ghost pirates and burning clipper ships going around in Sticksville right now, I'd say stranger — or *as* strange — things have happened. Besides, whether he had magic powers or not," October conclusively concluded, "Fairfax Crisparkle killed the Cooper boy, I'm sure of it."

"Well then," Ms. Fenstermacher said, an inscrutable little smile on her face, "thank you for a rousing presentation."

October's dad snuck back out of the class as Ms. Fenstermacher announced the next student presenter, so he didn't hear what Tanya Devonshire or any of the other students who followed her had to say, but I'll be honest: he didn't miss much. And though

October sat through all the remaining presentations, she wasn't able to pay much attention to them. Instead, she was feeling a mix of profound gratitude and extreme worry.

She was thankful that her father hadn't hugged her or exclaimed, "My baby girl!" or done something equally embarrassing. But she was also worried about that question Ms. Fenstermacher asked and her smile afterward. *What did it mean?*, October wondered. Would she have to watch her back as she left class today?

As it turned out, the only reason she had to watch her back as she left class was that her father eventually did that embarrassing dad thing. At least he waited until the school day was over, but he eventually did give his daughter a hug.

"I admit," he said, "I was planning a pretty serious grounding for you after you ended up in jail, but I'm really proud of you after seeing that history presentation."

"So proud you might not ground me at all?" October hoped aloud.

"Not *that* proud," he said, releasing October. "But maybe I could cut it down to a week."

"Tough but fair," October said. "But can I start it next week? I really need to see Yumi tonight."

"October . . ."

"I'll be back by ten," she said. "I have to talk to Yumi about jail."

"It wasn't really —"

"Please, Dad?"

Mr. Schwartz switched his grimace from one side of his face to the other, then back again. "Okay, but only because that presentation was so good. And I want you back by ten."

"Thanks, Dad," October chirped, which is something she almost never does, and kissed him on the cheek.

In all likelihood, she could confront Ms. Fenstermacher with the dead kids, get her arrested, and be back home by ten. That was possible. But everything needed to go smoothly. Given the Dead Kid Detective Agency's track record, October might have been in for more than a week's grounding. That is, if she survived the rest of the night at all.

You Can't Spell "Conspiracy" without "Piracy"

If I hadn't been so worried last night about my dad finding the dead kids and me hanging out in the living room, I could have planned things better. I'd panicked and told them to meet me at the Sticksville Museum, but a few hours before our scheduled pre-shakedown meet-up, I regretted not making plans to meet at the cemetery. You know, so the dead kids could help me bring supplies. A few mysteries in, I knew that rope, for instance, is always handy. You can never have enough rope. Just after nightfall, the dead kids were going to meet me at the Sticksville Museum to confront ghost pirate, history teacher, and *Battlestar* enthusiast, Ms. Fenstermacher when she'd likely be alone, and they were not going to bring that rope I now so desperately wanted.

When Dad left my locker bay to do his post-school rituals of marking, checking email, and whatever else he did, I put on my coat and mittens as quickly as I could and ran all the way home. Before Dad arrived, I needed to find some sort of weapon and leave for Yumi's. It wouldn't have been very helpful to have my dad walking in on me as I scoured the house for the best melee weapon. See, I had done this sort of thing before — twice now, I had gone to confront some culprit and both times I'd arrived completely unarmed and was taken surprised by a madman who was completely armed, with a rifle or baseball bat. Like the guys and gals on *CSI: Miami*, I wasn't going to get fooled again.

At home, I started in the kitchen. My first instinct was to grab a steak knife or something like that, but I worried I wouldn't be able to carry it without stabbing myself. I just knew I was as likely to cut myself open by accident on my way to the museum as fend off Ms. Fenstermacher. Still, there were other, less pointy objects in the kitchen that could be of use. I tried out the rolling pin but it made it look like I was living in a *Tom and Jerry* cartoon. My next stop was the garage. A tire iron or crowbar would be ideal.

Our garage was disappointingly bare of blunt automotive tools. Since Dad was sometimes the auto shop teacher, he'd taken most of the mechanic tools he owned and brought them to school. I'd forgotten about that. Lousy budget cuts were taking the most ideal weapons away from me. I also now had two shovels, but they were a bit heavy and impossible to conceal. However, the garage also contained, in addition to Rubbermaid containers of jigsaw puzzles and old school work, a little bit of sports equipment, which is how I found the croquet mallet.

I can't remember why we ever had a croquet set: neither Dad nor I could ever be considered posh. Maybe I once forced him to play-act scenes from *Heathers* with me? In any event, I was grateful to find the set. The mallets made the perfect weapon for a thirteen-year-old of limited strength and athletic ability. It was like a little wooden, play sledgehammer: conceivably, it could break someone's nose, but I could also lift and swing it without needing an asthma puffer immediately after. And if I held the hammer end just on top of my shoulder and slid the handle down my arm, into my palm, I could conceal the mallet in the sleeve of my coat. Thank you, Victorian aristocrats or whoever invented croquet, because you may have saved my life tonight.

I checked the clock on the microwave: 3:45. With my cro-quet mallet tucked in my coat, I turned to leave for Yumi's to kill some time until seven, when the museum would be closing for the evening.

On my way out the door, the phone rang. Against my bet-ter judgment, I picked it up.

"Hello. Schwartz residence?"

But somewhere, the telephone was still ringing. Which was when I recognized the ring. It wasn't our telephone; it was the old telephone, from Morna's old boarding house. I ran to my room so quickly, the mallet fell out of my coat and nearly tripped me up.

"Hello, this is October," I almost shouted into the phone, like I'd won a radio contest or something.

"Be careful," the woman's voice rasped.

"Mom?" I said. "Mom, is that you? How do you know what's happening?"

But the voice refused to answer, and my frustration with the thing just about hit its limit. Seriously. Stupid phone. If you *are* my mother, why are you trying to make me super emotional when I'm about to confront the person who's been trying to kill me? Why are you never around when I need you? In many ways, I kind of wished I was wrong and it wasn't my mother at the other end of the phone. But I couldn't worry about that now. I had girl talk to accomplish and (possibly) a history teach-er to brain. If I survived it all, I might seriously just throw the telephone into the river or something more dramatic. Set it on fire and shoot it from a T-shirt cannon into the garbage dump. As much as I wanted to know my mom, I couldn't take much more of the phone's head games.

☠   ☠   ☠

There wasn't much girl talk to be had at Yumi's, unless you're talking about the board game Girl Talk, in which you try to find which boy likes you by calling a series of boys on a special glam game phone. In which case, there was none of that, either.

(Tragically.) Mostly, we talked about the episode of *Twin Peaks* we were sort of watching and whether we thought we would ever like coffee more than Diet Coke and how Kyle MacLachlan used to be so supernaturally handsome.

The actual girl talk intruded when I forced the issue and asked Yumi directly about Stacey. In a super awkward way, too, like:

"So what's going on with you and Stacey?"

"I don't know," Yumi said, chewing on a black Twizzler. "I think my crush may have been half baked. Like I got sucked into Valentine's Day hype. After dancing with him, I just didn't feel it anymore."

"Maybe there really is a spark or something between people. Like in a romance novel," I said.

Yumi gave me the side-eye.

"Fine. I don't care. Makes my life easier if I'm not your third wheel."

"Let's just get back to *Twin Peaks*," Yumi said. "Agent Dale Cooper is looking murder."

"Are you still trying to make *murder* happen, Yumi?"

☠   ☠   ☠

The dead kids were on time, waiting for me when I arrived at the Sticksville Museum at seven. The end of the street was extremely dark, and the light from inside the museum was the only thing illuminating our general area.

"Big night," Kirby said, rubbing his palms together.

"Yeah," I said, "and it could get hairy. So even though you technically can't hurt Ms. Fenstermacher, I want us to try something."

"What?" asked Tabetha.

"I want the five of you to follow me, but hide around the corner. When I start talking to my teacher, I want you to surround her and link your arms. Just like a standing seance."

"What's a standing seance?"

"Just link your arms!" I said. "Make a pentagon that she

can't escape from. She's going to lie about things and she might try to run. Don't let her out of the pentagon!"

"This plan would sound way better if we called it the *pentagram*," Derek said.

"That's not the same shape," I said. "You should be like a human rope to confine her. Okay? Just be ready to make the pentagon when we start talking. And don't break it, no matter what lies she tells."

Closing time for the Sticksville Museum had already passed, so there wasn't much more time to waste. While I strode to the museum's front doors, the dead kids snuck around the side of the building and ghosted through the wall.

At the end of the front hall, it was not Ms. Fenstermacher, but the older docent, Mrs. Crookshanks — the one who'd subbed for my dad during his most recent depressive episode — sitting behind the information desk, her head down, immersed in some Sudoku.

"Sorry, we're closing," she said, when she heard me come in. Then she tilted her head to meet my eyes. "Oh, it's the little vampire girl. Miss Schwartz, right?"

I don't know if the constant zombie or vampire cracks were worse. Honestly, lady, goth has been around since the 1970s. It's not new.

"Yes. October," I said anyway, even though she was on my last nerve and I had a croquet mallet concealed in my coat sleeve.

"How's your father doing?" she asked.

"Much better, thanks. He's fine," I said, realizing how awkward this all was. After all, the longer my dad had been too depressed to work, the longer Mrs. Crookshanks had a sweet teaching job. But whatever. She called me little vampire girl. I couldn't care less about her job prospects.

"Well, even though we know each other, I still can't let you in. It *is* closing time."

"That's okay, I just wanted to talk to —"

Ms. Fenstermacher descended from the upper floor of the Cooper House and looked surprised to see me. (As *if* she

251

didn't know this confrontation was looming after that history presentation.)

"October," she said, "I'm surprised to see you here on a Friday night. I feel like after today's presentation, you could apply for a job here."

"I'll just leave you to it," the older museum worker said. She slid on her coat and left through the front hallway.

"Bye, Roberta," Ms. Fenstermacher called after her. "October, what can I do for you?"

From the corner of my right eye, I could see the dead kids huddled around the Black History display, which was looking sadder than usual after the ghost pirate's — or should I say, Ms. Fenstermacher's — theft. I subtly nodded, and the dead kids, invisible to her eyes, surrounded her in a circle (not a pentagon, I guess) and held hands. It looked like a really personal game of Red Rover was about to start.

"Brrr. It's cold in here," Ms. Fenstermacher noted. "Crookshanks must have turned the thermostat down when she closed up."

"You can drop the small talk, Ms. Fenstermacher," I said. "You know why I'm here."

"I do?" she said.

"I know you're the ghost pirate. I know you've been trying to kill me and have been stealing Sticksville's historic treasures."

"What are you talking about, October?" she said, panic creeping into her voice. "That's insane."

"Is it?" I asked, and ran for the staff washroom.

Ms. Fenstermacher moved to follow me, but she was clotheslined in her gut by Tabetha and Kirby's linked arms.

"What was that?" she said, panicking more. "Why can't I move? What's happening here?!"

By the time I returned with the Ziploc bag of the Cooper family letters, she was pawing the air like a terrible mime, frantically trying to break through the invisible force field around her. Cyril got a face-full of Ms. Fenstermacher's hands. He shot me a dirty look when her fingers rammed up his nose.

"Stop that," I said, throwing the bag to her feet. "Look at this."

She crouched and opened the bag. "The Cooper family correspondence? Where did you find it?"

"The toilet tank. They never left the museum," I said. "Probably like the rest of the stolen goods."

"October, I don't know what this is . . ."

My heart was now beating in my chest so quickly, it reminded me of when our gas-powered lawnmower would kick-start. Could my plan be working? And if it did totally work, was I going to have to club my teacher with a croquet mallet? I slowly lowered the mallet from my coat sleeve and hid it behind my back.

"For some reason, you're trying to hide what happened to Cyril Cooper and protect that witch, Fairfax Crisparkle. Why? Why, Ms. Fenstermacher?" I swear, I really wasn't trying to yell.

"October, you're talking crazy," she said, trying to move toward me again but was stopped by a lap bar made of Tabetha and Cyril's arms. "Nothing makes sense right now. Why can't I move?"

"If you're not the ghost pirate, then what was that smile in class about?"

"That smile in class?" She cough-laughed. "I smiled because I *like* you, October. You have great confidence. You're incredibly self-possessed. Especially given that you're a year younger than your classmates. That was a stellar presentation, October. Though now I'm beginning to think you may have too *much* confidence."

"Then where were you at the Valentine's dance when the ghost pirate showed up?" I asked, moving closer, my fingers polishing the handle of the croquet mallet. "Nobody could find you. Not even Mr. Santuzzi. He can find a student playing hooky from a floor away!"

"I was in the washroom on the phone with my mother," she said. "My father's quite ill. He was about to go in for surgery. It was a difficult — I don't have to explain myself . . . I didn't want to chaperone the dance that night. I can show you the phone record!"

Ms. Fenstermacher frantically pulled her flip phone from her jeans pocket and held it out for me.

"Please let me go," she cried. "How are you doing this?"

"So, you're . . . *not* the ghost pirate?" I said, feeling suddenly very unsure of everything. She was giving me her phone. I started to back away, trying to stuff the croquet mallet back into my coat sleeve.

"Don't let her out," Cyril whispered to the other members of the pentagon.

"October, are *you* a witch?"

"Who, me?" I said. Nervousness was setting in. What was I doing? I'd threatened my teacher. I'd be in prison until I was an old woman in my thirties.

"What's that behind your back?" she asked, leaning into Kirby's chubby outstretched arm.

"Ha, what? Nothing," I said, backing up further. *Please don't drop the croquet mallet, please don't drop the croquet mallet, please don't drop the croquet mallet.*

My mantra about keeping a firm, concealed grip on the croquet mallet was then interrupted. A massive crash of broken glass — like the explosion of a high-pitched bomb — screamed into the lobby. Then, before I could realize what had happened, Ms. Fenstermacher dropped to the floor like a puppet whose strings had been cut (and the puppet had then been spiked on the ground). A brick lay beside her head.

"Ms. Fenstermacher!" I yelled and rushed over to her unconscious body. This was all my fault. All my fault. "Break the pentagon! No more pentagon!"

The dead kids broke their circle to let me in and crouch beside her.

"What happened?" Morna shouted.

"Who threw that brick?" Kirby asked.

"How do I check her pulse?" I shouted.

Derek touched Ms. Fenstermacher's neck and wrist. "She's still breathing."

For a brief moment, relief washed over me, like a glass of water on a new sunburn. But seconds later, the relief evaporated like I'd just put on a sandpaper shirt. I felt the lacquered wood of the croquet mallet pulled under my chin, bruising the soft part of my throat. I could just barely see the blue stripes of the hammer to my right. I'd dropped it when I rushed to check on Ms. Fenstermacher.

Hot breath tickled my ear, and it was Mrs. Crookshanks's voice that announced, "You're coming with me, October."

Then I felt a damp rag pressed against my face. There was no way I was getting home before ten.

☠   ☠   ☠

21

The Plank Generation

As if you didn't already know, that damp rag was quite drenched in chloroform, a kidnapper's best friend (as kidnappers tend to have few real human friends), and it put October out cold. And as if you *also* didn't already know, our nearly forgettable docent and substitute teacher, Mrs. Crookshanks, was the ghost pirate. After all, she, too, is a museum employee. And apparently owns a Hawaiian shirt. Who knew? We'd all pegged her as more of a Christmas sweater type of lady, hadn't we?

When October finally came to, she realized her arms and legs were bound. Again. Another month, another situation in which October Schwartz was tied up by some villain. She also noticed, by the smell and air, that she was on the water and, in fact, on the deck of a boat, but a much more modern boat than the last one she'd been on. The dead kids, however, were nowhere to be seen, which wasn't reassuring. The last time she'd been kidnapped and bound by a criminal, October had awoken to the friendly, though corpse-like faces of Morna, Cyril, and Tabetha. All she could see this time was the damp wooden deck, its puddles of water already morphing to ice, and her crystallized breath in the dark clear sky. Understandably, she started to hyperventilate. Can one develop asthma through repeated stress?

Perhaps beckoned by the golden-retriever-like panting of our heroine, Mrs. Crookshanks emerged from the lower deck of the boat, clad in a brown fur coat. Like we didn't already think she was villainous enough. What had she planned next, to light an unfiltered cigarette on an orphan's dried skull?

"Mrs. Crookshanks?" October asked. The woman was definitely Mrs. Crookshanks, but October's eyes were still adjusting to the darkness out on the river, and the small silver-haired woman looked more like Dr. Zaius from *The Planet of the Apes* than a substitute science teacher.

"Yes, it's me," she said. "Though you may also know me as the ghost pirate. Welcome to my boat."

"Wait," October said, squirming up into a seated position. "You own this boat?"

"You might have seen it right next to the *Garage Sail* in the marina? How else do you think I knew when you were on the *Kingfisher*? How else would I have known when to set the fire?"

October was, of course, alarmed. And a little perplexed as to how Mrs. Crookshanks afforded a boat on a substitute teacher and retiree's limited income. Worse, she was unable to move and was face to face with a woman who thought almost nothing of burning a teenage girl alive.

"You must really hate history," October mumbled, not really knowing what else to say.

"I don't think so."

"Then why do all this?" October felt the cold suffuse her limbs. Mrs. Crookshanks had removed October's coat to tie her up and her black hoodie wasn't much help out on the river. "Why are you trying to kill me? And to prevent me from finding out anything about Cyril Cooper?"

Mrs. Crookshanks crouched down in front of her bound victim and jabbed her index finger toward October, who reflexively flinched.

"I've been onto you, girl. Ever since you walked into the museum," she seethed. "Asking questions about the Crooked Arms. About the MacIsaac family. You didn't think I knew what you were up to?"

October was, genuinely, bewildered. She knew what she was up to — solving the murders of her five dead friends — but she had no idea what that had to do with this unhinged museum docent.

"And Schlangegriff? Could you be more obvious?" Crookshanks yelled, getting to her feet. "Once I realized what you were doing, as a servant of the Dark One, I couldn't let you continue."

"Dark One?" October said. The nickname was coming up far more frequently than made her comfortable.

"Don't be a dolt. Fairfax Crisparkle. I thought you were a detective."

"Crisparkle." All the long, narrow pieces were falling into the right slots in the Tetris game in October's brain.

"Are they going to revoke your membership from the Nancy Drew Fan Club?" Mrs. Crookshanks mocked.

"Fairfax Crisparkle, is he still alive? What's Asphodel Meadows? How did you glow?" October unloaded all the questions that had stymied her for the past three weeks, though her most crucial question of the moment went unspoken: where were the dead kids?

"What do you think this is? A spy movie? *Spy Kids*?" That was probably not the spy movie anyone was thinking of. "I don't reveal my plot to you, girl. I am the one asking the questions."

And, as if to prove her interrogation authority, Mrs. Crookshanks pushed back the fur coat from her waist to reveal her ghost pirate cutlass, tucked through her belt. She pulled it from her waistband and circled behind October to give her a test poke. October nearly cried right then and there, given her history with Mrs. Crookshanks's pirate sword, but she decided, no matter what, no substitute teacher was going to make her cry.

Crookshanks, with her free hand, hoisted October to the standing position and October saw what the Fairfax Crisparkle devotee had in store. She was standing at one end of a fairly long yacht, nearly as long as the basketball court at school. From the port side of the ship, a diving board jutted out over the dark water of the river.

"Out of tradition, I'm going to make you walk the plank," she said.

"I'll scream," October said. Peering over the side of the yacht, October could see a nearly ten-foot drop to the water below.

"I hope so," her tormentor said. "We're in the middle of the river. Look how far we are from the marina."

Its lights were a distant glow.

"I'll swim to safety!" October said. No way was this old lady going to outsmart her.

"In this temperature?" Mrs. Crookshanks said, cutting the ropes from October's legs. "Good luck. You *do* remember it's February, right? Now march."

October, seeing no way out of the situation, stepped onto the board. She hoped the dead kids had some bright idea and were in the immediate vicinity. Otherwise, her high school career wasn't even going to survive its rookie year.

"This is stupid," October said, wary of the sword close behind her. "I won't jump. I won't. Just kill me. Why don't you just kill me?"

"There are a lot more questions when a teenage girl's dead body shows up with sword wounds all over it. A drowned girl prompts fewer inquiries," she said. "It's an old Crisparkle trick. Make it look like an accident."

Well, October thought, *at least I was right about Cyril's death.* Perhaps she was a pretty decent detective.

"Start walking," the museum docent said, jabbing her sword forward. "Get on with it."

"I kind of wish you were wearing your pirate costume," October said.

Mrs. Crookshanks dropped her arm. "Yeah, I thought about putting it on. There just wasn't time. It's a shame. The vest of halogen lights is really heavy, too."

October wasn't sure how much longer she could stall this woman. The dead kids needed to show up with the Coast Guard in the next minute or two.

"Before I push you into the Niagara River, I have to ask you," Mrs. Crookshanks asked. "What is your interest in Cyril Cooper?"

"It was just a history project." October sniffled.

"My eye, a history project. You know he died the same way you will. And we all know he was the Dark One's first victim."

"*He* didn't know that," October said, immediately realizing her slip-up. "I mean . . . I found his name at the Sticksville Museum."

"Oh my stars!" Mrs. Crookshanks gasped. October turned her head slightly to see the museum docent gazing at her with wonder like she'd just seen a dog that had done the Harlem Shake. "You can talk to him! You've talked to Cyril Cooper!"

"It was just a history project," October said again, but even she didn't believe herself now. Crookshanks tugged October by the hood of her sweatshirt and held the tip of the sword close to her face.

"You can talk to the dead, you little tramp. I should have *realized* you had a ghost assistant! You said something about spirits at the school. It explains so much."

October actually had more than one ghost assistant, and they were more like partners, but she wasn't about to volunteer that. Not with a blade so close to her face. She didn't want to over-excite Mrs. Crookshanks.

"I thought I'd read something about dead kids in your diary," she continued. "But I figured it was part of that wretched novel."

In October's mind, it was enough that Ms. Fenstermacher was trying to kill her. She really didn't appreciate the use of the word "tramp" or the insults about her writing. October wasn't commenting on *her* fashion choices, after all. Fur coat. Give me a break.

"Where's your ghost assistant now?" she asked.

October was asking herself that very same question. Cyril was supposed to have a crush on her; he had a funny way of showing it.

"I guess he can't swim." Mrs. Crookshanks laughed and cut October free from the ropes. "Can't have the police drag the river and find your arms tied behind your back. Keep walking."

And that, finally, is when the cavalry — pathetic as it was — arrived. In the distance, October could see Tabetha, Morna, Derek, and Cyril paddling a small rowboat hard, with their navigator Kirby perched on the bow like a wooden mermaid. October's survival mode suddenly snapped into action. Crookshanks hadn't spotted the rowboat yet.

"All right, I'm walking, I'm walking," October said, shuffling slowly along the narrow board. Only about a foot separated her Chuck Taylors from the edge. "But I'm going to scream and splash until I die. I'm going to make as much noise as possible."

Mrs. Crookshanks produced a remote control from a pocket in the fur coat. With her gloved hand, she pressed a button and Duran Duran's "Rio" blasted from the pleasure craft's speakers.

"We're just having a little party on the yacht."

A retro '80s party, evidently. October could practically hear her smile. October was smiling, too, but *inside* her face. The monster sound of the speakers would disguise the sound of the dead kids' approach nicely. October moved very, very slowly to the plank's edge as Crookshanks watched. She moved as little as possible, in movements that could still technically be considered forward motion. Soon, the dead kids had gently bumped up against the side of the yacht, and Cyril, ever the seaman, tied a rope around a hook on its side.

"We're coming up," Cyril said.

Tabetha started to say something, too, but October couldn't hear her, as Mrs. Crookshanks started to shout over the chorus of "Rio."

"Before you head to Davy Jones's locker, I just want to let you know, you may have stopped the McGriff boy, but not the rest of Asphodel Meadows," she yelled. "And when you die tonight, there will be no stopping us."

"Ms. Fenstermacher will stop you!" October shouted, though she wasn't sure why. Her history teacher didn't seem like the action-hero type. Then neither did a thirteen-year-old in too much makeup and T-shirts that featured overly sensitive bands.

"Fenstermacher? *That* bimbo?" Mrs. Crookshanks said. "She doesn't even think Crisparkle is *real*!"

The dead kids started to climb a rope ladder located about fifteen feet from where the diving board attached. They'd be aboard shortly. October turned to them slowly and stretched out her arms. She held her palms face out, connecting her index fingers and thumbs.

"What is that?" Kirby asked, near the bottom of the rope ladder.

"I don't unnerstan'. What's that s'pposed t'be?" Tabetha said.

"It's a *pentagon*!" October shouted.

"Is he here?!" Crookshanks shouted.

Realizing a ghost assistant or assistants were nearby, Crookshanks wasted no time in shoving October off the ship. Luckily, the dead kids had managed to park their little rowboat, as much as one can "park" a seacraft, right underneath the plank, so October avoided plunging into the icy river. However, she did drop about ten feet onto her rear into a hardwood boat, so there was still a lot of pain involved. She'd live, but she wouldn't be able to sit comfortably for several weeks. The rowboat shook on the surface of the water upon October's crash landing. The dead kids continued, unseen by Mrs. Crookshanks, up the side of the boat.

Not hearing any sort of splash or scream or thrashing, Mrs. Crookshanks hurried to the end of the diving board. (It would have been fitting if one of the dead kids just followed her out there and gave her a little push, but they couldn't do that because of those downer ghost rules.) She looked down to see October ten feet below, sprawled in the bottom of a wooden rowboat.

"The ghost of Cyril Cooper brought a lifeboat?!" Mrs. Crookshanks screamed, incredulous.

October Schwartz scrambled to her feet, which was a bit more difficult on the water than on solid land. But once she gained her bearings, she started up that ladder, following the dead kids. Apparently, one brush with death was not enough for her! Mrs. Crookshanks, seeing what October had in mind, hurried back down the plank and started toward the spot where the rope ladder attached to the boat's side. But one step off the board and she found herself stuck. She couldn't move forward, pressed against the chest of Derek Running Water, whom she couldn't see. She retreated, then bumped into another invisible wall (Morna MacIsaac). She was trapped inside the pentagon!

"I know you're there, ghost!" she shouted.

"Good job, everyone," Cyril said. "We've got her trapped."

That was not exactly the case. Her fur coat billowing behind her, Mrs. Crookshanks slashed wildly downward with her cutlass, cutting off Cyril's left arm at the shoulder. There was a lot of screaming that followed.

Mrs. Crookshanks pushed forward, through the space where she'd made her cut, and found all resistance had disappeared (what with Cyril's dismemberment). She ran over to where October was now clambering onto the deck like a beached walrus.

"Do something!" Morna screamed.

And, with split-second timing, the one-armed Cyril Cooper did. With his good (attached) hand, he picked up his severed limb and tossed it toward October in a Hail Mary throw. The arm flopped like a side of beef a foot or two in front of October's stunned face. She had no idea what Cyril expected her to do with this arm. She was so stunned that she barely noticed Mrs. Crookshanks bearing down on her like a freight train of fur and fury.

Luckily, October didn't have to *do* anything with Cyril's severed and, frankly, gross arm. Mrs. Crookshanks, running full tilt and unable to see any ghostly activity, tripped on the obstacle and fell face-first into the yacht's boom. If you're something of a sailor yourself and have ever knocked your melon on a ship's boom, you know it doesn't take much for that thing to cause some head trauma. Given the substitute teacher's relative velocity, the resulting bonk knocked her out cold. She crumpled in a heap, like the clothes of someone who'd just spontaneously combusted, at October's side. It's simple physics, folks.

Quickly, the dead kids checked to see that the woman was unconscious. Tabetha gathered the ropes Crookshanks had cut and discarded and passed them to October. As they all breathed a sigh of relief and talked about how, despite its success, they should never mention the pentagon again, October and Cyril oversaw the hog-tying of Mrs. Crookshanks.

"Think you can still make some of your trusty sailor knots with one hand?" October asked.

Cyril smiled. "I think so. But I might need your help."

"Just tell me where to place my finger," she said. "Also . . . this may be awkward timing, but, um, do you still like me? Like *like*-like me?"

He grimaced while pulling a knot closed.

"It's hard not to. You're just so clever, October. But don't worry."

"I'm a little worried."

"I can *like*-like you from afar. I understand why it's strange for you, so I'll try my best *not* to make it strange."

"Thank you," October said, trying not to blush. Luckily, the inhumanely cold weather helped to mask it. "And for saving my life, I'll let you drive the boat back."

"But I don't know how to steer this kind of boat," he said.

"It has a motor. You like driving cars, don't you?"

"Yes."

"Think of this as a car on the water."

Cyril's eyes lit up. "Excellent."

☠   ☠   ☠

22

The Crookshanks List

The telephone woke me on Saturday morning. I guess it was closer to Saturday afternoon, but whatever. I'd had a long night. This time, I recognized the ring immediately as that of the old black candlestick telephone I'd taken from the Crooked Arms about a month ago. So I refused to answer it. All the telephone ever offered were vague answers and half promises about the whereabouts of my missing mom and I was so *over* it. Sure, it had helped me in some of my darker moments, but the phone didn't help me one bit with Mrs. Crookshanks. "Be careful." As if I couldn't figure that out myself. I wasn't answering it.

By the fifth ring, though, I realized my dad was probably in the house, too, and wondering why I had another telephone in my room, so I kind of *had* to answer it, if only to shut it up. I rolled over in bed and pulled the receiver from its hook.

"Hello," I groaned.

"I'm sorry," the voice said.

"Ugh!" I shouted and hung up. Sorry about what? About never telling me *anything* of use? About how I nearly froze, then drowned last night? About how you're really my mom and you abandoned me when I was three and now you just call to talk like a raspy-voiced audio book of the hundred best fortune cookie riddles or something? Ugh was right.

Feeling a bad taste in my mouth, which could have been morning breath but was more likely a reaction to the phone call, I hauled myself out of bed and went to the kitchen. I felt sore all over, probably from free-falling onto my bum into a wooden boat, but I'd live, thanks to the dead kids.

Dad was doing the crossword and drinking coffee at the kitchen table.

"Ah. Sleeping Beauty finally emerges."

"You know, I had an eventful night," I said, taking a seat across from him and flipping most of the hair out of my eyes.

"You don't say." He swallowed a mouthful of coffee. "I was just glad to see police officers bringing you home as the *victim* of a crime rather than the *perpetrator*."

"That sounded wrong, Dad."

"I'd prefer not to have the police at my door at all, October." Dad's sarcastic tone had vanished completely.

Despite his disappointment with another visit from the police, the one thing (of many) it seemed I didn't need to worry about at the moment was my dad. Though I had somehow managed to get myself again kidnapped by a maniacal teacher, albeit a substitute teacher, I wasn't currently being blamed for any of last night's mishaps. I was more worried about what this Asphodel Meadows was, as it seemed to be connected to some (possibly living) witch. Plus, Mrs. Crookshanks had mentioned "others" — never a good sign. Who wants to hear about others? The dad situation, however, was under control. He even seemed to be in a generally good mood. The tie he was wearing (on a Saturday, like a lunatic) looked new. I didn't recognize it, and Dad only bought himself new ties when (a) he got invited to a wedding or (b) he got invited to a funeral, which suggested to me maybe he had started things up with Ms. Salmons again. You know, after she got me out of jail. That was fine by me. I wanted to get on her good side, since she'd probably be prosecuting Mrs. Crookshanks.

"How's the crossword?" I asked.

"I need a five-letter word for dry, heated bread," he said, lowering the paper.

"Toast?" I said. "You needed help figuring out 'toast'?"

"No. I was just waiting for you to wake up," he said. "So I could tell you that's what you are. Toast."

"Dad!"

"You are in *so* much trouble, October Schwartz," Dad said.

"People were trying to kill me," I explained.

"And that's why I'll give you a few days' grace before your punishment begins," he said. "Also, I need to figure out what this creative punishment will be."

"Fine," I sighed.

"What are your plans on this, possibly your *last* Saturday of freedom?" he asked.

"I don't know. I slept through most of it," I said. "I should probably check on Ms. Fenstermacher in the hospital."

"I think that would be very nice," he said, returning his attention to his crossword.

After I showered and changed, I visited the nearby convenience store owned by that Korean lady who was literally the first person I ever spoke to in Sticksville. They usually had an okay selection of cards. She was a first-generation immigrant, and I wondered if she knew she had moved into such a den of witchcraft and evil when she left East Asia for this southern Ontario town. I picked out a get well card that had a picture of historic Canadian rebel Louis Riel that read "Get Better *Riel* Soon,"

which was perfect for a history teacher. In retrospect, it's very strange I found it at the convenience store.

When I got back home, I wrote Ms. Fenstermacher a really long note. I knew it would be long when I started, so I printed really, really small, and even then, the last sentence got kind of smashed in. Here's what I said:

Dear Ms. Fenstermacher,

I'm so sorry you were hit on the head with a brick. I hope your head is feeling better now. But more than that, I wanted to apologize for accusing you of being the ghost pirate and, well, preventing you from moving anywhere. There is a rational explanation for that, I swear. And if you've heard any of the recent news, you'll know that your colleague, Mrs. Crookshanks, was _really_ the ghost pirate, and she worked at the museum and was a (substitute) teacher, too, so I wasn't that far off. She also threw that brick at the back of your head, so you may be happy to know that she's been arrested, and it was kind of thanks to me. (You're welcome.) Also, I don't want to sound like a kook, but I think she's, like, an acolyte or Belieber of that old-time witch guy you told me about (and who I'm pretty sure killed my history project subject, Cyril Cooper), Fairfax Crisparkle. I'm not crazy, but I've seen some things lately that make me think magic is for real. Anyway, I'm really sorry about your head, and you're probably my favourite teacher other than my dad, and I really appreciate the nice things you said about me while I was interrogating you. I hope you won't hold me binding you against your will against me when you are grading our final projects.

Get well soon!

Yours truly,
October Schwartz

On Sunday when I visited the hospital, I went up to the nurses' station four separate times. The first three times, I asked the nurse on duty which room was Ms. Fenstermacher's, as I was a student of hers. And they told me, but I didn't go in. Only on the fourth time did the nurse on duty, who'd seen me twice already, say, "She's in Room 116B, but she's sleeping now." So that's when I felt comfortable visiting. I snuck in her room and saw her head wrapped up in gauze like it was part of some papier mâché project, resting on the recently fluffed pillows, and left my card on the sliding tray table beside the bed.

☠ ☠ ☠

Monday at school was weird, as the semester was pretty much over, but no one felt calm or relieved. Maybe that's because Ms. Fenstermacher had been bashed in the head with a brick. Or because the substitute science teacher was an evil ghost pirate. Whatever it was, things were gloomy.

Before French, I visited my compadres Yumi and Stacey at their usual post by Yumi's locker. Yumi dropped her books and held her hands up like she was holding an invisible concertina below her chin.

"Schwartz! You survived another brush with death!" she said.

"What's up?" Stacey asked, retrieving Yumi's school stuff from the floor.

"Kidnapped and threatened by yet another person on the Sticksville Board of Ed's payroll, and one who has a fetish for dressing like a pirate, no less," Yumi said.

"How do you do it, Schwartz?" Stacey asked.

"Listen," I said, trying not to reveal anything, "I was just in the wrong place at the wrong time."

"I feel like you have this secret life," Yumi said. "You have to let us in on this, Schwartz. We're dying of boredom over here. Last night, Stacey and I read articles in *Reader's Digest* out loud."

"One day soon, I promise," I said. "I have to get to class now."

As awful as it felt to hide everything and lie to my dad or Ms. Fenstermacher, it felt way worse to deceive Yumi and Stacey. I'd have to do something about it sooner or later. Maybe the Dead Kid Detective Agency could use two more living members? Maybe Ms. Fenstermacher — assuming she didn't have significant brain damage — could be an adult member-at-large. These were all things to consider before I tried solving my next mystery.

I was removing books from my locker, wondering where I'd even start looking into Tabetha's past, when Ashlie Salmons strode by my locker. I could sense her presence from the strong aroma of berry lip gloss. That's when I did something I never thought I'd do.

"Ashlie, wait up!" I called, sliding the combination lock closed on my locker.

Ashlie turned in a perfect, fluid 180 on her red ballerina flats.

"Are you speaking to me, Zombie Tramp?"

"Yes."

"And why?" she asked. "Are you currently bleeding to death?"

"Uh, no," I said.

"Then I see no reason for you to speak to me."

Instead of speaking and making things worse, I just put the peanut-butter jar of money into Ashlie's perfectly manicured hands.

"What's this?" she asked.

"Eighty-seven dollars and sixty-five cents," I said. "Money that other kids raised to bail me out of jail. Can you make sure your mom gets this? She really helped me out."

"Is this a joke?" Ashlie began to soften.

"No," I said. "And I realize it's the end of the semester and too late, but if you ever need any more help with schoolwork, let me know."

"Why are you doing this?" she said, slowly creeping away. She held the jar protectively in her hands like it was an infant and I was a rabid mastiff. "Did Dr. Lagostina put you up to this?"

Dr. Lagostina! That sounded much more believable than me just spontaneously trying to be a better person!

"Yes," I lied. "He suggested I try to . . . um . . . make amends.

And I want you to know that you're pretty smart . . . and I'd be happy to tutor you any time."

"I'm just going to back away now," she said.

And that was the last I saw of her that day. We had a sub in history, but he seemed normal and totally non-homicidal, except for the fact that he had a soul patch. And while he didn't teach us much in the way of history, he did mention our grades wouldn't be in from Ms. Fenstermacher until she recovered from her head trauma, which was probably for the best.

☠   ☠   ☠

Later that afternoon, following class, I had a bout of déjà vu, all over again. Someone knocked on our door, which was unusual. (We have a doorbell.) And when Dad answered, two policemen stood on the other side. Strangely — or maybe not so strangely, as Sticksville wasn't that large a town — they were the same two police officers who'd come to question my dad after Mr. O'Shea died: the big guy who looked like a Victorian-era boxer and the younger brown guy. Though they both were in Arctic adventure gear this time, as it was nearly twenty below outside.

"Oh no. Not again," my dad groaned. "Come to illegally detain my daughter again?"

"Don't worry," the younger guy said, wincing. "We're not here to question or arrest anyone this time. May we come in?"

My dad gestured that they could, and the older cop with the waxed moustache placed my knapsack in my arms.

"We figured you might be missing this," he said.

One strap had been cut clean in half where Mrs. Crookshanks had hacked it apart, but it otherwise looked the same.

"Thanks," I said.

"This was among the items retrieved from Roberta Crookshanks," he continued. "At first, we thought it would be required as evidence, but Crown Attorney Salmons says she has an airtight case without it."

"So you get your stuff back," the other cop said.

"And did the museum get all *its* stuff back?" I asked, probably pressing my luck, requesting so much information from the police. But maybe they'd feel they owed me for the unlawful imprisonment.

"Their stuff was, technically, never stolen," the old-timey boxer said.

The non-time-travelling police officer explained further: "Though all the historical material was missing, it never left the premises. Crookshanks just hid it all in Rubbermaid containers with misleading labels in the museum's basement."

"As it turns out," the moustached cop continued, "we were wrong to even suggest you were involved in the museum robbery."

"Oh, that's okay," I said. "You didn't happen to find a necklace with the backpack, did you?"

Since the ghost pirate, who I now knew had been Mrs. Crookshanks, had taken the mysterious shack-sourced necklace — which I felt was fair to assume was a Fairfax Crisparkle original — I hoped there was (a) a possibility the police had recovered it and (b) a possibility I could convince the police it was mine.

"Whatever we found is in the knapsack. Are you missing a necklace? What did this necklace look like?"

"Um, strange," I said, remembering Cyril's not-so-vivid description. "It was strange looking."

"Did you want us to report it as stolen?"

"No, no," I said.

After they both shrugged with their whole bodies, the police officers were handed coffee mugs by my dad. He was very gracious to the organization that jailed his only daughter; I was right about how trusting of authority he was. I ran to my room to check if anything was missing from my bag. I unzipped the main flap and dumped the contents onto my bedspread. Luckily, my most important possession, probably — my *Two Knives, One Thousand Demons* composition book — fell out with the pens and collection of Shirley Jackson's short stories that I was reading. Mrs. Crookshanks had said she read through my notebook, so I figured I should check to make sure she hadn't torn out any pages or desecrated the journal in any other ways. Now, I don't want to get all Upworthy here, but not only were all the pages there, but a little scrap of paper fluttered out onto my bed, and what it said changed everything forever.

☠   ☠   ☠

Before Dad's surely draconian punishment measures took effect, I figured I should get in one more meeting with the dead kids before they disappeared for the next month. The full moon was looming. Throwing caution to the wind like it was a dead relative's ashes, I snuck out that Monday night while Dad was out at a volleyball administrative meeting, which I strongly suspected was code for a date with Ms. Salmons.

The dead kids spotted me from my trail of hot breath first. Derek, Kirby, and Morna were sitting on an overturned rotting log.

"October," Derek shouted, "how's the tailbone?"

"I can barely feel it because of how numb my entire body is in this cold."

Cyril and Tabetha appeared from the other side of the cemetery clearing.

"Cyril! Your arm's back!" I shouted.

He hopped over one of those low, poor person's tombstones and gave me a massive hug, using both arms.

"Ahem, get a tomb, you two," Kirby coughed, making the worst pun I (or anyone) had probably ever heard.

"Good news," I said to my assembled dead friends. "I got my bag back. And my journal."

"That's great," Morna said.

275

"So, that angry old lady is goin' to jail?" Tabetha asked.

"Yep," I said. "Though I'm lucky she tried to kill me, as what she did at the museum technically wasn't theft and wouldn't have landed her in prison. Unfortunately, the police didn't find any weird necklace, Cyril. I was hoping it might tell us more about your killer, Fairfax Crisparkle."

"So, yer sayin' this guy that killed Cyril really was a witch?" Tabetha asked. From the body language of her folded arms, I could tell she harboured (get it?) some doubt.

"According to local folklore, he was," I said, opening my backpack. "And Ms. Fenstermacher, my history teacher, if that's any endorsement."

"But why would this witch want to kill Cyril?" Derek asked, slapping the Loyalist in the back. A puff of corpse dust blossomed from his shoulders into the cold air.

"Clearly, Cyril saw something in that shack he wasn't supposed to see. Or took something he wasn't supposed to take," I said and retrieved three straws from the bag's inner pocket. "Like that necklace, or the book he burned."

"An' this Asphodel Meadows group is somehow connected t'him?" Morna asked.

"I guess," I said, "though I'm not sure how. Fairfax Crisparkle must have died about 200 years ago. But Mrs. Crookshanks talked about Asphodel Meadows like they were active now."

"And the German gent who killed Morna," Kirby gestured toward his Scottish friend, "was also connected to these Meadows, if I recall correctly."

Only Kirby would refer to Udo Schlangegriff as a *gent*. Morna's eyes shrunk with worry.

"So far two of your deaths have had something to do with Asphodel Meadows, and I'm willing to bet whatever our next case is, it's tied to them, too," I said. "Speaking of which . . ."

At that point, I hid the straws behind my back, shuffled them around and obscured their heights with my wool mittens. Then I presented them to my dead friends.

"Kirby, Tabetha, Derek — will you each draw a straw?"

Moments later, Tabetha was elbowing me in my squishy gut and circling Kirby, lowly chanting into his unamused face, "Drawing straws winnahhhhh, drawing straws winnah."

"There's no need to gloat," Kirby pouted.

"My personal opinion? We should get started on my mystery right away," Tabetha announced. "Think ya can start researching, living girl? Or maybe we jes' track down this Asphodel Meadows?"

"Yesterday, I would have thought that was impossible, but I think you should all take a look at this piece of paper. Mrs. Crookshanks left a shopping list of sorts in my composition book."

I took off my mitten and dug into my pocket for the list and passed the folded paper to Kirby. He unfolded it and the other four dead kids gathered around. As they looked it over, I began to explain.

"I'm guessing Asphodel Meadows is some kind of secret society or group dedicated to Fairfax Crisparkle. But I have no idea if he's alive or where he is or what they do. But since we've been seeing that red graffiti everywhere, I think we can assume Asphodel Meadows definitely exists."

"This list . . ." Kirby stuttered.

"What is it, Kirby?" Tabetha asked.

"Like I said, I don't know what Asphodel Meadows is, but I now know *who* it is."

Kirby read the list out loud for the benefit of the three illiterate dead kids:

Crookshanks
Schlangegriff
O'Dare
Burton
Fairweather
LaFlamme

"Recognize anyone?" I said, wrapping my arms around myself to stay warm. It wasn't just the weather making me cold.

"Like Crookshanks and Schlangegriff? Our two most recent nemeses?"

"October," Kirby said, "why is my name on this list?"

"An' who are all those other people?" Morna asked. "O'Dare?"

"I recognize the name Fairweather," I admitted, and I felt hot shame shoot up from my sneakers to my lower eyelids.

"And why is that?" Cyril asked.

"That's my mom's last name."

☠   ☠   ☠

Appendix A: Cast of Characters

October Schwartz: she's the protagonist of the book. If you're having a hard time keeping track of which one she is, you should probably put the book down right now. Enroll in a remedial English course or something. She's in nearly every sentence of the book.

Mr. (Leonard) Schwartz: October's dad and a teacher at Sticksville Central High School. He teaches auto repair and biology, and probably important life lessons to October, or whatever. He's suffered from bouts of clinical depression ever since October's mom left the both of them.

Yumi Takeshi: October's best friend at Sticksville. She shares October's interest in black clothing, eyeliner, and horror movies. She also comes as part of a two-friend package deal with Stacey.

Stacey MacIsaac: friend to October and constant companion to Yumi Takeshi. A lanky boy with an affinity for mismatched vintage clothing and percussion instruments. Book Two (*Dial M for Morna*) revealed he was related to October's dead friend Morna MacIsaac.

Ashlie Salmons: terror of the unpopular ninth grade girls at Sticksville Central High School. Loves include belts, boots, bangs, and bullying. She leads a small crew of mostly unpleasant young ladies. Her mother is a Crown attorney.

Ms. Fenstermacher: October's cool new history teacher (perhaps a little too cool to be a teacher), who replaced the sometimes-homicidal Mr. Page (see Book One for that story). She also works at the Sticksville Museum (former home of Cyril Cooper) and is Sticksville's biggest fan of *Battlestar Galactica*.

Mrs. Eileen Tischmann: the well-meaning but somewhat flighty music teacher at Sticksville Central High School.

Mr. Santuzzi: stern mathematics teacher at Sticksville Central High School, noted for his tight leisure suits, alleged toupée, and military past. He says things like "roger" and "lock 'n' load" when teaching lessons on factoring.

Dr. Lagostina: Sticksville Central High School's resident two-fer: part physician, part therapist. He, unlike most normal people, likes listening to people's problems.

Cyril Cooper: unofficial leader and oldest of the dead kids. He was from a Loyalist family who fled to Canada during the American Revolution; his possibly promising career in shipbuilding was cut short by a mysterious assailant. Cyril is fascinated by automobiles.

Morna MacIsaac: youngest of the dead kids, Morna was a Scottish immigrant who came with her family to Canada in 1910 for work and affordable land. Instead of finding much of either, the MacIsaacs lived in a boarding house called the Crooked Arms

until Morna was killed outside a local pub by a man named Udo Schlangegriff (who was posing as a *Titanic* survivor named Dr. Alfred Pain), as revealed in *Dial M for Morna*.

Tabetha Scott: dead kid who escaped slavery in the American South and ended up in Sticksville. She left Virginia via an ornithologist who helped them access the Underground Railroad, and settled in town with her dad. Bickers endlessly with Kirby and never hesitates to share her opinions.

Kirby LaFlamme: dead kid and one fifth of the not-so-famous LaFlamme quintuplets. During the Depression, he and his siblings were the inspiration for the LaFlammetown theme park. He was outlived by all his brothers, and he's fluent in both French and English.

Derek Running Water: the most recent of deaths among the dead kids, Derek lived with his mother in Sticksville, but became politically committed to the Mohawk Warrior cause with the 1990 standoff in Oka, Quebec, the events of which led to his death. Derek can be relied upon to provide explanations to the other dead kids for modern technology and terminology. But he's not great with directions.

Alyosha Diamandas: one of Sticksville's most persistent realtors. Alyosha feels a healthy real estate market is indicative of a healthy democracy. He's a fan of all houses, save the haunted kind. (He's had a few run-ins with the dead kids over the years.)

Crown Attorney (Cecilia) Salmons: mother of Ashlie Salmons who shares her daughter's taste in fashion, but also shares October's thirst for justice. (After all, she spends her days prosecuting criminals and such.) Has recently been romantically linked to Leonard Schwartz, much to October's chagrin.

Goth Hardware Clerk / Percy: the dark prince of Beaver Hardware, who wears the same thing stocking shelves of finishing nails as he would to a Ministry concert, and who sometimes offers friendly advice to October.

Mrs. (Roberta) Crookshanks: retired teacher who works at the Sticksville Museum with Ms. Fenstermacher, and sometimes acts as a substitute teacher at Sticksville Central High School. She's easily amused by the kids and their adorable goth subculture.

Olivia de Kellerman: fictional heroine of October's horror opus, *Two Knives, One Thousand Demons*. Fated to fight alone (with occasional help from her wheelchair-bound Uncle Otis) against hell's hungry hordes, Olivia likes sharp things and dislikes evil. She's basically a one-woman demon-killing army.

Appendix B: Passing References (Important Cultural History!)

The Amazing Race: wildly popular reality television contest in which duos, much like Phileas Fogg and Passepartout before them, traverse the globe through a variety of means and compete in a number of "culturally relevant" challenges along the way.

Angry Birds: series of video games in which players catapult choleric birds into the poorly constructed homes of their natural enemies, pigs. The game has since been franchised into television, amusement parks, and, yes, activewear.

Anne Rice: the goth high priestess of vampire fiction, this New Orleans–based author is the woman behind the super-sensual Vampire Chronicles series, which includes *Interview with the Vampire*, *The Vampire Lestat*, *The Queen of the Damned*, and more. Basically, the first author listed on any goth's OkCupid profile.

Are You Afraid of the Dark?: beloved Canadian children's television show that was like a kids' version of *Tales From the Crypt*. Each week, the preteen members of the Midnight Society sat around a campfire and told spooky (but entirely PG-rated) stories.

***Armageddon* (1998):** a Michael Bay/Jerry Bruckheimer movie epic in which only the world's best drillers (Rockhound, Bear,

Chick — you know their names) can save Earth from certain destruction by a giant asteroid. If you don't know the movie, you know its Aerosmith-penned torch song, "I Don't Want to Miss a Thing."

The Bachelor: a reality television show in which a single man must, over a course of weeks and episodes, eliminate potential romantic interests until he has winnowed them down to one woman who will (in theory) become his wife. Episodes frequently involve conversation about "finding the one" and "avoiding drama," and have inordinately high rose and hot tub budgets.

Baseball Furies: fictional (and terrifying) baseball-themed New York street gang featured in the greatest movie about fictional gangs ever, Walter Hill's 1979 *The Warriors*.

Battle Royale (2000): the ur-*Hunger Games, Battle Royale* is an over-the-top (and amazing) Japanese film in which a ninth-grade high school class is taken to a remote location where they must fight each other to the death. Your parents will never let you watch it.

Battlestar Galactica (BSG): a popular science-fiction television series about a fugitive fleet of humans evading and battling the Cylons, a robotic race that aims to destroy all humanity. Ms. Fenstermacher is a fan of the revamp in the 2000s (with a female Starbuck), rather than the original 1978 series.

Bauhaus: British post-punk musical group that are often regarded as the first goth rock band. Taking their name from everyone's favourite German architectural movement (super goth, right?), they recorded the unofficial goth anthem "Bela Lugosi's Dead" in 1979. They broke up in 1983, but members went on to solo careers and formed later bands, Tones on Tail and Love and Rockets.

Belieber: colloquial term for a devoted fan of Stratford, Ontario's favourite son, pop star sensation and underwear model Justin Bieber. Beliebers are not yet recognized by world governments as a legitimate religion.

Beetlejuice (1988): Tim Burton movie about a recently deceased couple who employ a dirtbag ghost named Beetlejuice (Michael Keaton, in possibly his finest role) to help them scare a new family out of their former home. Beetlejuice appears when you say his name thrice in rapid succession. (See also *Candyman*.)

"Billie Jean": one of Prince of Pop Michael Jackson's greatest singles is a song that basically mirrors a paternity test episode of *The Maury Povich Show*. During the music video, Jackson dances on a series of tiles that light up as he steps on them.

Bruce Willis: actor, singer, and bald-guy extraordinaire, Bruce Willis has been gruffly charming audiences since rising to fame on the television show *Moonlighting* in the mid-1980s. He is probably best known as action hero John McClane from the Die Hard (*Die Hard*, *Die Hard with a Vengeance*, *Only the Good Die Hard*, etc.) film series.

Candyman (1992): a horror film based on a Clive Barker story that concerns an urban legend come to life in Chicago. The Candyman, an artist who was murdered and had his hand replaced with a hook (but not necessarily in that order), will allegedly appear whenever his name is said five times in a mirror. (See also *Beetlejuice*.)

Carmen Sandiego: she's a "sticky-fingered filcher from Berlin down to Belize." First in a series of video games, then a game show and animated series, Sandiego was an international thief who robbed treasures and led detectives on a wild chase around the world, inadvertently teaching them valuable facts about world geography (or how to use a World Almanac) along the way. Has been known to both "ransack Pakistan" and "run a scam in Scandinavia."

Carrie Bradshaw: the lead character on the HBO television series *Sex and the City*, who wrote a newspaper column on the single woman's life in New York City and had an interest in shoes bordering on addiction.

Chaka Khan: the Queen of Funk herself, Chaka Khan (born Yvette Marie Stevens) has a decades-spanning career in music that began in the 1970s. She's best known for songs like "Ain't Nobody," "I Feel for You," and "Tell Me Something Good" (recorded with her early band, Rufus).

Christopher Walken in *Pulp Fiction*: *Pulp Fiction* (1994) is a very violent, very funny movie that you won't be able to watch until you're older, but all you need to know for the purposes of this book is that Christopher Walken's character, a former Vietnam prisoner of war, hides a gold watch in his bum for two years to keep his captors from finding it.

Criss Angel: the Marilyn Manson of illusionists, Angel (born Christopher Nicholas Sarantakos) rose to frame with his show *Criss Angel: Mindfreak*, during which he dazzled unsuspecting rubes with his mind-blowing (and sometimes violent) illusions. Like if David Copperfield shopped only at Hot Topic.

Cruella de Vil: the villain of the novel and animated film *101 Dalmatians*, de Vil is a glamorous older woman who, eschewing more typical pursuits like bridge or shuffleboard, endeavours to skin puppies for their fur.

CSI: Miami: the first spinoff of the *CSI* television series, which focuses on a Miami-based forensic team working to solve grisly crimes. The show is distinguished from its predecessor by the location, the frequency with which its lead character, Horatio Caine, removes his sunglasses for effect, and by the different song by The Who that serves as its theme: "Won't Get Fooled Again."

Dangerous Minds (1995): movie about a former Marine, played by Michelle Pfeiffer, who becomes a teacher at an inner-city, underfunded high school and finds her students involved in gangs, the drug trade, and uninterested in learning. But things turn around when she puts on a leather jacket and shows them that song lyrics are really just poetry with music. (See also "Gangsta's Paradise.")

Dark Shadows: television's longest-running vampire-centered soap opera. Airing in the late 1960s and early 1970, it was recently remade as a bad latter-day Tim Burton movie.

Doc Martens: shorthand for Dr. Martens boots. The black leather boots with distinctive yellow stitching around the sole have, at times, been the preferred footwear of punks, grunge fans, and numerous other youth subcultures.

Def Comedy Jam: a cable television series created by hip-hop magnate Russell Simmons that featured hilarious performances by black stand-up comedians and helped kickstart the careers of people like Martin Lawrence and Dave Chappelle. The super-profane comedy specials were often spoofed for the uproarious behavior of the audiences. Don't bother wondering about the show, though; your parents won't let you watch them until you're thirty . . . or maybe dead.

Doogie Howser, M.D.: Wait, you're a doctor and you're only sixteen? That's the premise of this early '90s television series, starring Neil Patrick Harris, that wild and crazy guy from the Harold and Kumar movies and awards show broadcasts.

Dr. Zaius: orangutan in the *Planet of the Apes* film who is something of a major authority in Ape City. You can identify him by his lustrous blond hair and pretty boss leather coat.

Duran Duran: English New Romantic rock band who took their name from a *Barbarella* character and who made a splash in the early 1980s with their fairly racy music videos. Duran Duran are best known for their classic '80s hits "Hungry Like the Wolf," "Notorious," and "Girls on Film." The music video for "Rio" mostly takes place on a yacht.

Errol Flynn: one of the original playboys, Flynn was an Australian-American actor best known for playing swashbuckler roles in Hollywood, be those pirates, Robin Hoods, or Don Juans.

The Empire Strikes Back (1980): the second Star Wars movie to be released (and fifth in chronological order), this is, like, the dark one where the bad guys (spoiler alert) temporarily win. The movie also features some space dogfights on an ice planet and lot of kung fu–style training for Luke Skywalker.

Face/Off (1997): at one point, John Travolta and Nicolas Cage were two of the most bankable movie stars in Hollywood and they made an action movie about face transplants directed by John Woo. You kind of want to see it now, don't you?

The Fast and the Furious: unstoppable action-film franchise that follows the dizzying highs and life-threatening lows of the world of illegal street racing. If nothing else, will probably be memorialized in the Smithsonian for introducing the concept of "Tokyo drifting" to the masses.

Fresh Prince of Bel-Air: early '90s sitcom starring hip-hop MC Will Smith as a street-smart Philadelphia teenager who got in one little fight and his mom got scared, at which point his mother made him move in with his auntie and uncle in Bel-Air, a wealthy Los Angeles neighbourhood. The show explored issues of race, class, and actor Alfonso Ribeiro's dance skills. (See also *Jazz*.)

Frogger: early video game (like, 1981 early) in which you play as a frog, attempting to cross a busy road. Basically, Jaywalking: Home Edition.

Funky Winkerbean: the titular character of a long-running comic strip about the gently humorous exploits of the gang at Westview High School. That is, until it took a real about-face in 1992 and became way more serious. Winkerbean himself looks like a slightly less-beatnik Shaggy from *Scooby-Doo*. (See also *Scooby-Doo*.)

"Gangsta's Paradise": hit song featured on the *Dangerous Minds* soundtrack by hip-hop recording artist (and later celebrity chef) Coolio that chronicles the various pressures and difficulties of a young black man growing up in urban America. (See also *Dangerous Minds*.)

Godzilla: giant lizard-like monster, borne of nuclear experimentaton, who starred (and continues to star) in a series of Japanese (and some American) films, typically wreaking havoc in Tokyo and other major metropolitan areas. She's been in more movies than King Kong and has atomic breath.

Good Charlotte: Maryland-based pop-punk band who almost singlehandedly launched the Hot Topic retail franchise. Twin brothers Joel and Benji Madden and a crew of emo-looking rockers rose to prominence in the early 2000s with singles like "Little Things," "Lifestyles of the Rich and Famous," and "The Anthem" (which, despite some petitions, did not replace "The Star-Spangled Banner" as America's national song).

Goose / Maverick: Goose and Maverick are the nicknames of fighter pilots played by Anthony Edwards and Tom Cruise, respectively, in action movie and Kenny Loggins music video *Top Gun* (1986). Other such nicknames featured in the film: Viper, Jester, Stinger, and Iceman.

The Green Hornet: fictional serial hero who is the vigilante alter ego of newspaper man Britt Reid; with his valet and confidant, Kato, he acts as a scourge to the criminal underworld. A 1960s Green Hornet television program featured a hot jazz version of

"The Flight of the Bumblebee" played on trumpet by Al Hirt, which may be the only reason to ever listen to jazz.

Grunge: musical and youth subculture popular in the early 1990s, deriving from Seattle, Washington. The music is best represented by the stripped-down rock music of Nirvana, Pearl Jam, and Alice in Chains, while the fashion is mostly Doc Martens and flannel shirts.

Harlem Shake: dance move that originated in Harlem in 1981 and grew in popularity through the 2000s. As all dance aficionados will tell you, that thing people are doing in those popular internet "Harlem Shake" videos isn't *really* the Harlem Shake. The real deal involves rapidly shaking one's arms side to side and looks not unlike a really rhythmic full-body seizure.

***Heathers* (1988):** dark comedy about an outsider girl (Winona Ryder, naturally) who tries to become one of the Heathers, her school's in-crowd, before she meets up with a weird boy (Christian Slater) who begins killing the more popular kids. This movie would never get made nowadays.

Henry Kissinger: American diplomat who served as National Security Advisor and Secretary of State during the 1970s. Won the Nobel Peace Price in 1973, despite widely being recognized as a war criminal.

Indiana Jones: Dr. Henry Jones ("Indiana was the dog's name!") is a dashing archaeologist who frequently rescues historical artifacts from villainous hands, all the while armed only with his wits and a bullwhip. But, like, in movies. This isn't a real guy.

Jack Dawson: protagonist of the film *Titanic*, Dawson (Leonardo DiCaprio) is a working-class Wisconsinite who wins third-class tickets to the doomed ship and, improbably, begins a romance with first-class (and engaged) passenger Rose (Kate

Winslet). Spoiler alert: he doesn't make it to Europe and dies of hypothermia after spending too long in the icy waters of the Atlantic. But if Céline Dion is to be believed, Rose's love will go on and on.

Javert: antagonist in the book and musical *Les Misérables*, Javert is a dogged police inspector who is, frankly, pretty obsessed with a guy who literally just stole a loaf of bread and really turned his life around afterward. (See also *Jean Valjean*.)

Jazz: not the overrated musical genre. In this case, Jazz refers to a character on *The Fresh Prince of Bel-Air*. One of Will's streetwise friends whom Will's Uncle Phil takes an immediate disliking to. You can most often see him being tossed out the front door of the Banks family's Bel-Air mansion. (See also *Fresh Prince of Bel-Air*.)

Jean Valjean: the yin to Javert's yan in *Les Misérables*, Jean Valjean struggles to go straight after a prison sentence for stealing bread. But try as he might, no matter what he does — becoming a socially conscious industrialist, funding orphanages and schools, lifting wagons off old dudes — his nemesis Javert will never let him forget he's an ex-con. (See also *Javert*.)

Jewel: Alaskan singer-songwriter behind the acoustic and soulful singles "Who Will Save Your Soul" and "Foolish Games."

Josie and the Pussycats: one of the best fictional rock bands of all time, the comic book characters first appeared in Archie Comics and tour the world as a cat-themed rock trio. Members include guitarist Josie, bassist Valerie, and drummer Melody, whose word bubbles are always decorated with musical notes.

Joy Division: British post-punk band that formed shortly after two of their members went to a legendary (but poorly attended) Sex Pistols show in 1976. The gloomy band recorded songs like "Transmission" and "Love Will Tear Us Apart," before their lead singer Ian Curtis committed suicide at twenty-three.

The surviving members later formed new wave electronic act New Order.

Kolchak: The Night Stalker: 1970s television series about a night-beat newspaper reporter, Carl Kolchak, who investigates mysterious crimes in his hometown of Chicago, often to discover supernatural forces — like werewolves, zombies, and at least one headless motorcyclist — at play.

Korn: wildly successful "nu metal" music group, who kind of combined heavy metal with hip hop (sort of?). You might not remember hits of theirs like "Got the Life" and "Freak on a Leash."

Kyle MacLachlan: actor who may be best known as Special Agent Dale Cooper from the slightly bonkers television series *Twin Peaks*, though he also appeared in *Blue Velvet*, *Showgirls*, and *Dune*, so he's basically forever enshrined in the world of cult movies. MacLachlan also had a recurring role on *Sex and the City*.

Limp Bizkit: The Monkees to Korn's Beatles, Limp Bizkit was another successful "nu metal" band, led by the perennially backward-baseball-capped frontman Fred Durst. Crank songs like "Break Stuff," "Nookie," and "Re-Arranged," and get ready to lose friends. (See also *Korn*.)

Little House on the Prairie: a series of eight children's books written by Laura Ingalls Wilder about frontier life in the American Midwest in the late nineteenth century. The books inspired a late 1970s television series and countless generations of children to wear bonnets and call their parents "Ma" and "Pa" (or "Pa" and "Pa" or "Ma" and "Ma," as the case may be). The bonnet thing may be an exaggeration.

Lord of the Rings (extended cuts): ambitious and special-effects-laden film adaptations of the J.R.R. Tolkien novels, directed by New Zealander Peter Jackson. While the original theatrical editions of the movies are each over three hours, the three extended cuts combined total over eleven hours of Middle Earth "goodness."

Louis Riel: Canadian politician and leader of the Métis people of the Canadian prairies. He led two resistance movements against the Canadian government (in 1869 and 1885) to preserve Métis rights and culture in the Canadian West. Following the second resistance movement, he was arrested and ordered executed by Canada's first prime minister, John A. Macdonald.

Magneto: irate master of magnetism in the X-Men comics, he is the proponent of a much more radical, violent take on mutant-human relations than his nemesis, the more diplomatic Professor Charles Xavier. You might remember him as Ian McKellen or Michael Fassbender, depending on which X-Men movie you watch. He inexplicably has a British accent despite very clearly being German. (See also *Professor X*.)

Marathon Man (1976): suspenseful movie in which a history student (Dustin Hoffman) and long-distance runner finds himself thrown into a shadowy world of espionage and elderly Nazis. During a key scene, Hoffman is tortured via some totally unnecessary dental surgery.

Memento (2000): that movie Christopher "Dark Knight" Nolan made before he was famous, about a man who has no short-term memory and can't remember what happened minutes before. It's shot in reverse chronological order. Don't worry; your computer isn't broken.

Mentos: brand of mint candies that were sold in the 1980s and 1990s using a vaguely European series of commercials in which individuals creatively work their ways out of unfortunate situations, inspired by partaking of "The Freshmaker" in their pockets.

Metallica: as opposed to all those "nu metal" bands listed earlier, Metallica is a real-deal heavy metal band, recording such heavy songs as "One," "Enter Sandman," and the album *Master of Puppets*. They've got so much cred, they were on Beavis's T-shirt.

Miracle on 34th Street (1947): classic holiday movie that mostly takes the form of a courtroom drama, during which the state of New York tries to demonstrate that Santa Claus is legally insane. Most likely, it served as the inspiration for countless defence lawyers.

The Misfits: American band who blended punk rock with horror film themes and imagery. They write songs about requiring skulls and their band patches (featuring skulls — it's a motif — with underbites) live on forever on punk kids' jean jackets.

My Bloody Valentine (1981): early slasher film about a group of teenagers in a Canadian mining town who throw a Valentine's Day party, in clear defiance of a murderer who really doesn't like Valentine's Day.

My Bloody Valentine (band): the phrase "my bloody valentine" also refers to an Irish band that was a pioneer in the "shoegaze" musical subgenre, identified by use of creative guitar distortion and totally not-exciting live performances.

Nancy Drew: seriously? You're three books into this series and you don't know who Nancy Drew is yet? Have you been paying attention at all?

The Nanny: popular sitcom of the 1990s in which a working-class woman (who was not without style or flair) from Queens, played by nasal-voiced comedian Fran Drescher, becomes the nanny of a well-to-do (and handsome!) single father's three kids.

Narnia: magical land of talking animals and mythical creatures featured in a series of books by C.S. Lewis, the most famous of which is *The Lion, the Witch and the Wardrobe* and the most bizarre of which is *The Last Battle*.

Never Been Kissed (1999): romantic (but fairly creepy) comedy about a journalist (played by Drew Barrymore) who poses as a student at her former high school to get the inside scoop on teen culture.

Ocean's Eleven (1960, 2001): whatever the era, both movies involve a gentleman thief, Danny Ocean, and his team of criminals who endeavour to cleverly rob multiple Las Vegas casinos at the same time. Bonus points if you can name all eleven actors who form the Ocean's Eleven.

Oingo Boingo: weirdo new wave/ska/funk band of the 1970s and 1980s that were notable for their use of horns and Halloween obsessions. The band is probably best known for their singles "Dead Man's Party" and "Weird Science" — and the fact that their lead singer and songwriter was Danny Elfman, now a fairly famous film composer.

The Oregon Trail: one of the earliest (but still the best) computer games ever made. In it, you bring your family along the historic Oregon Trail, travelling from Missouri to Oregon and learning about American pioneer life along the way. The goal: arriving in Oregon with as many surviving family members as possible. Your enemies: starvation, deep rivers, and typhoid. (One of your kids will *definitely* get typhoid.)

Patti Smith: basically the living embodiment of punk, Patti Smith is an American singer-songwriter and poet who exploded on the burgeoning New York City punk scene with her album, *Horses*, in 1975.

P.D. James: one of the most famous English crime writers of all time, Phyllis Dorothy James (the Baroness of Holland Park!) is the author of over a dozen mysteries featuring detective-poet

Adam Dalgliesh, among others including (in a change of pace) the dystopian novel *Children of Men*.

P!nk: singer-songwriter Alecia Beth Moore first exploded onto the music scene as an R&B artist with shocking pink hair and feminist jams like "There You Go" and "You Make Me Sick," but later became known for pop party anthems like "Get the Party Started" and "So What." Also, she lost her pink hair, which made her stage name all the more mysterious!

Pong: before video games looked basically like movies you can control, people were mesmerized by two dashes of light that slowly bounced a pixel between them in a crude approximation of table tennis in this, one of the first arcade games ever.

The Price Is Right: a television staple for people restricted to their couches due to terrible illness. Typically airing at noon, it is a game show during which contestants win cash and prizes by correctly guessing the retail price of various consumer products. Basically capitalist propaganda *par excellence*.

Professor X: comic books' diplomatic founder and leader of a school for gifted youngsters, which provides a sanctuary for mutant children. That sanctuary, ironically, frequently places them in life-threatening situations in their role of super-team, the X-Men. Portrayed in film by James McAvoy and Patrick Stewart, he also inexplicably has a British accent despite being born in the U.S. of A. (See also *Magneto*.)

Rancid: Tim Armstrong, Lars Frederiksen, Matt Freeman, and Brett Reed (or, later, Branden Steineckert) comprise an East Bay punk rock band that somehow straddles the line of commercial success and street cred. They've recorded punk rock hits "Salvation," "Time Bomb," and "Roots Radicals," among many others. Co-frontman Tim Armstrong can only go about four songs in concert before removing his shirt.

Reservoir Dogs (1992): cult crime film that was also the first movie directed by violence- and pop-culture-obsessed filmmaker Quentin Tarantino. The criminal protagonists of the movie use colour-based aliases (Mr. Blue, Mr. Pink, Mr. White) and wear identical black suits, white shirts, sunglasses, and skinny black ties.

Rocky Balboa: lead character of the Rocky boxing movies — which start off way sadder and grittier than you'd expect — portrayed by Sylvester Stallone.

The Rocky Horror Picture Show (1975): perhaps the ultimate cult movie, *The Rocky Horror Picture Show* is an intentionally campy musical that melds horror, rock 'n' roll, and gender fluidity. Film screenings are usually attended by moviegoers in costume and accompanied by routine actions and jeers from the crowd.

Rubik's cube: 3-D puzzle that is solved when each of the cube's sides is filled with a three-by-three grid of the same colours. The toy rose to popularity in the 1980s. I totally know a woman who can solve one within a minute.

Saturday Night Fever (1977): a dance film starring John Travolta that uses the disco scene of late 1970s New York City as its backdrop. Remembered for Travolta's white leisure suit and a kickin' disco-fied Bee Gees soundtrack, it's less remembered for being, like, a harrowing portrayal of working-class masculinity. (Because, y'know: disco.)

Scooby-Doo: clearly the spiritual predecessor to *The Dead Kid Detective Agency*, this immortal Hanna-Barbera animated television series features the Mystery Gang (Fred, Daphne, Velma, Shaggy, and talking dog Scooby) as they cross the country in a quest to debunk all supernatural mysteries, even if they have to eat a few massive sandwiches and break a few pairs of Velma's glasses along the way.

Sean Paul: Jamaican dancehall recording artist whose songs — "Gimme the Light," "We Be Burnin'," "Temperature" — are instant party generators.

She's All That (1999): teen rom-com starring Freddie Prinze Jr. and Rachael Leigh Cook that's like *My Fair Lady* meets *The O.C.* Big man on campus Zack accepts a bet that he can turn loserish art student Laney (who wears overalls and glasses, making her, basically, a sea-monster) into the prom queen. You can imagine how that works out.

Shirley Jackson: legendary American author of mystery and horror short fiction and novels who was an influence on writers like Neil Gaiman, Stephen King, and others. She's best known for the novel *We Have Always Lived in the Castle* and the short story "The Lottery," which is not an uplifting tale of someone who comes into great wealth by winning the lottery.

So You Think You Can Dance: televised dance competition during which happy-footed hopefuls compete as individuals and pairs in a variety of dance styles — contemporary, hip-hop, ballroom, jazz — and home viewers vote for their favourites. Often a training ground for *Step Up* movies. (See also *Step Up: Revolution.*)

Speed (1994): ridiculously fun action film with an even more ridiculous premise: a city bus is rigged with a bomb that will explode if the bus's speed drops below fifty miles an hour. Shut up and take my money!

Spy Kids (2001): first of a series of family adventure films directed by Robert Rodriguez in which two kids discover their parents are semi-retired spies and, through a series of mishaps, end up doing some high-tech (and not particularly realistic) spying themselves to save their parents. Based on a true story, I assume.

"Stairway to Heaven": a Meatloaf-length song by rock band Led Zeppelin that begins quite slow, then gets a little too fast, and chronicles the purchase of a very tall staircase. Despite the awkward tempo change, it remains a staple of high school dances, often acting as the final slow dance of the night.

Step Up: Revolution (2012): possibly the best and certainly the most political of the franchise, the fourth installment in the Step Up dance movie series featuring a new crew who use their dance-based flash mobs to heighten political awareness and fight gentrification in their Miami neighbourhood. (Yes, you read that correctly.)

Stevie Nicks: tenth-level sorceress and sometime vocalist in the rock group, Fleetwood Mac.

Sue Grafton: author of a series of mystery novels that double as important lessons on the alphabet: *A Is for Alibi*, *M Is for Malic*, *R Is for Regicide*, etc.

"The Summer of '69": unofficial Canadian national anthem recorded by Bryan Adams as an ode to a summer during which he was literally nine years old (a.k.a. the best summer of his life).

Swatch: Swiss watch brand that had its heyday in the 1980s and featured bold and colourful band designs.

Switchblade Romance (2003): unbearably tense and brutal French horror movie that, translated literally, has the more fitting title *High Tension*. After viewing, you will cringe every time you see a concrete saw on a construction site.

Tetris: a Soviet puzzle-based video game in which players must take differently shaped blocks that fall without explanation from the sky and rotate and slot them into as pleasing a flat horizontal line (with no gaps) as possible. Did you realize that each of the Tetris shapes is made of four squares? That's why it's called Tetris! Mind: blown.

Tom and Jerry: a cartoon cat and mouse who attempt to kill or maim each other in a long-running series of animated shorts. Jerry, the mouse, typically ends up getting the upper hand on Tom, due to society's anti-cat and anti-Thomas bias.

Tomb Raider: Lara Croft, the fictional star of video games (and later, movies and comic books) is a very athletic British archaeologist and adventurer who travels to ancient ruins and faces certain doom at every turn.

Twilight: superlatively popular book and movie franchise about the love triangle between a sparkly vampire, a Native American werewolf, and a sullen young woman. *That* old story.

Twin Peaks: short-lived 1990s cult television series that follows the aftermath of teenager Laura Palmer's murder in a small, bizarre Washington town. Like much of co-creator David Lynch's work, it looks at the seedy side of small-town America, and is really, really focused on coffee.

Uggs: popular brand of boot that look a bit like really plush space boots and look best when paired with really baggy sweatpants.

"Under the Sea": the most danceable song from the 1989 Disney animated film *The Little Mermaid*, it's the song performed by Calypso-loving crab, Sebastian, to convince mermaid Ariel to remain underwater (and not join the world of humans) by outlining how chill life is in the ocean.

Unsolved Mysteries: the television program most likely to give you nightmares, the program documented real-life unsolved crimes, conspiracy theories, and supernatural phenomena via interviews and re-enactments. For most of its run, it was hosted by Robert "Flying a plane is no different than riding a bicycle" Stack.

Upworthy: website for viral internet content frequently mocked for its alarmist and hyperbolic headlines, like "He Locked Seventeen Dogs in a Butcher Shop. What Happened Next Made Him Collapse in Tears."

Usain Bolt: only the fastest man in the world. Multiple gold-medal winner Jamaican sprinter Bolt is so fast, at the 2008 Summer Olympics, he destroyed the previous 100-metre dash record, even though he slowed down near the finish line to check an undone shoelace!

V.C. Andrews: American novelist Cleo Virginia Andrews is best known for her infamous novel *Flowers in the Attic*, but wrote a number of novels chock full of Gothic horror and skeevy family secrets.

Veronica Lodge: one third of the primary love triangle featured in Archie Comics, Veronica Lodge is a wealthy, strong-willed brunette who is a lifelong frenemy to her more kind-hearted blond counterpart, Betty Cooper.

Willy Wonka: fictional candy industrialist featured in beloved children's book by Roald Dahl, *Charlie and the Chocolate Factory*. Wonka employs slave Oompa-Loompa labour and wantonly kills children with unpleasant attitudes, yet is still admired by young readers everywhere.

Zumba: created by Colombian choreographer Alberto Pérez, Zumba is a dance fitness program that takes most of its elements from the world of dance and is done to a soundtrack of all your favourite current pop hits.

Evan Munday is the author and illustrator of the Silver Birch award finalists *The Dead Kid Detective Agency* and *Dial M for Morna*. He lives in Toronto, Ontario.

The Dead Kid Detective Agency Series

The Dead Kid Detective Agency
Dial M for Morna
Loyalist to a Fault

Get the eBook free!

At ECW Press, we want you to enjoy *Loyalist to a Fault* in whatever format you like, whenever you like. Leave your print book at home and take the eBook to go! Purchase the print edition and receive the eBook free. Just send an email to ebook@ecwpress.com and include

- the book title
- the name of the store where you purchased it
- your receipt number
- your preference of file type: PDF or ePub?

A real person will respond to your email with your eBook attached. And thanks for supporting an independently owned Canadian publisher with your purchase!